# BILLY

## MESSENGER OF POWERS

# BILLY

## MESSENGER OF POWERS

by

Michaelbrent Collings

## THE BORGO PRESS

*An Imprint of Wildside Press LLC*

MMX

Copyright © 2010 by Michaelbrent Collings

All rights reserved.
No part of this book may be reproduced in any form
without the expressed written consent
of the author and publisher.
Printed in the United States of America

www.wildsidebooks.com

FIRST EDITION

# CONTENTS

Chapter the First ................................................................................. 9
Chapter the Second ........................................................................... 25
Chapter the Third .............................................................................. 36
Chapter the Fourth ............................................................................ 59
Chapter the Fifth ............................................................................... 75
Chapter the Sixth .............................................................................. 89
Chapter the Seventh ......................................................................... 98
Chapter the Eighth .......................................................................... 108
Chapter the Ninth ........................................................................... 117
Chapter the Tenth ........................................................................... 132
Chapter the Eleventh ...................................................................... 143
Chapter the Twelfth ........................................................................ 160
Chapter the Thirteenth .................................................................... 171
Chapter the Fourteenth ................................................................... 183
Chapter the Fifteenth ...................................................................... 194
Chapter the Sixteenth ..................................................................... 209
Chapter the Seventeenth ................................................................. 223
Chapter the Eighteenth ................................................................... 235
Chapter the Nineteenth ................................................................... 246
Chapter the Twentieth .................................................................... 258
Chapter the Twenty-First ................................................................ 276
Chapter the Twenty-Second ........................................................... 284
Chapter the Twenty-Third .............................................................. 299
Chapter the Twenty-Fourth ............................................................ 310
Chapter the Twenty-Fifth ............................................................... 329
Chapter the Twenty-Sixth .............................................................. 340
Chapter the Twenty-Seventh .......................................................... 352
Chapter the Twenty-Eighth ............................................................ 365
Chapter the Twenty-Ninth .............................................................. 376
Chapter the Thirtieth ...................................................................... 392
Chapter the Thirty-First ................................................................. 398

Epilogue .................................................................................. 404
About the Author .................................................................. 406

# DEDICATION

*To Laura,*
**FTAAE**

*To My Dad,*
**For Teaching Me to Write**

AND

*To My Mom,*
**For Loving What I wrote**

# CHAPTER THE FIRST

*In Which Billy goes to a New School, and sees a Winking Frog...*

    Billy Jones was only fourteen years old the first time he died.
    On his first day at Preston Hills High School, *thirteen*-year-old Billy walked through the gate in the chain link fence that surrounded the school where he would be more or less incarcerated for the next four years. He looked around, trying to get his bearings, trying not to let the fear he felt show on his face. PHHS was larger than Preston Hills Middle School had been. It was two stories, with classrooms that Billy could tell were much larger than the middle school's rooms. The place was huge, with an air of permanence that made it seem as though it had been there forever, catering to the needs of the Older Kids who walked its halls.
    I'm actually in high school, Billy thought. But he didn't have time to decide whether that was a good thing or a bad one, because at that moment another student bumped into him.
    The boy was taller than Billy. Good-looking, too, which Billy instantly noticed because he wasn't so good looking himself. Billy wasn't *ugly* or anything; he knew no one had ever thrown up from just looking at him. But he was also aware that he was extremely small for his age—only a little over five feet—and his thick blonde hair was far too curly for comfort. Add his halo of golden curls to his diminutive stature, and he looked like a doll. A doll that apparently seemed to scream, "Hey, look at these cute curls? Wouldn't I be fun to punch?" to the school bullies. Not only that, but Billy's clothing was not exactly trend-setting. His family didn't have much money, and Billy mostly wore Salvation Army clothes. So for him "lookin' good" meant he was wearing clothing that had never smelled like mold or cigarettes.
    In contrast, the tall boy who had bumped into Billy and was now staring at him stood on the opposite end of the Coolness Spectrum. Unlike Billy's raggedly curly coif, the other boy had dark brown hair that was perfectly combed and styled. His clothing was

the latest fashion, and worn with the casual distaste that Billy knew only the rich can get away with. No backpack, either: the bigger kid had one of those khaki messenger bags that held half the books and cost ten times more than Billy's used six-dollar book bag. And the picture of perfection was completed by the boy's eyes: expressive green eyes that could probably grab any girl in the school with the force of a tractor beam.

Now, those green eyes were glaring at Billy. Billy involuntarily took a step back. "Sorry," he mumbled. He didn't know why he said that: the big kid had knocked into *him*, not the other way around.

Still, the boy nodded, as though considering whether to accept Billy's apology. Then he said, "I'm Cameron. Cameron *Black*."

For a moment, Billy felt a surge of hope. This was clearly one of the Popular Kids. And he was introducing himself to Billy! Billy had never managed to break into that prestigious group at Preston Elementary or Preston Hills Middle School. Maybe he'd lucked into making friends with one of them here. His first day! He caught an imaginary glimpse of himself sitting with the Popular Kids. Eating lunch with the Popular Kids. Getting invited to go out to the movies on Friday nights. Wearing all the Right Clothes and doing all the Right Things.

The daydream ended suddenly, as Cameron Black took a step toward Billy, looming over him. "Don't. Ever. Touch. Me. Again," said Cameron in a low but intense whisper.

Billy gulped. He nodded. The nod was a little more exaggerated than he meant it to be. In fact, it was more of a convulsive shiver, as though he had suddenly discovered his PB&J sandwich was actually made with boogers and pocket lint.

The shudder made Billy's shoulder move. Just a little. Just enough for his backpack to slide down a bit. As it did, Billy suddenly knew what was going to happen next, as though he was seeing the future through a crystal ball. But in spite of his foreknowledge of the coming catastrophe, he couldn't stop it from happening.

The backpack slid downward, hanging on the crook of his arm for one slow-motion moment.

The universe contracted, and suddenly the only things in it now were Billy, Cameron, and the backpack.

The backpack dropped, slowly, from Billy's loose arm.

It hung for a thousand years in mid-air, suspended between his arm and what lay below it. Billy wanted to scream, wanted to grab the backpack. But even a thousand years wasn't enough time for him to catch the falling bag. Its downward motion was inevitable, unstoppable, like a lead bar dropped from the top of the Empire State Building.

The backpack fell on Cameron's foot.

Billy watched it happen with horror. Something told him this new occurrence wasn't good. It was bad. Very Bad, in fact. He knew that his backpack was empty except for pencils and a few sheets of lined paper in a cheap three-ring binder. It couldn't weigh much. It was soft. But Cameron was now looking at him as though Billy had actually tried to hit him over the head with something a bit bigger and harder—like a car, or the state of Texas.

"Ow," whispered Cameron. Billy knew that "ow" usually meant "that hurt," but the way Cameron said it somehow sounded more like, "prepare to die."

Cameron grabbed Billy's shirt. The shirt tore a little, exposing Billy's thin shoulder. Cameron then pulled Billy to the left, yanking him between a few students who carefully stayed out of Cameron's way.

Moving precisely, almost carefully, Cameron placed Billy—all five feet nothing of him—in one of the lockers against a nearby wall. It was a close fit: if Billy had been a bigger kid—even a normal sized one, instead of the smaller than average thirteen year-old—he wouldn't have fit. But he wasn't a bigger kid. Just Billy. So he *did* fit. Like a hand in a glove. Or, rather, like a Billy in a locker.

Cameron poked a large finger into Billy's chest. "I'm closing the door now. Don't try to get out before first bell rings." He swung the locker shut, then looked in at Billy through the slats in the locker door.

Billy experienced a crazy moment where he wondered if those slats were there to keep kids stuffed in lockers from suffocating: after all, the *books* presumably didn't care if they had a draft of fresh air now and then. Was locker-stuffing so widespread at this school that they had actually designed the lockers specifically for it?

Billy's mind was ripped away from this horrifying train of thought by Cameron's voice. "And don't tell anyone that I did this. If you do, the only thing that will happen is that I'll make sure that something awful happens to you."

Like what? Billy thought.

Cameron leaned closer to the locker, and as though he had heard Billy's thought as clear as conversation, said, "Let your imagination run wild, kid."

Billy did. It wasn't a pretty sight. The image his brain coughed up involved a toilet in the student bathrooms, a blindfold, a rabid great white shark, and several baseball bats with nails sticking out of them.

Cameron moved away.

Billy waited. He thought about calling out and opened his mouth. Then he thought about angry sharks and pointy sticks and shut it again.

A minute later the first bell rang. Billy was officially going to be late on his first day at school. He pushed on the locker door to see if it would just spring open from the inside. It didn't, of course.

He began knocking on the inside of the locker, hoping some other late student would hear his tapping and let him out.

No one did.

He tapped harder.

Then gave a little shout.

Then he gave a bigger shout.

"Help!"

He banged on the door of the locker.

"HELP!"

He pushed with all his might on the inside of the door, bracing his feet against the back of the locker so that he could use his full body weight. This turned out to be bad timing on his part, because the door suddenly opened, and Billy lost his balance, falling to the sidewalk in front of the lockers.

The first thing he saw was his backpack, still laying where it had fallen about a dozen feet away.

Well, thought Billy, at least it didn't get stolen. Apparently the school didn't admit thieves. Just good-looking psychopaths who were proud members of the We Hate Billy club.

The second thing Billy saw was a foot.

It was right in front of him. The foot was wearing a clean white sneaker. Above the sneaker was an ankle-high sock. Above that was a bare ankle, which—as he knew ankles tended to do—gradually turned into a leg as Billy's gaze continued to rise.

Billy was only thirteen—his fourteenth birthday was still two months off—and he was, as his father put it, "young for his age." He knew that was code for saying he looked more like a sixth-grader than someone starting high school. And perhaps as a result of that, he hadn't really "discovered" girls yet the way that some of his classmates had. He didn't really get some of the jokes he overheard them telling, or the way they talked about them in the halls before class.

In spite of his admitted lack of knowledge, however, Billy *did* know what a girl's leg looked like. And this was definitely a girl's leg. A nice one, too.

Billy's gaze continued to rise up the leg, to the shirt, to the neck.

By the time he reached the girl's head, Billy felt dizzy. He wasn't sure if that was because of a lack of oxygen in the locker, or the fact that he was still on the ground craning his neck to see up, or because the girl was simply the prettiest girl he had ever seen.

The next moment, however, Billy was pretty sure that his dizziness was caused by the last reason, because his heart suddenly attempted to take a three-foot step to the left, not minding that there was a ribcage in its way. At the same time, Billy felt his stomach try to jump out through his face, and he was pretty sure that his toes turned inside-out.

In that fraction of a second, Billy knew he had "discovered" girls. Or at least, one girl. She was taller than Billy. No surprise there, *everyone* was taller than Billy. But instead of making her seem imposing, her height just made her seem lithe and graceful. Her brown hair hung to her shoulders in thick waves that shimmered in the sunlight. And her eyes were stunning: blue and beautiful, with an electric spark of intelligence and joy behind them that made it seem as though she were on the verge of laughing at a joke that no one else could hear. Billy noticed that the girl had a band-aid on one knee, and somehow this small blemish on the overall perfection of her image didn't make her any less attractive. Rather, it had the opposite effect, as though reminding Billy that she was indeed human, and so perhaps—just perhaps—there was a chance that someday they might....

Might what? thought Billy, and blushed brightly at the possibilities that lay behind the unfinished thought.

"I'm Blythe Forrest," said the girl.

Why does everyone in this school tell you their name first thing? thought Billy. Are they all crazy?

Still, being crazy—if Blythe was indeed crazy—didn't make her any less pretty.

Blythe's beautiful face wrinkled with obvious impatience. Somehow, this made her even cuter.

"Well?" she demanded.

Billy hopped dexterously to his feet, sending a suave look at the girl as he said, "I'm Billy. Billy Jones." He made it sound cool. He looked cool. He *was* cool.

BILLY: MESSENGER OF POWERS, BY MICHAELBRENT COLLINGS * 13

At any rate, that was what Billy *wished* had happened. In reality, he managed to lay there like a trout about to have its head cut off, and the only word he got out was "ahxgl" or something like it.

Blythe frowned. "Are you in the special class or something? What's your *name*?"

"Billy Jones," he finally managed. He tried to smile, but then remembered that his stomach was still trying to get out through his head, and clamped his mouth shut before he could blurt something stupid like "Did you know squirrels make cheese?" or "My moonbeam has peanuts," or worst of all, "You're the prettiest girl I've ever seen."

"Billy Jones?" she asked. Billy nodded, rather proud of himself for managing to maintain that level of muscle control. He felt like he had to go to the bathroom.

"Billy Jones," she said again. When she said it, she had a look on her face that Billy didn't like, as though she was trying out a dirt-flavored jawbreaker. A moment later she said, "Interesting. Your shirt's ripped."

Then she turned without another word, disappearing around a nearby corner like a strange, beautiful dream. One that smelled like strawberries.

The final bell rang. Billy was late.

He hurried to his bag and swept it off the ground, not bothering to dust it off. Then he pulled his schedule from his pocket, uncrumpling it as best he could while running at the same time. He didn't even know where he was running to at first, but figured that moving toward the school's center would probably be a good idea.

He managed to read the schedule as it bobbed up and down in his hands. History. Building B, Room Six.

Billy ran to his first class, trying to remember the layout of the school from the packet he and his parents had received three weeks before. Where is Building B? he thought as he rushed through the halls. The school, which ten minutes ago had seemed merely huge, now felt positively planetary in size. He half-expected to see small moons whipping through the halls, held there by the gravitational pull of the high school.

Then he remembered: Building B was the name of the second floor of the school. Of course, he thought. After all, saying "Second Floor" wouldn't make much sense, would it? Wouldn't want anyone knowing how to get anywhere, would we? Where would the fun be in that?

His internally voiced sarcasm, unfortunately, did not make time go any slower. So it was no surprise to him that when he finally found room six, out of breath from running up the stairs and then frantically dashing down the hallway that—thankfully—had a clearly visible sign saying "Rooms 1 thru 10," all the other students were already seated.

They looked at him, all of them moving at once like their heads were connected by some kind of control center.

Billy shifted uncomfortably. He again felt like he had to go to the bathroom. Only this time it wasn't because he was in the presence of the beautiful Blythe Forrest. It was because what felt like six hundred eyes were now staring at him, and each set of eyes was in a face that now held a smirking look that seemed to say "Ah-ha! Now I know who the Class Doofus is going to be!"

"Yes, may I help you?" said a voice. The sound cracked like a BB gun through the room. Billy turned to face the voice and was greeted by a new pair of eyes, dark brown and piercing, which looked at him with a mixture of impatience and annoyance. It was clearly the teacher.

She looked to be in her late sixties, but was still obviously strong and mentally agile. Her brown eyes glittered with not-quite-hidden knowledge. Her face was creased with age, and a permanent frown line pulled the edges of her thin lips downward. She was not particularly tall, but when she took a step toward Billy, he had the sense of being in the presence of a giant. He stepped back involuntarily.

"Well?" she demanded.

"Uh...," he managed. This was clearly not going to be a day where he could manage any sparkling conversation. Single-syllable grunts were apparently the only thing he could do on command.

"'Uh' is not an appropriate answer to my question," she responded, and this time her tone of voice brought to mind something with a higher caliber than a BB gun. A nuclear-tipped bazooka, maybe.

The class tittered. Billy blushed. He could feel his cheeks and the edges of his ears heating up as blood rushed to them.

The teacher silenced them with a glance. Billy suspected she could do this to serial killers and SEALs, let alone to nervous ninth-graders.

"I was late," he managed.

"Clearly," she replied. She held out her hand. Billy looked at it like it was an alien appendage. What was he supposed to do with it?

"Your schedule," the teacher prompted. Billy handed it over, noting how she seemed to frown at the fact that it had been crumpled into a pocket, rather than professionally laminated and framed.

She read it quickly, looking at it over the top of the reading glasses perched at the end of her nose. "Well, William Jones," she said after a moment, "at least you're in the right place, if not at the right time."

The class nervously chuckled again, and this time the teacher did not bother to use her Death-Stare to silence them. She just handed Billy his schedule, then pointed to an empty desk in the second row.

Billy moved toward it, and as he did his foot caught on something. He tripped, stumbling forward in a desperate attempt to keep from falling on his face.

The students' chuckles now turned to full-volume guffaws. Billy struggled to right himself, his arms flapping faster than hummingbird wings. He wished he was dead. Better yet, he wished he had *been* dead for a few hundred years, cremated, and the ashes buried under a small mountain on a frozen island in the middle of the Arctic Sea.

At least the day can't get any worse, he thought fleetingly. But he knew, even as he thought it, that this absolutely the wrong thing to think. Experience had taught Billy that no matter how bad things were, they could *always* be worse.

"Harold Crane!" shouted the teacher. Her voice had moved up in intensity from bazooka to intercontinental ballistic missile. The class silenced instantly. Billy held himself motionless, still in a half-crouch, petrified by the teacher's words. No one else in the class moved, either.

The teacher walked to a nearby student. The kid was a bit smaller than Cameron had been, but Billy could see that Harold Crane was clearly cut from the same kind of stock: thick chest, strong arms. His hair was dyed red at the tips, long bangs hanging artfully down over his eyes, which now had an innocent look pasted across them. He might as well have had "Born To Bully" tattooed across his forehead.

The teacher looked down. Billy and the rest of the class followed her gaze, and those close enough could see what she was looking at: Harold's sneaker pushed out in the middle of the aisle. That was what Billy had tripped on.

Harold's look of innocence faltered. He shrugged. "It was an accident," he said.

"Very well," said the teacher. "Be advised that if there are any more 'accidents,' they may result in 'accidental' visits to the Principal's office." Her gaze shifted to take in the whole class at once. "That goes for all of you."

She turned to walk back to her desk. As soon as her back was turned, Harold turned around and locked eyes with Billy. He made a quick slicing movement across his throat, then pointed at Billy before turning back to face the teacher as she swiveled toward them again.

Billy sighed as he dropped into the seat behind his desk, his book bag dumping unceremoniously to the floor with a dull thud. What was it about his existence that made people like Cameron and now Harold so angry? Had he offended them in a past life or something?

The teacher's voice—still commanding full attention, but softer now that she was not actively perturbed—reverberated through the room.

"I am Mrs. Russet," she said. Her tone of voice clearly communicated that they should pay attention. Billy suspected that the President of the United States would sit up a little straighter if he were visiting Mrs. Russet's classroom. "This is ninth-grade history, and I wish to make a few things very clear before we begin. First: I am the teacher that all the other teachers are afraid of. I grade hard, and I have been working here long enough not to care if that bothers some of the younger teachers here. Most of you will get average grades. This is nothing to be ashamed of. Average is not bad. A few of you will get better grades, and a few of you will receive excellent grades. These will be earned. You will have to work in this class, and work hard."

The whole class groaned collectively. Mrs. Russet silenced them again with what Billy was already starting to think of as The Look.

"There will be reading assignments every day. I will not grade these assignments, but there will be pop tests on them. The tests will go over not just the reading of the previous night, but may cover anything and everything learned to that point in the class."

Billy's nearest neighbor, a small, fair-skinned girl, looked like she might either pass out or throw up at this announcement. Nor was she the only one; Billy could see that most of the class looked visibly disturbed by the pressure Mrs. Russet was already bringing to bear.

"That is the bad news," she said. "There is, however, also some good news. The good news is that I will make myself available at any time—before school, after school, or weekends—to help anyone who feels they need extra assistance. I will not provide extra assistance for those in the class with excellent grades. They need no help.

But anyone else can come to me at any time and make an appointment for private teaching at a mutually convenient time."

Billy knew that he was likely to be one of the people who needed extra help. History had always been a tough subject for him. He was pretty sure that someone had discovered America at one point. He was also pretty sure that that person had been neither a giant squid nor a space-alien. Beyond that, however, the details always got sketchy. So he was at least a little heartened to find out that help would be available if—when—he needed it.

The momentary lightness was crushed, however, when Mrs. Russet reached into her desk and pulled out a sheaf of papers. She began handing them out.

The first student who received one gasped. So did the second and third students. Harold Crane—the red-tipped bully—was the first one to actually say something when he got his paper. "Pop quiz?" he asked. "It's the first day of school!"

"Thank you for that astute observation," answered Mrs. Russet dryly.

"How can there be a quiz on the first day of school?" Harold demanded.

"You all received orientation packets, did you not?" responded Mrs. Russet. She looked around the room for a moment, as though making sure no one disagreed with her statement, then resumed handing out the papers.

"You're going to test us on the orientation packets? How can you test us on the orientation packets?" Harold's cheeks reddened to the color of his hair-tips. Billy thought the kid looked like he might implode at any moment, leaving behind nothing but a charred desk and some tiny whiffs of red-dyed hair.

"The orientation packets were addressed to each of you, not to your parents. You should have read them, and you should be prepared to show that you understood what they said," said Mrs. Russet.

"That's not fair!" shouted Harold. A few of the other students muttered their agreement, and even Billy found himself nodding.

"Not fair, Mr. Crane? Why not?" The teacher broadened her gaze to take in the whole class. "I, too, received orientation materials. They included the names and pictures of each of you. Which I memorized. Along with as much of your background information as was available. Which is why I know what your previous grade average was, Ms. Conway." Mrs. Russet stared at a girl in the third row, then shifted her gaze to a mullet-haired kid behind Billy. "And it's how I know that you held the fifty-yard dash record at your old school, Mr. Carrey." She moved her eyes to Billy for a moment, as though she was going to single him out, too, but then seemed to think better of it. She looked at a large boy in the back of the class. "And it's how I know that you are the third of four children, Mr. Canter."

She looked around at the class, which was now silent. "Why did I do this? Because I received the information, and I did not want to waste it. You should have all done the same with your orientation information."

Mrs. Russet resumed handing out the papers. "And as for what is 'fair,' Mr. Crane..." she stopped a moment. "There is a 'fair' that comes to the county every summer. Other than that, 'fair' is not something that most of us will encounter very often in life. I will be fair in that I will only test each of you on information I know you have received. But your notion of whether that is or is not 'fair' is not something that will concern me."

She finished handing out the papers. Harold looked like he was thinking of something to say, but before he could, Mrs. Russet held up a hand. "The tests have been passed out. Testing has begun. Anyone speaking before all tests have been completed will receive a zero."

She sat down at her desk, folded her hands, and began methodically scanning up and down the room, watching the students with the precision of a spy satellite.

Billy fumbled in his bag for a pencil. Then he wrote his name at the top right of the page, and read the first question.

"1. Where is the Principal's office located? Please describe how to get there from the main Student Entrance."

Billy blinked. The words were familiar, he knew they were English, but he wasn't able to process them. Between his encounter with Cameron, his time in the locker, meeting Blythe, and the whirlwind introduction into history class, he had blown a fuse somewhere. He knew he had to focus. Billy had never been an "A" student, but he always tried his hardest. He would try his hardest here, too. But to do that, he had to calm down.

He closed his eyes for a moment. He took a breath, held it, then let it out slowly. It was what his mom—a checker at a nearby grocery store who he knew had to face at least six hundred crises per day—always told him to do when in danger of panicking.

It worked. Billy felt his heart rate slow down from Hyper-Speed to the level of You'll Have a Heart Attack Any Second Now. Another breath, and he relaxed further.

He concentrated on "seeing" the insides of his eyelids. At first, all he could see was pink. Then strobing flashes started to go off. He concentrated on *them*, and imagined they were space ships, carrying passengers into distant places. He imagined hopping onto one of them. It carried him into space, where nothing could hurt him, where he was alone and safe, where—

"Mr. Jones!"

Billy jerked, his eyes flying open as his name was called. Mrs. Russet was still at her seat, her gaze drilling into him once again. This time, her look was even more intense than it had been when Billy entered the class.

Billy waited, horrified. Did she think he'd been asleep? Cheating somehow? What?!

Mrs. Russet blinked a few times, as though she herself was uncertain why she'd called his name so loudly. Then her stare returned to its previous level. "Please stay after class, Mr. Jones," she said.

"But, I'll be late," he managed to squawk. His throat felt drier than the surface of the moon, which at least was an improvement over constantly feeling like he had to use the bathroom.

"I doubt you'll have to worry about that, but if it happens I'll write you a note," Mrs. Russet said.

Billy nodded, feeling the class's eyes on him once again. Mrs. Russet looked around at the class, apparently noting their attention as well. "The test is still in progress," she reminded them. Everyone looked back at their papers.

Billy looked down as well. He began writing, but knew when the papers were turned in that he'd failed his first test in ninth grade. And failed it miserably. His concern for what Mrs. Russet wanted to talk to him about consumed him, making it impossible for him to concentrate. He had tried his relaxation exercise again a few times, but each time he opened his eyes to find Mrs. Russet staring at him once again.

The test took the majority of the class period. After the tests were all collected, Mrs. Russet handed each student a World History book, copying down which student had which copy of each, and informing them that the books were to be brought to each and every class, no exceptions, even on scheduled test days. She gave them their first night's reading assignment as the class end bell blared electronically over the school intercom system.

The students all shuffled out, schedules clutched in one hand, new books in the other. Several of them cast final looks in Billy's direction as they left, ranging from concerned to amused. Harold

Crane managed to pantomime cutting Billy's throat one more time on his way out without Mrs. Russet seeing him.

Billy barely noticed. He was still dry-mouthed and terrified about the impending doom of a private conference with Mrs. Russet.

At last, all the students were gone. Mrs. Russet moved to the classroom door with a hand-written sign that Billy managed to read: "Please wait outside until door opens." She used some transparent tape to attach it to the outside of the door, then swung it closed.

As the door shut, Billy could sense that he was entering into dangerous territory. What could a teacher want with him? He'd managed to make it through the first nine years of kindergarten, elementary, and middle schooling without even being really *noticed* by any of the teachers, let alone being singled out in this way. He didn't know what was going to happen here, just that it wouldn't—couldn't—be anything good.

Mrs. Russet turned slowly to face him. A long moment passed, in which neither said anything. The teacher just looked at him intensely, and Billy did his best not to meet her gaze.

Mrs. Russet finally went and sat down at her desk. "Come here please, Mr. Jones," she said.

Billy dutifully did so, slinging up his book bag to his shoulder. Hopefully that would remind her he had to get to another class and whatever torture she had in mind for him would be brief.

As he approached her, Mrs. Russet did something strange: she reached into her desk and brought out a ceramic frog. It was a funny little figurine, the kind of thing Billy thought a person might find in a baby's room, or maybe at a garage sale, hunched between the roller skates that hadn't been worn in a decade and the broken video recorder. The frog was clearly eating something: insectile wings and the end of a thorax were hanging out of the large mouth.

Billy had barely a moment to register this before Mrs. Russet brought the frog to her lips. For a moment, Billy thought the teacher was actually going to *kiss* the frog, no doubt hoping that the kiss would transform the amphibian into a middle-aged male teacher with a bad comb-over who would whisk her romantically away to a magical library where they could read forever and would be able to torture students every Wednesday night at scheduled times.

She did not, however, actually kiss the ceramic frog.

What she *did* do was even more bizarre.

She turned the frog sideways, and *whispered into its ear*. Or where its ears would be if frogs had ears. Billy couldn't remember whether they did or not, and right now he didn't think that piece of information was nearly as important as the fact that his history teacher had clearly fallen clean off her rocker.

Billy couldn't hear what Mrs. Russet said to the frog, not clearly at any rate, but he felt something odd come over him. It was as though someone had stuck a hose filled with liquid nitrogen down his throat and then turned it on full blast. Coolness flowed from his heart outward, to his hands, his feet, and his head.

For a moment, Billy swayed on his feet. He blinked, and in that moment, he thought the ceramic frog *moved*. It seemed to grin around the wings and body of the bug it was chewing on. Then one of its great eyes closed and reopened in what Billy thought was a wink.

Billy's eyes bugged in amazement, and he involuntarily blinked rapidly a few times. When he re-focused his eyes, the frog was not moving at all. In fact, he saw no sign that Mrs. Russet had ever held a frog. In its place, she was holding a manila file folder marked "Jones, William W." on the side.

It's not the students who introduce themselves who are crazy, thought Billy. It's me.

For a moment, he wondered if he was really here. Maybe there had never been a bigger kid named Cameron Black, maybe the lovely Blythe Forrest had never existed. Maybe he was hooked up to a feeding tube in a mental hospital somewhere. But then he realized that would mean that he had never been shoved in the locker, had never fallen on his face in front of Blythe, had never tripped in front of the whole history class. That would be too good to be true.

So I'm really here, he thought. Too bad.

"What does the 'W' stand for?" asked Mrs. Russet suddenly.

"Uh, Walker," said Billy.

"Hmmm...," replied the teacher. She continued reading his file. Billy fidgeted. He snuck a glance at the clock, sure that the entire passing period must have passed, and that second bell would ring any second.

To his amazement, barely thirty seconds had passed from the end of class.

"Mr. Jones," said Mrs. Russet. Billy snapped his eyes back to her, not wanting to chance offending this force of nature.

"Yes, Ma'am?" he managed.

"Please hold out your hand."

Billy blinked again, unsure what this meant, but held out his hand nonetheless, palm downward. Mrs. Russet looked at his knuckles for a moment, no doubt marking the best spot to hit him with a ruler.

But she didn't hit him with a ruler. Instead, she put out her own hand, and held it above his for a moment. Then she extended her index finger, and touched it ever so lightly to the top of his hand. They remained that way for a moment, Billy completely unsure what was going on.

Mrs. Russet looked from his hand to his eyes, gripping Billy with a gaze stronger than an earthquake. "I have something very important to tell you," she said, her dry fingertip still resting atop his hand.

Billy waited. He nodded. It seemed like the appropriate thing to do. "Okay," he said.

Mrs. Russet licked her thin lips. She took a deep breath, then said, slowly and gravely, "Rainbow bears enjoy Ding-Dongs at Christmas."

Billy blinked again. His eye muscles were getting a workout today. "What?"

Mrs. Russet nodded as though he was contributing to her bizarre statement. Then she said, "Fleas do the limbo while wearing chopsticks."

Billy did his newfound blinking trick again. He also re-revised his previous theory about the school's insanity level. It wasn't the kids here who were crazy. And it wasn't him, either.

It was *everybody*.

Mrs. Russet withdrew her finger suddenly, and folded her hands on the desktop. She glanced at the clock. "I don't think you'll need a note, you should have plenty of time to get to your next class."

Billy just stood there, rooted to the spot by the sheer insane pressure of what had just happened.

"Don't forget to do your reading assignment," Mrs. Russet continued. After a long moment, during which Billy continued to pretend he was practicing for the Olympics in the Most Widest Eyes And Openest Mouth competition, she frowned. "If you don't hurry, you *will* be late. And I will not write a note for a student who is late merely because he is not intelligent enough to move his feet and legs in a rudimentary walking fashion."

Billy's body turned toward the door. His head came last, as though it wanted to keep looking at the crazy teacher as long as possible. At last, though, both his body and his head were moving in a semi-coordinated manner toward the door.

He pushed the door open, surprised to see how few students there were in the halls. It seemed like a million years had passed, but apparently it had really only been a minute or so. More students were coming out of the classrooms now, but no one seemed overly hurried, and Billy sighed in relief as he realized he probably would not be late to his second class.

The feeling of relief disappeared, however, when he cast a quick glance back into Mrs. Russet's room.

Once again, the teacher was holding the ceramic frog.

Once again, she seemed to be whispering to it.

And once again, Billy thought it winked at him.

Billy turned and walked quickly away, not knowing what else to do.

He did know, however, that this was the strangest day he could ever remember having, and that nothing could possibly top it.

Looking back, however, Billy would later think that he had only been half right about that.

# CHAPTER THE SECOND

*In Which Billy begins a Very Strange fourteenth birthday, and first Fights back...*

Billy's birthday fell on a day that was more than two months into the school year. It was in late October. This meant that he was one of the youngest kids in his class. If he'd been born one month later, he wouldn't have started school until the following year, making him one of the oldest kids in his grade. But as it was, his relative youth made his already-small frame even smaller when compared to his classmates' comparatively robust physiques.

Most of the time this didn't bother Billy too much. But it did mean that he could fit in a locker. And Cameron Black was only too happy to remind Billy of this fact at every opportunity.

Since that strange first day of school, things had proceeded fairly normally for Billy. He was getting mostly average grades, which his parents were satisfied with, if not overly excited about. But he was definitely getting above-average levels of attention from what Billy was coming to think of as the Torture Brigade. It had, of course, Harold Crane in it, as well as Sarah Brookham, a girl he'd accidentally spilled his milk on one day, and a few other people whom Billy had annoyed by having the audacity to live on the same planet they did.

And it went without saying that the founding member of the Torture Brigade was Cameron Black. He was in four of Billy's six classes, and seemed to figure in every minute of Billy's life. The locker-stuffing didn't occur every single day, but Billy could be sure that every single day *would* bring some new agony at Cameron's hands. It ranged in severity. Some days, Cameron settled for throwing dirty looks at Billy in the halls. Others, there would be a foot waiting to trip him at just the most embarrassing moment possible. And on others, Billy would be grabbed by the Torture Brigade and stuffed into an empty locker. Cameron said the same thing every time the locker-stuffing happened: don't move until the bell, and don't tell anyone I did it.

On the morning of Billy's birthday, he woke up the same as he did every other morning: wondering what the Torture Brigade was going to do to him today. This time, however, he had the added bonus of waking up to the sight of fire.

For a moment, Billy's sleep-fogged brain was not able to figure out the significance of the flame, and he almost went screaming out of the room looking for a fire extinguisher before he realized what the fire was: a candle. It was stuck in a blueberry muffin, which was being held only a few inches in front of his face by his mother as she sang "Happy Birthday" to him.

Billy sat up in bed and grinned wearily at his mom as she finished the song. His mother was a bit overweight, and had probably never been a beauty queen. But her face was kind, and usually had a smile for Billy, like it did now.

Billy looked around. "Dad?" he asked.

His mom's smile faltered for just a moment. "He had to go in early today, honey. A bunch of the other guys called in sick."

Billy smiled sadly, not wanting to add to the obvious distress her mother felt at his development. Neither of his parents made much money, because they weren't very educated: Billy knew that they hadn't even finished high school, though both of them had eventually taken high school equivalency tests that essentially allowed them to say they had graduated. His father had gone on to take some night school classes at a nearby community college while working day shifts as a janitor in an office building, and when Billy was ten his father had finally gotten a two-year degree. His father had then continued his nocturnal education, this time taking classes to become a certified paramedic, and only a few months before had managed to land a job with the Los Angeles Fire Department. This was great news, because it meant that for the first time in Billy's life his family was making enough money to cover expenses. But it was also terrible news because now his father was on call whenever he wasn't working overtime, trying to dig the family out of a huge load of debt that had accumulated over the years.

Not that it mattered, Billy supposed. Even when he was home, his father was so busy and overworked that he rarely said anything or participated much in the family's doings. It was almost like Billy was living with a stranger instead of a dad: someone courteous and helpful in a pinch, but not often there, and certainly not his first pick to talk over one's troubles with, be they a lack of stylish clothing, girls, or anything else. In spite of all this, though, Billy still wished things could be different when his father missed a birthday or had to cancel on a family outing. Which was most of the time.

Billy blew out the candle.

"What did you wish for?" asked Billy's mother, then waved her hands in mock terror. "No, don't tell me, don't tell me!" she yelled. "It won't come true if you do!"

Billy smiled and forced a laugh. He wasn't about to tell her what he'd wished for: either a set of huge arms that he could use to beat Cameron Black to a pulp, or failing that, just for a day that Cameron and the Torture Brigade were all sick at the same time, allowing him to get from class to class for a full eight hours without feeling like he was exploring a nuclear waste site in his underwear.

After the muffin was done, Billy's mother fed him a big breakfast. Billy ate most of it before his mother screamed, "Oh, it's seven-thirty! We'll both be late!" He and his mother got in their car—a beat-up fifteen-year-old rust bucket that usually worked—and she dropped him off at the main student entrance on the way to her job as a checker at the local grocery store.

Billy went to his locker and got his books for his first and second classes. He kept an eye out for the Torture Brigade, but strangely, none of them were around.

First period went fine. Mrs. Russet was as hard a teacher as she had claimed to be that first day, but had never brought out any ceramic toads again, and had never mentioned the strange interview of Billy's first day.

Second period, too, was fine. This was unusual, since it was one of the classes that Cameron shared with Billy, and Billy could always count on at the very least a few wads of paper being thrown at his face during class.

But nothing happened.

Nothing out of the ordinary happened in Billy's third class, either. Or his fourth. Or rather, nothing happened that hurt or scared or embarrassed him in any way, which actually *was* out of the ordinary for Billy. But he didn't mind this kind of unusual lack of activity a bit.

Billy began to smile a little. Maybe birthday wishes could come true after all.

He smiled even more when he saw what was on the menu for the school cafeteria at lunch: hot dogs and French fries. Billy's favorite cafeteria dish. His family qualified for free lunches from the school, since they didn't make very much money. Usually this meant that Billy was eating something that everyone called "Salisbury steak" but that he was pretty sure was actually cardboard and paste shaped into a patty and drenched in some kind of sauce that was made out of old tree bark. But hot dogs and French fries were good stuff.

Billy grabbed a lunch tray and got in line. As usual, he was alone in the cafeteria. Not that there were no other students in the room with him. Just he wasn't standing "with" any of them. He was on friendly terms with a few kids in the school, but none of them were actual "friends" of the type he could sit with during lunch. Especially since the Torture Brigade had let it be known early on that any friends of Billy's would risk their wrath. In spite of this separation from the other students, however, Billy generally found a way to enjoy his lunch: sitting at the end of one of the long cafeteria tables, he could pretend he was actually *with* whatever kids were sitting at that table, instead of just sitting near them.

Suddenly, he heard a chilling whisper in his ear. "I heard today's your birthday, Billy-willy."

Billy's blood immediately stopped circulating in his body. He knew Cameron's voice better than he knew his own. He started to turn, but stopped when Cameron whispered, "Don't even think about it, shrimp."

Billy felt a sharp pain in his right calf. He blanched. The pain came again. Cameron was kicking the backs of his legs with horrendous power. Right there in front of everyone!

Billy saw a teacher standing only a few feet away. Mrs. Russet was on monitor duty today, but she had her back turned. Billy thought about yelling for her, but knew from experience that Cameron would put on an innocent face and the teacher wouldn't see anything happening, so would ignore Billy's complaints.

Cameron started singing in Billy's ear, punctuating each word with another snap-kick to the backs of Billy's calves. "Happy [slam] Birth-day [slam] to [slam] you [slam]. Happy [slam] Birth-day [slam] to [slam] you...."

The kicks grew harder and harder, and Billy grit his teeth, praying for Mrs. Russet to turn around and catch Cameron in the act. But she didn't, and the pain in Billy's legs grew worse and worse, until finally he did the only thing he could think *to* do.

He dropped his lunch tray.

His hot dog and fries scattered across the floor, causing more than a few nearby students to scream and jump away as though the food were battery acid.

Mrs. Russet turned at the clatter. She frowned over Billy's shoulder.

Billy's heart leapt. She was clearly frowning at Cameron! Finally, someone had actually *seen* the Torture Brigade's leader at work.

In the next moment, his heart sank back down to its previous level, and then continued on a downward spiral, coming to rest on his big toe.

Cameron wasn't standing behind Billy.

In fact, the bigger boy wasn't anywhere to be seen.

The student now standing behind Billy was one of the seniors at PHHS: one of the Older Kids who ruled the school and didn't even notice Billy's existence.

Billy turned around and jumped: Mrs. Russet was standing right there.

"For goodness sake, Mr. Jones, I volunteered for lunch duty until one o'clock. Are you going to make me late?" With that, Billy realized that Mrs. Russet *hadn't* been looking at Cameron. She'd been looking at the large clock on the wall behind Billy.

Billy mumbled, "No, Ma'am," then stooped to clean up his mess.

Mrs. Russet waved him away. "No, no. Just go get another tray. The custodian will clean all this up."

Billy turned to leave, then halted when he heard Mrs. Russet say, "But don't you stand in line all the way through again. Just get a tray, cut in front to get your lunch, and go through to the cashier." Billy turned, shocked at this unexpected display of friendliness. To his even greater surprise, Mrs. Russet was smiling. Or, well, actually, *not* smiling. Billy was pretty sure the muscles in her face wouldn't be able to smile if you offered her a million dollars for a grin. But she wasn't frowning, either, which was the closest thing to a smile he'd ever seen Mrs. Russet do.

His suspicions that she was actually being nice were confirmed by her next words. "Happy birthday, Mr. Jones."

Billy smiled in amazement before turning away to get his tray. By the time he was back at the front of the line again, Mrs. Russet was gone and the spill had been cleaned up. There was no sign that anything had ever happened here.

Billy frowned. That reminded him. Where was Cameron? Billy had been *positive* that Cameron was the one whispering to him. But where was the bigger boy?

Billy showed his lunch pass to the cashier, who nodded him through, and continued into the cafeteria, craning his neck to see if he could find Cameron's face among the swarming throng of students.

The bigger boy was nowhere to be seen.

Billy sat in silence, positioning himself near the door to the cafeteria so that he could see the students coming in and out. Cameron was not among them. Billy started to doubt that any of it had ever happened. But when he raised his pants legs and looked at his calves, he could already see a row of deep purple bruises. The kicking at least had really occurred.

Finally, it was time for Billy to go to his locker and collect his books for his fifth-period class. He dumped out his uneaten lunch—he had completely lost his interest in food because of his curiosity as to where Cameron could have gone—then walked into the hall and up the stairs to the second floor hall where his locker was located. At the locker, he spun the combination lock to the first number.

Before he could spin the dial to its next location, he heard a sound that again made his blood turn to dust in his veins.

"Happy Birth-day to you..."

Billy swung around as fast as he could. This time, he saw what he had expected to see the first time: Cameron Black, grinning evilly from ear to ear. And not just him, either. The entire Torture Brigade was there in full force. Harold Crane stood behind Cameron, his thick arms crossed across his broad chest, his hair now died booger-green. Sarah Brookham was there as well, dirty blonde hair straggling across her face as her mouth worked up and down, chewing gum at world-record-setting pace.

Cameron shoved Billy up against his locker. "Try and get me in trouble, will you?" He pushed into Billy, leaning his whole body weight on the smaller boy. "Try and get old Russet to see me, huh?"

Billy gasped. It was getting hard to breathe. Cameron gave Billy a quick shake, causing Billy's head to snap back and hit his locker. Billy cried out quietly, his eyes crossing for a moment.

"Leave him alone!"

Cameron turned his head, not letting go of Billy, and Billy sagged as he saw the worst thing he could imagine seeing in this situation: Blythe Forrest.

Blythe was in three of Billy's classes, but since their first strange encounter she had never spoken to Billy. And now here she was, apparently taking an interest in him for the first time, and doing so because he needed *rescuing*. Billy would rather have been beaten up every single day and twice a day on Sundays than have Blythe coming to his rescue. Blissful fantasies that involved him asking her to come over to his place to watch a movie and ended in her declaring her undying love to him all shattered before his eyes. Girls didn't declare undying love to the little kid they had to rescue. It just wasn't done.

"Stay out of this, Forrest," snarled Cameron, turning his attention to Billy.

"Why should I, Black?" responded Blythe, striding fearlessly toward them.

Billy, watching this interplay, found Blythe even prettier now that she was standing up to Cameron. Of course, she was still rescuing him, so her increased beauty just made Billy more depressed about his overall predicament.

Cameron turned around to face Blythe again. Harold Crane and Sarah Brookham both moved as if to stop Blythe, but Cameron stopped them with a glance. "Don't," he said to his cronies.

Blythe glanced at the two other Torture Brigaders, disgust written large across her lovely face. "Yes, don't," she agreed. "You wouldn't like what would happen to you." She turned her gaze to Cameron. "Would they, Cam?"

Cameron growled, and Billy could feel the big boy tense. He was sure that Cameron was about to spring at Blythe.

Billy had one fleeting moment of thought, and it consisted of only two words: "Not her!" Suddenly terrified for Blythe's safety, Billy shoved Cameron, hard.

Coming from someone Billy's size, the shove wasn't much. In fact, Billy was so bad at shoving he actually missed. He was aiming to push Cameron in the chest, but his grip slipped, and he lurched forward, off-balance. His arms windmilled, and there was a sickening crunch as Billy's out-of-control elbow planted itself firmly in the middle of Cameron's nose.

Blood erupted from the other boy's face. Cameron cupped his hand below his nose, trying in vain to keep the red liquid from soaking his designer shirt.

"You made me bleed," he said. Oddly, he didn't sound angry. More…surprised than anything.

Billy looked at Blythe. She, too, looked shocked, her gaze riveted on Cameron's ruined face.

"MR. BLACK!"

It was Mrs. Russet. She was hurrying down the hallway like a freight train hauling anvils down a steep hill, an unstoppable force.

Billy sighed in relief. Cameron couldn't pretend nothing had happened *this* time. He was snuffling like a walrus with a head cold, blood soaking his shirt in a widening red cone.

*Billy: Messenger of Powers*, by Michaelbrent Collings * 31

Mrs. Russet looked at Harold and Sarah. "Leave," she barked. The two junior members of the Torture Brigade showed rare intelligence as they high-tailed it as fast as they could.

Mrs. Russet looked at Billy, then at Cameron. She swiveled at last to Blythe. "What happened?" she demanded.

Blythe appeared barely able to speak. "He...," she pointed to Billy. "He...*hit Cameron.*"

Mrs. Russet made a noise deep in her throat, something between a cough and a guffaw. "That's not possible," she said. She looked at Billy and Cameron again. "Is that true?" she demanded of Cameron.

"Well," managed the bigger boy. "I don't think he meant to. It was just a lucky accident for him."

"Lucky? Lucky?" The word seemed to enrage Mrs. Russet even more. "Get out of here, Black!" Cameron turned to go. "You, too, Ms. Forrest." Blythe hesitated a moment, but Mrs. Russet's furiously flashing eyes convinced her to go.

"And you," she said angrily, grabbing Billy by the shoulder, "you come with me."

She yanked him down the hall with her.

Billy couldn't believe it. How was this possible? He was being *punished*? Not only was Cameron not in trouble—again—but Billy *was* in trouble?

"But I didn't—" he began.

Mrs. Russet's mutterings cut him off. "Not possible," she said under her breath, casting a glance at Billy. "You didn't even Glimmer."

Billy tried again. "But he started it."

Mrs. Russet stopped in front of a room marked "Janitorial" and seemed to focus on Billy for the first time. "I don't doubt that for a second, Mr. Jones."

"But then," Billy said in a very small, very confused voice, "Why are you mad at *me*?"

Mrs. Russet's visage softened. Or at least, it got as soft as it could, which was to say it could have shattered diamonds but was now slightly less frightening than it had been a moment ago. "I'm not mad at you, Mr. Crane. I'm mad at Cameron Black."

She withdrew a small item from her pocket. It was a key, Billy saw. But it was unlike the keys he saw his parents and other older people use. It was old-fashioned and looked like it had been made by hand at an ancient forge: the kind a person would see in movies featuring underground dungeons in medieval castles. But where there was usually a circular piece of metal at the top of such keys, this one had been shaped to resemble a beehive.

Mrs. Russet pushed the key toward the keyhole to the janitorial closet. There was no way it was going to fit, Billy knew. The key was far too large.

But somehow, it did fit.

"Buster bumpkin bunny burps," whispered Mrs. Russet. She turned the key. A dazzling light speared out of the key, blinding Billy. Unseeing, he felt Mrs. Russet's hand on his shoulder.

"I'm not mad, Billy. But you never should have been able to touch Cameron. You see, he's a Black. But you did touch him. So we must find out why." The hand tightened. "Hold your breath," she said. "Take two steps forward, then one step back."

Billy did what she said. He did so automatically, almost as though he had no choice in the matter. Through the blaze of white light, he could feel Mrs. Russet moving with him.

A queer jerking sensation bounced up through Billy's frame, shivering him from head to foot. The breath he'd been holding burst out of him in a whoosh, and at the same time the blinding light dimmed. Billy blinked once, then *screamed* at the first thing he saw.

Because the first thing he saw…was a dragon.

Billy had never seen a dragon before, so he couldn't absolutely swear that what he was now looking at was a dragon. But it certainly *looked* like what Billy imagined a dragon would look like. It was the size of a two-story house, with overlapping metallic blue scales the size of tea plates covering its entire body. Great glistening wings flapped slowly, moving lazily and gracefully as those of a butterfly resting on a rose.

But this was no butterfly. The dragon's mouth was agape, teeth the length of Billy's forearm glistening with saliva that dripped in stringy lengths to the stone ground upon which the monster sat. The saliva spit and hissed as it touched the ground, etching acid courses through the rock.

The dragon spotted them almost at once. It hissed a warning, and a long tail that ended in a wickedly serrated point flicked over its head. Two small puffs of flame emerged from its nostrils, and then it inhaled deeply.

Billy knew what was going to happen next. He simply *knew* it. He and Mrs. Russet were going to be incinerated.

He screamed again.

Strangely, Mrs. Russet's only response was, "Oh, fiddlesticks. Artetha couldn't Imbue a key if the White King Himself helped her do it."

The dragon was still inhaling.

Billy was still screaming in terror.

Mrs. Russet held out her key: that strange key that she had used on the door to a janitorial closet that apparently was much more than a janitorial closet. She shook it like one would a remote control that wasn't working, then said, to no one in particular, "Artetha, if you are listening, I want you to know that I am going to drop a mountain on you the next time we meet."

The dragon stopped inhaling.

Mrs. Russet looked it square in the eye, and said, "Don't even think about it, Serba."

The dragon, still holding its breath, seemed to grin evilly, and made a noise, deep in its throat, that Billy would swear sounded like nothing other than a nasty chuckle. Then it opened its mouth to exhale.

And what happened next made everything else seem ordinary in comparison. As the dragon opened its mouth, not fire, but a thick liquid river of lightning spewed toward Billy and Mrs. Russet.

Billy screeched and dropped to the ground, skinning his knees and hands on the rock below. Mrs. Russet reacted differently. She whispered a quick word, and the rocky ground all around them shifted as though it had suddenly become water. A thick stalagmite erupted from the ground directly in front of them, and the dragonsbreath slammed into it with the sound of dynamite exploding against the rock face of a mountain. A shower of dirt and pebbles cascaded down all around Billy and Mrs. Russet, but the stalagmite had protected them from a painful electric death.

Billy could no longer see the dragon, but heard it inhale again, and wondered how many hits the pillar of rock could absorb before simply falling to pieces.

Mrs. Russet looked at him. "Stand up!" she snapped. Billy did so, surprised he was able to move at all.

BANG! Another explosion slammed shockwaves through Billy as the dragonsbreath hit the rock again. The pillar started to shimmy back and forth, clearly about to topple.

Mrs. Russet grabbed Billy as the dragon once more inhaled for a final, deadly strike. She held her strange beehive key against the back of the stalagmite as though it were a door, and turned the key, whispering again those nonsense words that apparently turned the key on: "Buster bumpkin bunny burps."

And a door appeared in the back of the rock.

Billy had thought nothing could surprise him further at this point, but a door appearing as though to meet the key's needs did so.

He didn't have long to think about it though. The dragon stopped inhaling. This was it.

"Hold your breath," hissed the teacher. "And remember: two steps forward, one step back." Then she yanked Billy forward with her, with him lurching against her unsteadily as they stepped into the dark doorway to nowhere just as the dragon exhaled lightning once again.

The sound was all around them, too loud to be believed, as the dragonsbreath exploded through the rock. But then it instantly muffled, as though heard from a great distance. "One step back," said Mrs. Russet, and her voice, too, sounded odd and strained. Billy realized his eyes were tightly closed. But he didn't open them. What new terror would he see if he did? He just scrunched them even tighter, and then stepped backward with Mrs. Russet, her bony, strong fingers sunk deep into his shoulder and giving him little choice in the matter.

And then, all was silence.

And a moment later, sounds came to Billy. Strange, alien sounds.

"Open your eyes, boy," said Mrs. Russet impatiently. "We're here."

Billy opened his eyes. And gasped.

"Welcome," said Mrs. Russet, "to Powers Island."

# CHAPTER THE THIRD

*In Which Billy arrives at The island, and is given the Test of Five...*

"This is what happens when you don't hold your breath" was the first thing Billy saw. It was written in ornate letters on a six foot tall bronze sheet that stood behind what looked like a shriveled mummy. Its mouth was open in a silent shriek and its eyes bugged out of its head, pupils staring in opposite directions like a chameleon. Billy stifled the urge to scream.

Instead, he managed to look at Mrs. Russet and stutter, "W-would I l-look like that if I hadn't held my breath just now?"

"Of course not," said Mrs. Russet, somewhat distractedly. "You'd be much shorter."

Billy reeled, trying to take in his surroundings. He and Mrs. Russet were standing in what looked like the lobby to a movie theater. Nearby, there were three lines of people, everyone in them waiting patiently as the lines moved toward three glass cases. Each case was about six feet tall and held in it what looked like a carnival fortune teller: one of those plastic mannequins that would give someone a card with their fortune on it in exchange for a quarter.

Mrs. Russet pulled Billy with her into the shortest line. "What are we doing?" asked Billy. "Where are we? Why are we here? Who are you? How did we get here? Why are we in line? What's that fortune teller thing? How—"

"Calm down," snapped Mrs. Russet. "Powers Island. To determine if you Glimmer. Mrs. Russet. By Imbuement. To stand and be counted. The Counter."

Billy looked at his teacher. The words were, once again, English. But as had happened so often in recent minutes, he didn't understand a word of what she was saying.

"What?"

"Those were the answers to your questions."

Billy thought furiously. He couldn't remember what he had asked. But he suspected that, even if he did remember, he wouldn't understand the answers anyway. Still, he tried again. Start with something basic, he thought, then said aloud, "*Where* are we?"

"Powers Island. Specifically, we're in the tower at the center of the island right now, in the Accounting Room."

Billy had been right: he didn't understand a word of that. Accounting Room? It sounded like someplace where there should be guys in suits with calculators, not a bunch of people in waiting in line for a fortune teller booth.

A sudden "pop" sounded behind them. Billy turned and saw a man appear out of thin air. He was dressed like a bobby—a British policeman—with a tall rounded cap and swinging a short nightstick with practiced ease. The bobby nodded at Mrs. Russet. "Lumilla," he said in a precise English accent.

Mrs. Russet nodded back. "Bellestus," she replied as the policeman stepped into another one of the three lines.

Billy's brain was quickly overloading again. He opened his mouth to fire another machine-gun cartridge of questions at his teacher, then decided to just wait quietly for a few minutes to see if anything remotely understandable happened. He closed his mouth and Mrs. Russet—Lumilla?—smiled at him as though approving of his decision.

They moved forward in their line, slowly but surely approaching the glass-cased mannequin before them. During the time they waited in line, Billy heard three more "pops" and turned to see three more people appear out of nowhere: a man in a three-piece suit; a lady with a stethoscope hanging around her neck and a round badge that said "ENT's are head and shoulders above the rest"; and what looked like a tribal warrior from darkest Africa, complete with ornate headdress and a thin bone piercing his nose. Each of these three arrivals nodded at Mrs. Russet with either familiarity or respect when they noticed her in line.

At last, it was Billy's and Mrs. Russet's turn to approach the mannequin. Mrs. Russet went first. She didn't have to put a quarter in the machine, just touched a button on the side of the case. The mannequin—which had a thick beard and wore a jeweled turban and a blouse made of glimmering silk—moved a rigid hand and a card dropped into a slot at the bottom of the machine. Mrs. Russet took it and touched it to her shirt, where it stuck tightly.

"Lumilla Russet—Dawnwalker" is what the card said.

Billy stood silently for a moment, unsure what to do. Mrs. Russet pushed him gently toward the machine. "Your turn," she said.

Billy walked forward hesitatingly, fearful of what was going on and what would happen next. Nothing had hurt him so far—though the dragon had seemed quite happy to try—but he still felt as if a meteor was going to fall on his head at any moment.

Unbidden, his mind cast up an image of Blythe Forrest, her beautiful eyes looking at him, her lovely face lit by a smile that was for him alone. His toes again felt like they were turning inside out, but at the same time just thinking about Blythe made him feel more...secure. Nervous, but happy and safe.

Billy stepped forward and pressed the button on the mannequin's case.

The mannequin's hand moved. It wavered, as though uncertain, taking much longer than it had with Mrs. Russet. But, at last, a card dropped into the slot. Billy took it.

"Billy," it said simply. No last name, nothing else on it.

"First time, eh?" said the woman who stood behind him in line. The lady doctor. She touched him gently on the arm. "You'll be fine," she said gravely, glancing at Mrs. Russet. "You're in good hands."

Billy knew that the words were meant to be encouraging, but for some reason they just made him worry that much more.

"Come on, we haven't all day for this. I'm getting far too old in the real world to spend all day on the island," said Mrs. Russet. She took the "Billy" card from Billy's hands and pressed it against his shirt. The card hadn't been sticky, Billy knew. But it stuck to his shirt like it had been super-glued there. Then Mrs. Russet took Billy's hand and walked him over to what looked like a nearby bank of elevators, the old fashioned kind with windows in the doors through which each passing floor might be glimpsed.

"What are those?" Billy asked, almost afraid of what the answer might be.

"Elevators," answered Mrs. Russet. She looked at him like he had just dropped fifty IQ points. "You know, little boxes that take people up and down in tall buildings?"

"But...I thought...," Billy stammered. His voice drifted off as one of the elevators dinged and opened. Mrs. Russet stepped in. Billy followed her, and the doors closed.

"What floor and department, please?" said a pleasant voice from a hidden speaker somewhere.

"Three thousand seven hundred sixty-eighth floor, Glimmer Detection and Decisionary Department," replied Mrs. Russet.

"It is my pleasure to lift you there. Would you care for a refreshing beverage or some kind of tasty treat on your trip?" asked the elevator. It began whirring, and Billy's stomach lurched as he felt the elevator begin to rise.

"No thank you," said Mrs. Russet.

Over three thousand floors? Billy thought. He did a bit of math in his head: at ten feet per floor, that was over thirty thousand feet, or about...*six miles*!

The elevator went up one level, and through the window in the elevator's door Billy caught a glimpse of what looked like a forest. A forest? he thought. How could an entire forest be inside a single floor of a building?

Then he realized that if there was a forest in the first floor, that meant that ten feet per floor was probably way too little. Who knew how high up they would be when they got wherever they were going?

"Are you sure you wouldn't like a treat?" cajoled the elevator. "I have very yummy snacks. Dell-Diddly-Delites?"

Another floor passed, and Billy glimpsed a herd of something that looked like pigs the size of dump trucks galloping by.

"Bing-Bing Belly Boomers?" continued the elevator as it picked up speed. The floors flashed by faster and faster, and the things Billy saw grew stranger and stranger. What looked like a truck-sized armadillo on one floor, a group of men and women in white coats chasing each other while holding what appeared to be huge butterfly wings on another, house-sized beehives stretching as far as the eye could see on a third. Then the elevator was moving up too fast for the floors to be seen, and they became mere flashes of light that strobed by as the elevator sped upward.

"Scuddle Snackers?" The elevator was really hard-selling its inventory. "Fizzy Floaters? Shakka-Shakka Shakes? Blue Lightning Crumpets? Candy bar?"

"Shut up," said Mrs. Russet. No more words came out of the speakers, but Billy felt for some reason as though the elevator were sulking.

Mrs. Russet swiveled to look at Billy. She tapped a spot on the wall of the elevator. It looked no different to Billy than any other spot on the wall, but when she did so, two softly-velveted seats emerged from the sides of the elevator. Mrs. Russet sat down on one, gesturing for Billy to do the same.

"You must have many questions," she began.

Billy nodded. He was afraid to actually *ask* any questions, since that just ended up making him more confused. But Mrs. Russet was looking at him expectantly, and he didn't want to irritate her, so finally he said, "What was the key?"

"This?" asked Mrs. Russet, drawing out that strange beehive key. "It is an Imbued Object." Billy stared at her blankly. "It means it is magic."

"Magic?" said Billy.

"No, magic," said Mrs. Russet.

"Magic?" asked Billy again.

"*Maqic*," she emphasized.

Billy couldn't hear a difference between the way he was saying the word and the way Mrs. Russet was. His look must have told Mrs. Russet this, for her brow furrowed. "Can't tell the difference between magic and magic, either," she mumbled, as though Billy had failed some kind of test. Then she re-focused her attention on him. "You can't hear the silent 'q'? Try it again: magic," she said, over-enunciating the last word as though she were trying to teach Billy a new language.

Billy, now thoroughly befuddled and maybe even downright bamboozled, shook his head. "It sounds like you're saying, uh, 'magic.'"

Mr. Russet shook her head. "Fine, for now we'll just call it magic, since you haven't been Determined yet."

Billy still didn't understand anything she was saying. But he felt some hope, because at least her words were starting to sound a bit more like threads of a normal conversation, rather than just a spewing of random words.

She held up the key. "This is a key that has been Imbued with magic."

"Imbued?" asked Billy.

"Imbued means that a Power—what I suppose you would call a wizard or a witch—has put a small piece of his or her magical essence into an object to give it certain special properties. In this case, a Power named Artetha put some of her essence into the key and made it magic. The key can take its possessor from one place to another through doorways in space and time that it creates. So the possessor is me, and I wanted the key to open a doorway to Powers Island—to where we now are—and that is what it did."

"But you wanted us to go to somewhere that we could almost be killed by a dragon first?" asked Billy slowly.

Mrs. Russet frowned. "No. Artetha makes, on the whole, very good keys. Unfortunately, she is occasionally a bit sloppy with her Imbuement process, so once in a while you might end up getting sent somewhere you didn't wish to go. The dragon Serba's lair, for example, or the surface of the sun." Mrs. Russet shrugged as though to say, "What can you do?"

Billy lit up as he made a connection. "Was the frog in your room on the first day of school imboobed?"

"Im*bued*. Yes it was."

"What did it do?"

"That's a bit complicated," responded Mrs. Russet.

"But the frog and the key are both magic?" asked Billy.

"Well of course," said Mrs. Russet. "Haven't you been listening to anything I've been saying?"

"And are you magic?"

"If by that you are asking am I a Power, then the answer is yes," said Mrs. Russet.

"Then is everyone here at Powers Island also magic?" asked Billy.

"Yes," said the teacher.

"But everyone I've seen, all the people in the line downstairs, they all looked…normal."

"Good heavens, Billy, what would you expect us to look like?" asked Mrs. Russet, a glimmer of amusement in her eyes. "We wouldn't get along so well in the rest of the world if we wore Greek togas or long robes and pointy caps that had stars all over them, now would we? Powers are all human beings. Or at least, most of them are. And those that are human all live in the world the same as you, and have jobs, and families, and everything else that makes a person a person." She shrugged, apparently suddenly realizing that she had dropped into what Billy thought of as his teacher's Lecture Mode. "At any rate, as an answer to your question, yes, everyone here is magic."

"So…," Billy gulped. "Am I magic?"

Mrs. Russet paused, seeming unsure for the very first time since Billy had known her.

At that moment, the elevator dinged. "Three thousand seven hundred sixty-eighth floor, Glimmer Detection and Decisionary Department," it intoned. Sure enough, it sounded piqued and offended.

"We're here," said Mrs. Russet, and stood to leave as the elevator door whooshed sulkily open, leaving Billy's question unanswered.

Billy followed her into a hall, and couldn't help but gasp. The hall seemed to go on forever. In fact, it extended so far that it actually dwindled to a pinpoint and disappeared in both directions.

More than that, though, the wall on one side was made of fire. It was bright and flickering, a living flame, but though Billy stood within mere feet of it, he could not feel any heat. He put a hand toward the wall, to see how close he could get to it before he could feel any warmth, but his hand was slapped away at the last second.

"Don't!" shouted Mrs. Russet. "You'll get it dirty."

"But...it's fire," protested Billy.

"And very clean fire," agreed Mrs. Russet. "Now come along."

Billy walked behind Mrs. Russet's quick feet as she sped down the hall. He looked to the other wall, the one not made of fire, and discovered it was a translucent blue. It looked familiar, but he couldn't place it. Then, suddenly, a large dark shape appeared in the wall nearby. It was indistinct at first, then its outline slowly sharpened as the shape came closer. Finally, the shape was completely clear. It was an enormous blue whale, about two hundred feet long, swimming through the wall and keeping exact pace with Billy and Mrs. Russet, one great eye staring unblinkingly at them. Billy glanced at Mrs. Russet, but she seemed to be paying no attention to the boy for the moment. So he reached out a hand and gingerly touched the blue wall. His fingers came back dripping wet.

"Is that the ocean?" he asked, awed.

"Of course it is," said Mrs. Russet. "What else would have a great blue whale in it?" She nodded curtly at the whale, which dipped its forequarters in return.

The whale then turned its huge eye to look squarely at Billy. Billy felt at a loss for a moment, unsure of what the proper protocol was when being stared at by a blue whale through a wall of water. He watched the whale for a moment as he walked, still trying to think of what he should do, if anything. Finally, he decided to follow Mrs. Russet's lead, and slowly and respectfully he bowed his head toward the leviathan. The whale seemed to consider this for a moment, then it winked its great eye at Billy and swam off again.

"What would happen if I put my head against the wall?" asked Billy, hurrying to catch up to Mrs. Russet.

"I shouldn't advise it," was Mrs. Russet's only reply.

Now that he knew that one wall was a raging—though cold and contained—inferno, and the other somehow contained an entire ocean in its structure, Billy wondered what the ceiling would look like if he looked up.

So he did.

And Billy saw something few people had seen from ten feet away and lived to tell about: the inside of a hurricane. Not the *eye* of a hurricane, the calm area in the center of the swirling winds where things were quiet and stable, but the actual hurricane itself. Billy could actually see masses of rocks, cars, pieces of buildings, and even some people being thrown about at great speeds directly above them, though for some reason none of the people up there seemed frightened. Quite the opposite in fact: Billy saw that they were all laughing and seemed almost to be dancing in the gusts and eddies that flung them about like autumn leaves in the wind.

The forces at work had to be tremendous, and yet, as with the wall of fire and the strangely contained sea to his right and left, Billy could feel nothing of the great forces only a few feet away.

"What is this place?" Billy whispered. He asked it of himself, forgetting in his awe that Mrs. Russet was even there, not expecting any kind of answer. But to his surprise, she did answer. And to his greater surprise, the answer she gave actually made some sense to him.

"It is a Convergence," she said. "A place where four great lines of energy come together, drawn here by the Powers who wield and shape them." She gestured to the wall at her right. "Fire." Then to her left: "Water." She pointed up and said, "The great Wind," and then down at their feet and whispered, "and the ever-growing power of Life."

Billy looked down for the first time—he had been so captivated by what was happening above and to his sides he had not taken care to watch where he was walking. Now he saw that below him were what looked like enormous leaves from some great tree, but so tightly overlapping that Billy could feel no difference in the floor's level where one leaf left off and another began. "What kind of leaves are they?" he asked, still hurrying to keep up with Mrs. Russet's rapid gait.

"They are the leaves of the Earthtree, just as what you see above is the Earthwind, and to the right and left you see Earthsea and Earthfire. Four of the six Elements in their rawest, most unrefined forms. We Powers take these Elements and use them to do what you call magic. They are the source of our strength."

She stopped suddenly, scrutinizing Billy as though for the first time. "Are you...*closer* to any of these? The gray wind, the red fire, the blue water, or the green life below you?"

Billy looked down. "Well, I'm standing on the plants, so I guess I'm closest to them—"

"Not physically close, you dolt. I mean do you *feel* as though you have any sort of special connection to one of these? Do you like one of them more than the other, perhaps?"

Billy looked at the walls of water and flame again, the swirling tornado of a ceiling, the veined green leaves below. Then, slowly, he shook his head.

Mrs. Russet looked a bit disappointed. To Billy's surprise, he found that he didn't want her to be disappointed in him. She was stern, even rude at times, but...she was also fair. She cared. She had been a good history teacher in school, making sure—by intimidation if necessary—that each student learned as much as he or she possibly could. Now Billy sensed that she was trying to teach him at this very moment, and that the things she was trying to teach were even more important than when and how Napoleon lost the battle of Waterloo. He just couldn't understand *what* those monumentally important things were.

"Well, no matter," she said. "We'll come to the answers soon enough."

She turned and strode off again. Billy followed her in silence. Occasionally a school of fish would swim by to his left, or he would glimpse a roof flinging through the storm above. Once he thought he glanced strange, shimmering, but faintly human shapes in the flames beside him. Only the leaves below were silent, still, and somberly immobile.

Suddenly, after what seemed like a year of marching, Mrs. Russet stopped. "We've arrived," she said. Billy was grateful for this announcement: his feet ached from walking, and he had a stitch in his side that was rapidly increasing in intensity. At the same time, though, he couldn't help being bewildered at Mrs. Russet's decision to stop. To his eyes, this part of the hall looked the same as had every other part of it.

"We've arrived where?" he asked.

"At your Determination," she answered. She pulled a small stone from her pocket and clenched it in her fist. A moment later, the stone expanded, lengthening out and increasing in size until it was a long staff of clearest crystal.

"Stand back now, Mr. Jones," said Mrs. Russet. Billy moved quickly back about five feet, and as he did so the old woman struck the end of her crystal staff against the leafy floor. The resulting sound was quite unexpected. Billy had expected to hear a dull thud, the sound one would normally hear when dropping a rock to a spot of grassy ground. Instead, a clear, bell-like tone reverberated up and down the corridor. It bounced off the walls, back and forth and up and down, changing in tone until it had traveled the entire range of a musical scale, like the most beautiful, voiceless song that Billy had ever heard. The sound dissipated until the song was no more, but it faded so slowly that Billy couldn't tell the exact moment when the beautiful song ended and the silence of the corridor began.

A long moment passed, during which neither he nor Mrs. Russet spoke.

Then a pair of legs dropped down into Billy's view.

He looked up to see a kindly-faced old man floating down from the maelstrom in the ceiling, landing gently in front of Mrs. Russet. The man seemed to be around the same age as Mrs. Russet, but neither stern nor sour as she could be. Rather, he seemed more like Billy had always imagined Santa Claus: eternal youth clothed in an old and happily chubby body.

The man wore clothing, Billy was sure, but he couldn't see exactly what kind of clothing it was, because from the neck down the man seemed to be dressed in wind: a swirling cloud of gray and gusting air that obscured what he was wearing and made him seem larger than he actually was. The man wore a piece of the storm above, and had brought it down into the hall with him.

The instant he landed before Mrs. Russet, the old man grinned, deep gray eyes twinkling. "Lumilla," he said, and bowed a sweeping bow before her.

"Tempus," replied Mrs. Russet, nodding her head.

"I'd ask if I might kiss your hand, but my ears are still ringing from the tongue-lashing you gave me last time I dared that question," said the wind-clothed man, Tempus. He turned to Billy. "And who have we here?"

"Who indeed?" whispered a voice. Billy, Mrs. Russet, and Tempus all turned to see another man enter the hall, this one stepping out of the wall of flame to Billy's right. Like Tempus, the man was clothed. And also like the wind-wreathed Tempus, the newcomer's clothing could not quite be seen. He was ringed in flame up to his neck, but the fire light dimmed as he stepped away from the wall and approached them. At last, it seemed to extinguish completely as he moved away from the wall, though Billy could still see the barest hint of a spark in the man's piercing eyes.

"Hello, Vester," said Tempus, holding out his hand in greeting.

Vester ignored Tempus's outstretched hand. He knelt next to Billy. He looked like a young man, in his early twenties perhaps, good looking and tall, with wavy brown hair of the kind that Billy wished he could have. The man was dressed in jeans and a T-shirt that said "Los Angeles Fire Department" across it, and just as Billy wished he could have the man's hair, he also looked longingly at the man's thick arms and muscled chest which fairly exploded through his t-shirt. Someday, he thought. Someday I'll look like that, and I won't need Blythe to protect me anymore. Instead, *I'll* protect *her*.

Then on the heels of that thought came another: Who am I kidding?

The man who had walked out of flame looked at Billy for a long time, then the corners of his lips perked up ever so slightly before he stood and took Tempus's hand. "Sorry, my friend," said Vester to Tempus. The fireman looked at Billy. "I was surprised to see Billy here, that's all."

Both Billy and Mrs. Russet started. "You know him?" asked Mrs. Russet in surprise.

"No," Vester said to her. "But I work with Mr. Jones, who is a paramedic in the fire department." He looked at Billy. "I was in his ambulance once. Did you know he has a picture of you taped to his dashboard? You're swimming in the picture. In the ocean, as I recall."

Billy's eyes widened. He remembered his mom taking that picture just the last summer, on a family trip to the beach. His father hadn't been able to be there, working as he so often was. His mom had taken a picture of Billy flying head over heels in a crashing wave, laughing as he struggled to his feet, covered in seaweed. "For your father," she had laughed.

Billy didn't know what surprised him more: the fact that this strange young man who could walk through fire knew his father, or that his often distant-seeming father had a picture of Billy in his ambulance, where he could see it while he worked.

Vester looked with apparent concern at Billy. "You all right?" Billy nodded mutely. Vester smiled, a reassuring, comforting smile. "It looked like you were having a good time in that picture."

Yet another voice was now heard, this one thick and phlegmatic, as though the speaker had a serious cold. "Of course he was having a good time. How could you not have a good time when in the water?"

Billy looked over and saw a man hanging in the wall of water, his hair moving slowly back and forth in the invisible currents that flowed through the great Earthsea.

The man stepped out of the water and into the hall. Billy looked at the man's feet as he entered the hall, expecting him to leave a wet trail behind him, but he didn't. His feet—and the rest of him, including his impeccable three-piece suit—were perfectly dry. Only his voice remained thick and unpleasantly wet. He looked at Billy. But where Tempus had looked at Billy with amusement and Vester had looked at him in a comforting and familial manner, this man's look was cold and deep as a midnight sea. "You are unDetermined," he announced gravely, more than a hint of distaste in his expression.

Tempus laughed. "I'm always surprised that you can know that sort of thing right off, Wade."

Wade looked at Tempus with contempt. "I am a Power of water. I see the boy's blood, and the blood tells much."

Billy shivered internally, unnerved by this aloof man talking coldly of his blood.

"Well," said Vester, apparently sensing Billy's discomfort. "We're just about all here, then, aren't we?"

"Almost," said Tempus, seeming to laugh even as he said this one word. "Just our favorite lass and we'll be ready."

"Ready for what?" squeaked Billy.

Mrs. Russet stepped toward him and put a comforting hand on his shoulder. "All will be explained in a moment, Mr. Jones."

"Mr. Jones?" came a voice, and Billy's skin crawled. He knew that voice. Or at any rate, he knew a voice very much like it. He turned behind him and saw a woman walking toward them. She was dressed all in black, a long black dress that accentuated the exaggerated sway of her hips as she walked, elegant black gloves that extended all the way to her elbows, and a string of black pearls that hung on a long white neck that was partially obscured by her thick black hair.

His eyes were drawn for a moment to a huge dark broach pinned on the side of her dress. It was a beetle, one of those types he saw in movies about mummies who came alive and killed folks. Usually with the help of such beetles. The beetle broach made Billy feel sick to his stomach.

"Mr. Jones?" said the woman again, drawing Billy's gaze to her eyes. Billy's skin continued to try to pry itself loose from his skeleton as she approached. She had green eyes. Green eyes that were very familiar.

"This is Eva Black," said Mrs. Russet. And then, almost unnecessarily, for Billy already suspected what she was about to say, she added, "Cameron Black's mother."

Mrs. Black stood close in front of Billy, eyeing him with what he thought was amused disdain. "Mr. Jones, I've heard so…much… about you." Then her expression of disdain turned to one of cold rage as she said, "You hurt my boy today."

Billy's skin stopped trying to run away without him and instead now felt as though it had frozen solid. He tried to say something, but nothing came out of his twitching mouth. Mrs. Black smiled and looked at Wade, the man who had come from the seawall. "UnDetermined?" she asked him, nodding toward Billy. The water Power nodded, and with that Mrs. Black turned to Mrs. Russet. "So that's why you called us, Lumilla?"

Mrs. Russet nodded. Mrs. Black smiled delicately, as though contemplating eating a rich chocolate truffle or drinking a cup of cocoa on a cold winter evening. Then she said the most horrifying words Billy had ever heard: "It will be a pleasure killing you, young man."

Billy didn't know what to say or do. He wanted to hide, but there was nowhere *to* hide in this hallway. And besides, he knew that running would be the wrong thing to do, a useless gesture.

On the other hand, this woman had just said she was going to *kill* him!

"Be careful, Eva," said Mrs. Russet. "He *did* manage to hit your boy, remember. And with no training or tutelage. Perhaps Billy is himself a Black, and perhaps he's even one whose good side you will want to be on some day."

Mrs. Black snorted derisively. "I hardly think so—" she began, but then stopped as the floor shifted below them all.

Billy let out a little shout—he was coming to expect the unexpected, but still couldn't contain the fear he felt as the leaves that had until now supported him suddenly parted, allowing him to drop downward through their suddenly flexible forms.

He screamed in earnest now, free falling through a mass of leaves, trying to grab them, to hold onto something—anything—that would stop him from falling. But his hands came up empty, cruelly cut by the edges of the leaves through which he was descending.

Then, quite suddenly, he landed in a pile of leaves as thick and soft as a king's mattress. It was almost a pleasant feeling, and would have been fun if he hadn't been so terrified.

Five matching thumps told him that Mrs. Russet, Vester the fireman, Tempus of the wind, Wade the water Power, and Mrs. Eva Black had also fallen with him into—what?

Billy stood up and looked around. It appeared as though he was in a great basket, woven of living vines, tight and secure. In the middle of the room stood a single table, long and thin, that reminded Billy uncomfortably of a table in an operating room. At one end of the table stood a lit candle, and at the other end sat a small bowl of water.

Behind the table stood a woman, a short, chubby woman whose age Billy couldn't quite make out. She seemed somehow both old and young at the same time. Her body was covered in leaves and vines and greenery that grew out of the very floor of the living basket in which they all stood. And when she moved toward Billy, she didn't have to walk: the living floor she stood on lifted her up and carried her close to him on shifting blades of grass that sprung up before her and then disappeared into the greenery as she passed.

"Good day, Billy," she said. "I am Ivy."

"Hi," said Billy. It was a single syllable, but under the circumstances he was rather proud of managing to say anything coherent at all. In fact, the simple feat of uttering the word made him feel rather heroic. Then he caught sight of Mrs. Black looking at him and his heroism disappeared, leaving him feeling more like a lobster being held over a pot of boiling water.

"As you've no doubt guessed," said Ivy, pulling Billy's gaze back to her, "you are here for a specific reason, Billy."

"Quite so," added Tempus with a windy laugh.

"Do be quiet, Tempus," said Wade. "We'll never get through this if you blather."

"Why *am* I here?" asked Billy.

"Yes," said Mrs. Black. "I'd like to know that, too. It seems fairly clear to *me* that this boy..."—and the way she said "boy" made it clear to Billy that she really wanted to say something else, like "worm" or "dog-doo that I stepped in and am about to scrape off my shoe with a shovel"—"...is a no-Power nothing—a mere human who is nothing more than a waste of our time."

Mrs. Black faced Mrs. Russet challengingly, and Tempus, Vester, Wade, and Ivy all joined her in staring at Billy's teacher.

Billy felt that had he been stared at like that by these four frighteningly strange people—or Powers, he supposed he should call them—he would have just poofed instantly into a Billy-shaped smoke outline and disappeared. Mrs. Russet was made of sterner stuff, though. Not only did she *not* poof into a Mrs. Russet-shaped smoky outline, she managed to look fairly irritated, as though she hadn't counted on having to answer any questions.

"Well," she finally said, "the greatest indicator that I saw was that he managed to punch your son, Eva."

"I *told* you," responded Mrs. Black coolly. "That was clearly luck."

"And I tell *you*, Eva, that no 'no-Power nothing' that I'm aware of has *ever* managed to harm a Black Power in all our history." Then, she added with a biting sarcasm, "I'm surprised to find that you know so little of your own history, Eva. But then, the Blacks have never been famous for their thinking." Billy still wasn't sure exactly what they were all talking about, but he felt a bit of pride, both that he had apparently managed something special in smacking

Cameron, and at the fact that Mrs. Russet was clearly sticking up for him.

"Still and all, Lumilla," said Wade, his wet, dripping voice oozing over Billy like a cold tide, "there *are* other tests which are less radical than the test of Five."

"Don't you think I know that?" snapped Mrs. Russet. For the first time, Billy thought she appeared a bit anxious. This did nothing to calm his already strained nerves. "I already gave him those tests."

"And?" asked Ivy.

"He didn't *fail* them," said Mrs. Russet. "Not totally, at any rate."

"Let's back up a moment," said Vester. He tousled Billy's hair and winked at him. Generally, Billy didn't go in for head-tousling, any more than he went in for diapers or a baby rattle. But at that moment Billy felt as though he could have hugged the young fireman, if for no other reason than because he actually seemed to recognize that Billy was more than a little frightened by the tempest of discussion that all seemed to be about him. "Lumilla, why did you give him any tests in the first place?"

"The first day I met him—the first day of school—I gave out a test—the written kind, not a Test of Power—to all my students. And before he started working on his test, Billy did...." Mrs. Russet's face screwed up as though she herself were trying to figure out what it was Billy had done.

"Yes?" prompted Ivy.

"Well, I'm not exactly sure *what* he did. But he closed his eyes, and suddenly I could feel something in the earth."

"You mean he was calling the Earthessence? He was going to do a first spell of some kind?" asked Ivy.

Mrs. Russet shook her head. "It didn't feel like he was controlling the Element. It was more as though the Earthessence were waiting for something. Expectant."

Eva Black laughed, a quick yip of a laugh that sounded to Billy as though a small dog had caught its leg in a trap and was now considering chewing the leg off to get out. "And for that," she said, "you summon five Powers to a Gleaning? Because of an indistinct *hunch*? Have you lost your mind, Lumilla? You could have simply been having indigestion for all we know!"

"Now, now," said Ivy, the greenery that cloaked the young/old woman writhing anxiously. "I'm sure there was more to it than that." She turned to Mrs. Russet. "What about the other tests?"

"Inconclusive at best," said Mrs. Russet.

"Really," said Eva. Her tone of voice left no doubt that she had a very low opinion of anyone else's opinions. Especially one that originated with Mrs. Russet. She looked squarely at Billy and said, "Robot fish wear Picasso's underwear."

"What?" asked Billy. No one answered. He realized that everyone in the room—Mrs. Russet, Eva Black, Tempus, Vester, Wade, and Ivy—were all staring expectantly at him. He felt like he should do some kind of trick or musical act or something. Unfortunately, the only trick Billy knew was the best way to get comfortable in a locker, and he had never learned how to play anything other than the kazoo. So he just smiled a nervous half-smile and waited for someone else to do something.

Finally, Wade said, "Interesting." He paused, then the water Power told Billy, "Did you know my koala rents paperclips for potato chips?"

Billy had a sudden, crazy urge to reply, "No, but if you sing the first part of it maybe I can follow along," but managed to ignore that impulse. Everyone was still looking at him, and he suspected that no one would think that was a very funny response to Wade's incomprehensible question.

At last, Ivy cleared her throat. "Well," she said. "I think we can agree that his Glimmer reaction to nonsense is minimal. What about pronunciation?" She looked at Billy. "Say 'magic.'"

"Magic," repeated Billy dutifully.

Eva tsk tsked loudly. "He certainly fails *that* test. Didn't say it with the silent 'q' at all." She turned an angry eye on Mrs. Russet. "I can't believe you've wasted my time like this. Perhaps you could try taking an antacid next time you feel inclined to bring in a nonPower for testing."

"I'm telling you, Eva, I felt something that first day. Something unusual. Something I've never felt before." Mrs. Russet stared at all the other Powers, challenge flashing from her eyes. "He needs to be tested. He needs a Gleaning."

Vester put a placating hand out. "I'm sure no one challenges your sensitivity in these matters, Lumilla," he said, casting a glance at Eva that seemed to say quite clearly "except her." But out loud he merely continued, "But do you really think it's worth the risk to do a Gleaning?"

Mrs. Russet crossed her arms. Billy recognized that movement. A student in her history class had once told her he needed another day to turn in a project that was due. Mrs. Russet had crossed her arms just that way, and Billy knew at that moment that the student's request was doomed. The crossed arms meant that Mrs. Russet had made up her mind and wouldn't be budged.

"I do think it's worth the risk to do a Gleaning," she answered. "I think it's worth that risk, and more. I'll be his Sponsor, if that makes a difference."

The other Powers in the room all looked visibly surprised by his announcement. Ivy nodded. "Well, if you're going to be his Sponsor, then the decision is yours." She looked at Billy, gesturing to the table in the center of the room. "Billy, please lay down here."

Billy looked askance at Mrs. Russet, who nodded, then he moved timidly to the tabletop.

Vester moved to stand by the candle at one end of the table. "Head up here," he said, pointing at the candle before him, "and feet down there," continued the fireman, nodding at the bowl of water at the other end of the table. Billy did as Vester told him, watching as the six Powers in the room took up positions all around him. Vester remained at his head, the watery Wade moved to Billy's feet. Eva Black and Ivy stood on either side of him, and Mrs. Russet and Tempus stood just behind Ivy.

Looking up at the group, he realized for the first time that all of them wore badges like his and Mrs. Russet's. Vester's, Tempus's, and Ivy's badges all said their names, followed by the word "Dawnwalker," just like Mrs. Russet's did. The badges that Wade and Eva Black both wore, however, said something different: "Darksider."

"What's a Dawnwalk—?" began Billy.

"Hush," said Mrs. Russet. She waited a moment as Eva, Tempus, Vester, Wade, and Ivy all closed their eyes at the same time and suddenly became motionless as statues. They even looked harder somehow, like they were no longer people, but perfect reproductions of themselves made of rock or steel.

Mrs. Russet looked at Billy. "Yes?"

Billy couldn't remember what his question had been, so he settled for what he figured would be a good second-place question: "What is going on?" He was surprised how calm he sounded, considering the fact that he was waiting to have who-knows-what done to him by people who had walked out of water, fire, a tornado, a tree, or just plain appeared out of nowhere, and that he was currently laying on what felt like an operating table in the middle of a room made out of a giant basket in the Earthtree, whatever *that* was.

Mrs. Russet sighed. "We can't always tell who is going to be a Power. Usually there are signs when someone is an infant: they call one of the six Elements to them and channel it somehow. A toddler will make waves appear in its wading pool, for instance, or perhaps a six-inch rain cloud will suddenly appear and hang over his or her crib for a week or so, raining the whole time." She glanced at the five other Powers, who were still standing motionless. "But occasionally someone will make it to an older age—around fourteen—before showing any signs of being a Power."

"But *I'm* fourteen," said Billy.

"Yes, I know," said Mrs. Russet dryly, and Billy blushed. Of course she knew that. Hadn't she wished him happy birthday at lunch? "At any rate, when the Power is discovered later, usually an older child will channel an Element, just the same as a baby who becomes a Power. But sometimes a young man or woman will just do what we call Glimmer. It means he is periodically coated in an aura of indeterminate power, one that no specific Element must obey. It's only visible to other Powers, and not even to all of them, so sometimes it's missed." She paused a moment, then said, "I thought I saw something like that surrounding you—just for an instant, the barest blink of an eye—your first day at school."

"And someone who Glimmers will become a—a Power—as well?" asked Billy.

"Sometimes," replied his teacher. "We don't understand Glimmering completely. Sometimes it's a one-time thing, and the child goes on to have a normal life, never aware of its brush with the Powers. Other times, the Glimmer returns. And then..."—Mrs. Russet exhaled as though suddenly quite tired—"Well, then the child is going to be involved with the Powers, either as a Power himself, or...."

"Or?" prodded Billy.

"Or in some other way. Let's just leave it at that for now." She cleared her throat, then continued. "Usually, someone who has Glimmered will be able to tell the difference between the words 'magic' and 'magic'—"

"The difference between magic and magic?" began Billy. "But—"

"Don't interrupt, Mr. Jones. And for *heaven's* sake, let's not have another back-and-forth where I say magic and then you repeat it back to me incorrectly."

Billy shrugged as though to say, "Okay." This seemed to satisfy Mrs. Russet, so she continued. "Another way to trigger a clearer Glimmer is to send the potential Power into total confusion. The easiest way to do it is to say something so completely nonsensical that the potential Power can't tell his feet from his forehead."

Billy's eyes lit up. "So when you said that stuff about golden bears and fleas being on fire, and when Mrs. Black said that thing about fish underwear...."

"Correct," said Mrs. Russet, looking at him with approval. "They were confusing you to see if they could trigger a Glimmer."

"But they didn't, did they?"

"No," answered Mrs. Russet. "And usually, that would be the end of it. But as I said, with you, that first day of school, in addition to almost seeing a Glimmer, I also felt something. Something highly unusual, something I've never felt before." She paused, her brow furrowing, clearly trying to figure out the best way to explain the rest to Billy. "As I've already explained, the Powers channel the Elements. Each Power has control, to a greater or lesser degree, over a single Element. Thus Wade," she glanced at the cold-faced "Darksider" who stood near the bowl of water at Billy's feet, "is a Power of Water. And Vester," she said, pointing to the fireman near the candle, "is a Power who controls the Element of Fire. Ivy, if you couldn't guess, channels and bends the Life Element—the Element that controls the earth's plants and living things. Tempus is a Power of the Wind and Storm. And as for me, I am a Power of Earth."

Another connection was made in Billy's mind. "The dragon! That's what saved us! You made that stalagmite that saved us from the dragon!"

This garnered a second approving nod from Mrs. Russet. Billy thought he might lift bodily off the table with pride. "Very good, Mr. Jones. I have a deep and—if I do say so myself—very powerful connection with Earth. And on that first day, when you had your eyes closed in sheer panic during the test, the Earth said something to me."

"What did it say?" whispered Billy.

"I don't know," she answered.

Billy realized then that she hadn't mentioned one of the Powers in the room. "What about her?" he asked, motioning to Eva Black. "What is her, uh, Element?"

Mrs. Russet frowned. "She is a Power of the Black. The Element of Death. As is her son, Cameron. Black Powers are the fighters of our world. The weakest of them is capable of fighting off dozens of normal people at a time, and the most powerful in our history have laid waste to entire cities. That's why I finally decided to bring you in here. Even accidentally, you shouldn't have been able to even *touch* Cameron Black. Not unless he wanted you to—which I doubt—or unless you were a Power yourself, most likely another Power of the Black."

"So I *am* a Power?" asked Billy, both excited at the idea of being someone magic and disturbed that the magic he likely had was such a gruesome one. Although, he realized, having power over Death would probably enable him to stop the bully attacks at school.

"I've already told you I don't know if you're a Power or not," said Mrs. Russet. "But we have to find out. And that's why we're here. Because there is a single way that is one hundred percent certain of determining whether a person is a Power or not."

"What way is that?" asked Billy, suddenly and inexplicably chilled.

"It's rather simple, actually," said Eva Black, her eyes snapping open. She smiled, the first genuine-seeming smile that Billy had seen come across her face. "I get to kill you."

Billy looked at Mrs. Russet. Eva Black had said that already, but he had figured—or at least hoped in his heart of hearts—that she was just trying to scare him, or was making some kind of very unfunny joke. Mrs. Russet just looked back at him. Billy suddenly knew: it wasn't a joke. Eva Black really *was* going to kill him.

He jerked into a sitting position before being pushed roughly back into place by something. He looked down and saw that vines as thick as his arm had emerged with lightning speed from the floor below him and wrapped themselves around his body, forcing him onto his back again.

"Ow!" Billy yelped, thrashing against the grip of the greenery. It did no use, however: all he accomplished was to scrape his body on the hard surface of the plants.

Mrs. Russet was shouting something at him the whole time, and it was only gradually that Billy became aware of what it was.

"...in no danger, Billy! Nothing is going to happen!"

"Nothing?" yelled Billy back at her. "This crazy woman just said she's going to kill me!" This sent him into a new frenzy, trying to get himself loose though he already knew that he could not escape from the plants.

"Let me explain!" she said, moving near him. She looked at Ivy, who watched with obvious concern on her face. "Ease up a bit, Ivy," snapped Mrs. Russet.

Ivy nodded, and though the vines didn't loosen at all, they became *softer* somehow, as though made of steel wire wrapped in soft cotton. Billy's struggles slowed a bit, though he still jerked spasmodically, his body refusing to just give up.

"It's okay, kid," whispered Vester. "I won't let anything bad happen to you." The young man smiled reassuringly. "What would I say to your dad if I did?"

Billy was not reassured. "Oh, well, since you put it that way. I'm sure that my dying would be real embarrassing for you. That would really put my death in perspective. Thanks a heap."

"Be silent, Mr. Jones!" snapped Mrs. Russet, in her most no-nonsense you-are-walking-on-thin-ice-and-if-you-don't-behave-yourself-right-now-you-are-looking-at-extra-homework voice. Billy, trained to perfection by two months of exposure to that tone of voice, instantly stopped yelling and went stock still. Mrs. Russet nodded. "I will explain what's going to happen. Whether you want to or not, it *is* going to happen, but you won't have to worry about being killed." She glanced around the room. "Almost everybody here has been killed at *least* once, for one reason or another, and you don't see us any the worse for wear."

Billy said the best and brightest thing he could think to: "Huh?"

"Remember how I said that confusion causes some people to Glimmer?" Billy nodded. "Well," Mrs. Russet continued, "that's nothing to what happens when they *die*. When you die, all kinds of things happen in your brain. And those things trigger the Glimmer in anyone who has any potential at all to be a Power."

"Not just a Glimmer," interjected Tempus, the jolly fat man still looking like he was thinking of a particularly good joke and was just waiting for the right moment to share it. "More like a Great Big Blaze."

Mrs. Russet nodded. "You've heard of out of body experiences? Where someone's heart stops or they die on an operating table but are resuscitated?" Billy nodded. "What generally happens to them?"

"Something about a light," he answered.

Mrs. Russet nodded. "Right. Some people think the light is God or angels. Other people think that it's just random electrical charges in the dying person's brain. But what it really is—though I'm not saying that God or angels aren't involved in the process—is that person's inner potential breaking out. It's the grand-daddy of all Glimmers."

She looked at Billy. "Do you want to hear more? Can Ivy let you up, or does she need to keep you wrapped up in weeds?"

"They're not weeds, they're—" began Ivy, but silenced herself when Mrs. Russet glanced angrily at her. "Never mind," she said.

"Well?" asked Mrs. Russet.

Billy thought for a moment. On the one hand, he wanted very much to bolt off the table and run like a frightened horse. On the other hand, he was now terribly curious.

And besides, he was in the middle of a big basket hanging from the Earthtree. Where was he going to go if he *did* manage to get off the table?

"I'll listen," he said.

"Good." Mrs. Russet nodded at Ivy, and immediately the vines unwrapped themselves from Billy's quivering frame, disappearing back into the leafy floor below the table.

"We need to find out if you Glimmer, Billy," said Mrs. Russet. "And the only sure-fire way to do that, is to be there when you die. Unfortunately, we don't know when that will happen naturally, so we have to…help the process."

Billy stifled the urge to jump up and try to run again.

"How do you do that?" he asked in a small, frightened voice.

"Easy, buddy," whispered Vester. His kind eyes looked softly at Billy, that deep spark glinting from within them, touching Billy with a feeling of warmth. "We won't let anything bad happen. I'll watch out for you."

"Just so," said Tempus with a smile. The old man's smile was so infectious that Billy couldn't help but crack a bit of a smile himself.

"So what's going to happen?" asked Billy.

Mrs. Russet looked around her at the other Powers in the room. "Eva is a Black. She bends Death. She is going to stop your heart. Just for a second!" she added hurriedly, clearly seeing Billy poised to jump again. "The instant she does it, we'll have our answer, and these other four," she gestured to Ivy, Vester, Wade, and Tempus, "will make sure you come right back. Vester is a Power of Fire. He'll make sure your heart starts beating, he'll conjure the spark that we all need to live. Wade will bend the Water in and around you to insure that your blood flows and your tissue lives. Tempus will breathe the Wind of life into you. And Ivy, as a Power who is intimately tied to Life itself, will guide and direct them." Mrs. Russet looked deep into Billy's eyes. "You *will* come back, Billy Jones. I promise you."

The logical part of Billy's mind wanted to scream out. To holler "Forget it, lady!" and then kick and punch and scratch and bite anything that came near him until he somehow escaped this crazy place. But the logical part of his mind was no longer in charge. In fact, it hadn't *been* in charge since Billy had seen the blue dragon. Only his instincts remained, and, somehow, they whispered to him that Mrs. Russet was telling the truth. That she could be trusted. That he would be safe.

"All right," he whispered. He lay back on the table, shivering involuntarily. The shiver turned into a shudder as Eva Black moved close to him. She licked her lips as though savoring a favorite memory, then reached down, and touched his chest. At the same time, Vester put one hand into the open candle flame at the head of the table, and lay his other hand on the crown of Billy's head. Wade, at the bottom of the table, put one hand in the bowl of water and lay his other hand on Billy's leg.

As they did this, Ivy and Tempus closed their eyes. The entire room shuddered, and seemed to pulse with barely-contained life.

Billy looked at Mrs. Russet. "I'm scared," he whispered, so quietly that he wasn't even sure she would be able to hear it.

"I know," she whispered back. She reached out and took his hand. "I know, young man."

"Touching," said Eva Black mockingly. Then her eyes flicked to Billy's. They were already brown, but as he watched, they turned a deep, dark black. Billy was reminded of the eyes of a shark: soulless and empty, driven by a search for one thing, and one thing only. Blood.

Then there was a sharp prickling at his fingers. It felt like a nest of ants walking across them. The feeling moved to his arms, then swarmed into his legs and feet, circling his chest. Then, at last, the sensation crawled into his chest, and burrowed into his heart.

Billy took a great, shuddering breath. Then breathed out.

He felt his eyes close, and then knew no more.

# CHAPTER THE FOURTH

*In Which Billy Lives, and becomes the Object of Prophecy...*

Flashes.
Images.
He heard a scream.
Darkness.
Then another scream, a hoarse whisper: "He is coming! He is returning!"
Darkness.
Flashes.
At last, Billy's eyes fluttered, then slowly opened. His eyelids felt like they each had a small piano strapped to them. He couldn't hold them open long enough to focus on anything, so they crashed shut again.
He tried to sit up, but couldn't.
Gradually, he became aware of a cacophony of voices, as though a thousand people were all talking at the same time.
He tried again to open his eyes. This time it worked better: the pianos had been replaced with small sacks of lead. It was still hard to keep his eyes open, but Billy managed.
What happened? he thought. Then: Oh, yes. I died.
He still couldn't see anything but fuzzy shapes, still couldn't make out any individual sounds in the angry symphony sounding around him.
Am I still dead? he wondered.
But no, he didn't think so. Billy wasn't exactly sure what staying dead would feel like, but he was pretty sure that it wouldn't be so loud and blurry.
Gradually, his eyes managed to focus.
He wasn't in the Earthtree anymore. Or at least, he certainly wasn't in the part of it that he had been in before dying. The beautifully woven room was gone. Billy now found himself curled up in the corner of what looked like a tiny cave. He didn't know where it

was, but could feel the weight of the earth above him and somehow intuited that, wherever he was, it was somewhere deep and unknown.

The sounds Billy had been hearing started to sort themselves out, gradually, as Billy looked around. The cave had no light bulbs or anything like that, but there *was* light. Billy looked closely at the wall nearest him and saw that there was some kind of moss-like plant coating the stone. The plant glowed dimly, casting a pale blue incandescence around the cave that allowed Billy to make out what was happening nearby.

Mrs. Russet, Ivy, and Vester stood in another part of the cave, looking down on something. Billy couldn't see what it was, at first, but then made out an arm cloaked in a swirl of air, and knew it must be Tempus. The four "Dawnwalkers" were here with him. Billy felt relieved at that.

Wade—the Power of Water—and the cruelly grinning Mrs. Eva Black were nowhere to be seen. Billy felt even more relieved about that.

Billy oozed slowly to his feet. His whole body felt as though someone had set him on fire, rolled him in dirt to put out the fire, and then set him on fire again. He ached with every miniscule movement of his mangled muscles. A small groan escaped him as he hobbled toward the small group in the middle of the cave.

The three Powers huddled around Tempus looked up for a moment, but only a moment, then leaned back over the prostrate old man. Billy, afraid to say anything, tiptoed closer to the group until he was standing right behind Mrs. Russet, and could see what they were all looking at.

It *was* Tempus, Billy knew. But the jovial fellow barely looked like himself. Gone was the jolly grin and the amused and playful eyes. Now, the old man was crumpled in a withered pile, his arms and legs twitching as though he had put his finger in a light socket while taking a bath. Tempus also looked gray, not the living grayness of the storm he had first emerged from, but a cracked, bleached gray that seemed to bespeak of coming death. The old man looked used up.

Tempus's mouth was moving, a frantic whisper coming from his lips. "He is coming, he is returning, he is returning, he is here...," he whispered, the words coming over and over from him.

Billy barely knew Tempus, so was surprised at how concerned he was. Even though Billy guessed he had himself been dead very recently, and even though he felt like he should be concerned about *that*—he imagined that dying, even for a little while, might have some sort of long-term effect on a person—Billy found himself forgetting what had happened to him and only worrying about the stricken old Power who lay in a huddle in the middle of the cave.

"He is coming, he is returning, he is coming…," Tempus kept whispering. The sound was haunted, fragmented. It sounded less like Tempus than like someone speaking *through* Tempus. As though a ghost had inhabited the man's body and was forcing him to speak. And hurting him terribly in the process.

"What happened?" asked Billy.

Vester glanced at him. "We were going to ask *you* that, kid."

"What do you mean?" Billy's confusion rose again. But he didn't have a chance to ask anything else because at that moment, Tempus cried out in a loud voice.

"HE IS HERE!"

The old man's body convulsed, every muscle contracting at once, then just as suddenly his body went limp. Tempus's eyes closed, and as they did the swirling wind that had surrounded him dissipated.

Billy was surprised to see that underneath that wind Tempus had been wearing a pair of long shorts and a disturbingly bright Hawaiian shirt. Not the kind of thing you would expect a Power of the Wind to be wearing.

But then, Billy didn't know what he *would* expect a Power of the Wind to wear, either. Then he realized that the shirt's Hawaiian landscape was shifting as he watched. The green trees were waving in the wind, the ocean behind them was lapping in and out. It was like watching a Tempus-shaped television where someone had adjusted the colors to look like a Piñata had just collided with a field of brightly-colored flowers.

Billy pried his eyes from the moving vista of Tempus's shirt, looking back to the Gray Power's face. For a second, Billy was sure that the old man was dead. But then Tempus's eyes blinked open, tears running down his cheeks as though he had been staring too long at the sun. "What happened?" he croaked. "Last thing I remember was Eva stopping the boy's heart…." His words drifted off. "Where are we?"

"In a mountain, or under one." answered Mrs. Russet. She paused a moment, then added, "I think."

"Huh?" asked Tempus. Billy was surprised at how good it felt to have someone *else* not know what was going on for a change. Tempus clambered awkwardly to his feet, Vester steadying the old man's arm as he did so. "We're in a mountain?"

Ivy nodded. "When Billy died, the Earthtree just…just…."

"It ejected us," said Mrs. Russet. Tempus looked like he still didn't understand, so Mrs. Russet elaborated. "The tree put us down, and then did its best to squash us."

"Bah!" Tempus replied. "Poppycock. Tummyrot. No green thing would try to harm us with Ivy in our midst. She wouldn't let it happen."

With that, Ivy let out a strangled cry, hiding her face in her hands as though ashamed. "It's true!" she wailed. "The branches were falling everywhere, all over the place. Vester had to…to…." She couldn't even finish the thought.

"I had to burn the branches before they hit us," finished Vester. He touched Ivy's arm softly. "You know I didn't want to, Ivy."

The young/old woman nodded, but didn't take her hands from her face.

Tempus harrumphed as though unsure what to say next. He looked around. "And where are the Darksiders?"

"Gone," said Vester flatly. "Eva had her hand on that nasty beetle broach of hers before we even touched the ground. It must have been Imbued. She grabbed Wade, and they had Transported away before you could say, 'help,' or 'take us with you.'"

"Not a great surprise there," said Tempus. "Eva always has been most interested in her own personal safety and comfort." No one disagreed with him. "Well," he finally said. "At least we saved Billy." He managed a wink at Billy. "Told you we wouldn't let anything happen to you." Then he looked around at the cave. "And I see that Lumilla had us swallowed in Earth to protect us from whatever it was that was happening up there, and," he pointed at the glowing moss in the cave, "Ivy has taken care to give us light." He bowed that old-fashioned courtly bow of his, wobbling only a little at the end. "My thanks for your consideration, ladies."

Mrs. Russet and Vester shared a glance. Billy could see that Tempus noticed. "What?" asked the Gray Power. "Did I say something funny? I certainly *hope* so. Could use a laugh right now."

Vester and Mrs. Russet finally looked back at him. "No, nothing funny," said Mrs. Russet. "But you were wrong on all counts. I'm not the one who made the ground swallow us up. And Ivy didn't make the Glowmoss grow."

"And as for Billy," Mrs. Russet looked at Billy with an expression that he couldn't really make out. It was as though she were looking at someone she didn't know…and perhaps didn't *want* to know. "We didn't save him."

"But…but he's *here*," protested Tempus.

"We know, Windwalker," said Vester. Billy noted that the fireman didn't do much talking. But when he did, everyone listened. Billy knew that some people talked to hear themselves speak, others talked to fill the silence that seemed to frighten them, and still others only spoke when they had something to say that would actually communicate or accomplish something. It seemed Vester was one of the last group, which was unusual for someone as young as the fireman was. Billy liked that, and it made him appreciate Vester even more. "But none of *us*," he nodded around the room, "saved Billy. Eva stopped his heart, and that was the very instant where everything happened. The world seemed to go crazy, the tree started shuddering. We were all spewed out of the Gleaning room, and you were knocked out on the way down. Then the tree tried to crush us—sorry, Ivy," he interjected as the statement brought a new round of wails from the Green Power', "and I did my best to protect us. But we were going to be killed, when all of a sudden...."

"What?" asked Tempus. "When all of a sudden what?"

"We ended up here," finished Vester.

"But how?" demanded Tempus. "*How* did we end up here?"

"None of us can quite figure that out," said Mrs. Russet. "And we didn't have a whole lot of time to think about it, since you started screaming right about then."

"And Billy? Who saved him? If Eva stopped his heart, and none of us were able to do our jobs, then he should be...."

Mrs. Russet shrugged as Vester moved to hug Ivy. She had stopped actively crying, but her eyes were still damp. She pulled a soft leaf off of the greenery that still covered her and used it to dab at her eyes.

"We don't know how Billy was saved, either," said Mrs. Russet. "We suddenly found ourselves in this place, and Billy was with us, unconscious but alive."

"Then Eva must have made some mistake. She must have killed him wrong," said Tempus.

Vester shook his head. "No, she did her job all right. I felt the spark leave him right as everything fell apart." He looked at Billy. "The kid was a goner."

Billy felt his knees buckle. It was one thing to have agreed to be killed, but he found that having people talk about it as actually having occurred was a whole different experience. Mrs. Russet managed to catch him before he fell over.

"Stand up, Mr. Jones," she said with her old sternness. Billy found that strangely comforting. Yes, he had by all accounts been killed. Yes, the Powers apparently had broken their promise that nothing bad would happen. Yes, they appeared to be in a cave deep under a mountain with no apparent way to get out. But at least Mrs. Russet was still as prickly as a cactus wearing a barbed wire skirt, so *some* things were still normal.

Billy stood. "What do we do now?" he asked. He looked at Mrs. Russet. "You said you were a Power of Earth. So can't you, like, make a hole open up, or snap your fingers and poof some stone stairway into existence?"

"Young man, I never 'poof' anything," she said indignantly. Then her expression softened. "But normally, yes, I could control the Earthessence and make it lift us from this place to the surface."

"Why don't you do that then?" asked Billy in what he hoped was a helpful tone.

Mrs. Russet frowned. "Because I can't. Something is stopping me."

"Stopping *you*, Lumilla?" asked Tempus incredulously. "But... you're one of the Great Powers. You of all people should be able to—"

"Yes, Tempus, I am well aware of what I am and what I should be able to do," snapped Mrs. Russet. "But the fact remains that I don't seem to have access to my powers here. Something is blocking me. Something that I've never experienced or even heard of."

"What about you, Vester?" asked Tempus. "Can you bend your Element to blast us out of here?"

Vester shook his head. "Not even if I had that kind of power at my control in the first place—I'm no Lumilla. But we're all blocked," he responded. He nodded at the greenery that sheathed Ivy. "See?" Billy noticed for the first time that the vines sheathing the oldish young—or was it youngish old?—woman were wilting and brown, as though they had gone too long without water or sunlight. Vester continued, "And look at you," he said, pointing at Tempus's outrageous clothing. "You've lost your wind."

Tempus looked at his beach shorts and magically moving Hawaiian shirt, his knobby knees and elbows still aquiver from his ordeal. He turned an embarrassed look to the group, shrugging as he said, "At least they're comfortable."

Then the seriousness of the situation seemed to bear in on the man of the Wind. "Then...then we're trapped," he whispered.

"Trapped?" asked Billy. "For how long?"

"Unless something changes," replied Mrs. Russet, "I'd have to guess," her eyes narrowed to slits as though she was performing some complex calculation in her mind, "forever."

"Forever?!" Billy fairly shouted the word.

"Well, not forever," granted Mrs. Russet. "Assuming we *are* under a mountain, erosion and the natural movement of the strata will likely bring us to the surface at some point. Say, a few thousand centuries or so."

Billy felt his knees go weak again. "But," he stammered. "But, we can't be here for a few thousand centuries. We just can't! It's my birthday!" As soon as the words came out, he knew how ridiculous they sounded. Like a man in front of a firing squad asking for a reprieve because he would miss his favorite TV show if they killed him.

Tempus, too, seemed to appreciate the absurdity of the moment. He chuckled. Then guffawed. Then laughed out loud. A moment later, Vester joined in, and then Billy, too, started laughing in spite of himself. Ivy chuckled daintily, and even Mrs. Russet managed to stop actively frowning.

Then the cave shook, a huge, rolling movement that reminded Billy of some of his least-favorite carnival rides. The ground bobbed up and down, and everyone struggled to remain upright.

This is what an earthquake feels like when you're *inside* it, thought Billy, and not just sitting in a room a few thousand feet *above* it. He wondered if he was going to die—again—in the next few seconds as the cave inevitably collapsed under the pressure of the shifting rock all around them. The way things were going, it seemed likely.

But he didn't die. In fact, quite the opposite happened. With a final heave, a wide rift cracked open on one side of the cave. The crack widened, bright light streaming through it as it grew. A moment later the cave stopped moving. Mrs. Russet moved toward the crack, which was taller than a man and about two feet wide. She gestured for the group to follow.

They did, Vester holding onto Ivy with one arm and guiding Billy with the other as they all stepped through the crack.

And found themselves on a beach.

Billy looked behind him in time to see that they had come out of a huge rock, fifty feet to a side. As he watched, the crack through which they had come sealed itself off, the sound of stone scraping on stone loud and dry in the still air. Then the stone sank down into the sand with a rumble, lower and lower, foot by foot, until the beach sand covered it up and there was no trace it had ever existed there at all.

"We're at the Lagoon," whispered Ivy.

Mrs. Russet nodded. Then she dug her feet into the sand she was standing on and closed her eyes. She smiled. "Can you feel it?" she asked.

Billy watched as the other three Powers also closed their eyes. "Our powers aren't being blocked anymore," said Vester with a sigh of relief. He pulled a matchbook out of his pocket, and struck a match. He touched the flame with a fingertip, and when he drew back his hand the flame moved off the head of the match, staying on his finger. As Billy watched, the flame took on the shape of a tiny horse, which pranced and reared about Vester's palm. Vester smiled, and the stallion whinnied in return. It sounded like a miniature explosion. Vester held out his arm, and the fire-horse ran up its length and then lay down on its tiny haunches, resting on Vester's shoulder.

"Yes," nodded Tempus. He drew in a great breath, and then exhaled. A miniature tornado came from his mouth, picking up water from the nearby waves and creating a waterspout about a foot in diameter that swirled up a few feet before losing cohesion and disappearing. A moment later, gray wind coalesced around his vacation outfit. Billy—and everyone else—breathed a sigh of relief at that.

Tempus turned to Billy. "I think you have some explaining to do, my boy."

"But, but I didn't—I mean, I don't think I did anything," stammered Billy.

"He was dead, Tempus. Remember?" said Mrs. Russet. "At least for part of what happened. So he's not likely to be able to answer any of our questions." She paused, frowning. "Still, I think this merits a trip, especially given what was happening to you in the cave, Tempus."

"What do you mean?" asked Tempus. "I don't remember anything until all of you were looking at me and then a second later we ended up here. You said I was knocked out."

"I also said you started screaming," Mrs. Russet reminded him.

"You don't remember what you said?" asked Ivy, surprise clear on her face.

"What I *said*?" Tempus's confusion visibly continued to grow. "What are you talking about, Ivy?"

"He doesn't remember," murmured Vester to Mrs. Russet.

She nodded in agreement, then said to Tempus, "You were Prophesying, Tempus. You were saying, 'He is coming. He is here.'"

"Who's coming? Who's here?" asked Tempus.

"Exactly what I'd like to know," responded Mrs. Russet. "And that's why we're going to take a trip. I think we have to tell the

Council what's happened here. To see if anyone else has Prophesied, or if anything else unusual happened on Powers Island during Billy's Gleaning."

She turned to face Billy. He fidgeted under the force of her stare. "Because of what happened, we couldn't tell if you Glimmered or not, Mr. Jones. But regardless of that, one thing is certain: what happened during your Gleaning has never happened before, to anyone."

"You're forgetting something," said Vester quietly. All eyes turned to face him. "Tempus didn't just say 'He is coming, he is returning.' At the end, the last thing Tempus said was 'He is here.'" The fireman turned to Billy. "And I don't think he was talking about me."

"An Object of Prophecy," whispered Ivy, awe clear in her voice as she gazed at Billy.

Mrs. Russet pursed her lips. "All the more reason to get this before the Council." She picked up a handful of the sand below them, then blew on it. It swirled in her palm, drawing more sand from the beach below. The mass grew and grew, until finally it took the shape of a long flat plate the size of a small boat or car. Its shape shifted fluidly as more sand swept up to join it. Billy felt like he was watching a sand sculpture build itself.

At last, the lines of the sculpture solidified into an aerodynamic shape that reminded Billy of a high-powered race car. Five deep grooves or slots marked its topside, but other than that the shape was featureless. Clearly its maker didn't care one bit for unnecessary decoration or complexity, but nonetheless Billy got the impression that it was a ship of some kind, and he suddenly realized that the grooves on top of the craft were deep enough and about the right size and shape to fit one seated person.

"Vester?" Mrs. Russet asked. Vester nodded, then touched the sand mass. Fire ringed it, a flash of light so bright and heat so sharp and intense that Billy was sure his eyebrows must have been singed off.

What was left after he blazing heat died down was a craft of perfectly transparent glass, glowing bright red with the heat of Vester's Fire.

"And Tempus?" Mrs. Russet continued. Tempus raised his hands, and a cold breeze came from nowhere, cooling the glass structure. The wind then warmed, and swirled around the group on the beach.

Suddenly, Billy felt the same wind like strong arms beneath his own, lifting him bodily onto the glass vessel, and placing him gently in one of the deep grooves in its surface. Sure enough, the groove was actually a seat of some kid. Billy expected the glass would be hard and uncomfortable, but found it to be the opposite: it molded to him as though designed specifically with his body in mind.

The wind stayed with him, holding him fast to the surface of the strange ship like an invisible seatbelt as Mrs. Russet, Vester, Ivy, and lastly Tempus himself floated into position on the glass vehicle.

"Everyone ready?" asked Tempus. No one answered. "Then here we go. Next stop, the center of Powers Island and a meeting with the Council."

The Windwalker shuddered a bit when he said the last bit about "meeting with the Council."

Billy felt a thrill of fear, communicated to him by Tempus's own clear nervousness at being near the Council, whatever that was.

But a moment later, Billy's fear was gone, replaced by total panic as the glass ship lifted high into the sky above the peaceful Lagoon. It lurched forward, and Billy suddenly knew what "fast" was. It wasn't a car, or a train, or even a Mach-speed fighter jet.

It was a glass craft, high above a mysterious island, speeding toward something Billy could not even guess at.

The great glass vessel streaked high above the island, allowing Billy a view of the entirety of it. Powers Island appeared to be fairly small, only a few miles from side to side. In the middle of it was a structure so tall and wide that he knew it must be the place he had first appeared when he came here. The tower was made of huge stones, set so closely together that Billy suspected that no cement or mortar was needed to hold them together. And the tower was mind-rendingly tall, so tall in fact that it eventually disappeared from view, because it went so high that it disappeared into the middle of a swirling mass of turbulent clouds that covered that portion of the island. Long, thick vines wrapped around the tower, the living branches of what Billy now knew was the Earthtree supporting the impossibly tall edifice.

Billy looked down over the side of the glass ship. Actually, he looked *through* it: so perfectly clear was the glass that he might as well have been floating on thin air.

As he had done in the elevator, Billy was moving so fast he couldn't make out many details. Much of Powers Island was covered by small forests, dotted here and there by miniature mountain ranges that thrust up from the body of the island like skipping stones on the surface of a pond.

There was also an impossible range of weather occurring on the island, Billy saw: on one end of it a fierce blizzard raged, on another a hurricane swirled in one confined space. Still another spot was host to a lightning storm, and the rest of the island gleamed in the deep burnished glow of sunlight.

There were houses, too. Billy glanced small concentrations of buildings, like small towns or villages. From his vantage point, they mostly looked normal, although Billy guessed that most small town he was aware of wouldn't occasionally see someone fly skyward on a gust of air, then zoom off to cavort and play in a nearby tornado.

The glass airship banked suddenly, and Billy would have thrown up if he had had anything in his stomach. He was silently thankful that Mrs. Russet had earlier turned down the elevator's offer of snacks. He wasn't sure what a "Shakka-Shakka Shake" or a "Blue Lightning Crumpet" would look like after being barfed all over the side of an invisible glass aircraft, but he guessed it wouldn't be pretty.

The crystalline craft was now hurtling directly toward the great tower at the center of Powers Island. The building loomed larger and larger in front of Billy. He gulped as it neared, because he suddenly realized that there were no windows or docks or whatever might be a good way for the ship he was in to actually get in*side* the tower.

He looked away from the huge structure that was rapidly approaching, and found himself looking down at a pair of what appeared to be men made of rock that were punching each other near the base of the tower. He was reminded of the Rock-em-Sock-em Robots he'd seen on television: two little robots in a boxing ring that kids could "fight" with until one of the robots' heads popped off. Those robots, however, had been only a few inches tall. The rock monsters below were well over one hundred *feet* tall, and the sound of their crushing blows was enormous. Billy winced each time the wrecking-ball of a fist of one giant would impact the body or face of the other. Below that noise, he could hear faint yells, and realized that the giants were standing in the middle of a Coliseum-like arena, with what looked like thousands of people shrieking in excitement at the spectacle in their midst.

"What is that?" he screamed over the roar of the wind all around them.

Vester looked down. "Boxing match," he replied.

Just then, Billy heard something like a sonic boom. He looked at the rock-boxers and saw one of them hit the other with a powerful uppercut that sent the losing giant's head right off its shoulders. The head—which looked as huge as that of the Statue of Liberty—flew directly upward, propelled by the enormous force of the blow.

Billy inhaled in terror as he realized that the head was on a course that would intercept the glass craft. He looked around in panic, but no one else in the ship seemed particularly concerned. Mrs. Russet and Ivy were having a quiet but intense-seeming conversation in the front of the ship, Vester was shouting what sounded like congratulations to the winning rock giant, and Tempus was apparently asleep, his eyes closed and elephantine snores coming from his open mouth.

Billy's eyes narrowed as the giant decapitated head sped toward them. He inadvertently hunched his shoulders up around his ears, certain he was about to die yet again.

But at the last second, there was an enormous explosion as the flying head burst into a million fragments. Each tiny piece of rock hung in the air for a split second, then each of *those* pieces transformed from rock to flame, creating a sphere of fireworks that lit up the sky before trailing slowly downward.

"Way to go, Polonium!" shouted Vester, leaning precariously out over the side of the crystalline ship. He pumped his arms wildly. Put a soda can in his hands and surround him with a few college buddies and he would look like he was watching a pay-per-view sporting event on TV. He leaned back in and smiled at Billy. "Now *that's* how you win in style," he said.

Billy was about to ask what exactly he had just seen, but he only got as far as "What was th—?" before going silent and clutching the side of the ship in terror.

With his attention drawn to the bizarre spectacle below, and then their brush with Death by Giant Head, Billy had momentarily forgotten the reason he looked down in the first place. He remembered now, however, as he saw that the glass ship was mere feet away from the huge, solid tower, heading at crushing speed at a blank wall, and showing no sign of stopping.

He started to scream, but the scream was left behind as the ship banked sharply upward, impossibly fast, and now they were traveling parallel to the line of the tower, at a ninety degree angle to the earth below, vertical as a rocket escaping the planet's atmosphere.

Billy kept screaming. It seemed the only really appropriate thing to do. He screamed as long as he could, then when he ran out of breath, he inhaled and screamed some more.

He ran out of breath again, and inhaled to scream still more, but at that moment Tempus appeared to finally awake. "That's enough of *that*," he murmured, and waved a hand.

Billy screamed. But this time, no sound came out. He knew he was hollering and shrieking—he could even feel himself grow hoarse with the effort. But no sound whatever escaped his lips. He stopped screaming his silent scream a moment later, and chanced a glance below them.

The ground was thousands of feet away. *Miles* below them. It receded farther and farther, faster and faster. Powers Island itself shrank to half its size, then a fourth, then an eighth. Then it contracted still further until it was a mere pinprick in the ocean, and then finally disappeared altogether. At that very instant, Billy felt something wet and cloying all around him. A bright flash illuminated everything, and he realized that they were flying through the roiling storm he had earlier seen ringing the tower, keeping it from being viewed above a certain height.

Electricity crackled in the air, lightning crashing within what seemed like inches of the ship. Still completely silenced by Tempus's spell, Billy couldn't give voice to his fright, but continued to look around in terror.

Vester reached out and tapped him on the shoulder. "Watch this," the fireman grinned. He reached out a hand, and lightning arced out of the sky, lancing down until it hit Vester. Vester clenched his fist at the same time, as though catching a fast fly ball. The lightning dissipated, and Billy couldn't help but crane his neck to see as Vester opened his fist, revealing a small ball of electricity. The ball sparkled and crackled with contained energy, then shrank down for a moment before expanding again. Just as the match flame on the beach had done, the energy formed itself into the shape of a horse, which galloped up Vester's shoulder to join the other horse. The two equines—one made of fire, one of lightning—pranced across Vester's shoulders and arms, and Billy couldn't help but laugh a silent laugh.

Vester smiled. "We're safe as houses," he said. Then, pointing up, he added, "And we're almost to the top."

Billy looked skyward.

It was true. They were, at last, almost to the top of the tower. The top, like the rest of it, was twined in the think branches of the Earthtree, which joined together at the top of the building to form a bower of sorts. A waterfall flowed from the top of the tower, flowing off the side of the stone tower, its spray gradually dissipating and losing itself in the force of the ever-present storm below it.

The craft finally slowed as it flew over the lip of the tower, touching down gently on a soft mat of greenest grass that sprang up impossibly from the bare stone of the tower. Once more, Billy felt himself gripped—gently, but firmly—by the wind and lifted out of the craft. The others, too, were lifted up and set softly on the stone ground that constituted the top of the tower. Then Mrs. Russet clapped her hands, and the glass craft suddenly lost cohesion, falling instantly into a large pile of sand again, the sand then flowing over the side of the tower and disappearing into the vast emptiness below.

Billy looked around. The top of the tower was enormous, hundreds of feet in diameter, so he felt no sensation of being particularly high up, even though he knew he was many thousands of feet above the earth. The wood of the Earthtree cradled the tower in branches that moved of their own accord, not twisting with the wind but constantly shifting and joining to create beautiful shapes, a living work of art. Nearby, a straight river flowed, the one that fed into the waterfall that Billy had seen earlier. As far as he could see, the river bisected the tower perfectly, and he suspected that it somehow ended in another waterfall on the *other* side of the tower, though that would mean the river was moving in two directions at the same time. That would have been impossible anywhere else, but here....

Strange, beautiful flowers grew at the edges of the water, and Billy had the feeling that if he were to lay down among them, he might never wake up, but would sleep forever and dream only of beauty and light.

"Come on then," said Mrs. Russet, walking toward the center of the tower. Billy could see something in the distance, which gradually resolved so that he could make it out. It was a crystal dais, a raised platform of that appeared to be made of purest diamond, glimmering and glinting as the sun's rays kissed it before shattering into a million shards of rainbow and light.

The dais was perfectly round, and around its circumference sat seven chairs. Actually, they were thrones, more ornate and beautiful than any furniture Billy could imagine gracing a head of state in the "normal" world.

One of the thrones was dark red, and appeared to be carved out of a single enormous ruby. On it was a pillow, maroon and gold of deepest velvet that made Billy sure that sitting in it would be nothing but bliss.

Another of the thrones was blue, and it moved like the waves of the sea, slowly ululating and pulsing while still somehow managing to hold the general shape of a chair. Lovely many-colored shells and coral coated it, and Billy even thought he could see tiny sea creatures—shrimps and damselfish and wrasses—floating within the chair.

The next throne was carved of brown marble and dark granite, exquisitely inlaid with fine etchings of gold and silver, and sporting carvings that looked to Billy like some kind of writing, though in a language that appeared both ancient and alien.

Following that was a green throne, one that grew from the branches that wound around the dais. Its living frame writhed ever so slightly, as though the chair was waiting impatiently for its master or mistress to come and sit on it.

And the last two chairs were the most beautiful of all, though completely opposite in many ways. One was black as deep space, absorbing the light so completely that Billy almost couldn't make out the details of its structure. It looked as though it were formed of a million tiny black pearls, all held together through some dark force. Billy shivered as he looked at it. This chair, alone among them all, seemed like one he would not care to sit in. Beautiful, but a throne of fear.

But as frightful as the black seat was, the throne to its left was just as beautiful and more. It was purest white, gleaming with a brilliance that outshone even the diamond platform on which it sat. Billy couldn't tell what it was made of, but every so often the chair would flash, exploding in a rainbow of colors that reminded Billy of mother-of-pearl, only a million times brighter.

"What is this place?" he asked, surprised to find that he could speak again. He glanced at Tempus.

The old man shrugged. "I figured that you weren't screaming any more, so you could have your voice back."

"This is the Council Seat, atop the Diamond Dais," answered Mrs. Russet, disregarding Tempus's aside. Billy looked at her when she said this. Her voice had changed somehow. It was deeper, more resonant. As he watched, she walked toward the dais. Before her, the stone floor of the tower shifted like liquid, forming stairs that allowed her to step gracefully onto the top of the diamond platform before they sank back into the stone as though they had never been.

Mrs. Russet walked to the center of the dais. She withdrew a stone from her pocket. Once more, the stone changed in her hands, becoming the same crystalline staff she had used before to summon Vester, Tempus, Wade, and Eva Black at the time of Billy's Gleaning.

She touched the staff to the exact center of the dais. No sound came forth this time. Instead, a dazzling rainbow of colors emerged. The display was so bright, it should have blinded Billy, but it didn't. Rather, it seemed to heighten his sense of sight: everything suddenly appeared clearer to him, the colors more vivid, like he had been seeing in pastel his whole life and now at last could see the bold colors of an oil painting.

Mrs. Russet closed her eyes. "I summon the Council," she intoned.

Almost immediately, a voice responded. The voice seemed to come from everywhere and nowhere at once, as loud as a wave crashing down, yet silent and piercing as the whisper of a friend. "Who summons us?"

Mrs. Russet stood tall, gripping the crystal staff with a confidence and strength that belied her years. "It is I," she said, "Lumilla the Brown, Power of Earth and Councilor of the Powers."

The light from her staff flared even brighter with this, as the disembodied voice came again: "And why are we summoned?"

"Because I believe that the White King, long prophesied, has at last begun his return," answered Mrs. Russet. She paused a moment, as though weighing her next words carefully. Finally, she said, "And I believe I have found his forerunner: the Messenger who will go before the White King and prepare us for the final battle."

Mrs. Russet took in a great breath, apparently steeling herself to say what followed. She looked right at Billy, her dark eyes piercing him to the soul. "I believe I may have found the boy who will destroy us."

# CHAPTER THE FIFTH

*In Which Billy meets the Council, and the Diamond Cracks...*

Destroy? thought Billy. She's not talking about *me*, is she?

He looked over at Vester, and saw that the youthful fireman looked just as surprised as Billy did. So did Tempus, for that matter. Ivy was the only one who seemed as though she knew that pronouncement had been coming. Billy remembered that she and Mrs. Russet had been engaged in deep conversation on the ride from the Lagoon to the top of the Tower. Was this what they were talking about? he wondered.

Apparently Tempus also had questions of his own, for he looked at the green-garbed woman and asked, "Ivy? What is this that Lumilla is saying?"

Ivy looked almost helpless, shrugging her shoulders as she said, "It's not for me to say, Tempus." She nodded toward the diamond podium where Mrs. Russet still stood. "The Council is convening."

Billy followed her gaze and saw that, over each of the colored thrones, a light of the same color as that throne was beginning to appear. Soon, there were six glowing orbs: green, blue, gray, red, brown, and black. All but the black one cast a beautiful glow, leading to a many-colored rainbow dance that played across the diamond podium like a symphony of tone and hue. As for the black orb, it seemed to grab whatever light passed near it and pull it in, as though seeking to extinguish the very existence of all around it.

Billy looked at Vester. "What's going on?" he whispered. "What's the Council?"

"The six strongest Powers, the governing Masters and Mistresses of each of the Elements," replied Vester.

Billy looked at the thrones. "Six Elements?" he asked. Vester nodded. "Then," asked Billy, "why are there *seven* chairs?"

Vester pointed at the one chair that did not have a light-orb glowing over it. "That one is the White Throne. Only the White King may sit upon it."

"The White King?" asked Billy. "What's—"

"Shush," whispered Ivy. "They're here."

Billy looked up, and saw that the orbs were slowly shifting, changing from circles into glowing shapes that gradually resolved themselves into human figures.

Only the brown globe maintained its shape, but it moved toward Mrs. Russet, who had remained standing where she was during the dance of the lights. The brown globe overtook her, seeming to merge with her, then obscuring her figure for a moment before re-coalescing into what was recognizable as Billy's teacher. Only where before she had been wearing a pale blue blouse and no-nonsense ankle-length skirt, she was now clothed in an outfit that was brown from top to bottom, a beautiful cloth with what appeared at first to be intricate stitching. But when Billy squinted, looking closer at the cloak, he saw that the stitching was really something else, something far more marvelous and breathtaking.

"What is that?" he couldn't help but whisper, tugging on Vester's shirt and pointing at what he saw.

"The Outlines of History," whispered Vester in return. His voice had taken on a hushed, almost awed tone. "Lumilla the Brown is the greatest Power of the Earth—perhaps the greatest Power alive today. And the earth is the repository—the resting place—of most of the past. So when she is in her fullest power, here on the Diamond Dais, Lumilla is cloaked with the knowledge of that past. She—" he continued, then interrupted himself. "Look there!" he half-whispered, half-shouted, pointing at Mrs. Russet's cloak. "I think it's—yes, yes it is! It's the Battle of Gettysburg!"

Billy looked where Vester was pointing, and, sure enough, could just barely make out the shapes of two great armies clashing in a field, their dark outlines barely visible against the brown background of Mrs. Russet's velvet cloak. The two armies of the Civil War came together in a fury of fire and smoke, then were swallowed up in the ever-changing pattern of the cloak.

Billy kept watching, mesmerized by the scenes he saw unfolding. He saw a man at what looked like an ancient printing press, making a thick book. He saw a man in a wheelchair, talking into a dozen microphones, the eyes of those around him showing clear relief and happiness, his words—though Billy could not hear them—buoying them up in times of great need. He saw a man on a horse, riding among frozen troops in a wintry fort, shouting courage to them, urging them to great heights of bravery. He saw a woman moving among the poor and hungry of the world, ministering to them in her own infirmities.

The images swirled, deeper and deeper, faster and faster as Billy watched. A rocket ship taking off, a great medieval army marching across a field, a dark flash of men walking across a parade-ground, heels kicking high in unison as they saluted the screaming man beside them. And more and more, faster and faster. Billy felt himself falling into the threads of the cloak, helpless, suddenly consumed with the urge to know, to see...everything.

A hand clamped itself around his wrist, dragging him back from the abyss of History. It was Vester. "Don't look too long," he whispered in Billy's ear. "The Earthessence is powerful. Almost everything goes into it eventually, but if one looks upon it for too long without the right preparation, the secrets it yields can be too much. Men and women have lost themselves in History, and forgotten that they are creatures of the present, and ever bound for the future."

Billy withdrew his attention with difficulty as Mrs. Russet walked regally to the brown throne, casting her cloak around her in a dark blanket of History as she sat. He looked around at the others who were now appearing from the orbs above their thrones.

The first to appear was a man from the orb of Gray.

"Dismus the Gray, Power of the Wind," breathed Tempus. "The greatest of my kind."

Just as Mrs. Russet had been cloaked in brown, so Dismus the Gray wore an outfit of deepest gray, rich in tone. But where Mrs. Russet's cloak had been deep and solid, Billy saw that Dismus's cloak seemed ethereal, as though it might disappear at any minute, and the Gray Councilor along with it. And when Billy peered into Dismus's cloak of wind, he saw sights he did not understand: people in strange clothing, odd buildings the like of which he had never seen, each visible for only a fleeting moment before being lost in the wispy winds of Dismus the Gray's cloak.

Billy looked at Tempus questioningly. "Just as the Brown Earthessence bears in it all History past, so the Gray Windessence brings with it glimpses of the future, glances of what is to come, or what may be." Tempus looked at Billy, his expression one that appeared to be a mixture of affection and fear for the Gray Councilor who had just appeared. "The Grays are the Prophets, the Seers of our people."

Next came the Red Power. Billy noticed that Vester's eyes lit up as a beautiful young woman appeared in the orb. Her body was as the flame that clothed her, lithe and sinuous, never seeming to be at rest. Her eyes were like two rubies set in fire, bright against her pale face. "Fulgora, the Red Lady," said Vester. Billy looked at his new friend: the young fireman's words were not the hushed awe with which he had spoken of the Council, nor were they the comforting tones that he usually used when speaking to Billy. No, Vester spoke in a tone of voice that Billy had only heard rarely, a special kind of timbre and tone that immediately conveyed the fireman's feelings toward the Red Councilor.

He's in love with her, Billy thought. He wondered whether the beautiful Fulgora returned the sentiment, or even knew of Vester's love. But Vester seemed lost to the world when she appeared, whether the woman knew of his love or not.

Billy peered into her flame-cloak, but seemed to see nothing this time. Apparently flame was not a power that came with knowledge of the past or future. Perhaps there was nothing to be seen....

Then Billy's jaw dropped. He couldn't believe what had suddenly appeared as he watched Fulgora's cloak. It was...*him*. A Billy Jones of flame, but still clearly him. He saw himself on his eighth birthday, a wonderful day where his father had actually managed to show up and stay the whole day with the family. Then that image faded in the fire and he saw another image: this time a more recent one, of himself being bullied by the ever-present Cameron Black. Then that one, too, disappeared, replaced by something more pleasant: the flickering outline of Blythe Forrest as she had appeared to him in the terrible, embarrassing, and perfectly wonderful moment when he first laid eyes on her. She seemed to look at him, peering forth from the fires of the Red Lady's garb.

"What am I seeing?" he wondered aloud.

"Memories," said Vester. "As powerful as flame, as quick to come and go as lightning, they can warm...or they can burn." The fireman, too, was looking now at the Red Power's outfit, and Billy wondered what memories Vester was seeing, and how many of them featured the Red Lady in them.

Billy spared one more fleeting, longing glance at the image of Blythe Forrest in the flames, before he was again drawn to the appearance of a new Councilor: the Blue.

The Power appeared as a form out of the white spray of a breaking wave, not there at all and then suddenly solid. His outfit was a shifting mass of water, for he was cloaked in what Billy now could guess was the Earthsea itself. And when he looked in the man's watery cloak, Billy saw gold, gems, rubies. Then the cloak shifted, and Billy caught a glimpse of himself, only much larger than he really was: well-muscled and tall. Blythe was under his arm, giggling with delight as they walked down the halls of school together.

A hand covered his eyes. "Even more dangerous than the Power of the Earth," said Vester. "Water is the resting place of the world's most hidden treasures. And so the Blue Powers have the ability to influence our minds with the subtle promise of riches, of power, of influence, and none can do this better than Nehala the Blue. He is a wily one, like a fox that will smile at you while all the while planning how to catch and eat you." Vester shuddered, almost overwhelmed with revulsion.

Of course, Billy thought. Vester is fire and this Nehala is water. Of course they won't like each other. Natural enemies.

Another flare drew Billy's gaze to the last two orbs. Out of one, the green one, coiled thin tendrils that grew and grew. The tendrils budded new tendrils, which turned to flowers, which in turn ripened into fruit that fell from the vines, disappearing before they hit the pristine Diamond Dais. Then the vines withdrew for a short time, as though asleep under a blanket of snow, before starting the cycle again. Finally, the vines ran together and became muscle and sinew, a man being created from the living greenery of the Earthree itself. Billy watched in wonder at the sight. The man that finally became flesh sat at his throne. He looked right at Billy and smiled.

"My name," he said to Billy, "is Veric the Green."

Billy was surprised. He had been wondering that. Could the Green Power read minds?

At the moment Billy thought this, Veric shook his head. "We of the Green cannot read minds. But we do sometimes sense feelings, and I have lived long enough to guess the likely questions that flow from your confusions." He smiled again at Billy, then looked at Ivy. "Hello, Ivy," he said.

The young/old woman curtsied, her living dress flaring out and appearing to add to the depth of the bow. "Hello, Father," she answered.

Veric looked around at the seated Council. "All here?" he asked.

"Not yet," replied Mrs. Russet. Or, rather, Lumilla the Brown. Billy had trouble thinking of this as his history teacher when she sat in the brown throne, a living tapestry of all history swirling about her. The old woman nodded at the black throne. "We wait on Death."

"As do all creatures, great and small. All shall come to It eventually, and It is the greatest Power, which all other Powers serve," replied a voice. Billy hoped the voice didn't belong to who he thought it belonged to, but sure enough, as the orb reached out, its inky darkness seeping into the light that surrounded it, it gradually took human form, and became Mrs. Eva Black. She looked venomously at Billy as she took her seat.

"A great Power," agreed Mrs. Russet. "But the greatest? I think not."

"Do you claim Earth to be greater than Death?" asked Mrs. Black haughtily.

"I do not claim it is, nor do I admit it is not," responded Mrs. Russet. Then she nodded at the White Throne. "But I think we all can admit that the White is the greatest Element, and the White King the greatest Power of us all."

"Shall we agree to that? Shall we indeed?" taunted Mrs. Black. Billy hated it when she talked. It was like the angry edge of her voice was amplified when she sat in her throne.

He noticed that she, of all the Council, wore only her regular clothing. As though the Death Power was one that wore no adornment, and came with no more than what it was. Billy shivered, and thought, And what it is, is quite enough. Adornment or not, Mrs. Black was clothed in her Element, and that Element was indeed dark and frightening.

"The White King exists," said Mrs. Russet, in a tone that brooked no argument. "And he *will* come again."

"If you say so," said Mrs. Black.

"Please, ladies, please," said Veric, the Green Councilor. "We are not here to argue the truth or legend of the White King. We have convened the Council for another purpose, have we not?"

He looked at Mrs. Russet, who nodded. She looked at Billy as though she were waiting for something. He didn't know what she wanted, so he stood there, rooted to the spot. "Well," she finally said. "Don't just stand there like a stick figure." She gestured for him to come to stand in the middle of the Council.

Billy gulped. "Go on, my boy," said Tempus. The jolly old Power of the Wind was grinning impishly at him. "No one has ever died in the midst of a Council session." He winked. "At least, I don't remember it ever happening, but then, we Wind folk have short memories."

Billy gulped again, hardly reassured by what he hoped was Tempus's joke. But he managed to make his feet take several leaden steps toward the Diamond Dais. He didn't have the benefit of Mrs. Russet's power, so no stone steps rose to help him climb gracefully atop the raised podium. Instead, he had to clamber awkwardly up the side, no mean feat considering that the smooth dais was over half his height, with no handholds to help him.

He looked over at Vester, hoping the fireman would see his trouble and give him a lift, but Vester was still staring at Fulgora, the Red Lady, apparently lost in love by the mere fact that she was near.

Billy continued trying to hoist himself up, but instead just felt increasingly foolish. Here six of the most powerful people in this strange new world were waiting for him, and he was hanging off the edge of a diamond platform like a half-paralyzed monkey trying to climb a coconut tree. His ears burned, but he refused to give up.

Suddenly, he felt something give him a boost, pushing him up by the seat of his pants. It pushed a bit too hard, in fact, sending Billy up over the lip of the stage, where he landed with an "oof."

He glanced at Tempus, and the old man winked as though to say "You're welcome, kiddo."

Billy rolled his eyes at the gray man's sense of humor. Then he slowly got to his feet. He felt incredibly awkward, standing in the center of this circle. Not only because it was a focus of the earth's great Powers, but because no matter which way he was facing, he had at least two of them behind him. He had never before wondered what the back of his head looked like, but he suddenly had a crazy thought: I hope my hair is combed.

Then, on the heels of that thought came another: Sure, you wouldn't want these six wizards or Powers or whatever they call themselves to think you didn't comb your hair this morning. I'm sure that would make a huge difference in whatever earth-shattering decision they're about to make.

He faced Mrs. Russet. While not exactly what he would call a "friendly" face, she at least had a face that he was used to, and more importantly it didn't come with the almost frightening beauty of the Red Lady, or with the *completely* frightening look of Mrs. Black. He could feel the Death Power's eyes fairly burning a pair of holes in the back of his neck, and resisted an urge to drop to the floor of the podium like a kid in a fire drill.

"Very well, then, Lumilla," said Veric, the kind-seeming Green Power. "You have us here, and you have this boy. The question *we* all have, I think, is why?"

Mrs. Russet looked slowly around the ring. "We all know of the Prophecy. Of the return of the White King, and the ending of our world."

The Council members each nodded, some looking somber, others—like Mrs. Black—just looking bored or annoyed or both.

Mrs. Russet took a breath, then said, "I believe that the One Prophecy has begun to come to pass."

At this, the Councilors all sat up straight in their thrones. "Explain yourself, Lumilla," snapped Nehala, the Blue Power.

Mrs. Russet held forth her crystal staff. She touched it again to the Diamond Dais, and Billy saw something rise up from below, ascending through the diamond like an air bubble in the ocean. Then the object emerged from the diamond.

It was a book. A deep brown book that looked heavy as lead, and thick as all of life itself. He knew somehow that this book, like Mrs. Russet's deep-colored cloak, held the sum of History in its pages. That it had come at Mrs. Russet's call from the very center of the earth, and that in its pages he could find out anything that had ever happened before, from the beginning of existence to the present day.

"The Book of the Earth," said Mrs. Russet. She opened it, and read. "In the fourth Age of our Power, the White King came." Mrs. Black snorted in derision at this, but Mrs. Russet ignored her. "He was the all-Power, the one Power who has ever been a master of all the Elements, and he ushered in an age of peace that lasted a generation."

"Folklore. Myth," said Mrs. Black. Billy noted that the Blue and Gray Councilors nodded in agreement.

Mrs. Russet frowned at them. "Do you dispute the Power of Earth here in the presence of its heart?" Billy again felt like dropping to the ground, this time because he sensed that an all-out fight was on the verge of breaking out, and he knew for a fact that he didn't want to be in the middle of it.

Mrs. Black and the two other Powers backed down, saying nothing. Mrs. Russet nodded. "As I was saying...." Her eyes went back to the book, reading from its pages. "And after the White King worked his Power upon the face of the world, he was loved and revered, until," she turned a page. Billy thought he could almost hear the sound of the continents shifting when she turned the pages of that great book. "...until his closest friend attacked him, mortally wounding the White King. The King, in the midst of his pain, Prophesied. He Prophesied that he would return. And that before he did, a boy would come forth, a boy who was of the Power, but held none in his control. A boy that the Earth would protect, and that Life would seek to reject. A boy with Death in his past, but Hope in his present."

She looked at Billy. "I believe this is that boy."

Billy was unprepared for the chaos that followed this statement. All the Councilors, it seemed, erupted from their seats, several of them literally, Nehara the Blue rising up on a small, agitated water spout that burst from his throne; and Dismus the Gray whipping about the Diamond Dais in a whirlwind that sprang into existence out of nowhere.

Billy noted that only Fulgora, the Red Lady, remained calm, her sparkling eyes watching everything as though she were waiting for something, waiting for a special, perfect moment to occur. Billy had no idea what that moment would be, just that he got uneasy watching her. The fact that Vester loved her made Billy want to like her automatically, but he couldn't help but be spooked by her for some reason.

The rest of the Council, though, was screaming and yelling at the tops of their lungs. Billy caught snatches of the exchanges, but couldn't focus on any one thing in particular.

"Impossible! The White King is a legend...."

"How do you know this? Explain yourself, Lumilla!"

"If Lumilla says it, I'm inclined to...."

Around and around they went, a dizzying barrage of conversation that flew over and around Billy as though he were an innocent bystander in the middle of a firefight between two hostile armies.

Nor did it seem at all likely that the arguing was going to stop any time soon. Instead, the verbal combatants seemed to be increasing the energy of their attacks. Louder and louder the Council became, until suddenly there was a great noise that silenced all of them.

The Diamond Dais bucked under Billy's feet, sending him falling down hard to the shining floor below him. He heard a scream, but couldn't tell where or who it came from. Then the ground rolled again. He heard a great cracking far to his left, and thought with horror that it sounded as though one of the great stones that made up the great tower had separated from its moorings and would crash down to the island below.

Again the ground swayed and rolled below Billy. He looked over and saw Vester, Tempus, and Ivy reel, trying to remain on their feet. The tiny blue and red horses made of lightning and fire which were still riding across Vester's shoulders reared up in fear, then galloped into his pants pockets and disappeared.

Billy had no time to reflect on the strangeness of the scene, because another great shiver ran through the ground. To Billy's horror, the dais upon which he was so precariously perched began to crack below his hands and knees. A long, jagged fissure appeared below him, and Billy rolled to one side as the dais split in two, a four-inch crack running the length of the platform.

Billy's roll to the side was an instinctive move, nothing he consciously decided, but the move saved his life, as a long diamond shard erupted through the crack in the Diamond Dais, right where Billy had stood only a moment before. It speared four feet into the sky, a frighteningly sharp diamond shaft with a razor point at its tip.

The ground continued its roller-coaster movement, and Billy almost rolled right off the podium, but caught himself at the last moment. He looked around in panic as the ground continued to quake. Several of the Councilors, he saw, were holding strange objects in tightly-clenched fists. Fulgora the Red was clutching a red rose, her mouth moving as though she were speaking rapidly, though Billy couldn't hear what she was saying. Mrs. Black was rubbing her scarab broach wildly, clearly hoping that it would do something; just as clearly disappointed that whatever she was hoping would happen hadn't happened yet.

And Dismus was.... Billy blinked. The Gray Councilor was still whipping around the dais at full speed, but now he seemed out of control, as though something else was moving the wind, and he no longer had any say in its movements. The old man was swirling around the group faster and faster, in tighter and tighter circles... and he had an electric toothbrush in his hands the whole time.

He's worried about *cavities*? Billy thought in amazement as the ground rolled him around again, his body loose and limp as a piece of yarn. I don't think gingivitis is really an issue right now.

Then he remembered what Vester had said while Billy was caught in the cave. Tempus had asked where the Darksiders that had been a part of Billy's death—Mrs. Black and the cold Blue Power, Wade—had disappeared to. Vester had mentioned that Mrs. Black's broach was Imbued, and that she had grabbed it, then grabbed Wade and they had both disappeared.

Of course, Billy thought. The broach, the rose, and Dismus's tooth brush must all be like Mrs. Russet's beehive key: they must be Imbued Objects that can take them away from here.

Billy certainly couldn't blame any of the three from trying to get away; he was quite certain that he would be doing the very same thing if he'd had any such magical object. But he did wonder why the objects weren't working for the three Powers.

Then, just as suddenly as it had begun, the quaking stopped. Billy looked at Mrs. Russet, who alone among the Councilors had remained calmly seated at her throne during the great shaking of the tower. That made some sense, Billy realized: surely as a Power of Earth an earthquake wouldn't particularly concern her. But then he noticed that the knuckles of the hand that still held her crystal staff were white and strained. She was afraid, too, he realized, and that thought alone was enough to scare him as much as anything that had happened this day. Mrs. Russet did *not* get scared. She could make others uneasy at times—during surprise quizzes, for example—but did not get scared herself.

Slowly, though, as everyone became more or less sure that the ground had stopped its violent flinging about, the Councilors settled back to their seats, sinking onto them with a mixture of relief and tightly coiled fear. Billy spared a glance to where Vester, Ivy, and Tempus had been before this all started and saw the three Powers climbing out of a net-like lattice of soft vines. Evidently Ivy—or perhaps her father, Veric, the Green Councilor—had called the plants up to protect them from the shaking.

For a long moment, all were silent.

Then Mrs. Russet picked up the Book of the Earth again. She opened it, then read in a somber voice: "And before the White King comes, shall come the Messenger. And with him, the Earth shall shake, and the Seats of Power shall tremble, and there shall be a great rending, even as of a diamond splitting in two."

She looked pointedly at the Diamond Dais on which the thrones all sat. The crack that had opened below Billy stretched the length of the podium, interrupted only by the gleaming spire that now thrust skyward out of its center. Billy noted that the diamond shard was so clear, so perfectly formed, that he could see through it and gaze upon many-faceted images of the Powers who sat on the other side.

"I think," said Mrs. Russet after a long silence, "that we can dispense with the idea that the White King is a legend." She shut the book with the authority and awful certainty of a landslide crashing down. "I also think," she continued, "that it appears certain that this boy," and here she gestured at Billy with her crystal staff, "is the Messenger foretold."

There was another long pause. Then Fulgora said, "Not necessarily." Her lips, as flame red as her throne, moved slowly, her words deliberate and careful. "He may be the Messenger," she said. "Or this may have been coincidence."

"Coincidence?" shouted Dismus the Gray in shock, the electric toothbrush still whirring in his hands. "That wasn't a coincidence! That was prophecy! And I should know! I'm of the Wind!" He harrumphed as though that settled the question, then seemed to notice his toothbrush for the first time. "Not only did the Diamond Dais crack, but the Wind was spinning me—*me*—without my being able to do a thing about it." He shook his toothbrush at them all. "And my Transport key didn't work. Nor did yours or yours," he continued, looking at Mrs. Black and at Fulgora the Red in turn. "Don't deny it! I saw you grab your broach, Eva, and Fulgora still holds her rose in her hand! Something blocked us, something I've never heard of or felt before." He took a few deep breaths, visibly calming himself. "I think Lumilla is right, and I *don't* think," he added, looking at Fulgora, "that this is a mere coincidence. That would strain belief."

And with that, Dismus crossed his arms and sat back on his throne of air, swaying ever so slightly as the wind of the chair moved him back and forth in its eddying breeze.

"I agree that if this is a coincidence, then it is an extraordinary one," said Fulgora. "But then, we don't notice *ordinary* coincidences anyway, do we? So a coincidence, when anyone speaks of it, does tend to be an *extra*ordinary occurrence. Nevertheless," she said, holding up a hand to silence Dismus, who appeared about to go flying about on his tornado again, "I do agree that the odds against this being such a coincidence are high. But there *is* one other alternative." She gazed around the Council. "You all know of what I speak. Of *whom* I speak."

"Wolfen was not the Messenger. He was exiled over twenty years ago, and no one has heard of him since," said Mrs. Russet.

"Wolfen the White was not exiled," snapped Mrs. Black. Then, in an almost piteously sad voice, she said, "He left us." Then she straightened. "But I heard the prophecy at the boy's Gleaning. 'He is returning,' Tempus said. I believe he has. I believe that Wolfen is coming, if he is not already among us." Billy heard Ivy gasp fearfully at this, and wondered who this Wolfen person might be.

Mrs. Black continued. "And as for this boy, I don't think this Billy Jones is a Messenger, or even a mere Power. We're wasting our time with him."

"Then how do you explain what just happened?" asked Mrs. Russet indignantly, waving to the cracked dais and three diamond spires in its center.

"I don't know," said Mrs. Black, arms crossed. "It bears looking into. But to suggest it's because of him," she nodded at Billy, "is premature, if not just foolish."

The Councilors again erupted in a cacophony of disagreement, each trying to speak louder than the others. Veric stretched out a thick arm, the vines that made up his throne curling about him like infatuated snakes. "Silence!" he hollered. The others all quieted immediately, as much in surprise as out of a desire to obey, thought Billy.

"I think that the Council should not be bickering like schoolchildren. At the very least, not in the presence *of* children."

"At long last, Veric, you have said something I can agree with," said Mrs. Black. Veric looked momentarily pleased. The look disappeared, however, when Mrs. Black stood. "I am not going to waste my time in arguing, or in remaining here any longer." She touched her broach, clearly preparing to leave. Dismus, too, stood, and withdrew from his watery cloak a small seashell, apparently ready to follow her.

"Beware, Eva," said Mrs. Russet. "This discussion will continue without you. If a vote is held, we will still have the necessary majority."

"Not in this," said Mrs. Black. "As for this Billy Jones, he is nothing. He has not Glimmered, and has shown no power. More important, if you dare to declare anyone other than Wolfen the White as the foretold Messenger—and the rightful leader and King of all Powers—I will see to it that all Darksiders will leave Powers Island. The Truce will be over, and heaven help you."

She spoke a word, and disappeared with the loud sound that Billy had come to expect with such appearances and disappearances. A moment later, another clap sounded as Dismus exited also in a swirl of watery mist.

The remaining Councilors looked stricken. Billy didn't understand exactly what was going on, but he knew it was something awful. Something even worse than earthquakes, or dragons shooting lightning at you. Even worse than dying in the basket of a great tree.

Mrs. Russet turned slowly to look at Billy. "Tempus, Vester, Ivy," she called.

The three stepped closer to the dais, but did not step up onto the platform. Apparently that was reserved only for the Councilors and those that were specifically invited.

"The Council has much to discuss," she said. "Some of it is not fit for young ears, and some of it is not fit for anyone, but must be discussed nonetheless. Please take Billy and wait—all of you—in the anteroom until we call. The key word to get in is 'Transport.'" Her look never wavered from Billy's eyes. He didn't know what to do. He felt like he should do something, say something brave or heroic or at least make *some* statement. But nothing came to mind. All he could think about was how awful he felt.

That and the fact that his nose was suddenly incredibly itchy, but there was no way on earth he was going to scratch it right now.

"The Truce has been on the verge of collapse for years," continued Mrs. Russet. "I fear that this last set of events may finally break it. But regardless, we must decide a few things."

Her eyes grew, if possible, even more intense. "Not least of which, we must determine what to do with Billy Jones."

# CHAPTER THE SIXTH

*In Which Billy hears of the White King's Fall, and Wolfen's Rise...*

Billy clambered down from the dais and was taken by Vester, Ivy, and Tempus to a nearby outcropping of stone standing by the river that bisected the tower. The stone was roughly cubic in shape, about eight feet on each side, and was of the same type of rock as the tower itself. It looked like it had been carved out of the solid rock of the tower, then put on top of it as an afterthought, but there was no seam that Billy could see between the tower and the strange outcropping before which they now stood.

Vester looked at the rocky cube, unsure. "Anyone here ever been in the anteroom?" he asked.

"I have," said Ivy. She walked to the rock, then touched it with a finger. She traced her finger lazily across its surface in a few sweeping strokes. Billy watched her, curious to see what new strangeness would erupt.

Ivy saw him watching, and misinterpreted his look as one of questioning what she was doing. "Didn't you hear Lumilla?" she asked. "I'm writing the code word on the rock. Otherwise, we wouldn't be able to get in." As she said this, her finger stopped moving. Billy suddenly saw a dim gold outline in the rock, along the path where her finger had moved. "Transport," it said, and Billy had a moment to see that Ivy had put a smiley-face in the middle of her "o" before the word faded, and a beautiful golden doorway appeared in the face of the rock.

"Come on," said Ivy, and opened the door. She stepped through, followed by Tempus.

"Good thing," murmured the older man. "I need to put my feet up."

Vester nodded to Billy, gesturing for him to go through ahead of him. Billy smiled, then stepped through the portal.

He didn't know what to expect upon stepping through. Some jarring convulsion of light, or an explosion of color, or some strange smell that he would later find out was Eye of Newt or Pancreas of Dragon or something.

But he definitely did *not* expect a cozy, brightly painted room that had a pot-bellied stove in one end of it, a bar at the other, and about three dozen bean bags all around. One entire wall was a great window, which allowed an awesome view of a snow-filled vista, as though the room they were in was on the top of Mount Everest.

A blizzard raged outside, but unlike the blizzards that Billy had seen on television or read about in books, this one had snowflakes that looked to be about eight inches in diameter, each one a beautiful and distinct marvel of ice sculpture that danced in the fierce wind outside. Occasionally a group of the snowflakes would blow together, seemingly at random, to form a shape of some kind: a polar bear, an ice castle, a Christmas tree, and on and on in a never-ending flurry of beauty and prismatic light.

Tempus was already flopped in a beanbag, his arms splayed out to the sides in total exhaustion, as though he had run a marathon. Billy suddenly realized that he, too, was getting tired. How long had it been since Mrs. Russet first took him from school and brought him to the hall with the walls of water, wind, and flame? It felt like hours and hours. He hoped it hadn't been too long, because he knew that if he wasn't home when his mom got off her shift at work, she would panic and probably call out the police to look for him—if she didn't place a direct call to the President of the United States asking for the Army to start a house-to-house search.

Vester moved immediately to the bar. "Anyone want anything?" he asked.

"Cocoa," replied Ivy immediately, settling down into a dark green bean-bag that immediately sprouted flowers which she picked and began braiding into a small wreath.

"Make it a double for me," said Tempus.

Vester nodded. He turned to Billy. "And you?" he asked.

Billy realized that his mouth was parched. Just the thought of something to drink made his lips feel even drier. "I'd love something," he replied.

"What's your pleasure?" asked Vester. "You can have anything you want, pretty much, as long as it's cocoa." He laughed at Billy's surprised expression. "This place was designed by a pair of Councilors many centuries ago, when the Council was first formed. One of them was a Gray Power, a very powerful one who could see farther into the future than any other Gray Power before or since." He reached below the bar and brought out two steaming mugs of cocoa. Billy didn't see him make anything, the mugs were apparently just waiting for him down there, as if—naturally—by magic. Ivy and Tempus each stood and took one of the mugs, then sat back down in their bean bags. "Many of that Gray Powers' prophecies are recorded as some of the most accurate and powerful that have ever been."

Vester frowned as he withdrew another hot chocolate from under the bar and sipped at it. "Unfortunately, the sight of the future also drove him mad. Apparently he didn't like what he saw. But one thing in the future that he saw and *did* like was hot chocolate. So when he designed the anteroom, he and the Brown Power who helped him make this place made it so that there would always be hot chocolate available for the asking." He winked at Billy. "And you look like you could use a Vester Special."

Vester reached under the bar and withdrew a large mug. This one was heaped with whipped cream that practically spilled out of its sides, the tops of the cream sprinkled with chocolate shavings and colorful sprinkles. A fat marshmallow sat on top.

Vester looked around. "Now, where did I put...?" he began, then snapped his fingers. Billy heard a tiny neighing sound, then the minute red flame stallion that Vester had conjured earlier galloped out of the fireman's pocket, and back up to his shoulder. Vester held out his hand, finger pointed at the marshmallow on top of Billy's cocoa. The fire horse galloped down Vester's arm, across his hand, then leapt a great leap across to the marshmallow, where with a final whinny it disappeared in a flash and a puff of smoke, leaving behind a perfectly-toasted marshmallow. Vester pulled a maraschino cherry from under the bar, placed it on top of the whole concoction, then held it out to Billy.

Billy took it, and tried a sip.

It was the best hot chocolate he had ever tasted. It was as though there was yet another Element of Power—the ChocolateEssence—and Billy was pouring liquefied Chocolate Power directly down his throat. It tasted so good that he sank into the nearest beanbag without even thinking about it. You just couldn't drink this hot chocolate unless you were sitting in a comfy chair. Billy suddenly understood why they were at a top of a mountain, with a pot-bellied stove in the room: the whole anteroom was *designed* around the central idea of hot chocolate. And everyone knew, somewhere deep inside them, that a perfect hot chocolate was impossible without soft seats and a pot-bellied stove with a fire somewhere near, so you could be comfy and warm while looking out at a beautiful snowblizzard.

It was a moment of pure bliss.

Unfortunately, it was shattered when Tempus said, to no one in particular, "I wonder what the Council is going to do about our young Mr. Jones?"

Billy was wondering the same thing. But before he could say anything, Vester frowned and said, "I'm more worried about what Eva said, about Wolfen returning."

"Do you think it's really possible?" asked Ivy, her voice quavering.

"Who is this Wolfen guy?" asked Billy.

"Well, it's a bit hard to explain," began Vester.

"Nonsense," snorted Tempus. The old man's indignant tone was somewhat marred by the brown chocolate cocoa mustache he now wore, and the dollop of whipped cream on the tip of his nose. "It's not hard to explain at all." He looked at Billy. "Wolfen is pure evil."

He sat back with a smug smile, as if to say, "There, I told you it would be easy."

Vester cleared his throat. "Yes…well…that's true, but I suppose it might help Billy to know a *little* more than that. Just by way of background," he hurried to add as Tempus's face grew stormy. Tempus, almost sulky, buried his nose in his hot chocolate again.

Vester, too, took a long sip. "It was a bit before my time, really, I was younger than you were when it all happened, Billy." His eyes grew far off. "To understand what happened then, however, I must tell you a bit of our history. You know there are six Elements: Earth, Wind, Water, Fire, Life, and Death. In the beginning of the Powers, it is said that the Powers waged war upon one another. Wind Powers would snuff out Fire, Fire would blister and destroy Life, Earth rose up to choke Fire, the Water made mountains into rivers, and Death…Death waited and added to the chaos, to collect her spoils."

Vester drank a bit more of his chocolate, then put the mug aside. He looked out the window into the swirling snowflakes, and shivered, though Billy knew the fireman's shudder had nothing to do with the cold outside.

As though they sensed Vester's agitation, some of the giant snowflakes flinging about outside the anteroom joined together to form into what looked almost like a skull before exploding from one another and re-joining the mass of the blizzard.

"At any rate," continued Vester, "eventually the Powers formed into two opposing sides: the Darksiders and the Dawnwalkers. No one knows why they came to be called that, but that is what they called themselves, and it continues to this day." Vester gestured at the badge he wore, the one Billy had noticed at his Gleaning. "Dawnsider," it said.

"They warred with one another, those two frightful armies. They laid waste to each other, and to the earth itself. You may have heard that a long time ago, all the earth's continents were joined together in an enormous land mass called Pangea. The world's scientists believe it broke apart millions of years ago because of the natural movement of the earth. We Powers believe that in reality, the fracture occurred during the time of these wars."

"You believe?" asked Billy. "Wouldn't you know? I got the feeling that the big book Mrs. Russet had out there was like, the ultimate history book. Couldn't you just look in there and find out for sure?"

"The Book of the Earth," nodded Tempus. "It contains much of history, for most of what has happened to the sons of men and the daughters of women has happened on the earth. But there are some things it does not contain: the history of the seas, for example. And as Vester said, the wars of the Powers ripped chasms in the planet. Earth herself was broken, and like many badly injured things, she cannot remember all that happened to her during that age of destruction."

"Oh, it was a dreadful time," said Ivy.

"You were there?" asked Billy in shock.

"No, but some of the oldest trees on Powers Island still whisper of it, of their grandparents who were seedlings when it all came about. Only Earth itself has a longer memory than the trees." She shuddered. "The stories the trees have told me are horrifying."

She couldn't continue. Vester picked up as Billy listened raptly. Even the somewhat scatter-brained Tempus was listening attentively, his hot cocoa forgotten, the whipped cream on his nose dripping off slowly.

"Finally, one of the Powers rose and managed—by force in some cases—to stop the fighting."

"The White King," breathed Tempus.

"Just so," said Vester. "He was called the White King because, just as what we see as white is really a combination of every color in the spectrum, the White King was the first—and only—Power who could control not just one Element, but all of them. He could not get the Powers to abandon their allegiances as Dawnwalkers or Darksiders, but he managed to forge an alliance of sorts, which we call the Truce. He called forth the strongest Power of each Element, and together those six wizards joined together, under the White King's direction, and created Powers Island. He formed the Council, with one seat for each of the Elements, and one seat for himself. There the Powers could join and peacefully sort out their differences and make the rules that would govern the Powers. The White King tried to encourage the Powers to forget their differences and be as one, but there was a great disagreement that he could never overcome."

"What was it?" asked Billy, enthralled.

"The purpose of the Powers," said Tempus. Billy looked at the man. "To put it simply, the Darksiders believe that the Powers should rule the world, and subjugate all those who have no control of the Elements. The Dawnwalkers believe that the world of normal humans should govern itself, and that the Powers should not intervene in that world, but should only exercise their control over the Elements when among their own kind."

"So the White King sat upon the Diamond Throne at the head of the Council," said Vester.

"He judged in goodness and light," added Ivy.

"Yes, but he was betrayed, it seems. One of his closest friends stabbed him grievously," said Vester.

Billy almost spilled what little remained of his hot chocolate as his hand went to his mouth. "Someone murdered the White King?" he gasped.

None of the Powers in the room answered for a long time. Then Vester shrugged. "No one knows, really. The Book of Earth has confused accounts. Some say that he was murdered, others that he did not die, but went away into a land of his own making, there to walk eternally in the peace that he so craved."

"But there were prophecies," said Tempus, leaning forward. The stove's firelight reflected off the Wind Power's gray eyes, giving them a strange glow. Gone was the silly man in the Hawaiian shirt. Tempus was speaking now, not as a mere Power of Wind, but as a Prophet, speaking of other Prophets. "Prophecies that the White King himself made. That he would one day return. That he would come, and would save our world, and would do so by destroying it." Tempus shook himself, awaking from his half-trance. He grinned that impish grin of his. "Prophecies can be funny things, though. Quite open to interpretation."

"And that is where Wolfen comes in," said Vester.

"Oh, do we have to speak of him?" asked Ivy.

"I'm afraid so," said Vester. "I think that Billy will need to know of him in days to come."

"So now *you're* a Prophet, eh, Firewalker?" asked Tempus with a wink.

"No, it's not prophecy, just a normal feeling I have," responded Vester seriously. He turned to Billy. "After the White King disappeared, the Truce remained intact—barely. The Council held together, though disputes are not unusual. Part of what has held them together all these years is Powers Island itself." He looked around the room, as though it were the entirety of the island. "There are always a certain number of Powers here...around twenty thousand or so. If there are not enough present, then more Powers will be summoned to the island. The number is split evenly, so that there are always an equal number of Darksiders and Dawnwalkers." He indicated his badge. "That's why we all go to the Accounting Room, and what it means to be Counted."

Billy remembered something Mrs. Russet had said. "That's the room in the tower where I first appeared. With the fortune teller things that gave me this." He indicated his own badge, which said only "Billy" on it.

Vester nodded. "Right. The 'fortune teller things' are the Counters. They magically determine the alignment of every person who comes to Powers Island—whether that person is a Dawnwalker or a Darksider. That way, we can make sure that the numbers of Dawnwalkers and Darksiders on the island are always equal."

"Why do they need to be equal?" asked Billy.

"Because that way," answered Vester, "if either the Dawnwalkers or the Darksiders decide to void the Truce, there will likely be immediate destruction of a large number of the world's Powers, on both sides."

"It's a terrible way to keep peace," said Ivy.

"True," said Vester. "But neither side will risk the destruction of so many of its subjects at once. Powers Island, if ripped apart, would probably weaken both sides to the point that they might never rise again. No Power, of the Dark or the Dawn, would ever risk that...until Wolfen."

Ivy had stopped weaving her wreath of flowers some time ago. Now, at the mention of that name, the wreath seemed to wilt in her hands.

"Wolfen was an incredibly gifted Power," continued Vester. "He ascended to the Council when he was only a few years older than you, Billy, sitting for a decade on the Black Throne. He was a Darksider, and everyone knew that he was for subjugating humanity. But after a period of rule, he disappeared for several years. When he returned, he claimed that he was the Messenger of the White King—the man foretold to lead in a new age—and called all Darksiders to his side. To war."

"And they came?" asked Billy.

Vester nodded. "Yes, many of them."

"But what about the balance here on the island?" asked Billy.

Vester shrugged again. "It happened so quickly that many of the Powers didn't know it had happened until it was almost too late. And many of those who *did* know simply couldn't believe it was happening, it had been so long since open hostility had been present among the Powers. Wolfen had somehow managed—all by himself—to craft his own island, Dark Isle. He and his followers gathered there, and then...." Vester drew a deep shuddering breath. He couldn't go on.

"They attacked," Ivy said simply.

"It was a terrible, terrible war," said Tempus. "The Dawnwalkers were unorganized, unprepared to face a militant onslaught. Many of us were killed. Many more...." Tempus's face grew even more gray. He reached to the hem of his shirt, and drew it upward. Billy gasped. Tempus's stomach was a mass of terrible scars. But unlike most scars, these scars glowed a pale blue. "We were marked and herded like cattle, to be servants to the servants after the war ended and the Darksiders ruled."

To Billy's relief, Tempus lowered his shirt, and seemed to lapse into almost comatose silence.

"Wolfen lost, eventually," said Vester. "But not before wreaking great destruction on our world. He was captured, and tried, and sentenced to death. But the Darksiders were still many, though leaderless. They offered to re-institute the Truce, if Wolfen's life would be spared." Vester grimaced. "The Council agreed. Full privileges were restored to the Darksiders, and the Dawnwalkers no longer feared torture or destruction in captivity." He paused, then said, "Personally, I think they made a mistake. They should have killed Wolfen when they had him."

"Vester!" said Ivy reproachfully.

Vester looked evenly at her. "If you had lost *your* father to the man, maybe you would understand my feelings better, Ivy."

Ivy's voice immediately softened. "Oh, Vester, I didn't mean...."

He waved her off. "No matter. The Truce has continued. No Dawnwalker has ever confirmed that Wolfen is even still alive, let alone that he is contacting anyone amongst the Powers. And the Darksiders, of course, claim not to have heard from him since his exile."

"What about the Dark Isle?" asked Billy.

"It disappeared," said Vester, "the day Wolfen was captured."

"And no one knows where it is?" said Billy.

"Perhaps the great Powers of the Blue Water might. But the Water Powers tend to align themselves with the Darksiders, so they would hardly volunteer to tell a Dawnwalker, would they?"

"That's not fair of you, Vester," said Ivy. "Until we have some proof that they are conspiring with Wolfen—"

"That's a foolish policy," snapped Vester. "Proof will only come when we're attacked, and then it will be too late!"

Before Ivy could respond, the door to the anteroom opened. In the doorway stood a strange creature, gnarled and knotted. It stood on two legs, but where a head would have been on a man, there were only masses of branches and leaves. And instead of arms, there were two thick branch-like appendages that sprung out of the middle of what Billy could only call its trunk. "Billy Jones," it said. The voice came from somewhere inside the creature, resounding as though in a drum, and its voice was deep and dark with hidden knowledge. "The Council has decided your fate."

# CHAPTER THE SEVENTH

*In Which Billy Meets Wolfen, and goes back Home...*

Billy's stomach churned. His *fate*?

Then Ivy said, "Oh, Father," in a tone both amused and mildly reproving.

The tree-like creature chuckled. "Allow me my small diversions, Ivy." Then, to Billy's amazement, the creature exploded in a mass of blossoms, tiny flowers of every color that fell slowly to the ground and then disappeared.

Ivy stood from her bean bag, rolling her eyes at Billy. "My father is like that," she said.

"Did he—did your father just explode?" asked Billy.

"Oh, no, that wasn't my father. It was just one of his Fizzles," she answered. Then, when she saw Billy's confused look, she added, "A Fizzle is a non-living creature that some of the Powers can manage. Like Vester's little horsies made of lightning and fire."

Billy glanced at Vester in awe. Vester held up a hand. "Mine are just little Fizzles. Can't make them talk, and they have to be touching me or else they disappear within seconds." At that, the tiny electric blue horse ran out of Vester's pocket and re-assumed its perch on the fireman's shoulder. It looked around for a moment, as though trying to find the other horse, the one of fire that had sacrificed itself to perfectly toast Billy's marshmallow. Then, not finding its friend, it moved with tiny crackles of electric hooves to Vester's other shoulder, where it settled down to sleep.

"But my fate?" asked Billy. "What does it mean, 'The Council has decided my fate'?" He was dismayed to hear his voice—which was already too high for his own liking—starting to sound like a squeaky door.

"Could mean anything, my boy," answered Tempus, who rose creakily to his feet, taking a last sip of his cocoa before reluctantly putting the mug down on the floor. "Could mean they're just sending you home, could mean they're going to shower you in gold and call you the new White King, could mean they're going to feed you to a wyvern."

Billy's insides lurched. Vester frowned. "That's not funny, Tempus." He looked at Billy. "The Council hardly ever feeds anyone to a wyvern anymore."

The three Powers in the room watched Billy as his face went through about three hundred different expressions, ranging from uncomfortable to worried to downright terrified. Then they laughed, and Ivy hugged him.

"Oh, you are a fun one, Billy Jones," she said. She linked her arm through his. This close, Billy thought she looked much younger than old. He wondered what her real age was. If Veric, the Green Councilor, was her father, then she couldn't be *too* old. But it was hard to tell. Her face had the same ageless quality as some plants: looking at it you couldn't tell if it was one year old, or fifty. She squeezed Billy's arm tightly. "Come on, let's go see what the Council has planned for you."

Billy looked at his hot chocolate, which he still held. "What do I do with this?" he asked.

"Just put it down anywhere," answered Ivy. "There are Fizzles here who do the cleanup." And as she said that, Billy saw a tiny creature come running out from under the pot-bellied stove. It looked something like a tiny stone snowman, its body made up of three small rocks stacked atop one another. But instead of stick arms and no legs, this little creature had about a dozen pairs of minute stone appendages sticking out in all directions, which it seemed to use interchangeably as hands or feet as the situation warranted.

The Fizzle scuttled along the ground, then hoisted Tempus's cup in its small arms/legs, and precariously made its way across the anteroom floor, disappearing around the corner of the bar. There was a popping sound, and Billy knew that the rock Fizzle had just Transported to wherever the dishes got cleaned.

Billy put his mug down. He wanted to see if the same Fizzle would come to take his cup, too—anything to avoid finding out what the Council had to say to him—but Ivy drew him cheerfully back out onto the roof of the tower.

Outside of the anteroom the sky was now overcast, the tower completely cloaked in the eternal clouds that writhed about its heights. There was no sign of any beautiful blizzard, even though when Billy looked back through the open door to the anteroom, he could still see the wonderful snowflakes outside the cozy room, doing their magical dance. Several of the snowflakes appeared to swirl together into the form of a hand, waving goodbye as he watched.

Then Tempus and Vester stepped through the door. Vester shut it behind him, and as soon as he did, the golden door disappeared, leaving behind only the solid rock mass. Billy shook his head. He didn't know if he would ever get used to such things.

Ivy drew him toward the Diamond Dais. Billy saw that it was still split in two, with that strange crystal spire sticking up in the middle of it. He had unconsciously expected that the dais would have been fixed somehow, so was a bit surprised to see that it was still cracked and marred.

The Councilors all sat on their thrones, watching Billy, Ivy, Tempus, and Vester approach. Eva Black and Nehara the Blue Power had apparently not returned after leaving, since the thrones of Death and Water stood empty. But all the others were there: Veric, the Green Councilor of Life; Dismus, the Gray Councilor who represented the Wind; Fulgora the Red, the beautiful Fire Councilor; and Mrs. Russet—Lumilla the Brown. The four of them sat rigidly, looking very official and more than a little scary to Billy.

Billy caught himself gulping. He tried to imagine that Blythe Forrest was watching him, and managed to straighten his back and put on a brave face. This time, at least, he didn't have to climb up onto the top of the diamond platform on his own. A soft ramp of leaves rose up before him. He glanced at Ivy, who squeezed his arm and winked. He smiled in thanks.

His smile disappeared, however, as Ivy withdrew her arm from his and gave him a gentle nudge toward the platform. Billy walked up the leafy ramp, and stood at the edge of the platform.

"Mr. Jones," said Mrs. Russet. Billy turned to face her. "We have a bit of a problem. Most people who come here arrive because they have Glimmered, or have shown a Power. You have done neither, at least not in a way that we can verify. Ordinarily that would mean you would not remain here. We would send you back to where you live, with a spell over your memory so that you would never remember any of this, or would think it merely a dream."

Billy was surprised to hear how much Mrs. Russet's words dismayed him. As frightening and strange as this day had been, it had also been wonderful and exhilarating. He couldn't bear the idea of never remembering the anteroom and its hot chocolate, or the amazing boxing match between rock giants, or the three new friends who now stood behind him.

His concern must have shown on his face, because Mrs. Russet's expression softened. "Don't worry, Mr. Jones. We're not going to do that to you. Events of the day have convinced us that we must keep an eye on you, and test you to find out if you are a Power, or a normal human being, or something else entirely. So we are going to declare you unDetermined, both as to whether you have control over one of the Elements, and as to your eventual affiliation with either the Darksiders or Dawnwalkers."

"But I don't want to be a Darksider," Billy blurted without thinking about it. He immediately snapped his mouth shut, ashamed of his outburst.

Mrs. Russet nodded approvingly. "Well, that will be decided at a later time, if at all. As I said, for now you are unDetermined."

She stamped her crystal staff against the diamond floor in front of her earthy throne. Billy felt a warm sensation on his chest and looked down. The badge he had worn since he had arrived at Powers Island was changing. It had only said "Billy" all this time. But now the badge brightened, the word "unDetermined" appearing after his name.

"What does unDetermined mean?" asked Billy.

"Normally, it means that someone has Glimmered, but we haven't determined what Element they control," replied Mrs. Russet. "In your case. Well...," she shrugged. "It means we really don't know anything at all about you. But what we have decided to do," she continued, waving her staff to indicate that the decision was coming from the whole Council, "is treat you as though you *have* Glimmered."

"And what does that mean?" asked Billy.

"That you will be tested," replied Mrs. Russet.

She reached into her robe, and withdrew a small brown band. She gestured for Billy to approach. When he did, she held out the band, and the thing literally leaped through the air, attaching itself to Billy's wrist, becoming a seamless bracelet. It felt like plastic, but pulsed with strange warmth, as though it were alive. "The bracelet means you are unDetermined. But it is Brown because I—a Brown Power—am your Sponsor," said Mrs. Russet.

"My Sponsor?" asked Billy.

"I will be your guide and adviser through the testing process," answered Mrs. Russet.

Billy heard Tempus whisper, "Lucky," in a jealous half-whisper. Mrs. Russet glared over Billy's shoulder at the old man. "What?" asked Tempus, trying to look innocent and failing dismally. "Well, my Sponsor was a Power named Dopey the Blue." He shuddered. "At least, I think that was his name. It was what everyone else called him, anyway."

"Returning to business," said Mrs. Russet, with a warning glance at Tempus. The old Wind Power fell silent, his toe scratching absently on the ground in front of him, looking to Billy like a little kid whose mother has just scolded him.

Mrs. Russet took Billy's hand in hers. "I know this is all very strange to you, Mr. Jones. But the events of today are unusual." She looked at the crack in the Diamond Dais, the strange spire in its middle. "There are prophecies that seem to be coming to fulfillment, and you seem likely to be at the middle of them."

"Unless Eva Black was right, and it is really Wolfen who is the Messenger, and he has come back," interjected Fulgora, the Red Councilor still mesmerizing in her beauty even as she spoke words that obviously discomfited the rest of the Council.

Mrs. Russet looked at the Red Lady, frowning. "I do not think that is so. I certainly hope that it is not. Wolfen is in exile, and I hope never to hear from him or of him again."

There was a murmur of agreement from Veric the Green Councilor, as well as from Dismus, the Gray Wind Councilor.

Then, at that moment, a noise like rushing wind came from the Black Throne. The dark orb that had heralded Eva Black's arrival reappeared. As before, it grew, coalescing into a human form. Mrs. Black soon could be seen, and then her outlines solidified into the woman that Billy was already coming to fear and loathe.

But she looked very different now. Gone was the aristocratic sneer, the disdainful gaze. Now, she looked distraught, even afraid. Her hair, previously so perfectly combed and styled, was a bit mussed, with stray locks of hair now billowing around her face. "Stop," she said. "Don't go forward with the boy."

"We told you," said Mrs. Russet angrily. "You left, and we were forced to make decisions without you."

"But, but," said Mrs. Black, almost whimpering. Billy saw the other Councilors' eyes narrowing, clearly surprised at how Mrs. Black was acting. Their surprise grew as she started to sniffle. "But Wolfen...," she began, then began crying in earnest.

"What of him?" demanded Veric, his leafy arms crossed in front of his broad chest.

"He appeared to me," sobbed Mrs. Black.

"WHAT?"

Billy wasn't sure who screamed that. Maybe everyone. Certainly every person nearby was now on their feet.

"He appeared to you?" demanded Mrs. Russet. Then, without waiting for an answer, she turned to Vester. "Vester, get to the Accounting Room. Find out how many Darksiders are on Powers Island. We may have to evacuate if Wolfen is attacking."

"No, no!" shouted Mrs. Black. "You don't understand. He's not here to take his rightful place as Lord over all Powers." Everyone paused, staring at the destroyed-looking Death Councilor. "He's here to…to…." She shook her head, clearly not able to believe what she was about to say: "…To swear allegiance!"

"What?" said Mrs. Russet, shocked.

Before Eva Black could say anything more, a rainbow of color appeared over everyone's heads. It was like watching a nebula in deep space, a writhing cloud of many-colored gases that swirled in upon themselves. A rushing sound, like a sandstorm blowing a great dust cloud in front of it, emerged from the sight. And then a man floated down, dropping gently to the Diamond Dais beside Billy.

"Great Powers," whispered Veric in a quiet curse. "It's him. It's Wolfen."

Billy shrank away from the man beside him, but at the same time couldn't help but look closely at him, fascinated by the person who had caused so much havoc and fear among the Powers. Wolfen appeared to be in his mid-fifties, a wiry, lithe, tall man with a full head of salt-and-pepper hair that hung down to the middle of his back, tied tightly into a braid. He wore a black suit of soft-looking cloth, with a velvety white cloak draped over it. His eyes were green, crackling with intelligence, and his face was twisted with the remnants of a life lived in the shadow of hatred for those around him.

He looked at Billy. "Are you the boy?" he whispered.

Billy took another step back. He felt Mrs. Russet stand up from her throne, holding her crystal staff aloft. "Do not touch him!" she shouted. "He is not one of yours. You were exiled, sentenced to death should you ever return to Powers Island or speak to any Power again!"

Billy grew aware that Veric the Green and Dismus the Gray Councilors were also on their feet, the two of them standing close to Mrs. Russet, all of them tensed for battle. Fulgora, the Red Councilor, stayed on her throne, watching with interest, but without apparent fear.

Wolfen held up his hands. "I am not here to fight, and I have not broken the terms of my exile," he said quickly. "The terms of the exile were not that I could never return, or speak to another Power. It was that I could never return *except* to this one place, the Diamond Dais, where the combined might of the Council would keep me from doing any more harm." He paused, his eyes downcast, repentance and sorrow written large across his face. "I am very sorry that such a thing was necessary, and even more sorry that it was necessary because of things I myself did."

He looked up. "And it is for that reason that I have come here today. I have heard the rocks speak this day. I have heard the waves shout their secrets, and the trees whisper their words of warning, and I knew that prophecies were being fulfilled. I suspected that the Messenger was coming." Wolfen looked at Billy. "Is this he?" he asked. "The Object of Prophecy, the Messenger of the White King?"

Mrs. Russet paused, taken aback by Wolfen's meek and mild countenance. "We don't know," she replied simply. "He may be."

Wolfen bowed deeply to Billy. "If you are, I wish you well, my boy. For if you are the Messenger, then difficult times are upon the Powers."

He looked at the other Councilors. "But he is in no danger from me." Wolfen went down on one knee, kneeling on the diamond platform, and bowed his head. He rested his hands on the faceted ground below him. "I have been exiled, and I have kept the terms of the exile. I further swear allegiance to the Council and to its rules."

As he said this, the Diamond Dais began flashing, pulsing like a strobe light. Then the flashing stopped, and the entire dais changed from clear to a deep, lovely green.

"He speaks the truth," whispered Dismus the Gray Councilor, shock apparent in his eyes. "The dais only glows green with the power of truth."

Wolfen nodded. His hands still touching the dais, he continued. "I know that it will do little to pay for the great harms that I have done, but I wanted you all to know. I have kept my exile. I will continue to keep it as long as it is in my power to do so, and will never put my will above that of the Council or the terms of the Truce." He looked over at Billy, a surprising kindness in the Power's eyes, and said, "And this boy has nothing to fear from me now, for I have truly changed my ways of old."

Billy saw Mrs. Russet looking down, staring at the dais, clearly waiting for it to change. But it stayed green. She finally looked up at Wolfen, appearing unsure what to say.

"Wolfen...," she began, but could go no further. Billy tried to imagine what was going through her mind. How would she respond to someone who had apparently single-handedly started a war that killed and enslaved so many people?

Wolfen slowly stood. As he did so, the Diamond Dais returned to its original crystalline transparency. He bowed deeply to Mrs. Russet, Veric, and Dismus. Then he turned to Fulgora. "Still as beautiful as ever, Fulgora Candil. May your fire burn always bright."

Then he swiveled to face Mrs. Black. She was still sobbing, her face buried in her hands. He walked to her, laying a hand softly upon the crown of her head. "Eva," he whispered. "I was wrong. Hate was wrong, the War was wrong. I have seen that in these long years alone." He ran his hands along her hair. "Don't be sad, Eva. There must be hope, even in Death. The Truce is a thing of hope, and I hope that you will forgive my transgressions."

Mrs. Black pulled away from him suddenly. "No!" she screamed. Her face was streaked with tears and dark lines of makeup had run down her cheeks. "I don't know what they've done to you, but I don't believe this. I don't believe you! I don't!" She rubbed her dark broach and disappeared without a word, leaving Wolfen with his hand still out, standing before an empty black throne.

Wolfen sighed. He turned back to Billy and the three Councilors who stood behind him on the dais. "I am sorry. She was one of my supporters. She stood with many of the young Darksiders that I corrupted. Forgive her, her sins are not of her own making. They are mine to bear."

Wolfen nodded at Billy, sadness in his eyes. Then he bowed once more to the assemblage, and without making another move, he disappeared.

No one seemed to even breathe, surprise reigning supreme for a moment. Then Mrs. Russet shouted, "Where did he go? Fulgora, can you sense where he went?"

The Red Councilor stood and went quickly to where Wolfen had been standing. She closed her eyes for a second, then shook her head. "No, the fire of his passage is already cold." She opened her eyes again. "But then, Wolfen always could mask his trail." She sat back on the ruby throne once more, her red lips pursed in thought.

Veric, Dismus, and Mrs. Russet all sat back down on their thrones as well. Finally, Dismus asked, "What are we to do?"

"The Diamond Dais will not brook a lie," said Veric the Green.

"I know," said Mrs. Russet. "This day will certainly have a long entry in the Book of Earth." Then she shook her head. "We will have to watch Eva Black. I don't know what will come of this for her. She may do what Wolfen said. Or she may not."

"Wait a minute!" shouted Vester, startling Billy. He looked over to see the fireman leaping up to the dais. "You don't actually *believe* him, do you?!" he shouted, fury visible in his eyes and flushed cheeks. The tiny blue horse on his shoulders bucked and reared angrily as Vester spoke.

BILLY: MESSENGER OF POWERS, BY MICHAELBRENT COLLINGS * 105

"Vester," began Veric the Green, but he was cut off by Vester's angry shout.

"No! That monster just dances in here and says 'I'm sorry' and you idiots are going to...."

"You forget yourself!" shouted Mrs. Russet, drawing herself up. She touched her staff to Vester, and the man went rigid, paralyzed and still as stone. Only his eyes moved, still flashing with unmasked rage. "This is the Diamond Dais, and only the Council and those it invites may walk upon it." She crooked a finger, and Vester slid backward to the edge of the dais, still held rigid by Mrs. Russet's spell. "I know you have suffered. Many of us here have also suffered, and many of us here worry about what just happened. But the Diamond Dais says that Wolfen was telling the truth."

She gestured with her staff, and Vester could move again. He shivered: clearly Mrs. Russet's spell had not been comfortable for him. But he didn't say anything, and slowly climbed down from the podium under the force of her withering gaze.

Mrs. Russet switched her attention to Billy. "Mr. Jones," she said. "You probably have little understanding of what is happening right here, and I am afraid that the Council must discuss this immediately."

She touched his bracelet. "This will turn blue and grow cool when you are to return for your first test. When it does, get immediately to the nearest doorway. The bracelet is a Transport object, like my key, and will bring you to your first test when it has been prepared for you. Open the door—make sure no one is watching, mind you—and say the word 'elephant.' Then take two steps forward and one step back. And remember to hold your breath!"

"But what about—" Billy began, but before he could finish the sentence, Mrs. Russet had tapped his shoulder with her staff. Billy felt himself get dizzy, and closed his eyes for a second, remembering vaguely to hold his breath.

When he opened his eyes, he found himself back at school, standing in front of the janitorial closet through which Mrs. Russet had taken him to Powers Island. The door was still open, and Billy was half-surprised not to see the island inside of the room. But it was filled only with brooms and mops and cleaning supplies.

He stared dumbly at it, his mind still reeling. Then there was a sizzling sound. He looked down and had a moment of panic as he thought he had suddenly caught on fire, but then realized it wasn't his shirt that had spontaneously combusted. Rather, it was his "Billy—unDetermined" badge that he had worn throughout his time on Powers Island. The name tag burst into flame, reminding Billy of one of those movies where spies get a message that self-destructs after it's been read. Then, with a last puff of white smoke, the badge was gone, as though it had never existed, as though the entire trip to Powers Island had never been.

What am I supposed to do now? he wondered. A moment later, a red hummingbird appeared in front of his face. He knew it wasn't a normal hummingbird, because this one was made of gems: a tiny diamond body and emerald head, with crystal wings so thin they were almost invisible. It was a Fizzle, he realized.

The hummingbird opened its mouth, and to his surprise, Mrs. Russet's voice emerged. "Don't just stand there, Mr. Jones. Get to class!"

Billy looked at a nearby clock on the wall.

It read 12:45. According to the clock, his entire trip to Powers Island and back had only taken a few minutes.

"Move it!" shouted the hummingbird, still sounding like Mrs. Russet. Then it flew right at Billy, exploding into shimmering particles of dust only a few inches from his nose. Billy sneezed violently, blowing what was left of the Fizzle into the janitor's closet. Like Billy's name tag, the magical creature was gone and it almost seemed as though it never had existed in the first place.

Billy looked around.

The school bell rang.

Students entered the hall on their way to their after-lunch classes.

Billy still didn't move. How could he move, how could he possibly go to something as mundane as a *class* after all that had just happened to him?

Then he remembered that Blythe Forrest was in his next class.

Well, he thought, maybe I *could* go on to class. Just for a little while.

He walked hurriedly to his locker. And as he went, his thoughts were torn between thinking of Blythe, and wondering how exactly he was going to be tested, and when it would happen.

Students jostled into Billy as they hurried through the high school halls. One of them shoved him roughly out of the way, and Billy sighed.

He was back home all right.

*Billy: Messenger of Powers*, by Michaelbrent Collings * 107

# CHAPTER THE EIGHTH

*In Which Billy has Lunch, and then goes to a Test...*

When Billy got to his after-lunch class, he was almost positive that he would find out that it wasn't the same day he had left on. He *knew* that he had been on Powers Island for hours and hours. He went to the class, and stood for a moment in the doorway, half-expecting his math teacher to shout, "Billy, where have you been, we've been so worried about you!"

But the only thing that happened was that his math teacher—a fat man who wore suspenders every day even though his pants were two sizes too small for him and who was, appropriately enough, named Mr. Angle—said, "Take your seat, Billy."

Billy sat down, putting his book bag under his desk. He couldn't believe it, but apparently almost no time had passed here while he had been on Powers Island.

He looked around. The other students were already at their seats, paper and pens out and ready to take notes on the oh-so-boring boring lectures that Mr. Angle relished. Billy spied Cameron Black and couldn't help but look at the bigger boy. Cameron's nose was a little swollen where Billy had managed to hit him in the hall.

Does Cameron know about what happened on Powers Island? Billy wondered. Does he know about me? About Wolfen?

Cameron caught Billy looking at him and made a rude gesture.

Well, Billy thought, whether I'm a Power or not, at least I can comfort myself with the thought that some things will never change.

Billy swung away from Cameron, and was surprised to find that someone else was now staring at *him*. Blythe Forrest looked away as soon as he caught her looking, but he was positive that she *had* been looking at him. Billy repressed an urge to check if his pants were unzipped. Why was she looking at him? His tongue immediately felt thick and dry as a rock in his mouth, and his eyelid started twitching.

Blythe started scribbling on a sheet of paper, which she tore off her notebook and then crumpled up. She waited for a moment until

Mr. Angle's back was turned, then threw it under-handed in Billy's direction. Billy reached to catch it, but of course he missed. The paper ball bounced off his outstretched hand and hit him in the eye.

"Ow," Billy said as the paper landed on his desk and rolled onto his lap.

"What?" said Mr. Angle, swinging around to look at the class. No one spoke. Mr. Angle adjusted his suspenders, which were fire-engine red today, reached under his belly to hitch up his tiny pants, and then turned back to the chalkboard, writing the day's geometry problems.

As soon as his eyes were off the class, Billy's hand darted down to grab the piece of paper Blythe had thrown. He uncrumpled it quickly, flattening it out on his desk so he could read what she had written.

When he saw it, his eyes narrowed in confusion. It read, "When computing the length of a right triangle, remember that A squared plus B squared equals C squared. Also, this equation can be done backward when figuring...."

Billy looked at Blythe. She was staring at him, clearly waiting for a response. He held up the paper, then shrugged and shook his head, trying to mime that he didn't understand. She was giving him help with his homework?

Blythe's eyes rolled, and she made a flipping motion with her wrist. Billy frowned, even more confused. He shook his head again. Blythe mouthed something. It took Billy a second to realize what she was saying. When he did, his ears started to burn with embarrassment. "Turn it over," she was saying.

He flipped the piece of paper over. There, on the other side, was the message that Blythe had sent to him. Billy wanted to curl up and die. Again. And not be brought back this time. The prettiest girl he had ever met was now sending him a note, and he hadn't even thought to turn the paper over?

"Are you okay?" was what the note said. Billy, his cheeks burning with feverish humiliation, seriously contemplated not looking at her again. He thought it might be better to just avoid her gaze until after class, then run out without looking at her and put an end to his embarrassment by throwing himself in front of a school bus or something.

Instead, he turned around and looked at Blythe, though it took all the courage he had.

Blythe was still staring at him, waiting for a response. He held up her paper again, this time holding up the side with her message to show he had managed to find it. He nodded, and mouthed, "I'm okay."

Blythe smiled and nodded. "Good," she mouthed back. She looked as though she might have said something more, but before she could, Mr. Angle turned to the class.

"Yesterday we talked about quadrilateral figures," he began, his nasally monotone instantly sending half the class into a group coma. "Today, we will move on to the scintillating world of parallelograms, with all the magic of their parallel lines and incredible angles...."

Mr. Angle continued droning, but Billy didn't hear a word of it. Blythe had *smiled* at him! He forgot the humiliation of being rescued by her, the embarrassment of not reading her note right the first time, he even forgot the incredible world of Powers Island. It all disappeared in a beautiful face and a pair of red lips that curled up at the ends when he said he was fine.

Billy felt warm all over. He didn't meet Blythe's gaze when the end of class bell rang, because he knew he was still blushing with happiness. Even when he tripped on the way out of class and spilled half his books from his backpack, it didn't matter.

She had smiled at him.

The effect wore off during the last class of the day. Billy had forgotten his homework, and got a zero grade for his forgetfulness. Worse, though, was that he realized that even though not much time had passed here in the normal world while he had been on Powers Island, time *had* passed for him. He was incredibly tired after his adventures, and his head drooped repeatedly to his desk. The teacher finally had to ask him if he wanted a pillow, prompting the entire class to laugh—thank goodness Blythe wasn't in that class with him. And even after that embarrassing rebuke, Billy could barely hold his eyes open.

He rode the school bus back home, let himself into his family's apartment, and fell instantly asleep on the sofa. The next thing he knew, his mother was shaking him. "Wake up, Birthday Boy," she was saying.

Billy blinked, unsure for a moment what she was talking about. Who was Birthday Boy? A moment later, he realized she was talking to him, and sat up in surprise.

It's still my birthday? he thought in amazement. But didn't that happen a million years ago?

But no, it *was* still his birthday. His father came home about an hour later, and though he had to leave soon after he got home, there was time for the family to eat a rare dinner together. It was Billy's favorite: his mom's home-cooked pizza and garlic bread, with fruit punch to drink.

After dinner, there was a cake, which his father insisted on lighting while holding a huge red fire extinguisher he'd brought home with him for the occasion.

"Make a wish!" shouted his father in mock anger. "And you better get all the candles out on the first try, or…"—he mimed pulling the trigger on the fire extinguisher, aiming the spout at Billy like a fat red and black ray gun.

Billy grinned sleepily. "I don't know if he'll be able to, dear," said Billy's mom, clearly a bit concerned. "Look how tired he is."

"You okay?" asked Billy's father. And to Billy's surprise, his father sounded much more worried and…involved…than he had in a long time.

Everything's fine, Billy thought. I was almost fried to a crisp by a blue dragon, and was taken to a place called Powers Island where I found out I may be someone who destroys a world full of wizards. Oh! And I died, too! So it's been a pretty normal day.

But he didn't—couldn't—say any of that. Instead, he just grinned as broadly as he could and managed a weak thumbs-up. It was convincing enough for his folks, though, since his mom immediately launched into a tone-deaf rendition of "Happy Birthday" before watching Billy blow out his candles and then insisting that he cut the cake.

The cake was great, made of three whole layers of chocolate, and enough fudge topping to float the Titanic. Billy's present was equally wonderful: a cool watch that not only told the time, but also had a stopwatch, five alarms, and a thermometer. He hugged his mom and thanked her, grateful that he was old enough now that he wasn't required to add an embarrassing kiss on top of the hug, and then turned to his father.

"Fourteen," said his father, with a strange, far-away look in his eyes. "Did you know that a long time ago, that was old enough to be considered a man?" Billy hadn't known that, and he didn't really know how to reply. Thankfully, his father made it unnecessary to do so. He held out his hand and shook Billy's somberly, then said, "I think you're well on your way."

Billy tingled all over.

He went to bed a little while after his father left for another shift, barely able to keep his sleepy eyes open, his new watch on one wrist and the brown bracelet Mrs. Russet had given him on the other.

BILLY: MESSENGER OF POWERS, BY MICHAELBRENT COLLINGS * 111

He kissed his mom good night, and slept, and dreamed. But he didn't dream of Cameron Black pummeling him, or of his new watch, or even of Powers Island. He dreamed of a note and a smile. He dreamed of Blythe Forrest, who had protected him, and asked if he was all right. He dreamed about a friend.

The next day, he arrived at school five minutes early, and was the first one seated in history class. Mrs. Russet was writing on the chalkboard. She nodded at him when he came in, but other than that she gave no sign that she had ever done anything other than teach Billy or occasionally scold him in the halls for being too slow to get to his classes.

Billy was disappointed. Wasn't Mrs. Russet supposed to be his Sponsor? Wasn't she supposed to be guiding him through a series of magical tests? How could she be writing homework assignments on the board?

He looked at his bracelet. Still brown.

Harold Crane and Sarah Brookham came in the class together a minute later. The two members of the Torture Brigade glared at Billy, and Harold flicked an imaginary booger at Billy as he walked by. Billy flinched. Even though he had been to an amazing place, and knew things that almost no one else in the world knew about, he also knew that he was still at the mercy of Cameron, Harold, and Sarah. The locker-stuffing wouldn't stop. It would probably get worse, actually, since Cameron wasn't likely to forget that Billy had managed to give him a bloody nose.

To Billy's surprise, though, when he accidentally bumped into the bigger boy during the passing period between first and second classes, Cameron didn't shove him into a locker or pound him. Instead, the bigger boy punched him mock-playfully on the shoulder. "Don't worry about it," said Cameron. He laughed, the sound a bit nasally since his nose was still swollen.

Maybe he found out I'm a Messenger, or an Object of Prophecy, or whatever I am, thought Billy. Maybe now he wants to be friends.

Then Cameron leaned in close to Billy and whispered, "My turn is coming soon, human."

The way he said "human" froze Billy's heart. He knew instantly that Cameron, like his mother, was a Darksider. And he knew that Cameron now knew that Billy had been to Powers Island.

Most of all, he knew that Cameron still hated him.

But for some reason, Cameron didn't do anything else. He just laughed that nasty laugh again, and moved on down the hallway, leaving Billy to worry when the next meeting of the Torture Brigade would be held, and what dastardly plan of torture and destruction they would hatch.

After his fourth class of the day, Billy meandered to the lunch line, as he always did. He got his lunch—today it was a repulsive mass of intestinal-looking goo that the cafeteria somehow managed to call "spaghetti" with a straight face—and went to a table, as he always did. He sat alone, as he always did.

But then something different happened. "Hey," said a voice. An orange plastic lunch tray slapped down on the table beside his tray, and before he could fall over dead from the shock of it, Blythe Forrest sat down next to him.

"So, did you get in trouble with Mrs. Russet yesterday? You bugged out of fifth period before I could talk to you."

She popped a straw in her juice box and sucked the box dry in a single intake, as though she did this every day. As though she sat next to the least popular kid in school all the time. As though she actually wanted to know something about Billy.

Don't blow this, thought Billy. Be calm, be calm. You survived a blue dragon attack yesterday, you can survive this.

"I'm okay," he said.

Way to go! he thought. Two whole words without a single mistake!

He thought about saying something else, but then decided not to press his luck.

"What did Mrs. Russet do to you?" asked Blythe. She took a huge bite of the disgusting spaghetti-like substance, managing to slurp about a pint of it into her mouth without getting a single speck of tomato sauce on her chin. Billy thought he had never seen anything quite so cool.

"Nothing," he said. "Just, you know, gave me a talking to."

"Ugh," Blythe said, shivering. "I think I'd rather get hit by a garbage truck. Speaking of which..."—she took another gigantic bite of her food—"...You managed to slug Cameron pretty good. His nose looks like he got stung by a bee." She laughed. Billy laughed, too. He sounded like an idiot to his own ears, laughing like a moron just because Blythe was laughing.

She didn't seem to mind, though. She even looked pleased when Billy laughed. At least, he thought she did. Though his experience with girls was so limited—meaning nonexistent—that he could have been mistaken.

"Anyway, I'm going to see you next period, right?" she asked. She took another bite of food, and Billy realized in amazement that she had managed to eat her entire meal in three huge bites.

"What?" he asked, momentarily distracted by the petite girl's ability to put down food like a Sumo wrestler.

Stupid! he thought. Stupid, stupid, stupid! First rule: pay attention to what the girl says, even *you* know that, you idiot!

Blythe rolled her eyes. But she didn't seem too irritated. More like she was amused. "You're going to next class, right?" Billy nodded. "Cool," she said. She picked up her tray. "See you there."

"Wait!" Billy shouted.

Blythe had already turned toward a trash can, but she turned back around. "Yeah?" she said.

Billy didn't know what to say. Actually, he *did* know. But he couldn't believe he was actually going to do it.

"Uh, I was wondering," he began. "That is, well, uh...." He wanted to ask her if he could walk to class with her. But he didn't know how to say it in a good way. "Can I walk to class with you?" sounded like something a three year old would say. But he couldn't think of anything more suave. His mouth worked up and down, and he was sure he looked like trying out for an open spot in the National Idiots Association, but he couldn't stop it, and couldn't manage to say a word.

Blythe waited for a long couple of seconds. Then she looked at the wall clock. "Look, it's almost time for class, and I can't wait around here all day while you learn how to talk. You got something to say?"

Billy couldn't do it. He couldn't make *any* words come out of his mouth, let alone make the *right* words come out.

He shook his head, his entire soul aching with remorse at his inability to make his voice do what he wanted it to.

Blythe grinned mischievously at him. "Okay, well, I'm going to be at my locker in five minutes. If you learn to talk before then, maybe we can go to class together."

And then she was away in a puff of strawberry-smelling air, going to another table where a group of popular girls sat giggling. A few of them glanced in Billy's direction, and he wondered if what had just happened was some kind of dare or something. Maybe if he went to Blythe's locker in five minutes she'd be waiting with a can of spray paint to write the word "loser" across his chest in big letters or something.

Billy shook his head. No way she actually *wanted* to talk to him. No way at all. This had to be part of some mean trick. Maybe the Torture Brigade was behind this.

But Billy knew that no matter how slim the possibility was that she really wanted to be friends with him, he was going to go to her locker anyway. He'd take his chances.

Four minutes and fifty-three seconds later—he timed it with the stopwatch feature on his new birthday watch—he was standing in front of Blythe's locker, waiting for her. His mind raced, frantically trying to work out two things at once: what he was going to say to her, and the best way to dodge out of the way of spray paint, just in case.

He saw Blythe a second later, coming down the hall with three or four of her friends. One by one, the other girls pealed off to their classes, and soon Blythe was coming directly toward Billy. She was smiling almost shyly at him. And he didn't see a can of spray paint anywhere near her.

Oh my gosh, thought Billy. She actually wants to walk to class with me. With *me*!

His heart started hammering against his rib cage. Faster and faster, harder and harder.

She was within twenty feet of him. Still smiling. Still no spray paint.

A cool feeling tingled along Billy's arm. He thought for a moment he must be having a heart attack, his body shutting off before the sheer impossibility of walking to class with Blythe could take place.

But then he realized what was *really* happening. It was much, much worse than a heart attack.

Oh, no, he thought. Not now. Not *now*.

He looked down at his wrist.

The bracelet was blue. It was time for his first test to see if he was a Power.

Billy looked at Blythe. She was only ten feet away.

His heart stopped hammering at the inside of his body. It stopped beating entirely as Billy smiled, then waved quickly before turning away from Blythe.

He had a momentary glimpse of her face, which seemed confused and angry and upset as he turned away.

But the blue bracelet was almost burning him, it was so cold. Billy had to find a doorway, and fast. He turned a corner, running into the boys' bathroom as quickly as he could. There was no one in it. He ran to one of the stalls and opened the door to the toilet. He didn't know if a stall door counted as a door for purposes of a Transport spell, but he had to get to the test before the bracelet froze his arm off.

He swung the stall door open, said "Elephant," and then took two steps forward and one step back. He remembered to hold his breath at the last second as the world exploded in bright light around him, and he once again felt the jerking sensation of instantaneous travel.

The whiteness dimmed. Billy expected to find himself in the Accounting Room in the tower, where he would be issued a "Billy—unDetermined" tag.

But he wasn't in the Accounting Room.

He didn't think he was even in the tower.

He didn't think he was even on Powers Island.

In fact, he wasn't even sure if he was still on the planet earth.

He heard Mrs. Russet's voice: "Welcome, Mr. Jones," she said. "Welcome to your first test."

# CHAPTER THE NINTH

*In Which Billy is Tested, and is Saved in a Most Surprising fashion...*

Billy was standing on sand. But it wasn't like beach sand, or the sand he had played with in the play areas at school when younger. This sand was infinitely finer and softer. Not only that, but there was also the fact of its colors. The sand was deep purple, but as Billy watched, its hue shifted and the sand became blue. Then red, then yellow, and then green before going back to blue again.

And the sand wasn't the only thing that was an odd color: when he looked down at the ground, Billy saw that he himself was glowing as well: a pale blue aura surrounded him, extending about three inches from his body in all directions. He used a blue-glowing hand to touch his also blue-glowing leg. He half-expected a flash of light or a crackle of electricity to hum through him, but he saw and heard nothing out of the ordinary, and the only thing he felt when he touched his leg was that his knees were knocking in fright.

Billy looked up, and saw only a starry sky above him. It had been day at school when he left, so it may have been that wherever he was, was simply located on the other side of the earth, where it would be dark. He didn't think so, however. He'd never heard of anywhere on earth that had such color-changing sand.

Also, wherever he was, he could see three moons above him. One was blue, and cold and forbidding as ice. One was red, a deep furious color that made Billy feel as though he stood below an angry eye. The last was white, and had rings around it like Saturn, rings of every color that Billy could think of. The ringed moon was so close that it took up half the sky, and Billy felt as though he could reach out and touch it if he wished.

He looked down, between the sand at his feet and the bejeweled sky above, and saw dark mountains all around. He was in the center of a small valley that curved upwards on all sides so that Billy essentially stood in the middle of a huge stony bowl.

He turned around and around, marveling at the sights, and wondering if he was supposed to be doing something. Had his test already started? He had figured that this wouldn't be like tests at school, where he just had to make sure to bring a "Number 2" pencil and he would then be given instructions. But for the life of him he couldn't figure out if he was supposed to try to figure something out, or just stand where he was and wait.

"Mrs. Russet?" he called out.

His voice sounded strange, empty and weak, as though it was only traveling a short distance before being snuffed out by some unseen force. If he screamed, he knew, the sound would not travel past his own ears. If he was in trouble, he could not expect help to find him.

"Mrs. Russet!" he hollered again, this time a bit more anxiously. He had heard her voice when he first came here, he knew it. So where was she?

"Mrs. RUSS—" he started, but this time was surprised by the sudden appearance of his history teacher. She was dressed all in brown, as she had been on the Diamond Dais. But this time she did not wear her cloak with the history of earth etched upon it in moving threads. Rather, she wore a simple robe, almost like a toga. He also saw that she, too, was surrounded by the strange thin blue glow that enveloped Billy.

"It's the testing robe," she said, in response to Billy's questioning look at her attire. Her voice, too, sounded strangely disconnected, far away and thin. The teacher waved a hand. "I know, it's old fashioned, but the Powers do go in for traditional looks on some things."

She looked around, pursing her lips. "Well, this is a pretty place, if I do say so my self."

"If you say so yourself?" Billy asked. "Did you *make* this place?"

Mrs. Russet shrugged. "I know, the shifting color sand may seem a bit gaudy to some, but as a Brown Power it's so rare that I get to indulge in an all-out display of color." She picked up a handful of the sand at their feet and let it sift through her fingers, watching as the tiny particles shifted through their range of color as they fell.

Billy saw that the sand fell somewhat slower than he had expected it would, drifting featherlike to the ground below.

"Where is this place?" he asked.

Mrs. Russet reluctantly shifted her gaze to him. "I already told you, it's the place of your first test."

"So what am I supposed to do?" he asked. "Make a sand castle or something?"

Mrs. Russet pursed her lips. Billy felt like smacking himself. Who did he think he was talking to? This was the Brown Councilor, one of the six strongest Powers in the world! More important, it was his toughest-grading teacher! So how could he even think of being sarcastic to her?

Mrs. Russet apparently was thinking along the same lines, since she said, "That's quite enough of that tone, Mr. Jones. Unless you'd like to be left here forever?"

She raised her hand dramatically above her head, as though about to disappear. "No, wait!" Billy cried.

Mrs. Russet dropped her hand. "Manners?" she asked. Billy nodded humbly. She nodded her approval in response. "As to your question of what you must do for the test," she said, "first and foremost, you must survive."

At this, Mrs. Russet clapped her hands.

"*Survive?*" hollered Billy. He probably would have said it again, but what happened next was so stupendous and frightening it took his breath away.

The color-shifting sand beneath his feet started to pulse rhythmically, rising and falling as though it covered a huge giant who was breathing deeply. Then the sand at the center of the small valley started to swirl around and around, like a whirlpool. The whirlpool increased in intensity, and a hole started to open up in its center. The whirlpool grew wider and wider, steadily expanding until it was only a few feet from Billy and Mrs. Russet. Mrs. Russet started to move away from it. Billy didn't follow for a moment, dumbfounded.

"I would seriously consider stepping away from the edge," said Mrs. Russet, her dry tones goading Billy to movement. "It's going to be quite deep."

Billy managed to move, stumbling backward over red-green-yellow-blue sand, not daring to look where he was going, attention riveted by the display unfolding before him.

The whirlpool of sand continued swirling and whirling, until it was as wide as a football field. Billy looked down the funnel that the whirlpool had created, and saw that it went down as far as the eye could see.

"Mr. Jones?" said Mrs. Russet.

"Yeah?" answered Billy, his gaze still planted firmly on the sand vortex that spun downward to infinity.

"Mr. Jones, pay attention!" she snapped. Billy turned to face his teacher. "Good. Your attention is critical for this—and, indeed, every—test. I am your Sponsor, so I will tell you a bit of what is going to happen."

"Thank you," mumbled Billy. In his amazement and fear at what had just happened, he had momentarily forgotten that he was there for a test. Now he did his best to ignore the eddying sand behind him and focus on Mrs. Russet as she continued to speak.

"As you may have guessed, you are not on Earth," she said. Billy didn't respond. He *had* guessed that, but didn't think it was a good time to show how smart he was. Besides, a two-year-old would have been able to tell that this wasn't Earth. "Where you are," continued Mrs. Russet, "is a small meteor created in another galaxy expressly for the purposes of this test."

"How are we breathing?" asked Billy. "I mean, there's no air in space, right?"

Mrs. Russet nodded. "Indeed," she said. She pointed at the pale blue glow that surrounded both her and Billy. "This is an air supply," she said. "The point of this test is to see if you have any control over the Element of Earth, so I have isolated you from everything else as much as possible. There is no water here, no life other than you and me, no fire, and no air other than this little bit that surrounds us. And that will be gone within a few minutes, so you will have only a limited time to pass this test."

"So what do I do? What's the test?" demanded Billy, his sudden nervousness at the prospect of suffocating on a meteor in another galaxy lending desperation to his question.

"Again," answered Mrs. Russet, "the primary objective is to survive."

"But survive *what*?" asked Billy again.

"Survive that," answered his teacher, nodding over Billy's shoulder.

Billy turned around, and his face grew pale.

Up out of the maelstrom of swirling sand, something had appeared. Something terrible and ugly, massive and strong. At first all Billy could see was two long legs, pulling the monster up from the bottom of the sand whirlpool at the center of the valley. Each leg was as long as a bus, with eight joints that allowed the legs to bend as flexibly as a monkey's tail. The legs were a deep gray, thick and gnarled, and Billy could tell instantly that they were made of some kind of stone. The legs had no feet. Rather, each leg ended in a single, wickedly curved stone claw: a nasty hook that tapered to a sharp point.

The two legs sank their claw-feet into the mouth of the maelstrom, hauling up the beast that was behind them. The two front legs were followed by two more, then two more, then two more. When it had finally pulled itself to the surface of the vortex, Billy could make out a total of ten legs along the rock beast's thick body. The horrible fiend looked like a great scorpion, but each leg had one of those terrible curved claws in place of a foot, and the monster's body was the size of an eighteen-wheeler big rig.

Like a scorpion, the beast had a tail, and the tail was articulated so as to allow it to curve in any direction. Rather than a scorpion's barb, however, the tail ended in a trio of spikes that pointed in three different directions. Billy could tell just by looking at it that the three spikes would enable the beast to strike someone standing in front of it, by stabbing forward over its head—or where a head would have been if it had had a head—as well as allowing it to skewer attackers that stood on either side by sweeping the tail back and forth and using the two spears that pointed to its right and left.

Billy did what he thought was sensible under the circumstances. He did his best to faint. Then, in the middle of the action—he'd actually gotten his eyes to roll back in their sockets and was halfway to the ground—he thought that fainting might not be a good idea after all: who knew what a giant ten-legged rock scorpion would do? Maybe it would leave him alone. But then, maybe it would eat him, and if that happened Billy wanted to be awake to at least try to make a run for it.

Billy knew that in space, there was no air, so no sound could travel, and therefore he was surprised that he could hear the sound of the scorpion's ten legs thudding against the earth as it turned to face him. Then he realized that the vibrations were traveling through the sand, and through the very bones of his body. He gulped as the massive stone that constituted the monster's head turned a baleful glare upon him. The beast had no eyes, but its rock-head was pitted and cratered in such a way as to make it appear as though the scorpion had dozens of them. All of them were staring their blindly unblinking gaze at Billy, and to make the horrific image complete, there were two car-length mandibles on the bottom of the thing's head. Billy couldn't see a mouth, so he knew that those serrated jaws would have no other purpose than to tear, rend, and destroy.

The monster was on the other side of the vortex, the subterranean sand tornado standing between it and Billy. Billy didn't have any time to be relieved, however, for at that instant the whirlpool stopped its motion, and the many-colored sand rose back up again to a level plane.

Billy turned to run, and found that he had already gone as far as he could go: the bare stone cliff face that surrounded all sides of this valley was right behind him. He swung back to face the hideous rock scorpion, and saw it scuttling towards him with huge lumbering strides that were surprisingly lithe and quick coming from a monster made of what must be over twenty tons of rock.

The monster reared up on its back four legs, its mandibles snapping against one another so hard that tiny plumes of dust flew up from them each time it happened. It was only a few feet away, and Billy threw up his hands in a futile protective gesture as the monster threw itself forward, its front legs arcing in to hook into Billy's flesh on both sides before tearing him apart.

Billy closed his eyes and waited for certain death.

And, surprisingly, certain death didn't come.

He opened his eyes. The scorpion was as still as...well...stone. Its two front legs were only a few feet away on either side of Billy, but the monster was utterly motionless, appearing to be suddenly lifeless. It was as though some insane sculptor had crafted the nightmare creation, decided very sensibly that no one would buy it, and had catapulted it into space where it came to rest on this lonely rock.

Billy couldn't believe his luck. Then he realized that Mrs. Russet—whom Billy had quite forgotten about in the terror of coming face-to-face (or face-to-rock) with the monster—was staring at him. She was tapping her foot impatiently in the sand, tiny puffs of dust coming up in a beautiful rainbow of particles before settling to the ever-changing ground.

"Are you quite finished?" she asked.

"But...I mean...that is....," was all Billy could say. He felt, deep inside, that any terrified running and/or screaming and/or almost fainting he may have just done was totally justified under the circumstances. Apparently Mrs. Russet thought differently, though. She had the irritated look of a person caught in the checkout line of a supermarket behind someone who has coupons for everything and wanted to pay for it all with bags of uncounted pennies.

"Now, as I was saying," she said when Billy had managed to stop himself from blathering, "this test is the Test of Earth. This creature," she said, gesturing at the rock scorpion, "is a Fizzle. A Fizzle—"

"I know what a Fizzle is!" said Billy, almost triumphantly. "Ivy told me. When we were in the anteroom. It's...," he furrowed his brow, trying to remember exactly what Ivy had said. "It's a non-living creature that some of the Powers can make out of their Element, right?"

Mrs. Russet nodded. "Very good, Mr. Jones. But I suspect she did not tell you quite everything about Fizzles. For instance, each Fizzle requires some energy on the part of its maker. Right now, I am concentrating on two things: holding this rock scorpion together, and keeping it from moving."

"What do you mean, you're concentrating on keeping it from moving?" asked Billy. "I mean, it's just *you*, isn't it? Fizzles are like remote controlled robots, right?"

Mrs. Russet nodded again. "For the most part, yes. But there *is* always a danger when creating a Fizzle that the magical creature will take on a bit of its own personality and life."

Billy remembered how Vester's Fizzles—the blue and red horses—had pranced and danced on their own, as though they were living creatures. He nodded at what Mrs. Russet was saying. "So you mean, some Fizzles aren't totally under the control of the Powers that make them?" asked Billy.

"Correct. The greater the Fizzle, the more danger there is that the Fizzle will break loose and simply do what it wants to. For a lower level Power, the danger inherent in that is minimal, for its Fizzle will disappear unless the Power is touching it. However, for a greater Power—such as myself, if I may be so bold—there is a bit more danger involved if the Fizzle breaks free of its maker's power. Because in that case, the Fizzle will continue to exist for quite some time, and there may be...unfortunate consequences when such a Fizzle is allowed to do what it wishes. For example," she eyed the rock monster. "Eugene, here—"

"Its name is *Eugene*?" asked Billy incredulously.

"I made it, I can name it anything I want," replied Mrs. Russet indignantly. "I had a fish named Eugene once, and I've always liked the name. Now don't interrupt. We haven't got a lot of time before your air runs out."

Billy noticed how she didn't say "before *our* air runs out," and was filled again with that silent dread that he was coming to recognize so well.

"Eugene is quite a large Fizzle, and I imagine that if I were to lose control of him, he'd probably do quite a lot of damage to anything—or anybody," she added pointedly, looking at Billy, "that was anywhere nearby."

"Well," said Billy with a forced smile. "It's a good thing you won't let that happen, ha, ha." He literally said that, said "ha, ha." He was trying for a reassuring laugh, but just didn't have it in him. He didn't think that was a sign of cowardice; he imagined even Rambo or the Terminator would probably have trouble laughing when standing between the hooked talons of a giant scorpion rock monster named Eugene. Plus, he had a very bad feeling about the way Mrs. Russet pursed her lips when he said hopefully that she would never let the monster out of her control.

Sure enough, Mrs. Russet's next words did nothing to soothe Billy's fears. "As you can see, Mr. Jones, there is nothing but sand and rock all around you. If you are a Power of Earth, it is very likely that your control over that Element will show itself now."

"Why now?" he managed to squeak.

"Because people with the potential to do so are most likely to become Powers when their lives are in danger," she responded. She turned to the cliff wall nearby, took out her beehive key, and inserted it into a keyhole that appeared at that moment. She turned the key, whispered the words that would activate the key, opened the door that appeared, and put one foot through into the blackness beyond.

"You have about three minutes of air left, I should think," she said. "Good luck." Then Mrs. Russet took a deep breath, stepped through the opening in the rock, and was gone, the cliff face sealing behind her as though she had never existed.

Billy had little time to notice all this, because the instant Mrs. Russet wished him luck, the rock monster moved.

It shook itself, as though confused. Its head moved left and right, throwing off whatever traces of magical control had kept it from tearing Billy apart. Then the monster refocused on him.

The monster reared up, its terrifying body standing on only one set of legs, the front legs curling and grasping at space eighty feet over Billy's head, then the beast came crashing down with terrible speed, hurtling toward Billy.

Billy rolled away at the last moment, barely missing getting crushed by the impact of the scorpion's body on the colored sand. The beast shook itself, dazed, then looked around to see where Billy had gone.

Billy was running across the valley floor, weaving between the scorpion's huge legs, which were set like curved pillars in the ground. The sand below him pulled at his feet, making forward motion difficult, but Billy tried as best he could. He was aided, at least, by the fact that this place had lower gravity than Earth, so he was able to take great jumping strides and move faster than he normally would be able to.

The scorpion spotted him, and immediately the stone leg nearest to Billy raised up and then slammed down, narrowly missing him. The leg pulled up, leaving a curved crater in the sand where it had impacted. Again it smashed down, and again Billy barely missed becoming a Billy-kabob as he rolled away at the last second.

At last, he was out from under the scorpion's body. But Billy was hardly free from danger. He looked over just in time to see the three-pointed tail whistling down at him, its tips so sharp that he thought he could see moonlight reflecting off them.

Billy ducked, rolling through the sand ungracefully, frantically trying to figure out how to get out of the mess he was in.

What would Mrs. Russet do? he thought. The answer his brain coughed up wasn't at all helpful: She never would have let herself get in this situation in the first place, dummy.

Billy almost sighed. Here he was, a bizillion light years away from his house, about to run out of air if he didn't get pulverized by a rock scorpion first, and his subconscious mind was being sarcastic to him. He just couldn't get a break.

As if to answer that, the scorpion took another swing at him, which if it had hit would not only have broken Billy, it would have shattered him into a million twitching pieces. Billy ducked out of the way at the last second, however, and the spiked tail buried itself in the nearby rock wall. The scorpion pulled at it, but was clearly stuck, giving Billy a few precious seconds to run as fast as he could toward the other end of the tiny valley.

Come on, think! he shouted at himself. If I'm a Brown Power, what do I do?

He supposed that Mrs. Russet would have created an impenetrable rock fortress around herself, or made a great wave of rocks come ripping through the ground to crush the scorpion into sand. Most likely, she would have just thought about the scorpion dissolving, and it would have happened. But Billy had no idea how to make any of those things occur. He tried imagining them, hoping that was all he would have to do, but the only thing that happened was that the scorpion had time to pull its tail out of the cliff. The beast wheeled around on its many legs, again bringing itself to face Billy, and once more, the monster started lumbering after him.

Billy began wheezing. He thought at first it was just exhaustion from running across the sand, jumping and ducking and rolling to avoid the attacks of a homicidal space monster made of meteor. But then he realized it wasn't mere physical exhaustion: his air supply was running out. He glanced down at his legs, which were pumping madly through the rainbow sand. Sure enough, the blue glow that had surrounded him was rapidly fading.

WHUMP! WHUMP! The scorpion's footfalls were coming louder now, as though the titanic monster was angry that Billy had the nerve to stay alive this long. It came at Billy like an express train, and Billy once again had to roll away from a downward-curving leg. Sand exploded all around him, getting in his hair and eyes. The hooked leg had missed him by bare inches, and was still stuck in the ground right in front of him.

What Billy did next was insane. It was purely crazy.

It was also the only thing he could think of.

He took two huge steps, then *grabbed the leg*. He wrapped his arms and legs around it as tightly as he could. There were small craggy pits in the rock-leg, allowing Billy some foot and handholds.

The scorpion's jaws clicked together again, the vibrations rattling Billy's own teeth in his head. The monster pulled its leg out of the sand, taking Billy high up into the air with it. It shook its leg, trying to dislodge Billy, who was holding onto the leg with the tenacity of a woodland tick.

Billy refused to budge. His hands cramped, his leg muscles locked in quivering pain, but he wouldn't let go. The scorpion shook harder, trying even more forcefully to dislodge him, but that didn't work, either.

The monster paused, as though gathering its thoughts for a moment. Then Billy could swear he saw some of the thing's eyepits widen with an idea. The rock monster hobbled on its nine unencumbered feet to the nearest cliff wall. It raised Billy up, and then he realized that the monster was about to scrape him off against the rock of the wall.

Billy saw the cliff face coming at him and knew that he was a goner. He concentrated as hard as he could on the rock wall that he was now speeding toward, trying to will it into becoming soft as pudding, or blowing into a million pieces, or turning to sand. Something, anything that would save him. But nothing was happening. He finally gave up wishing for specifically rock-related things to happen, and just settled for a more generic wish that *anything* would happen. Just so long as it would save him.

At that moment, Billy was suddenly gripped by a surprising feeling of calm. He was going to die here. There was nothing he could do about it. But he was at peace. As though nothing could really harm him, nothing could touch him. He didn't know where the feeling was coming from, but he didn't care. It was delicious as fruit to a starving man, this feeling, and Billy actually closed his eyes to savor it.

Then there was a noise.

It wasn't a big noise, but nor exactly could it be called a small noise. Not a sharp noise, but nor was it a soft noise. It wasn't particularly loud, but it was hardly quiet, either. It was as though the very stuff sound was made of were being released from a container, where it had been confined for a thousand years, and was now calmly but firmly making its presence known throughout the universe.

Apparently, even though it had no ears, the scorpion heard the noise as well, because it stopped trying to scrape Billy off its leg. Its head began moving back and forth in a rhythmic pattern, reminding Billy of a snake being charmed by some kind of wise man.

Billy had very little time to enjoy this strange reprieve, though, because his air finally ran out. He inhaled, but no air came into his lungs. His suddenly stricken body tried to cough, but no air came into it. The dark void of space had no oxygen to provide, and whatever air Billy had been given as part of his test was now gone.

Darkness started swirling in at the edges of Billy's vision, and then he saw something, a bright light in the middle of the tunnel around the edges of his sight. At first he thought it was just another star, hanging between the three huge moons above him. But no, it couldn't be a star, because it was moving. Faster and faster it came, growing larger in Billy's sight.

The noise, that strange noise that he had been hearing, now grew louder as well. And as it did, Billy was amazed to see the colored sand below him starting to move as though in eddies of air. But that couldn't be, could it?

But it was! Billy suddenly felt a cool blast of rich, wonderful air hit him in the face. He inhaled deeply, the air as wonderful to him as the hot chocolate had been in the anteroom on Powers Island. He felt his muscles rejuvenate as oxygen flooded his air-starved lungs.

With the air, he felt something else that he had not felt since coming to this strange place of his testing: he felt sound. It seemed strange, to think that sound could actually be *felt*, but it was true. As the air came from who-knew-where, it brought with it the sounds that had been absent from this meteor in space, and the sound it brought was as tangible as concrete to Billy. He could hear his own breathing, he could hear the sift of sand below his feet, he could hear the scraping of rocky joints as the scorpion swayed nearby, still dancing to the silent music that held it captive.

And through all this, the star that sped towards them grew. It grew and grew, and began to take shape. Billy blinked. He would have rubbed his eyes had his arms not been clasped so tightly around the rock monster's stony leg. He couldn't believe what he was seeing.

A new sound greeted him. It came from the star that wasn't a star. It came from the thing that Billy couldn't believe he was seeing.

The sound was a neigh. A great, loud whinnying that Billy imagined might be what the horses of medieval times might have sounded like as they carried their knights to battle.

The sound came from the shape in the sky above them. From the star that was not a star. It was a horse. But what a horse! It was the purest white, from the tip of its hard-breathing nose, to the ends of its hooves, which appeared to be made of white marble. A golden horn emerged from the horse's forehead, a sharp-tipped swirl of bright color that seemed almost out of place on the snowy beast. Two enormous feathered wings emerged from its body, flapping in huge, powerful arcs. And instead of a horse's tail, the incredible animal had a trio of platinum-colored flails that were both beautiful and terrible to look upon. Billy knew somehow that the tails could flay the skin from off an enemy, and sincerely hoped the Unicorn—no ordinary horse, he could see that now—would view him as a friend.

As it flew, the Unicorn's legs galloped through the nothing of space, and with each downward movement, sparks flew from the marble hooves, making it look as though the animal ran on a path of fire. Billy could actually feel the heat of it from his tenuous perch. He could also feel the source of the air that had saved his life: with each downbeat of its wings, the Unicorn gathered wind and threw it downward, flooding the area with air of its own making.

The scorpion monster suddenly stopped its dance. It looked at Billy maliciously for a moment, then turned its head to look upon the Unicorn that was flying towards it. The scorpion made a noise other than the grumble of rock on rock for the first time: it screamed. The sound was like an avalanche or an earthquake, a clear warning cry that Billy understood instinctively: Stay away, the scorpion was saying. This place is mine. This *boy* is mine.

The Unicorn reared its feet in midair and answered with a battle cry of its own. And again, Billy felt like he could understand what the Unicorn was saying. The feeling was deeper than it was with the scorpion's challenge. It was deeper, and more powerful, as the Unicorn seemed to say, This place is not yours. This boy is not yours. Nothing is yours, for all of Creation is mine.

The scorpion screamed again, a shout of anger and frustration. Without looking at Billy, it pounded its rocky leg into the wall of the valley, a tremendous strike that shook Billy's skeleton and made his teeth rattle in his head. Billy's grip loosened and he fell to the soft sand below, the wind knocked out of him by the impact. He heard the thumping of ten legs scuttling into position over him, and saw that the scorpion was above him now, its four hindmost legs backed up onto the cliff walls, its front two legs reared up in challenge before it. It was protecting its prey, and would not allow any other beast to challenge it in this, the monster's own domain.

The Unicorn, now only feet from the scorpion, screamed its battle cry once more and attacked. It sped toward the scorpion, its horn lowered, a frightful golden spear. The scorpion riposted, its two hooked front legs swinging through the air in front of it, trying to knock the Unicorn to the ground.

The Unicorn wheeled in midair, its legs pushing it out of range of the strikes at the last second. It gave two great beats with its wings, and suddenly Billy felt himself in the middle of a great wind. The sudden rush of air threw him back to the edge of the valley, pinning him to the high cliff wall. It was so strong a blast that even the scorpion was pushed back for a moment. Then the monster pushed forward and lunged again at the Unicorn.

The Unicorn dodged once more, and as it did, it clapped its fiery hooves against one of the scorpion's forelegs. The scorpion shrieked as the leg glowed bright red, then began to actually melt, long gobbets of molten rock flowing down and splattering to the ground below, only feet away from where Billy stood. The lava-like rock splashed against the colored sand, instantly fusing what it touched into colored glass, creating a stained-glass floor of beauty in the midst of the battle.

The scorpion screamed again, and Billy thought that this time the sound carried a new feeling: fear. *What are you?* the monster seemed to be saying.

And the Unicorn's reply, which Billy seemed to hear in his heart, was, *To you, I am Death.*

The scorpion attacked again, swinging its barbed tail at the flying stallion in desperation. The Unicorn dropped its head and met the tail with its golden horn, and the tail exploded in a beautiful nova of color that drifted down. Billy saw that the colors floating down all around him were in fact budding flowers of every kind: roses, petunias, lilies, ever kind of flower that Billy had ever heard of, and more that he could not identify.

The scorpion was now cowering, trying to press itself into the wall of the valley, like a cockroach trying to find a crack to escape into when the lights come on. But it was no use, there was no escape from the onrushing Unicorn. The great steed continued to blast the rocky monster with bursts of cyclonic wind, and heat blazed from its marbled feet. The scorpion chattered, a whining keen that spoke only of fear.

The Unicorn tossed its white-maned head contemptuously, then wheeled in the air for one last, deadly attack. It dove at the scorpion, which tried one last time to knock the horse from the air with its maliciously curved legs.

The Unicorn wheeled, easily avoiding the scorpion's strike, and then turned at the last second. The Unicorn's three tails of platinum whipped about and struck the scorpion across the back. The scorpion shrieked in pain, then reared up on its hind legs, arcing its rocky back in agony.

The monster froze, solid as it had been when Mrs. Russet's power held it in stasis. Then it began to rumble, the sound beginning deep within the monster's body and rolling outward in long waves. Fissures appeared in the frozen monster's body, and then with a sharp cracking sound, pieces of the rock beast's body began to separate and fall away.

Billy covered his head and ran out from beneath the scorpion, two-ton boulders crashing into the colored sand all around him. He wheeled to one side, narrowly avoiding being crushed by a falling piece of the scorpion's once terrifying jaws. Billy's legs pumped desperately, terror giving him new strength, and he threw himself out of harm's way only an instant before the entire body of the scorpion exploded in a shower of rock and dirt.

Billy lay for a long moment, face down in the sand. He was amazed to still be alive, and he resolved right that instant not to be afraid of asking Blythe to walk to class with him ever again. Life was just too short.

Then he gasped as a pair of crackling marble hooves thudded into the sand only inches from his face. Billy looked up. The Unicorn stood before him, huge and kingly. It pawed its front hoof impatiently.

Get on, it seemed to say. I haven't got all day to kill monsters and wait for you to climb up.

"But, you're too tall," Billy began.

The Unicorn knelt down, dropping one wing to the ground, creating a ramp of sorts. Billy climbed up the wing, then awkwardly sat astride the huge animal.

The Unicorn shook itself, and Billy had to grab its mane to keep from falling. The hair was thick and strong, yet at the same time felt as soft as velvet. Billy wanted to bury his face in the Unicorn's mane, but knew somehow that the great animal would not permit that. Permitting such an action would not be dignified, and this horse was dignity personified.

The Unicorn reared back, screaming a triumphant cry at the remains of the rock monster that had been created by Mrs. Russet and then dispatched with so little effort by the Unicorn's powerful attacks. Then the white animal hunkered down, and with a tremendous bursting of its powerful muscles, it launched itself high into the space above the barren rock where Billy had been supposed to have his test.

I passed the test, he thought suddenly. I survived.

The Unicorn looked back at him, as if to say, You know that's not true..., the test was not passed, you were simply saved.

And Billy did indeed know that was true, though he couldn't say exactly where his certainty came from.

Then those thoughts were left behind as the Unicorn beat its wondrous wings and the meteor was left far behind them in the blink of an eye.

Where are we going? Billy wondered.

The Unicorn looked back at him, and again Billy seemed to feel the words the Unicorn would have said: You'll see, Billy. You'll see.

# CHAPTER THE TENTH

*In Which Billy is taken to a place he Knows Well, and a Challenge is Issued...*

    The universe sped past Billy and the Unicorn, faster and faster, until the stars fused together and became one continuous streak of light. Billy thought he glanced planets here and there, and streaking comets. Novas exploding in bright soundless light, and the pure darkness of black holes.
    Then the beautiful lights slowed. Billy saw Saturn pass by, its rings almost as beautiful as those of the great moon that had overshadowed the valley of his test. He saw the giant ball of gas that was Jupiter, and the relatively small red planet he guessed must be Mars.
    Then, a familiar green and brown and blue orb came into view. Earth. Home. The Unicorn upon which Billy sat galloped (or was it flew?) toward the planet, and Billy's hair whipped around his head in a halo of curls in the impossible wind that accompanied the Unicorn's flight.
    They entered the earth's atmosphere, dropping like liquid flame through the outer reaches and then into the highest clouds that hung miles above the earth's surface.
    Still farther they fell, and Billy couldn't help but laugh at the sheer exhilaration of the feeling. He was flying! The downbeats of the Unicorn's wings sounded like claps of thunder, the flaming hooves crackled like electricity, and Billy was riding the storm.
    The Unicorn flew above the waves of the sea, so low that its wingtips touched the still waters, leaving perfect dimples in the surface of the water that collapsed and disappeared an instant after they passed. Billy could see his reflection in the sea, a phantom version of him that lived below the waves, and disappeared as soon as Billy rose up high.
    Then he saw, far ahead, a familiar cloud cover. A looming pillar that extended high up until it could no longer be seen. Powers Island.

Billy thought at first the Unicorn would take him there, but it veered to the side at the last second. It took him higher again, into the clouds. Billy blinked moisture off his face, not able to see anything. Then he suddenly *could* see again, and glimpsed another island. But where Powers Island was beautiful, enjoying the presence of all seasons at once, and gifted with all manner of flora and fauna, this island was dark and forbidding, made of craggy cliffs and iron-colored beaches. Icy waves pounded at the cliffs that ringed the island. The waves were cold-looking and terrible, dark surf pounding against the treacherous rocks that encircled the island. And when Billy squinted, he thought he could see hundreds of black shapes swimming just below the surface of the jagged ocean.

Sharks, he realized. The place is surrounded by sharks. Then he thought, It's Dark Isle. This has to be Dark Isle, the place Wolfen made during the War of the Powers.

He knew it had to be true. What other place could look so terrible and forbidding?

Then a lash of rain whipped across Billy's face. He blinked, and when he opened his eyes, Dark Isle was gone, lost in the mists that surrounded him and the Unicorn.

The Unicorn continued to flap its wings, and flew them over earth and sea, over mountain and valley. At last, it landed in a place that Billy would never have guessed it would leave him.

It dropped him on the roof of his school. Billy sat atop the Unicorn, unsure.

This can't be all, he thought. I mean, take me through the universe, show me Dark Isle, and then...take me to school?

But the Unicorn shook its body, its skin rippling as though it was trying to get rid of an annoying fly. Billy didn't move. The Unicorn shuddered again, dislodging Billy from his perch. Billy fell to the side, rolling down the Unicorn's outstretched wing, and then falling to the rooftop.

Without another sound, without another look, the Unicorn shot into the air. It pounded its wings only a handful of times before it was too high to see.

Billy looked around him. After all that he had seen, the return to school was almost too unsettling to be believed. He wondered how he was supposed to get down from the roof. A moment later, he saw that there was an access door nearby. He figured it would have to be locked, but when he tugged at it, the door opened and he lowered himself onto the ladder below. He climbed down, and found himself in the janitor's closet, the same one that Mrs. Russet had taken him through to get to Powers Island. The door was locked, but it was designed to keep students out, not to keep them in, so Billy was able to unlock it from the inside and step out into the hall.

He looked at his birthday watch. Once again, only a few minutes had passed. Which meant that he was late for his after-lunch class.

He ran to his locker, managing to avoid the hall monitors who prowled the school, waiting with itchy fingers to give detention to students found in the halls without a pass. He grabbed his bag and hurried to his math class.

The door was open, which was lucky for him. Mr. Angle's back was turned, and Billy was able to slink in and take his seat without the teacher noticing. Mr. Angle turned around and checked his seating chart to make sure no one was absent, then began droning about rhombuses.

Billy sneaked a glance behind him. Cameron Black was, strangely, nowhere to be seen.

But Blythe was staring at him. Billy smiled and waved halfheartedly. She smiled back, and Billy's hopes soared. He had been so worried that she would be angry with him for abandoning her the way he had.

She wrote something on her notepad, then crumpled it up and threw it at Billy. To his pleasant surprise, he managed to catch it this time—no embarrassing misses in front of Blythe.

He uncrumpled the paper, and this time he also managed to turn immediately to the correct side, disregarding the math notes on the other side of the page. This time, however, he wished he *hadn't* been able to find what she wrote.

"You're a jerk," the paper said.

Billy's shoulders slumped. He looked back at Blythe, but the beautiful girl was now studiously avoiding his gaze, focusing so intently on Mr. Angle that you would think she was actually interested in what he was saying. This, Billy knew, was a total impossibility: *no one* could actually be interested in what Mr. Angle was saying. Which meant Blythe hated him.

His shoulders slumped even further. He had blown it. Forget almost being killed by a space scorpion. He had failed the test that really mattered.

A moment later, Mrs. Russet appeared at the door to Mr. Angle's class. She looked around, spotting Billy in an instant.

"May I help you, Mrs. Russet?" asked Mr. Angle tremulously. Apparently he was as scared of her as were her students. He hitched at his tiny pants nervously, and one of his suspenders popped off unnoticed.

"I would like to speak to Mr. Jones if I may," she answered.

"Well, yes, of course," Mr. Angle managed, even though she had already turned away and begun walking down the hall.

Billy snatched up his books. He threw one more glance at Blythe and was disheartened that even the novelty of his getting plucked out of class didn't get her to look at him. He hurried out of the class and into the hall.

Mrs. Russet was walking hurriedly in front of him, her old legs moving with the energy of a twenty-year-old marathoner. Billy struggled to keep up, barely managing to keep her in sight before she turned the corner and entered her classroom. The history room was empty.

She wheeled on him the second he entered. "Close the door," she snapped. Billy jumped at the sharpness in her voice. "Please," she added, as though aware of the terrifying effect she could have on people. "This is my free period, so we shouldn't be interrupted."

Billy closed the door, and when he turned back around he thought for sure that Mrs. Russet was going to want to know what had happened during his test. But she didn't. Her face was ashen, and the words that came had nothing to do with Billy's test. "What have you seen in the halls today?"

"What do you mean?" asked Billy incredulously. After all that had occurred, she wanted to know what he had seen in *school*?

"Did you see anything in the halls?" she demanded again.

"I don't know," answered Billy in confusion. "The hall monitors, and a bunch of Gummie Bears were stuck to the ceiling in this one part of the hall. How do you think someone can get a Gummie Bear up there?" he began, but his voice petered out when he saw the venomous glare that Mrs. Russet was directing at him. He gulped. "What's going on?"

Mrs. Russet shook her head. "I don't know. The Book of Earth has something I've never seen before, not in my lifetime, at any rate."

"What?" he asked.

"A blank page," she responded.

"So it has a blank page, so what?" he asked.

"You don't understand, Mr. Jones," Mrs. Russet said. "Everything that happens on the lands of the world is written in the Book of Earth as it happens."

Billy wondered if that included *everything*, including that one time he had picked his nose during class in first grade and everyone saw him doing it and made fun of him. Then he tore his thought away from that embarrassing moment. There were more important things happening right now, he knew, even if he didn't understand exactly what they were. "So what does a blank page on the Book of Earth mean?" he asked.

"I don't know. But the last entry is you going through the doorway to your first test. After that...," she shrugged, unsure in a way that Billy wasn't accustomed to seeing her be. "It's as though the history of today hasn't been written yet. As though something so monumental is going to occur that it will change the very fabric of our world." She shook her head, and murmured to herself, "The last time this happened...."

"What?" asked Billy. Mrs. Russet looked at him as though she didn't know what he was talking about. "The last time this happened...what?" he reiterated.

"The last time the Book of Earth was blank was during the time of the first Wars of the Powers, the time of the breaking of the earth, the rending of the continents. The time before the Truce, when all was chaos." She looked hard at Billy. "The time directly before the first coming of the White King."

Now, at last, she asked Billy what he'd been expecting her to ask from the beginning: "What happened during your test?" she said.

"Didn't you see any of it?" he asked, a bit surprised. He had thought she would ask for his impressions of what happened, or something, rather than opening with a blanket question.

"Do you think I would be asking if I had?" she answered.

Billy nodded, then told her as best he could what had happened. As he did, Mrs. Russet's brow furrowed ever more deeply. She interrupted occasionally, asking him a question when he was being unclear, but for the most part she remained silent. When he was done telling her what had happened, she pursed her lips in thought and was very quiet. She remained that way long enough that Billy wondered if she was doing something magical, or perhaps had just fallen asleep with her eyes open.

Finally, she reached into her pocket and withdrew a small cigarette lighter. She flicked the wheel, and flame emerged. Billy looked at her questioningly, and she explained, "Relax, Mr. Jones. I've not taken up something so opprobrious as smoking. We simply thought it would be best to have a way to keep in quick contact with each other." Then she looked at the flame and said, "Vester."

"Yes?" came the fireman's voice after a moment, emerging from the small flame as though he were standing in the room.

"I need you," said Mrs. Russet. "Can you come to me?"

"Just a sec," answered Vester's voice. The flame was silent for a few minutes, then it suddenly elongated and crackled. There was a puff of acrid smoke, and Billy's friend appeared beside him in the class. He was dressed in his work clothes: a blue uniform with a shiny badge on. "Sorry, I was on call and had to arrange for someone else to cover."

He looked at Billy. "Hey, sport," he said, then looked back at Mrs. Russet. "What's going on?" he asked.

"A great many things," she said. "I need to go to Powers Island, and I think I might need Billy while I'm there. But I don't want to take him to the Council with me...not right away. And I don't want him left alone on the island, either, so...."

"You want me to baby-sit," finished Vester.

"Hey!" said Billy in protest.

"Sorry, I meant 'youngman-sit,'" said Vester with a grin.

"Stop horsing around," said Mrs. Russet. "This isn't the time." She paused, calming herself. "But yes, that's exactly what I want you to do."

"Fine with me," said Vester. "I was hoping to catch the Challenge match at the stadium anyway." He punched Billy in the arm. "You in, kid?" he asked.

"Uh...," Billy answered. It was his standard answer now, but at least he was growing to accept the fact that sooner or later in most conversations he was going to be reduced to monosyllabic grunts.

"Great," said Vester with a smile. "When do we go?" he asked Mrs. Russet.

"Now," she answered, withdrawing her beehive key.

"Remember, kid," said Vester to Billy.

"I know, I know," said Billy. "Remember to hold your breath. Two steps forward and one step back."

"You're a pro," said Vester.

"Come *on*," said Mrs. Russet impatiently. Billy thought for sure she would use the key on the door to the classroom, but instead she went to one of the supply cabinets at the back of the classroom and opened it with her Imbued key. She whispered something under her breath as she did so—probably the same nonsense-sounding magic words that she had said the first time she took Billy to Powers Island—and then stepped into the cabinet, followed by Billy, with Vester at the rear.

They appeared in the Accounting Room, greeted as before by the nasty view of the mummy warning of terrible death if one Transported without holding one's breath. This time, however, Mrs. Russet didn't bother to stand in any of the three lines to the Counters, the carnival-like fortune tellers that dispensed the name badges to everyone on Powers Island. She shoved her way to the front of the nearest line, pulling Billy and Vester along behind her. A few people in the line looked at her questioningly, but immediately moved aside when she said, "Council business."

She, Vester, and Billy each got their name tags. Billy's still said simply "Billy—unDetermined," but he thought when it appeared in the Counter machine, the badge had said something else for a moment. He had no time to wonder about it, though, as Mrs. Russet immediately turned to him and Vester. "Keep him close," she said to the fireman. "Something odd is happening, and I don't know what."

"I'm not a baby, you know," said Billy, a bit peeved that everyone seemed to be acting like he was in need of constant watching.

"Yes, I do know that, Mr. Jones," said Mrs. Russet. Then she looked at Vester and repeated, "Keep him close." Then she turned without another word and got onto one of the elevators that opened to the Accounting Room.

Billy heard the elevator's voice say, "What floor and department, please?" in its normal cheery voice, then it continued in a sulky tone, "Oh, it's you," as the doors shut and Mrs. Russet went to wherever it was she was going.

Must be the same elevator we went to the Hall of Convergence in, thought Billy.

Then he felt Vester guiding him to another elevator. It opened. "Whaddya want?" said the elevator in a distinctly New York accent.

"Stadium," answered Vester. "I'm not too late for the start of the Challenge, am I?"

"Nah," answered the elevator as the doors closed. "Still got a few minutes. Say, 'dja hear the one about the two guys that ran into a bar?"

"No," answered Vester warily.

"Yeah," said the elevator. "It was weird, because you'd think the second guy woulda noticed it after the first guy walked into it. But BAMMO! He walks right into it! Harharhar!"

Vester laughed weakly at the joke, nudging Billy to do the same.

"Better laugh," whispered the fireman to Billy. "Some of the elevators can get testy if you don't laugh at their jokes. We don't want to end up in the Room of Destruction or the Department of Experimental Chaos."

Billy laughed as hard as he could. "Tone it down a bit," murmured Vester. Billy scaled his laughter down to a chuckle.

"Hey, you're all right," said the elevator. The doors slid open; apparently they had arrived at wherever they were going. "You can ride in me any time, kid."

"Thanks," said Billy. He followed Vester off the elevator, and could hear the thing chuckling to itself as it moved away.

The place they had gone to was familiar-looking to Billy. It reminded him of the concession level at a baseball or football stadium.

"Where are we?" he asked Vester.

"Powers Stadium," answered his friend. He grabbed something from a passer-by and handed it to Billy. "Hot dog?"

Billy took the hot dog. He was a little disappointed that the treat wasn't something more, well, exciting than a mere hot dog. Something a bit more magical was in order, he thought.

"Eat me," said a voice.

Billy almost dropped the hot dog. He looked at it. The hot dog had suddenly sprouted two tiny eyes and a mouth. "Mmmmm...," it said in a sultry whisper. "I'm so tasty. Steamed to perfection, with just the right amount of mustard. Nothing would give me more pleasure than to be eaten by a wonderful young gent like yourself."

Billy's eyes crossed in surprise. He looked at Vester with upraised eyebrows. The fireman was already biting into his own hot dog, which sounded like it was moaning in pleasure. Vester looked at Billy. "What?" he asked.

"Please," whispered Billy's hot dog. "I can just imagine the ecstasy of being crushed between your molars, the sublime pleasure of being slowly dissolved in your stomach acids...."

Vester started off through the throngs of people that surrounded them. Billy quickly looked around, spotting a man with a tray of hot dogs nearby, each of them extolling its culinary virtues to passers-by. He put his own hot dog on the tray and hurried after Vester, resolving never to eat anything on Powers Island before making sure it wasn't going to start talking to him.

Billy caught up with his friend as Vester was walking out into the open part of the stadium. Billy gasped. It *was* a stadium, but it was enormous, dwarfing any other sports arena. There must have been a hundred thousand seats in the place, most of them filled with chatting people. The center arena was big enough to put three football fields in it, and the whole thing was covered by a huge pool of water, waves slapping up against the protective walls that lined the space and kept the nearby spectators from being drenched. Periodically throughout the water there were pillars, big enough to stand on, their tops about five feet higher than the water below.

Atop many of the pillars there were small pyres, a few sticks arranged in a teepee and set ablaze. And on two of the pillars stood a man and a woman, each dressed in a bright red suit of what looked like armor. Their red metal faceplates were closed, so Billy couldn't make out their faces, but the two armor-clad figures waved at the crowd, which roared its approval.

Billy realized that this was the arena he had seen the "boxing" match in earlier, the two rock giants pummeling at each other amongst the screaming people. But at that time, the place had appeared to have sand in it. Where had the great pool of water come from?

Vester started walking down a set of nearby stairs, craning his neck for a good seat. As he did, something clicked in Billy's thoughts. "Hey," he said. "I thought that there were only supposed to be twenty thousand people on Powers Island at once."

"There are," answered Vester.

"But," Billy said, "this place is huge. It has to have a hundred thousand people in it."

"Yeah, but most of them aren't here," said Vester. "They're just watching the Challenge Match." And with that, the fireman stepped into a row full of cheering people...and stepped right through them. Not "through them" in the sense that Billy would walk through a crowd, ducking and moving to avoid being trampled. Vester literally passed right through the people sitting in his way as though they were ghosts. Billy gulped, not wanting to follow his friend anywhere that required walking through people, but realized he preferred that to being left alone in the middle of a strange place on Powers Island.

He took a deep breath, then walked into the aisle, following Vester. He passed through ten or twelve sets of legs, their owners not seeming to mind that Billy was walking through their smoke-like appendages, though several did holler at him to move it because "You're blocking my view."

Finally, he got to where Vester was. His friend was holding down a fold-out plastic chair that was apparently the universal standard issue for sports stadiums—even on Powers Island. "Take a load off," said the young fireman.

Billy almost fell into the proffered seat. "I don't get it," he said.

"Don't get what?" asked Vester, finishing off the last bit of his happy hot dog.

"Pwease help," said a voice that sounded like that of a toddler. "Pwease, pwease help." Billy looked around for the source of the voice. He finally saw a tiny last piece of a hot dog, evidently left over from the seat's previous occupant, sitting on the ground in front of him. As soon as Billy looked at it, the food whispered, "Pwease finish me. Pwease eat me." Billy shuddered, then nudged the hot dog away. "Nooooo," it cried in a small voice.

"Well?" repeated Vester. "What don't you get?"

"Anything," said Billy, praying that no more food would talk to him. He felt slightly sick, and knew he was going to have nightmares about talking hot dogs tonight.

"Well," said Vester, looking around, "the people are mostly Projections. It's like watching a show on TV, only in reverse. Instead of a real show being broadcast into what you see on TV, the Powers all around the world are broadcasting themselves into the stadium." He shrugged. "If the show won't come to you, then you just go to the show." Then he winked. "At least, that's how it works if you're a Power."

That explained how Vester had walked through everyone, thought Billy. Aloud, he said, "How can you tell if the person you're walking through is really there or not?"

Vester's eyes glimmered with mirth. "If you feel something when you walk into them, and they yell at you to get off their toes, then they're really there. The uncertainty is part of the fun."

"Okay," said Billy. "So are these...Projections...all of the Powers in the world?"

"Probably most of them," said Vester. "I was going to be Projecting here myself, if Mrs. Russet hadn't asked me to baby-sit—er—hang out with you."

"And what exactly are we going to see?" asked Billy.

"Geez, you don't know anything, do you?" said Vester good-naturedly. "Powers Stadium is where we Powers come to see our version of sporting events. Usually, the players are Powers who are competing to achieve some objective, or they're controlling Fizzles who do battle."

Billy snapped his fingers. "So those two rock giants we saw—the boxing match—those were Fizzles," he said.

Vester nodded. "Right-a-roni, my friend."

"And is that what they're going to do?" asked Billy, gesturing at the two armored people on the pedestals in the arena.

"Not exactly," answered Vester. "I mean, they are, but it's a bit more complicated in this case. This is a Challenge, which means that someone thinks they should be a member of the Council. So he's challenging the current Councilor to a match of magic. The greater Power will win, and either ascend to—or keep—the place on the Ruby Throne."

"Then that means," said Billy, looking at the armored woman far below.

"Yeah," said Vester, eyes aglow with that look of dumbfounded affection Billy had seen in them before, when Billy had stood before the Council on the Diamond Dais. "It means that the woman down there is Fulgora."

# CHAPTER THE ELEVENTH

*In Which Billy sees the Dead, and War Begins...*

Billy's breath caught in his throat. "What's going to happen?" he asked.

"You never can tell," answered Vester. "Not in a Challenge."

"But, it's not...I mean, no one is going to get hurt, are they? I mean, it's not dangerous, right?" he asked. He didn't know Fulgora, but the Red Lady was beautiful, there was no denying that, and it seemed somehow wrong to Billy that a woman so beautiful could be in danger.

Vester looked at him seriously. "Billy, have you seen anything since you came to Powers Island that seemed to tell you that there is any magic without danger?"

Billy was silent. Even the Transport spell that he was coming to accept as commonplace could mummify you if you didn't hold your breath. Vester was right, he knew. There had to be an element of danger in any spell, just as there was always a danger—however slight—whenever you turned on the stove or got in a car to go to a friend's house. Even the smallest conveniences came with a price.

He turned his attention to the arena. "What's with the water? And the little fires?"

Vester spoke distractedly, reminding Billy again of his father. His father spoke in that same voice when explaining the finer points of a football game to Billy: like he was there, but not there.

"The fire is because Powers generally need their Element to work their magic." Vester withdrew the matchbook from his pocket, the one he had used to create a small horse of flame. "I strike a match, I can control the fire it makes. But I can't *create* the fire. So that's why the fires are set on the podiums. And as for the water all around them, that's because Water douses Fire." He seemed to sense Billy's confusion, because he amplified that thought. "No one Element is supreme. It's like a big game of Rock, Scissors, Paper. Water can often destroy Fire. So in a Challenge, the most dangerous anti-Element is placed nearby. Only the strongest of the Powers will be able to practice their magics while in the midst of such danger. It's just one more way of proving the strength of the winner, and their right to the Council seat."

"So who's the Challenger?" asked Billy, nodding to the armored man who was still waving to the crowd. It was hard to tell at this distance, but Billy rather thought the red-suited man looked much, much larger than the diminutive Fulgora.

"That's Napalm," answered Vester. "That's what he calls himself, anyway. Thinks it makes him sound tough. His real name is Clarence Underweather, if you can believe it." Vester snorted. "He's a twit." Then, reluctantly, he added, "Good magicker, though." He cupped his hands around his eyes like a three year old looking through "binoculars," clearly trying to focus better on what was going on below, then the young fireman bolted to his feet. "Hey, foul!" he called out. A roar went up from the crowd, as though in agreement.

"What happened?" asked Billy.

"You didn't see?" said Vester incredulously. "How could you not see what just happened?"

"It's around a million feet away," answered Billy, a bit perturbed. Maybe it was just the talking hot dogs, but he felt on edge, and not in the mood to be reprimanded for his lack of knowledge of this world. "I can barely even see that there are *people* down there, let alone seeing some foul that I probably wouldn't recognize even if I *could* see it."

"What?" said Vester. Then, sheepishly, he said, "Oh, I forgot. You don't know about Close-Ups in the Stadium. Do this." Vester again put his cupped hands to his eyes, motioning for Billy to do the same.

"No way," said Billy. That just looked too stupid.

"Okay," shrugged Vester. "You're missing out, though." He swung his cup-handed gaze back to the arena, sitting forward on the edge of his seat. "They're starting."

Billy looked around, embarrassed, then reluctantly put his hands to his face. As soon as he did, he almost jumped out of his skin. Suddenly he could see the arena as closely as if he was standing right next to it.

The pillars stood about five feet above the level of the water that covered the arena floor. Each pillar was a few feet from the next, so that you could get from one to the other if you jumped, but a miss would mean the jumper would fall to an immediate soaking.

Billy realized, too, that there were shapes moving through the water. Long, dark shadows moved sinuously among the pedestals, like thick underwater snakes. Billy didn't know what they were, but he suspected that finding out would be a deeply unpleasant experience.

Vester's voice came from beside him, and Billy was surprised to see that when he turned toward his friend, he could see the Stadium in its regular size, with his friend still sitting right next to him. Apparently the Close-Up spell only worked when you were watching the central arena. "Here we go," said Vester.

As he said this, a spark shot up in the middle of the Stadium, like a miniature firework or a flare. As soon as it did, both Fulgora and Napalm moved. Each jumped quickly to the nearest podium with a flame on it. Napalm, moving more heavily than the lithe Fulgora, nevertheless reached one of the open flames first. He put one hand in the open fire and lifted, pulling the fire away from the sticks as though it were a solid mass. The flame danced in his hands, and a moment later it solidified into several bright balls.

Napalm held out his other hand, large and heavy in a red gauntlet, and pointed at Fulgora, who was still trying to jump to one of the fires. The spheres of flame belched from his hand, roaring toward Fulgora at a tremendous speed. Billy gasped as the first ball struck the Red Lady on the chest, knocking into her in mid-jump.

Fulgora fell backward with the force of the blow, and Billy gasped, thinking she was surely going to fall into the sea of water below her. Apparently whatever the creatures under the water were, they were thinking the same thing, because they immediately began closing in on her.

Fulgora didn't fall into the water, though. She managed somehow to fall back onto a nearby podium, arms windmilling as she struggled to keep her balance. The next ball of flame struck her then, actually helping her as it shoved her backward onto more solid footing.

"Stupid," murmured Vester. "Napalm might have had her if he had only thrown one flame at a time."

More balls of flame were speeding toward Fulgora, however. She barely had a moment to throw up her arms in front of her. The next fireball ricocheted off her, and she sent it hurtling back at Napalm, its speed even greater than it had been. Napalm had to dive aside at the last second as the trajectory of the ball curved in mid-air, coming not at the armored man, but instead hitting the podium on which he stood.

A roar went up from the crowd as Napalm's pillar blew into tiny pieces, destroyed by Fulgora's return attack. Vester smacked his hand into his palm. "Atta girl," he said.

But Napalm was far from finished. He had managed to retain control over his fire when he jumped, and now hurled a new barrage of fireballs at Fulgora. This time she was prepared, however, and deflected them harmlessly skyward, where they exploded into a display of fireworks. She also managed to reach some flame on a podium nearby her, and sent one huge fireball hurtling directly at Napalm, who barely managed to get his arms up in time to shield himself from the blast.

"How long can this last?" asked Billy.

"As long as it takes," said Vester, not taking his eyes off Fulgora. "Each time you do magic, it saps a little bit of strength out of you, so sooner or later you're going to just collapse or fall dead asleep on the spot. The bigger the spell, the harder it is to sustain."

"And how big are the spells they're doing?" asked Billy.

"Medium," said Vester. "Stuff that even I could do. This is just the warm-up."

Sure enough, Napalm threw one last fireball at Fulgora, then switched tactics. His supply of flame depleted, he jumped to another podium of fire, quickly snatching up the bright living flame. But instead of using it, he instead hopped to another podium, then another and another, gathering up a large mass of flame each time, until almost half the fires in the arena were circling above him in an eerie orbit of light.

"What's he doing?" asked Billy. "Why does he need all that fire?"

"He's getting his ammo ready," answered Vester distractedly. "It's much harder to make your Element into more Element, so making the available fire bigger would take a lot out of him. He's grabbing all he can for one huge blow."

Sure enough, Napalm had stopped moving now. He raised his hands in the air, and the circling flames above him arced down in lacey lattices of fire, rimming his body with a deep orange and red aura.

Fulgora, meanwhile, had not been idle. She, too, had been moving as quickly as possible, gathering up flame of her own. Instead of it circling above her, as it had with Napalm, however, hers was flowing sinuously around her: a deadly serpent of auburn and gold. But Billy was dismayed to see that it seemed she had much less fire at her disposal than did Napalm.

Napalm, too, seemed to sense this, as his body language took on a taller, more victorious posture. He raised his arms again, and the flames that enveloped him rose and then arced in a solid bridge toward Fulgora. The Red Lady held up her arms for a moment, and the movement of Napalm's fire began to slow.

"Wow," breathed Vester.

"What? What's happening?" Billy asked, vaguely aware that he was gripping the edges of his seat with sweaty palms and white knuckles.

"She's trying to take control of his flame," said Vester. "It's terrifically tough to take control of an Element that's under the influence of another Power. If she can do it, though, Napalm's finished. He won't have enough fire left over to put up any kind of serious challenge."

But Fulgora, Billy could see, was weakening. Slowly Napalm's fire crept toward her, at first an inch at a time, then a foot at a time, then moving quickly across the arena. Fulgora bent down, her body being forced into kneeling by the intensity of her energy as she fought the onrushing flame. At last, however, her concentration must have broken, for the bridge reached her. It rapidly encircled the Red Lady, a solid ring of fire that rose high enough it almost shielded her from view of the audience in Powers Stadium.

"What's he doing? Is he nuts?" Vester murmured to himself. "That fire's almost close enough for her to touch. If she *does* manage to touch it, she can steal it for sure, and then he's got nothing."

But the ring of fire was *not* close enough for Fulgora to touch. She reached for it, but could not quite manage to lay a finger into the swirling halo of flame around her.

Then, suddenly, the fire ring jumped higher. It thinned out as it grew, becoming almost transparent, but it went higher and higher, taller and taller. It began spinning more rapidly. Billy glanced at Napalm. The Red Power was clearly giving this all he had: rivulets of sweat were running down beneath his helmeted head, and his arms shook with the physical exertion of his mental attack.

Fulgora could now be seen quite clearly through the tall, thin wall of rapidly spinning fire that Napalm had cast around her. She was turning around on her confined podium, clearly unsure what to do. The fire cylinder sped its rotation, the revolutions it made going faster and faster, until it was a veritable tornado of fire. The water below Fulgora's pedestal began to boil, water steaming upwards.

Billy couldn't hear her, but he suddenly saw Fulgora lurch, apparently off balance. She crumpled to her knees, appearing to cough and choke.

"Great Powers," said Vester. "He's suffocating her." And instantly Billy understood. Just like a firestorm in a huge forest fire, the flame ring that Napalm had created was sucking all the oxygen from the area in which Fulgora stood. And that didn't only mean that Fulgora could not breath: it also meant that the meager flame she had managed to wreathe herself with was dying out, deprived of the air it, too, needed to survive. To make matters worse, the steam rising from the boiling water below the Red Lady was now thick and wet. The flames around her flickered, puffing up wreathes of steam as they slowly waned. She touched them with one shaking hand, clearly trying to add her power to them, to keep them alive so she could continue the fight. But she couldn't do it. The flames wavered, spat several desperate sparks around her, then flickered out in dismal defeat.

"No, no, no," Vester was whispering. He clutched at Billy's arm. Billy could only imagine what his friend was going through right now. How would *he* feel, if it was Blythe down there, in the middle of that deadly cylinder? He shuddered at the thought.

"It's okay," he said to Vester. He knew it must sound lame to the older man: Billy wasn't even a Determined Power. He didn't know what he was talking about. But he still had to try to give some comfort. "I'm sure she can...."

But before he could finish the thought, the crowd gasped as Fulgora, with one last effort, fell to the podium, her arms and legs hanging limply over the sides. Billy could see the beasts in the water below—who were apparently impervious to the great heat that was all around them—lunge upward to snap at her dangling limbs. They looked like huge, grotesque eels, their gaping jaws lined with razor teeth. Their mouths snapped shut with audible clicks, missing the unconscious Fulgora's fingers and toes by scant centimeters.

"Let it be! It's over!" shouted someone from the crowd of onlookers. "She's done, you've won the Challenge, Napalm!" The rest of the crowd quickly took up the cry, pleading with the armored warrior below to show mercy. Napalm showed no inclination to do so, however. His heavy, muscled arms raised even higher, their trembling matched only by the Red Power's apparent determination to not only win the Challenge, but destroy his rival.

Billy looked at his friend, expecting Vester to join in the shouts. But clearly the young fireman was clinging desperately to hope. "She's not gone, she's not gone, she can't be. She's not gone." It sounded almost like a chant, a prayer that if Vester said enough times would turn out to be true. Billy felt tears springing unbidden from his eyes. Somewhat they were for the lovely lady below them, who was being crushed so unmercifully below the angry power of Napalm's fire. But mostly they were for Vester, his new friend who already felt like he was as close to Billy as anyone outside his own family had ever been.

He touched Vester's shoulder, feebly patting it. He felt like he was patting a dog, knew it wasn't helping anything, but couldn't help but continue. It was something, at least, and he couldn't stand to do nothing. He wished he could help Fulgora more directly, but this gesture to his friend was all he knew how to do.

Then, abruptly, a gasp went through the crowd. Billy felt rather than saw Vester tense, and he quickly turned his attention back to the arena.

*Fulgora was rising.* She stood slowly, clearly crippled by pain and lack of breath, but just as clearly determined that this Challenge not yet come to an end.

The Red Lady reached out her gauntleted hand, grasping for the fire that had drawn so close. Napalm, seeing this, rapidly moved his hands. The loop of fire drew away from Fulgora, but at the same time increased the speed of its turning, sucking the air out of the circle now so fast that the air could be heard rushing from the top of the cyclone.

Fulgora faltered again, and it seemed to Billy that this time it *must* end; that this time it *had* to be over. Next to him, Vester was rocking back and forth in his seat, now almost rising up, now hunching far down, his body clearly incapable of expressing the depth of the fireman's emotions.

Then, with one last great gasp, Fulgora stood. She tottered to the end of her podium, almost falling into the writhing water below. She stopped herself, though, blinking rapidly, her head shaking as though she was trying to wake from a particularly vivid nightmare.

Then, she jumped.

"No!" shouted Vester, lunging to his feet.

Billy saw at once that Fulgora was not going to make it to the nearest pedestal; that her jump was going to fall dreadfully short of the safety of that marble podium. Her doom was certain, and a great wave of pained noises racked the arena as the onlookers suffered with her in anticipation of the end.

But then the gasps of pain turned to gasps of astonishment as everyone, including Billy, realized that Fulgora had not been trying to make it to the next pedestal in the first place.

She had been trying to make it to Napalm's circle of fire.

Billy didn't know what was happening, or what the Red Lady could be thinking. Even if she managed to touch Napalm's fire and wrest control of it from him, she would still fall inevitably to her doom in the watery sea of death below.

And sure enough, Fulgora was falling. But she stretched as far as she could as she dropped. Reaching forward, apparently pulling herself by force of will.

One finger. One single, solitary finger. It touched Napalm's ring of fire, and suddenly Fulgora was no more.

There was a flash of light, a glare so bright that the sun itself would have been embarrassed to be compared to it. Billy blinked his eyes, blinded for a moment, looking away to save his eyesight.

And when he managed to look back, he—along with a hundred thousand others—gasped in awe.

Fulgora was still falling. But slowly. Because she had sprouted wings.

"Great Powers," Vester whispered again.

The wings flapped once, and as they did, Fulgora changed. Her armor elongated, becoming great red scales, overlapping and tight as brass bullet casings. Napalm's ring of fire disappeared, being pulled into Fulgora's changing form.

She grew, and her armored face metamorphosed into something animalistic and fierce, with gleaming red eyes above a ridge of stony spires that ran the length of a long, sinuous snout. Her body elongated, a tail sprouting from her hindquarters. The wings pounded, taking on a deep red hue, carrying her instantly above the range of the sea monsters below.

Her form solidified, hardening to something like burnished metal. It was a shape Billy knew. A shape he had seen before.

Fulgora had become a dragon. Not a blue one, not like the one he had seen with Mrs. Russet, the dragon Billy's history teacher had called Serba. No, this was a gleaming red dragon.

Someone in the audience screamed as the dragon that was Fulgora beat its wings again, ascending to a new height so that it could look down upon Powers Stadium. The dragon screamed, and the roar permeated Billy's body, making his heart stutter in his chest, his eardrums almost bursting in his head.

He could see that Napalm had fallen to his knees atop his podium. The challenger's fire spent, the remaining pyres nothing but cold piles of charred coal, the armored man cowered, utterly powerless under the terrifying gaze of the red dragon.

Napalm screamed as Fulgora licked her lips. The dragon opened its mouth, and a gout of fire spewed forth, a white-hot blaze that scorched Billy from hundreds of feet away. The tip of the fire undulated forward like a long tongue, licking at the quivering shape of Napalm.

Billy, like almost everyone else in the stadium, was on his feet. He glanced at Vester. The fireman appeared stunned, his face utterly drained of blood.

"No one has ever become a dragon before," he murmured in a dazed voice. "At least, no one who's ever become human again."

The dragon opened its mouth once more, and Billy was sure this was it: the dragon was sure to broil Napalm in his own armor.

A ferocious roar came again, that terrifying sound even worse this time. And with it, the dragon spoke, its voice still recognizably Fulgora's, but with a deep and alien timbre that chilled Billy's insides.

"Do…you…YIELD?!" screamed the red dragon.

"Yes!" shouted Napalm, his voice cracking with hysteria and terror. "Yes, yes, by the Elements, I swear it, I swear it!"

The dragon folded its wings and swooped down at Napalm, who screamed and covered his eyes. But instead of eating the challenger, as Billy half-expected her to do, Fulgora stopped at the last second. She beat her powerful wings once, hard, and the blast of hot wind she generated blew Napalm right off his podium. Up over the water he sailed, flying limply through the air and crashing into the first row of seats beyond the water. Billy could hear the crunch of Napalm's impact, and knew that it was made all the more painful since all the Powers who appeared to be seated there were really Projections, so Napalm smashed into a row of plastic seats rather than comparatively soft laps.

The challenger lay groaning and moaning in a limp pile of armor and bruised bones as Fulgora roared triumphantly overhead. The baleful red eyes of the dragon looked around the stadium, as though seeking anyone else who might issue a Challenge.

No one did.

Then Billy watched in awe as, almost softly, the dragon winged downward and settled upon one of the podiums below. It coughed a burst of flame from its mouth. Then it shivered, as though suddenly cold. Another burst of flame seemed to explode uncontrolled from its maw, and with it a great puff of smoke. The smoke wrapped itself like a living cloak around the dragon, obscuring her from view. It settled like fog over a meadow, dissipating slowly.

And when it was gone, so was the dragon.

All that was left was a motionless form, draped lifelessly over the stone pedestal.

Vester was on his feet instantly. "Fulgora!" he screamed.

In an instant, a trio of Powers were at her side: two gray-clad Wind Powers and one red-robed Power of Fire. They floated on a current of air to hover beside Fulgora's pedestal. The Red Power touched her wrist and neck, feeling for a pulse. "It's faint," he said in a voice that was audible to all in the arena, "but she's alive."

Now a new round of buzzing conversation began. Billy caught snatches of it all around him. "Thank goodness," and "Did you ever see such a thing?" and "A dragon! By all the Powers, a dragon!" being the most common refrains. Vester appeared to hear nothing, his eyes glued to Fulgora as her limp form was floated by the Wind Powers over the water that had surrounded her tiny podium, and off to a side gate which opened for her and closed once she was inside.

"Recovery Room," said Vester. "That's a good sign. They don't send people there unless they're hopeful."

"Goodness gracious, did you ever see such a thing?" huffed a nearby voice. Billy turned. It was Tempus, the Gray Power who had been at Billy's Gleaning. The old man was weaving through the aisle toward them, crashing over, through, and around Projected—and several non-Projected—Powers to get to Billy and Vester.

His characteristic Hawaiian shirt—the moving landscape on this one a bright green and blue and looking more like someone had been explosively sick all over him than like he was going on holiday—flapped as he stumbled toward them. He was also wearing violently pink shorts that barely came down to his bone-white thighs, his knobby knees clacking together as he ran. "Oh, pardon me, was that your head?" he would ask when walking through one protesting Projection. "Sorry, just need to get over a few more of you," he would murmur as he balanced on top of another Power who was actually there. To Billy, the surprisingly agile old man looked like an ancient polar bear, hopping from ice flow to ice flow in the Arctic Circle.

He finally reached Billy and Vester, puffing violently as he reiterated to them, "Did you ever see such a thing?"

"No," said Vester shortly before turning back to look at the closed door to the Recovery Room as though hoping it would pop open at any second and Fulgora would walk out.

"Me neither," said Tempus. "Did you see how they just floated right out to her! In the middle of a Challenge, like they had to rescue an unDetermined child?"

Vester turned an almost-angry gaze on the old Wind Power. "Yes, Tempus, that was really unreal," he said sarcastically.

Tempus shrank a bit before his gaze. "Oh, and there was also the dragon thing, too, of course."

"Of course," said Vester, still clearly biting back incivility only through super-human effort.

Billy watched the short exchange like a spectator at a world-class ping-pong match, the volleys almost too fast to be seen.

"What happened?" he finally managed to interject. "I mean, she won, right? Fulgora is still the Red Councilor, and Napalm can't ever Challenge her again, can he?"

"She won all right," whispered Vester.

"Indeed she did," said Tempus. And then, as if Billy hadn't seen it all ready. "She actually *became* a dragon. And a fully-grown one, no less!"

Billy was beginning to sense that what had happened here was very unusual, even for a place where the elevators joked, rock giants boxed, and hot dogs begged you to be eaten in disturbingly desperate voices. "So becoming a dragon is a big deal?" he asked, though he already knew the answer.

"Yes," said Tempus, "In much the same way as Eurasia is a big island, or a blue whale is a rather large animal, or a redwood is just a tiny bit bigger than a mustard seed, or—"

The Gray Power broke off quickly as Vester again aimed an irritated look at him. Billy was almost grateful; he liked a good metaphor as much as the next kid, he supposed, but he had gotten the point pretty early on.

Tempus leaned in to whisper to Billy as Vester returned his undivided attention to his vigil over the Recovery Room. "Dragons are what Powers become when they don't want to die."

Billy was getting even better at his monosyllabic responses now. He had practiced them enough that he was in danger of losing his amateur status, so when he said, "Huh?" this time, it was a "Huh" that would have put a world class "Huh"-er to shame.

"Huh?"

Tempus's eyebrows went up. It looked like even *he* was impressed at how well Billy could communicate the complex thought, "I'm sorry, I haven't the slightest inkling of the beginning of an idea of what the heck you're talking about and the only way I could have less of an idea is if I went back in time to a point before you had said anything at all on this unknown subject and therefore not only didn't know any details about it, but was completely unaware that said subject even existed" in a single "huh?"

"Well," Tempus said, "I don't know if you've noticed, but time doesn't pass exactly the same here on Powers Island."

"I had heard something about that," said Billy dryly.

Tempus nodded gravely. Apparently he was better at sensing confusion than sarcasm. "It does, it's true. Usually, it moves much quicker here than for the rest of the world. The White King and the Great Gray Prophet who were the principal architects of Powers Island made it that way, to hide us from the rest of the world."

Billy looked questioningly at Tempus. He was now getting so good he was even able to dispense with the "Huh"s and communicate total confusion in a single glance.

"What I mean is," Tempus said, "well, you could say we are currently in a slightly different dimension. So something that appears to happen over a course of hours here, takes only a few seconds or minutes back home. So naturally some Powers would rather be dragons or sylphs or sprites or werewolves or such."

Billy blinked. He had been following Tempus up to that last little bit. And had the old man said *werewolves*? "I'm sorry," said Billy, "I don't really get you."

"Get me?" asked Tempus absent-mindedly. "I'm not a present. How could you get me?"

Billy was saved from trailing after Tempus's wildly rambling train of thought by a sudden commotion in the stadium. Everyone was on their feet, straining to look at the Recovery Room. The doors had just opened, and Billy could literally feel everyone at Powers Stadium—even the people who weren't really there—holding their breath. They all gasped disappointedly, though, when what emerged wasn't Fulgora, but merely one of the Gray Powers that had borne her on his Wind into the room in the first place. "They're still diagnosing," he said, again in that strangely-amplified voice that resounded throughout the stadium. Billy realized he must be doing something to the air to make it carry the sound everywhere, something that a Wind Power would surely be able to do.

"Where was I?" asked Tempus when they sat down again. "Oh, yes. Passing time and dragons." He looked at Billy. "If time passes quickly here, and doesn't in the real world, what does that mean?"

"Uh," said Billy dully, "it means that time passes fast here, but slow there?"

"Exactly!" crowed Tempus. "But more than that, it means that if you spend a lot of time here, you go back there and even though *you've* grown by a few minutes or hours or weeks, the *rest* of the world hasn't." The old man paused, trying to figure out the best way to explain. "You ever see a kid who literally just seemed to grow overnight? To grow a few inches and put on twenty pounds?"

Billy nodded. Cameron Black sprung instantly to mind. His eternal tormenter had seemed to grow hugely in the two months since school had started.

"Well," said Tempus, "that may be one of two things." The old man held up two liver-spotted fingers, ticking off the choices. "One, that he had a growth spurt. Or two, that he or she is a young Power who spent several months on Powers Island for training, then returned to the rest of the world's time only a day later. But he grew in those months. His *body* didn't know that only a day of 'real' time had passed. It had experienced a month of growth. And that means, ultimately, that a person who spends a great deal of time at the island...." He trailed off expectantly, clearly waiting to see if Billy would put this last piece together.

Billy thought. So someone got old here, but no time passed for the rest of the world? And that must mean.... "So someone who stays here a lot will seem to age faster, and die sooner."

Tempus laid a finger on his nose. Correct, the gesture told Billy. "Exactly. Me, for example, I know I look like I'm around fifty," (and here Billy couldn't help but think Tempus was being very generous to himself), "but my birth certificate shows that I was born in St. Andrews hospital in Illinois only forty-five years ago." He looked at his body, then back at Billy. "I think we can agree that my non-Power friends believe I've led a very, well, colorful life that has aged me prematurely."

Billy couldn't help but laugh. But then he grew sober. "So if I stayed here...."

"You'd age, too, faster than your friends, faster than your parents, faster than everyone. But don't worry," he hastened to add. "Most people don't spend that much time on the island, except perhaps when doing testing or involved in special training of some kind or other. So the difference is usually negligible."

"Why did the White King and," Billy tried to remember what Tempus had said, "the Great Gray Prophet make Powers Island that way?"

"So that it couldn't be found by non-Powers, of course," gruffed Tempus. Apparently he didn't have as much patience for other people's conversational tangents as for his own. "But we're talking about death and dragons right now." He rubbed his hands on his Hawaiian shirt absent-mindedly, as though trying to smooth out wrinkles. It didn't help much. Billy thought the shirt still looked like someone had managed to barf in the shape of palm trees.

"So some of us Powers seem to age. And even though, really, we still get our allotted lifetime of experiences—whether on Powers

Island, or back with the real world—some of the Powers don't like the idea of aging—and dying—before everyone else in the normal world. So they try to take refuge in something that lives forever." He eyed Billy. "Can you guess what that might be?"

Billy shrugged. He had no idea. "The sun?" he guessed, more to say something than because he thought it was the right answer.

"The *Elements*," Tempus said gloatingly, pleased with himself. "The Elements are always there, in some form or other. They are self-perpetuating in a way. So the Powers who want—wrongly, I think—a form of immortality must *become* their Elements." He paused, sobering suddenly. "I believe this is an affront to nature, and to the One who created all Elements." He shrugged then, adding, "But some disagree."

"So these Powers who want to live forever, they become Elements?" asked Billy. "They become Fire or Water? Or Earth or Wind?"

"No, that's impossible," said Vester, causing Billy to jump. He hadn't even been aware the fireman was listening to the conversation Billy and Tempus were having. "No one can be Fire. A human is a human, and Fire is Fire. Two different things."

"Quite so," broke in Tempus, looking a little miffed at Vester for interrupting the old man's lecture-like teaching of young Billy. "But still they try. And some—a very few, mind you—manage to become something that is close to an Element. An embodiment of it, something more than human, but less than pure Element."

"Like a dragon," said Billy.

"Yes," said Tempus, clearly pleased, though Billy wasn't sure if the old man's happiness sprang from Billy's cleverness or from his own skill at teaching. "Like a dragon. Dragons, being closer to pure Element, have greater control over that Element than any but the greatest Powers. More importantly, they live much, much longer. Some say they live forever. But," he added, with a bit of a frown, "that's hard to verify, since forever hasn't happened yet."

"So, Fulgora became a red dragon, and—"

"And that is absolutely astounding!" shouted Tempus. "No Power in recorded history has managed to become so close to Element, and then actually manage somehow to return to human form!" He looked at the closed doors of the Recovery Room. "Fulgora must have been truly desperate. Either that, or," he lowered his voice, clearly not wanting Vester to hear what he said next, "or much more ambitious than we dreamed." He spoke in normal tones again, then said, "Either way, she did something amazing. She will probably be on the Council for the rest of her life, since I can't think of anyone who would be crazy enough to Challenge her again after today's spectacle. Though," he added, eyeing the still-closed Recovery Room, "the rest of her life might not be a very long time."

"Don't talk like that," Vester snapped. He was clearly angry at Tempus now. His eyes blazed like the fire he controlled. "Don't ever say that. She's strong."

"Of course, my boy, of course," Tempus said placatingly, his hands up. "I didn't mean any harm. Just get carried away sometimes."

Vester's hands balled into hard-knuckled fists at his sides, and Billy worried for a moment that the fireman might take a swing at Tempus. He didn't want that to happen. Not only was he fairly sure that one hit would cause the knobbly Tempus to shatter into a million brittle tatters of bone and vomit-shirt, but he couldn't bear to see his two friends fight.

"I'm sorry, Vester," said Billy. "It's my fault." He looked at his feet, embarrassed. "I just don't know anything about anything," he said. He suddenly felt genuinely stupid. If he only understood these things—things which were apparently common knowledge among the Powers—Tempus wouldn't have had to explain all this to him, and Vester wouldn't have gotten so angry.

But to his surprise, Vester's anger subsided instantly. He clutched Billy in a sudden hug. "I'm sorry, too, Billy. It seems you've arrived in this world with no warning. Everything must be terrifying to you." The young fireman let go of Billy, giving a smile to Billy, then smiled at Tempus, too. "Sorry to you too, my friend," he said.

Tempus waved off the apology, but was clearly happy to hear Vester say that. Billy felt his insides move back to their normal position, overwhelmingly glad that Vester wasn't going to knock Tempus's head off like a Rock-em-Sock-em rock giant.

"Have you seen Ivy?" asked Vester.

Tempus nodded. "I did for a minute, but she was called away by something. I think there's a meeting of the Council happening right now, and sometimes her father wants her there during meetings so she can run needed errands or deliver messages."

Vester nodded and turned back to look at the Recovery Room.

Billy was going to look, too, hoping that Fulgora would come out soon. But before he had looked for more than a moment, something very strange and very frightening occurred.

A small explosion rocked the middle of the arena. Nothing huge, not on the scale of Fulgora's dragon breath, or even Napalm's fire bombs. But it sent a discernible noise through all of Powers Stadium. The noise appeared to come out of nowhere, but when Billy looked at the arena, he saw in Close-up that several of the monstrous eel creatures that had menaced Napalm and Fulgora were now floating belly-up in the water below the podiums, clearly dead.

He looked back up, planning to ask Vester what had just happened, but before he could do that Powers Stadium suddenly emptied substantially. About half the audience just disappeared, most of them just fading into nothing in the blink of an eye, and the rest using Imbued keys of varying shapes and types to open glittering doorways which they used to Transport themselves to somewhere unknown.

"What the—" Vester began.

Then, out of nowhere, a new crowd appeared. Not fifty thousand, nowhere near the number of Powers who had just Transported or unProjected themselves out of the stadium. Just a few thousand, perhaps, but enough that the new arrivals were noticeable in the crowd. They arrived with that characteristic "pop" of a Transport, all of them appearing almost at the same instant. The new arrivals looked around for a moment, apparently getting their bearings, then moved as one.

One of them had appeared nearby Billy. The creature—not a person, Billy now saw, but something else—had mottled skin, a dull, faded lattice of green and brown. It reminded Billy of grass that had been left unwatered a bit too long. The creature's skin also appeared flaky, making Billy think of some kind of weird full-body dandruff. The hair on the creature was similarly ill-looking, a diseased patch of mangy locks that curled in sticky clumps around its slightly misshapen head.

The eyes, though, were what really stood out, and what really frightened Billy. They were huge, far too large for its head, and subtly faceted, making the creature look almost insectile, like the world's biggest walking bug.

"What's that?" Billy managed to stutter out.

The creature zeroed in on his voice, and started to stumble towards Billy.

"Is that what I think it is?" said Tempus.

"Zombie!" shouted Vester. He grabbed Billy's hand. "RUN!"

Similar shouts went up through the whole of Powers Stadium. Billy glimpsed several of the creatures—zombies, Vester had called them—advancing on cowering Powers who were so panicked they couldn't even move. The creatures reached out grasping fingers, and the instant they touched the quivering men and women, the people fell over instantly. Whether they were unconscious, magically immobilized, or something even worse, Billy couldn't tell. But he knew he didn't want whatever it was to happen to him.

He ran with Vester, Tempus huffing behind them to escape the zombie that now pursued them. Billy glanced back and saw that the creature seemed solely interested in him and his two friends, oblivious to everyone else in its path. But whenever it bumped into an unProjected Power—someone who was really there, as opposed to spectating from afar—that person slumped over instantly.

"Do you have a Key?" yelled Tempus.

"Yes, but we can't use it," hollered Vester in response.

"*What?*" screamed Tempus incredulously.

"We have to get to the Recovery Room!" answered Vester.

"Are you insane?" puffed Tempus. The old man's knobby knees were a blur of motion as they ran.

Vester jerked Billy's hand, yanking him up a stairway that Billy saw would lead to a mezzanine that would take them near the Recovery Room. Billy instantly understood what the fireman was doing, but he didn't like it. Vester needed to get to Fulgora. The fireman was risking his—and Billy's and Tempus's—safety to make sure the love of his life was all right.

Billy saw Tempus shake his head resignedly. He apparently knew, like Billy did, that Vester would not be persuaded to leave without Fulgora. The Gray Power turned for a moment and moved his arms in a subtle motion. A small whirlwind erupted in front of the rapidly-approaching zombie, whipping it around in a circle and then flipping it ten feet back, gaining them some time. Billy could also see that all through the stadium, other windstorms and fires were blazing into existence, as well as trees with writhing branches that blocked the zombies' forward motion as other Powers tried to defend themselves long enough to escape. A few waterspouts erupted from the pool in the arena, as well, raining streams of water that flushed some of the zombies down into the lowest levels of the stadium.

In the midst of all of this, the thing that frightened Billy the most was the panicked look on Tempus's face, and the fear that flitted in Vester's eyes. If these two Powers were afraid, what chance would a mere boy like Billy have to get out of this alive?

And then the world exploded.

# CHAPTER THE TWELFTH

*In Which Billy sees the Hidden Place, and trips into Flame…*

A moment later, Billy realized that the world hadn't really exploded. Not quite. But it seemed to.

There was some kind of detonation, a roar so huge that the sound waves themselves knocked Billy off his feet. A sudden hail of pebbles rained down on and around him, plinking on the plastic seats of the stadium. Billy saw that their zombie pursuer had been knocked down by the blast as well, allowing Billy a moment to look around and see what new terror was being visited on them.

As he did, the ground bucked and heaved. Billy heard the sound of stones shearing away from one another. There was a huge thud as a twenty foot high stone landed within mere feet of him. The good news was that it squashed the pursuing zombie flat. The bad news was that it ripped away a large chunk of the stadium, leaving a gaping hole where seats had been. Billy almost fell into the vast crevasse, and was only saved by Vester's quick hand snaring him away from the abyss.

There were more thuds all around, more rocks falling from the sky. Vester yanked Billy back into motion, still heading for the mezzanine, as Billy looked up. The falling stones were coming from the tower that loomed over Powers Island. The very blocks that made up the huge structure were cracking off and plummeting to the ground below with nuclear blasts of sound. So far, the tower itself hadn't collapsed, still mostly held together by the great branches of the Earthtree that provided its support. But Billy wondered how long it would be before the entire structure fell to the ground, crushing everything below it to oblivion.

"Come on!" yelled Vester. "Keep up!"

He yanked Billy forward, Billy's shorter legs pumping as fast as they could to stay abreast of his friend. Billy heard Tempus say a word that his mother had told him was Not Nice, and then muttered something else under his breath. As soon as the Gray Power did so,

Billy felt a gust of wind at his back, propelling him forward. The wind increased, and now he, Vester, and Tempus were all being borne forward by a pillow of air, moving faster than they had been running.

"Thanks, Tempus," said Vester.

"You Fires are all so impetuous," was all the old man said in response, but he was smiling. The smile dissipated, though, when they got to the mezzanine, and were faced with hordes of screaming people, zombies plowing through them and leaving unmoving bodies behind. Tempus's forehead wrinkled in concentration as he made the wind upon which the three of them rested whip through and over the crowd, narrowly avoiding the clutching hands of several zombies.

As they passed, Billy could see that no two zombies were alike. Some were short, some were tall, others fat, some so thin they looked like skeletons. But all had that same flaky, grotesquely colored skin, and all of them had huge eyes that seemed to look everywhere at once.

"Now might be a good time to get your fire ready," said Tempus. "Just in case."

Vester pulled out his matchbook and struck a match. It sizzled to life, and immediately he pinched the flame between his fingers and put it in his pocket. "Ready as I'll ever be," Vester said to the Gray Power.

The three of them continued to rocket forward at speeds that alarmed and exhilarated Billy. The space between the mezzanine floor and the beginning of the next level up was limited, and Billy nearly had his head scraped off on the ceiling a few times as they rose to avoid being grabbed by zombies or knocked into by fleeing Powers.

He also thought he could hear several hot dogs moaning that they had been abandoned before being properly eaten. "Woe is me!" screamed one particularly frazzled frankfurter. "Never more shall I know the bliss of being rolled around in someone's mouth, the pleasure of being sent into his stomach, through his intestines, and at last taking the final step of my journey into—" Thankfully, someone stepped on that hot dog before it could finish its thought, squashing it into a reddish paste and putting it out of its misery.

At last, Billy and his friends reached the doors to the Recovery Room. Because no one had been near here, the area was relatively quiet. Pandemonium still ruled in Powers Stadium, and huge pieces of the tower were still plunging to earth, but Billy was relieved that there were, at least, no zombies nearby.

*BILLY: MESSENGER OF POWERS*, BY MICHAELBRENT COLLINGS * 161

As soon as they touched ground, Vester was off and running, Billy and Tempus close behind him as the young fireman ran to the closed Recovery Room doors. He pulled at them, but they were locked. Vester immediately reached into his pocket and grabbed his flame. The small fire elongated and rounded into a recognizable shape: a fire axe. Vester swung it expertly in a great sideways arc that bit deep into the locked door before him. Another swing, and the door splintered into two large, smoking pieces.

Vester collapsed the fire axe like a telescope between his two hands, and put the fire back into his pocket again. Then he ran into the room, Billy and Tempus close behind.

Fulgora was there, still unconscious, laying on a white bed in the middle of the room. No one else was with her; apparently anyone tending her had not felt bound by any kind of doctor-patient loyalty and had fled before Billy and his two friends arrived.

Vester gathered Fulgora tenderly into his strong arms, holding her tight against his chest. One of the fireman's hands, Billy saw, was now also clutching something tightly, though Billy couldn't see what. Then the fireman opened his fist, and Billy saw what he had been holding: a small glass marble, the kind Billy had played with when younger. It was bright red, with a streak of orange in its center.

"Ready?" asked Vester.

Tempus nodded. Vester looked at Billy. "I don't have to tell you, do I?"

"Hold my breath," Billy said dutifully.

Vester nodded, then maneuvered the marble between his thumb and forefinger. With a flick of his thumb, he tossed the marble into the air. It flew in a straight line for about two feet, then disappeared in midair with a tiny flash of light.

Then....

Nothing happened.

"Well?" said Tempus.

Vester grimaced. "I'm no Artetha."

"You made the key yourself?" Tempus said incredulously.

Vester looked almost embarrassed—no mean feat with all the destruction going on within mere feet of them. "I like to make stuff," he said.

"Stuff that doesn't work!" roared Tempus.

"Just give it a second," said Vester. Sure enough, as soon as he said that, a shimmering circle of flame about seven feet in diameter sprouted into life at the same spot the marble had disappeared. Vester looked triumphantly at Tempus. "See?" he said.

"Next time we use a professionally made key," said Tempus. He stepped toward the fire-ringed Transport door. Then he paused. "Where are we going?"

Billy had wanted to know the same thing, but had been too worried about everything going on around them to ask.

"Someplace safe," said Vester. That reassured Billy. Then Vester added, "I hope." That did *not* reassure Billy.

But then a new round of screaming and thuds started filtering into the Recovery Room. A zombie peered in through the ruined door, and spotted them. It immediately started moving forward, its huge eyes leering evilly at them.

"Last one in's a rotten egg!" shouted Tempus. He ran through the fire door and disappeared with a flash of color only slightly more vivid than his Hawaiian shirt and pink shorts.

"Go!" shouted Vester, shoving Billy at the door and then jumping simultaneously through as well, still holding Fulgora tightly to him. Billy held his breath, and jumped.

The first thing he was aware of upon landing wherever it was he had landed was that it was somewhere very, very hot. As usual when Transporting, Billy had been blinded by the light that always accompanied the move, so he had his eyes scrunched tightly shut. The wave of heat that hit him felt like he was inside an oven, about to be broiled at around six hundred degrees.

Then Billy opened his eyes, and realized that he had no such luck: he wasn't in an oven. He looked around, proud of himself for not screaming inadvertently at what he saw. But no matter how much he craned his neck to the left or right, there was no denying where he now found himself.

He was standing on a rocky ledge.

And the ledge was on the inside wall of an active volcano.

As it had done the last time he left Powers Island, Billy's "Billy—unDetermined" badge disappeared with a puff of smoke and a sizzle of flame. But Billy hardly noticed the noise, since it was drowned out by the far greater sound of the volcano. Everything seemed to be crackling with heat, and far below the narrow ledge on which they stood, magma bubbled and burbled like thick red soup in a huge deadly bowl.

"Why is it always a volcano or a blizzard? Just once I'd like to be transported into a room made completely of pillows, or maybe a planet whose only inhabitants are giant ice cream sundaes with sprinkles," Tempus was saying to no one in particular, even as Billy and Vester were just stepping through the doorway. Billy looked behind him and saw that the fire ring through which they had stepped was shrinking, now only half the size it had been when they stepped through.

And suddenly, he also saw a hand, mottled green and gray, that gripped the side of the fire. There was a sizzling sound as flesh burned, but the hand just clung all the tighter, physically pulling the ring of fire wider, wider.

Wide enough to let the zombie that had seen them in the Recovery Room at Powers Stadium step through. As soon as it was through, the fiery doorway disappeared behind it with a snap. Billy, Vester, Tempus, and the unconscious Fulgora were now trapped on the ledge with the creature.

Tempus yelled incoherently. He then followed that up with "Zombie!" As though anyone on the ledge needed that pointed out to them.

The creature looked around with its two huge eyes, a bit disoriented. Then it zeroed in on Billy and started toward him. As before, it moved purposefully, though Billy did notice that it had a tendency to stumble occasionally, as though not fully in control of its own muscles.

Billy backpedaled frantically, looking for some avenue of escape. But he was already backed up to the edge of the ledge. Below him, the lava burbled hungrily. Billy didn't know what would be worse, falling into lava or being touched by a zombie, but he hated the fact that he had to think about such things. He longed suddenly for the days when his worst fears involved being whether he would be put in a locker or have a spit wad blown at him through a straw.

The zombie was close now. Tempus and Vester were screaming at one another to do something.

"Make fire!" shouted Tempus.

"My hands are full!" responded Vester. "Make wind!"

"If I blow the zombie away, I might blow Billy right off the edge!" Tempus screamed back.

The zombie was within feet of Billy now, still lurching forward. It reached out a disgusting finger. Billy saw that the creature's nails were discolored and rotting, as were the monster's teeth, which Billy saw far too clearly as it grinned an evilly triumphant grin.

The finger was inches away. This was it. Billy closed his eyes and did his best to prepare for whatever was about to happen. He thought of Blythe, and for once the thought did nothing to make him feel better. He was about to die in a volcano, touched by a zombie. Things couldn't get much worse.

Then there was a shuffling, slithering noise to Billy's right. He mentally yelled at himself for thinking that things couldn't get much worse. That was just asking for it.

And sure enough, things were, in fact, looking even worse now. Because there was something hideous growing out of the bare rock right next to Billy. It was awful enough that even the zombie paused, looking at the fearful monstrosity that swelled to huge proportions beside Billy in a matter of seconds.

Billy couldn't really tell what it was, but it reminded him more than anything of a Venus flytrap. Only this one was about twenty feet tall, and its green-toothed mouth was six feet or more across. The plant hissed, and its mouth swiveled blindly toward Billy.

Sure, thought Billy. It wasn't enough that I was going to either be boiled in lava or knocked out by a zombie. Now I also get to choose Door Number Three: a painful death by plant-eating!

The zombie was still smiling widely, its eyes dead and black, its dark, rotting tongue licking its lips in anticipation of coming mayhem.

The smile disappeared less than a second later. In fact, the entire *zombie* disappeared. Because the giant flytrap suddenly snapped forward, not toward Billy, but toward the zombie. The zombie had a single instant in which it screamed, a thin high-pitched wheeze of a scream that came from deep within its rotten lungs. Then the scream cut off as the flytrap snapped shut around it.

The flytrap straightened up to its full height, the mouth at the apex, and chomped once. Billy had never been very fond of people who chewed with their mouths open. But he determined at that moment that he would rather sit in a room with a thousand open-mouthed food chewers than listen to the sound of a giant Venus flytrap chomping on a zombie ever again.

The flytrap chomped once more, then something strange happened. The plant heaved and bucked, and its entire body shivered. The plant's body turned gray, as though it had aged a thousand years in one instant. It withered and wilted. And as it did, Billy saw why. The zombie's fingers curled around the edges of the flytrap's mouth, forcing the plant open. Apparently the zombie's touch worked on plants as well as people, and the Venus flytrap was now as immobile—and perhaps dead—as had been those in Powers Stadium who were unfortunate enough to be touched by one of the zombies.

The zombie in the flytrap's mouth had been partially crushed, but didn't appear to mind. It glared down at Billy, looking angrier now than it had before, as the flytrap's mouth slowly lowered toward Billy.

Billy reacted instinctively, not really meaning to do what he did. But suddenly he found himself at the base of the flytrap, his arms around the plant's vine-like trunk, pushing as hard as he could. The zombie, seeing what Billy was trying to do, screamed its horrid scream again. It pushed even harder against the mouth of the flytrap, trying to force it open far enough that the zombie would be able to jump out.

It almost made it. But the second before the creature could get itself untangled from the immobilized plant's toothy grip, Billy heard a wonderful sound: the sound of tearing roots.

The flytrap lurched slowly to one side. Billy redoubled his efforts, pushing even harder. All the time spent trying to get out of lockers had thankfully built up his pushing muscles, so with a last ugly ripping, the flytrap slowly toppled over the side of the ledge, the zombie still in the huge plant's mouth.

Together the two monsters plummeted downward, and at last fell into the lava below. They disappeared with a hiss and a gout of flame. Billy breathed a sign of relief. Then he turned to look at Vester and Tempus, who were looking at him with a mixture of shock and relief.

"Well," Tempus finally managed, "*that* was a stroke of luck."

That comment, delivered in Tempus's typically scatter-brained tone, made Billy want to laugh. But before he could, the edge of the ledge that he was standing on suddenly started to crumble below his feet, no doubt weakened by the roots of the Venus flytrap, and still further weakened by the action of the plant and the zombie being ripped out of it by Billy's desperate pushing.

Billy wheeled his arms around in huge circles, his feet suddenly standing on ground that had the consistency of a waterfall. He scrabbled to stay on top of the ledge, but then the entire section he stood on fell away, dragging Billy down with it. Billy screamed, but there was nothing he could do. He was falling, falling, falling. Doomed to be burned alive in the lava.

Then, suddenly, Billy felt something grab his feet. In the next instant he found himself strangely indignant, his fear suddenly elbowed aside by anger. What? he thought. It's not enough for me to get almost crushed, zombie-touched, plant-eaten, zombie-touched again, then fall into lava? Something *else* has to happen, too?

He looked down at his feet, then, and saw something thick and green winding serpent-like around them. That was what he was feeling. But before he had a chance to figure out what the green stuff was, his downward fall was jerked to a stop. Billy felt his feet slam out from under him, and felt the green stuff tighten around them. He screamed as he resumed falling again, then screamed even harder when he bounced upward, feet first, then bounced back down, then back up, like he was being suspended over the lava pit on a rubber band or a bungee cord.

So now, on top of almost dying at least twenty different ways in the last minute or so, Billy was also in danger of losing what little he had in his stomach.

Slowly, however, the bouncing came to a halt. Billy was now hanging head-down, his feet held tightly by the thick green substance that had wrapped itself around them. He looked down (or, rather, he looked toward his feet, which was, in fact, up) and saw that the stuff around his feet was some kind of huge, elastic vine that went up to the side of the ledge.

Billy felt a jerk, and the vine started to pull itself—and Billy—upward. It reeled itself into the face of the volcano ledge like a fishing line. Finally, Billy felt his feet grabbed by a pair of strong hands. He was pulled up over the side of the ledge, and saw Tempus smiling at him as the old man hauled Billy to safety.

"Like I said," said Tempus with a wink and a smile. "*That* was lucky."

"Lucky nothing," said another voice. "That was extremely difficult."

Billy looked toward the sound of the voice, and smiled. "Ivy!" he shouted happily.

Sure enough, it was the Green Power, the chubby young/old woman who had been there at his Gleaning! She smiled wearily back at him, her hand clutching tightly to one end of a vine that looked an awful lot like the one that had just saved Billy from being fricasseed. The vine pulled up and wrapped itself around her, joining with the rest of the foliage that cloaked her.

"Where did you come from?" asked Billy.

"I showed up at the same time you guys did," said Ivy. "No one noticed me, though. Not surprising, what with the zombie appearing."

She weaved suddenly, as though about to topple over. Tempus moved quickly, the old man putting a steadying arm around her waist and helping her to the ground.

"Thanks," said Ivy gratefully. "The zombie's effect on my plant, and then my plant's death in the lava…." Her voice trailed off, showing clearly how exhausted and weak the Green Power was.

"Thanks," said Billy. "Thank you so much. I would have… well…you know."

Ivy smiled, still exhausted, but obviously trying not to let it show. The spells she had cast to save Billy's life must have taken nearly everything out of her.

"How did you know to come here?" asked Tempus.

"Vester showed me this place years ago," she said. "He told me to come here if there was ever...."

"A war," said Vester, completing her thought. Billy looked over at the fireman. Billy's friend was finally stooping to put the still-unconscious Fulgora down. Vester glanced at Ivy as he did so. "Still think I was being silly?"

"War?" asked Tempus. "Whatever do you mean?"

"Isn't it obvious?" said Vester. "That little explosion in the stadium was a signal. All the Darksiders on Powers Island disappeared at that instant, so that they could launch an attack on the Dawnwalkers." His voice was bitter, the loss of Vester's father years before clearly coming to the surface again. The fireman looked at Tempus. "I scoped out this hiding place years ago, just in case I needed it." He grimaced. "I hate being right sometimes."

"I know the feeling," said Tempus. The old Gray Power grew suddenly wistful. "One time, I bet my friend Typhoon—that wasn't really his name, just a nickname. I forget what his real name was. Anyway, I bet him that I could hold my breath for over a minute with my head immersed in a giant barrel of pickle juice. Of course, that was before *everyone* was doing it, and Typhoon—John! That was his real name...."

Tempus's voice suddenly dropped off as he realized that everyone was looking at him. He shrugged, embarrassed. "Sorry," he murmured. "Nervous rambling." Tempus looked at Ivy. "Where did you come from?" he asked.

"The top of the tower," she answered, laying her head back against an outcropping of rock, using it as something of a pillow. Vines snaked out from her outfit to cover the rock, making it more comfortable for her. "The council was meeting when it happened."

"When *what* happened?" demanded Vester in a tone that scared Billy more than a little. As though it could sense Vester's rage, the volcano they were in rumbled, and a spurt of lava jumped twenty feet up from the steaming pool of magma below the ledge. Billy unconsciously moved farther away from the edge of the ledge.

Ivy looked almost sick, as though she couldn't bear to say what had to be said. But finally she pushed the words out. "It was Wolfen," she finally managed with a dead-sounding voice. "He appeared on the Diamond Dais while the Council was meeting. They were talking about you," she said, nodding at Billy. She broke off from her train of thought. "Is it really true that you were rescued by a Unicorn?"

Billy nodded, and Tempus started visibly. "A *Unicorn*?" He harrumphed. "Impossible. They're imaginary."

"Apparently not," said Ivy.

"They are, I tell you," insisted Tempus.

"Tempus," said Vester warningly, and the Gray Power went silent. Vester touched Fulgora's forehead. "It's cool," he said to himself. Then he looked at Ivy. "What happened when Wolfen appeared?" he asked, his tone almost angry.

"He demanded that the Council abdicate and turn over the ruling of all Powers to him," said Ivy.

"Ridiculous!" bellowed Tempus. He looked like he would say more, but another near-murderous look from Vester silenced the older man.

Billy felt deeply afraid. He didn't know Wolfen, but he knew he'd felt odd at meeting him atop the tower, and knew that his friends hated and feared the man. So the fact that he was demanding control over all the Powers couldn't mean anything good.

"But, how is it possible?" asked Tempus in a quiet voice. "He swore fealty to the Council. He promised he had not broken the Truce, or done anything in contravention of the laws of his Exile. He promised, right there on the Diamond Dais, and the Diamond Dais turned green! The sure sign that he was telling the truth."

"I don't know how he did it," said Ivy wearily. She sounded like the weight of the world was on her shoulders. Billy went to her and sat beside the rock she was laying on. He didn't know what else he could do, but sensed she was appreciative of his gesture of support, however small it was. "I only know what I saw," she continued. She shuddered. "Wolfen appeared, and demanded the Council abdicate, and they refused. It was only a partial Council. Just my father, and Lumilla the Brown, and Dismus the Gray."

"So Eva Black and Nehara the Blue Councilor were conveniently absent when everything went crazy," said Vester.

"And what made the tower crack?" asked Tempus.

Ivy paled visibly. "Wolfen went insane with fury when the Council refused his demands. And all of a sudden there were explosions, and fire raining down, and the tower started to break apart right there. Dozens of zombies appeared out of nowhere, and started ransacking whatever they could."

"Then he's broken the Truce," whispered Tempus, as though trying to convince himself that it had actually happened.

"Not just that," said Vester stridently. "He's started a war."

"Let's not be hasty," said Tempus, but his heart clearly wasn't in his protestation.

"I'm not being hasty. The Darksiders all disappeared, the Dawnwalkers were attacked, and Wolfen was behind it all. War has come upon us again. Whether we like it or not."

"Oh, Vester," said Ivy, and Billy could suddenly see tears in her eyes. "It's much worse than that."

All eyes on the ledge swiveled to face her. Ivy was drooping, looking as wilted as one of her plants. She turned a dull gaze to Billy. "Zombies were *everywhere*."

Billy just looked at her. He didn't understand.

Great tears dripped from her eyes now, and Billy could see that they were green. They trailed down Ivy's cheeks and the plants that she wore reached up to wipe them away. "The zombies," she said. "There were too many of them. I got away, because they weren't interested in me. But," she gulped, fighting to get the words out. They wouldn't come.

Tempus patted her on the head, smoothing her vine-laced hair. "It's all right," he whispered. "It's all right, my dear. Take your time."

Ivy paused for a long second. She closed her eyes, obviously struggling for composure. Then she opened them again. "The zombies... they touched the Council."

She looked at the group, ending with her eyes on Billy. "Dismus, the Gray Councilor, was touched first. My father tried to stop them, but there were too many of them." Her voice choked off again, before she managed, "My father, and Lumilla—"

"What's happened to Mrs. Russet?" asked Billy, dread sinking icy tentacles into his spine.

Ivy gulped. She sat up straighter, and had to take a deep breath before she managed to say the last thing, the worst thing, the most terrible sentence that Billy had ever heard in his life.

"The zombies got them. They're gone."

# CHAPTER THE THIRTEENTH

*In Which Billy begins a Quest, and must go back to the Beginning...*

"What do you mean, they're gone?" squeaked Billy. "Like, 'I've gone to the supermarket' kind of gone?"

Ivy's eyes were closing as she struggled to stay awake. Billy remembered what Vester had told him at the Challenge: that it took tremendous effort to increase the size and strength of an Element. And here Ivy, in short measure, had Transported herself, then used her energies to make two huge plants to rescue Billy from a zombie and then from becoming a French-fried Billy in a lava pit. She must be exhausted, on the verge of collapse.

Still, Billy had to know what Ivy had been talking about. "Ivy," he said loudly. "What do you mean 'gone'?!"

But it was no use. Ivy's eyes closed. Billy shook her gently, then a bit harder. He would have shaken her even harder—say, hard enough to make her head pop off—had it not been for Tempus's hands, softly prying Billy away from the unconscious Life Power's form.

"Easy there, my boy," soothed Tempus. "I'm sure she meant something more than 'gone to the supermarket' gone, but less than 'gone to Heaven' gone. Lumilla and Veric and Dismus are all extremely tough. You don't get to be a Councilor without being tough. And tough Councilors are very hard to kill, or even hurt."

"But...." Billy searched for words that would ease his fear. None came to him. Nothing could have happened to Mrs. Russet! He knew he should also be concerned for Ivy's father, Veric, the Green Life Councilor; and for Dismus, the Gray Wind Councilor. But all he could think of was Mrs. Russet, his teacher. He pictured her crossed arms, scolding the entire history class for not being able to tell her King Tut's favorite color, and strangely the image made him smile a bit. Surely such a fearsome human being as a high school teacher couldn't be harmed by anything less than a nuclear missile with a Kryptonite tip.

He looked at the side of their ledge, the raggedy edge marking where part of their resting spot had disintegrated and nearly dropped Billy to his death.

"What's a zombie?" he asked, searching for some way to change the subject. He had to distract himself until Ivy woke and could give them more information, he knew, or he would go crazy with worry.

Vester, standing nearby, gave an involuntary shudder at Billy's question. "A zombie is a Power that has been taken over by another Power."

"Like they're possessed or something?" asked Billy. Once again, he was venturing into that huge area he was starting to think of as Stuff-I-Don't-Know-Land.

"Or something," said Vester. "Zombies are created when a Black Power—a Death Power—uses its Element to invade another Power's body."

"You mean," Billy gulped, "when a Black Power kills them?"

"Not just that," said Vester. "Some of the most powerful Death Powers can actually hold back—or even reverse—the onset of Death. So you become," Vester's eyebrows came together as he tried to find the right words. "Dead, but not dead. Dead but still moving."

Billy didn't understand. How could a person be dead but still moving?

His face must have shown his confusion, because Tempus went into lecture mode again. He started absent-mindedly smoothing at his Hawaiian shirt, and again Billy was for a moment distracted by the moving landscape on the shirt, the magic that animated it both fascinating him and making him wonder what kind of person would want to make the tacky things in the first place.

"Zombies are dead Powers," said Tempus. "They were outlawed under the terms of the Truce, years ago." His face got that faraway look in his eyes. "Some of the Black Powers discovered that they could use the dead like some of us use magical keys. The Black Powers could actually put a portion of their essence into a dead body—"

"You mean Imbue them?" asked Billy. He remembered that Mrs. Russet had said that about her beehive key, that it was an Imbued Object, which a Power had put some of her essence into to make it able to do magic.

"Exactly, exactly," said Tempus. "Quite so, quite so." Billy almost smiled. Tempus's airily scatter-brained tendencies were already as much a part of Billy's life, it seemed, as putting on clean underwear every morning. "But Imbuing isn't just a process of making something magical, it's actually putting the spell-caster's *power* into the object. Some Powers, like a Power named Artetha, for instance, have great talent at Imbuing keys. Artetha made Lumilla's—Mrs. Russet's—beehive key. You see, Artetha is a very strong Power of Fire, and she can travel with the speed of light, breaking through time and space in an instant. So when we say she is Imbuing a key, what we really mean is that she is putting a small piece of her*self* into the key, and thus gives that key the power to help others travel as she can."

"So Mrs. Russet couldn't do a Transport spell without her beehive key?" asked Billy.

"Oh, she could," said Vester. "But it would be much harder, and using an Imbued key doesn't sap her energy at all. Better all around to use a key. Plus, using an Imbued key means that if she arrives into the middle of difficulty—a magical battle, for example—then she's at full strength. Plus," he added, looking darkly at Vester, "when you do a Transport spell on your own, or using your own *unprofessionally crafted* key—or marble—you might find yourself with a misfire. So you could land in the wrong place, or not go fast enough, or get touched by a zombie." He said this last very pointedly, clearly still upset by the marble debacle. Vester apparently didn't notice, however, since he was now sitting by Fulgora, tenderly cradling the unconscious Red Lady's head in his lap.

"So the zombies are Imbued," prompted Billy after a moment.

Tempus returned his gaze to Billy. "Yes, yes, they're essentially Imbued Objects. Like the keys, they are Imbued with some of their maker. Therefore, logically, if the maker of something is a Death Power, then what you get is something that carries death in its very touch."

"Then that means...." Billy couldn't finish his thought for a moment. It was just too fearful. Ivy had said that the zombies had touched Mrs. Russet. So the thing Billy said next was the easy conclusion to that line of thought: "Mrs. Russet—and all the other Powers in the stadium who were touched—they're...they're...*dead*? Like Ivy's plant?" he added, thinking of the huge flytrap that had wilted upon eating the zombie.

Tempus frowned and chewed his lip thoughtfully. "Not necessarily," he said at last. "Most Imbued Objects don't have the full strength of their makers. So most zombies can't kill with their touch. They're more likely to induce paralysis or a coma or mere unconsciousness. Though some, more powerfully Imbued," he continued unhappily, "could conceivably cause death."

"Then, we don't know what happened to Mrs. Russet. Or Veric the Green, or, or...."

"Dismus," prompted Tempus. "Dismus the Gray Councilor. No, we don't know what happened to them. We only know what Ivy said before she had to recuperate her strength." He smiled, a clearly faked grin that Billy knew was solely for his benefit. "But, as I've said, Lumilla and the others are tough, so I wouldn't worry yourself overmuch, at least not now."

"Why would anyone even want to make something as horrible as a zombie?" asked Billy.

"Well, for one thing," answered Tempus, "they make excellent manual workers for certain jobs. Not for everything, mind you. You wouldn't want a zombie babysitter, for instance, or a zombie gardener. Not unless you like dead and rotting tomatoes—which aren't as bad as they sound, by the way. This one time, I was at a very popular little restaurant on Powers Island, a nice old place called GreenPower Inn...."

His voice drifted off as a moan sounded nearby. Both Billy and Tempus looked over and saw that it was Fulgora. She moaned again, twitched, then fell silent once more. Vester, still holding her head in his lap, felt her pulse, then put his hand on her forehead. "I think she's coming out of it," he said. But to Billy's ears, the statement sounded like it was more hopeful than realistic.

"As I was saying," Tempus finally said. "Zombies are wonderful at certain things. Harvesting diamonds, for instance, or digging ditches. Some of them have even served as legislators, though not as often as you'd think." He smiled, probably remembering some rambling anecdote about a zombie mayor or something. Billy was glad not to hear the whole story, however. He was more interested in the details of what made a zombie, because he suspected that he would be seeing more of them.

"So zombies are slaves," he said.

"Correct," replied Vester. "Very good, my boy. We'll make a Power out of you yet," he said, clapping Billy on the shoulder. "Yes, they're slaves. But they're also the bodies of the dead, so you have two very disturbing things: one, that someone wants a slave. After all, if you want a slave to mine your diamonds, then you're probably going to end up wanting a slave to tend your garden, and that a zombie cannot do. So...."

"So you're going to try to make slaves out of non-zombies—er, people," said Billy.

"Yes," agreed Tempus. "And the second disturbing thing about zombies is that the bodies of dead Powers are used to make them.

Throughout recorded history, one of the things that has been seen as an abomination to all people everywhere has been the desecration of the remains of those who have gone before."

"It's a disgusting practice," said a weak voice.

Billy jumped, then said, "Ivy! You're awake!"

Ivy grimaced at Billy's shout. She looked like she had a serious headache. "Zombies are an affront to Life," she said, her hands pressing at her temples. Then, slowly, with Tempus's and Billy's aid, she sat up. She looked at Fulgora. "How is she?" she asked. Before waiting for an answer, one of Ivy's clothing-vines snaked toward Fulgora, touching the Red Lady's cheek. "She'll live," said Ivy confidently.

Vester looked extremely relieved at this news. "Can you tell us any more?" he said to Ivy. "About what happened at the tower?"

Ivy shook her head. "Not much. The zombies touched the Councilors, and I saw a few of the creatures put objects—they must have been Transport keys—on Lumilla and Tempus and my Father."

"How do you know they were Transport keys?" asked Tempus.

"Because the Councilors all disappeared," snapped Ivy. "And I'd prefer to think they were Transported, instead of just disintegrated or some such."

"Prisoners of war," said Vester quietly. Everyone looked at him.

"Vester," Ivy began warningly. But Tempus silenced her with an upraised hand, the old man's usually jolly face unusually somber.

"Ivy," he said. "I know you don't want it to be so. The Life Powers are—happily—eternally optimistic about others' motives. But there aren't enough Black Powers in the world to have created so many zombies, unless they've been planning this for some time. And the Darksiders *did* all disappear. And you yourself saw Wolfen on the tower."

"But the Diamond Dais, like you said, it was green. Wolfen wasn't lying when he swore fealty, when he promised he hadn't broken the terms of his Exile," said Ivy.

"I know how it looked, my dear. But if anyone could fool the Diamond Dais, it would have to be Wolfen, that craftiest of Powers." Tempus looked at Vester. "I believe you were right, my fiery friend. We're at war." He sighed, and smoothed his shirt again. "And Lumilla and the others are likely prisoners."

Billy, in a sudden flash of insight, remembered the scars, those terrible glowing scars on Tempus's stomach. From the last War of the Powers. He suddenly realized that on those occasions that Tempus had rubbed at his stomach, the old man wasn't habitually smoothing his shirt, he was feeling his *scars*. Billy trembled at the thought of his good friend undergoing the horrible tortures that would leave such vivid reminders after so many years.

"Then what do we do?" asked Ivy in a small voice.

"We burn everything."

Billy turned. He half-expected Vester to have said something like this a while ago, but the voice he heard wasn't Vester's.

"Fulgora!" said the fireman, tenderly helping the woozy Red Lady to her feet. "We were so worried," he managed to say, his voice almost choked with emotion.

Fulgora looked around her. "Chikurachki?" she asked Vester.

"What's Chikurachki?" blurted Billy. "Some kind of spell?"

Fulgora looked vaguely amused and more than a little irritated, as though the young Power was not used to people speaking unless she had specifically invited them to do so. "It's the name of this volcano," answered Vester. "It's in Russia."

Billy was almost disappointed by that answer. He had though "Chikurachki" must be a spell name or a code word or something. But no, just a volcano.

"Good job," said Fulgora. "Uhhh...," she continued, looking at Vester. Billy saw the fireman's shoulders slump, and realized with horror that the Red Councilor didn't even know his friend's name!

"It's Vester," said Billy, almost shouting the words. Then he added just as fervently, "And he saved your life!"

"Really?" asked the Red Lady in a tone that scorched Billy's ears. But she looked at Vester with something like interest in her eyes. "And how did you save me?" she asked amusedly.

"Um, well," said Vester. Billy was somewhat disheartened to see that Vester talked to Fulgora almost exactly the same way that Billy talked to Blythe. Both he and the firemen sounded like cavemen that had been run over by woolly mammoths one too many times. Billy had thought he would surely grow out of that kind of reaction to girls. So the fact that the very brave and clearly strong and smart fireman couldn't put a sentence together in front of his true love was fairly depressing.

"What do you remember?" asked Tempus, the Gray Power jumping to his friend's aid.

Fulgora's eyes narrowed. "I remember that horse's behind Napalm Challenging me. And I remember that he ringed me with fire. And then...." She struggled to remember more, then at last shrugged her lovely shoulders. "Nothing."

"My dear," said Tempus. "You became a dragon."

Fulgora laughed, a deep, throaty laugh that seemed even to Billy like the promise of a beautiful tomorrow. And if it affected *him* like that, couldn't imagine how such a laugh would affect Vester. He sneaked a glance at his friend. Sure enough, Vester looked like he was about to go into a happiness-induced coma.

"Don't be ridiculous," said the Red Lady. "No one has ever become a dragon and then come back."

"You did," blurted Vester. Fulgora looked at him sharply. Vester looked down, apparently suddenly discovering something incredibly fascinating about his shoes. "My Lady," he added.

"Indeed," said Tempus. "You won the Challenge, but were unconscious. So when the zombies attacked—"

"Zombies?" said Fulgora in a near shout. "Zombies attacked?"

"Yes, dear," said Tempus patiently. "I thought you heard us talking about that, and that's why you said 'We burn everything' when you awoke."

"Oh, that," said Fulgora dismissively. "I say that all the time when I wake up. I just like the sound of it." She focused an intense look on Tempus. "So what's this about zombies?"

"There was an attack," said Tempus haltingly, even the old Gray Power apparently not completely immune to Fulgora's charms. "Zombies—we think led by Darksiders—came into the stadium and attacked."

"How do you know it was the Darksiders behind it?" demanded the Red Lady.

"Well," answered Ivy, slowly rising to her feet, "aside from the fact that only Death Powers can make a zombie, and most of them are Darksiders, the fact is that zombies also attacked the Council at the same time, and carried away all the Dawnwalkers."

"Impossible," scoffed Fulgora.

"Not impossible," insisted Tempus. "It happened, as sure as the wind on my face. And Vester," he added, pointing at the fireman, who was still examining his feet like the secrets of the universe were written on his sneakers, "risked his own life to save you from the undead creatures."

Fulgora looked at Vester with a new look on her face. Not appreciation, exactly, but Billy thought she looked interested in hearing more of Vester's part in her rescue. But she didn't ask any further questions. Instead, she murmured, "I must find out more."

And with that, she suddenly strode to the edge of the ledge and jumped off.

Billy heard himself holler and lunge forward in a vain attempt to stop Fulgora's suicidal leap. He missed, though, and saw her plunge downward, hitting the lava below and disappearing instantly.

He lost his balance then, and might have followed her right off the edge, had Vester not snatched him back.

"She's all right," said the fireman. "She's a Red Power. The lava won't hurt her. She's probably Cresting." Then, off Billy's confused look, he explained, "It's a spell that some Reds can do. Riding the fires that heat the earth. She'll pop out in some other volcano, or a hot spring somewhere."

"But," stuttered Billy, "she didn't even *thank* you."

Vester shrugged. "She's a Councilor, and perhaps one of the most powerful Reds ever. Why would she even talk to me?"

Billy suddenly knew what he looked like to other people, hopeless and wallowing in self-pity, however well-warranted it might be. He didn't like it. "Hey," he said to Vester. "You were looking down so you didn't see, but," he winked, "she almost smiled at you."

"Really?" asked Vester, for all the world looking like he was Billy's age again. Then his shoulders drooped. "Well, that's probably because she remembers seeing me in school."

"You went to school with her?" asked Billy, incredulous.

Vester nodded. "Yeah, we were both in college together. I knew she was on the fast track to become the Red Councilor even then. She was in my biology class with me." He grimaced. "I didn't get very good grades; was always the one who kept everyone after class because I had about a thousand questions about the things I hadn't understood about the teacher's lecture."

Billy knew what *that* was like. Occasionally he had made his own elementary school class late for recess when he'd had a last minute question or two. Facing thirty kids who hated your guts for making them lose the prime spots in the line for the swings or the slides was worse than facing a firing squad.

"Well," said Billy, still trying to console his friend. "You saved her, and that's the truth. She's bound to remember that even more than biology class."

Vester shrugged.

"I hate to interrupt this little 'chin-up' session," said Tempus after a moment. "But I *do* want to point out that we are currently hiding in a volcano without any kind of plan for the future."

"I like the idea of hiding," said Billy. And he did. Hanging on a precipice hundreds of feet over boiling lava was a huge improvement in his eyes over being chased by zombies, though he wasn't sure whether he liked it better than being chased by murderous giant rock scorpions in space. He decided he'd have to call that one a tie.

"Actually," said Ivy brightly, "we *do* have a plan."

"Really, young lady?" asked Tempus.

"What plan?" said Vester, always more to the point than the Gray Power was.

Ivy's brightness dimmed almost instantly. "I'm not sure."

"So," said Tempus slowly, "we *do* have a plan, but we're not sure what it is." Ivy nodded. "I'm afraid I don't see the difference between that and not having a plan at all," said Tempus.

Billy agreed. Wasn't a plan something you knew you were going to do—or at least something you knew you were going to try? How could they have a plan and not know what it was?

"Let me explain," said Ivy.

"Please do," answered Vester. There was a burble nearby, and a small pocket of lava popped open in the wall near to the precipice. Vester absent-mindedly walked over and put his hand in the flowing lava, looking like he was as refreshed by that as most people would be by putting their feet up and enjoying a cold drink.

"On the tower, right before Lumilla was, well, touched," said Ivy, "she managed to say something."

"Was it 'Argh, I'm about to be zombified'?" asked Tempus.

"No, but that would have made more sense," said Ivy. "What she said was, 'Tell Billy—'"

"Tell *me*?" asked Billy incredulously. "Tell me what?"

"Well, I'm going to tell you if you'll let me," said Ivy. "She said, 'Tell Billy to go to where you're empty when you should be full, and say the words you've heard me say to the jumper that never quite eats.'"

Everyone was silent for a moment.

Finally, Billy said. "Why would she tell you to tell me that?"

Ivy shrugged. "I don't know. Like I said, the words don't make any sense to me."

"No, not the words," Billy said. "I mean, why would she want to tell *me*?" Everyone looked at him blankly. "I'm just a kid. Not even a Determined Power, maybe not a Power at all. So why would Mrs. Russet bother telling you to give me a nonsense message right in the middle of a life and death struggle with the undead?"

"That is a good question," said Vester.

Tempus cleared his throat. "Yes, Tempus," said Ivy. "If you have something to say, just say it. Let's do away with the pauses while you wait for us to realize how smart you are, shall we?"

Tempus frowned good-naturedly. "I don't wait for you to realize that. I assume that you already know it. In any case," he continued, "I think that the reason she shouted the 'nonsense' is quite clear."

Everyone looked at him. Clearly it wasn't clear to anyone except him. Which, Billy realized, made some sense: nonsense might appear more sensible to someone who was so prone to speaking a great deal of nonsense himself.

"Don't you see?" asked Tempus. "She wants us to do something. Something important."

"So why not just tell us what that is?" asked Ivy.

"Code," murmured Vester.

Tempus nodded at the fireman. "You don't really remember the last war," he said to Ivy. "But there are certain things one doesn't do in such a conflict. Go trick-or-treating behind enemy lines, for instance, or shout 'Magical Bomb!' in a crowded theater on Powers Island. And one more thing you don't do is scream out 'Hey, there's something terribly important that needs doing, and here's what it is' while you're standing in the middle of the enemy's army." He smiled playfully. "It rather gives away one's plan of attack, wouldn't you agree?"

"So she gave Ivy a code? A clue of what we have to do?" asked Billy.

"Exactly, my boy," said Tempus.

"But why for me?" asked Billy.

Tempus shrugged his shoulders in an exaggerated gesture of ignorance. "Who knows? Perhaps because it was the only thing that came to mind. Maybe because she panicked. However," he said, looking piercingly at Billy, "I tend to think that it's because you are something very special."

"I'm not special," said Billy.

"Yes, you are," said Vester. "You had to be, or else Mrs. Russet wouldn't have risked her life for you." He pulled his hand from the lava where he had been holding it, and when he pulled out his hand he also pulled a long string of the molten stuff with it. In an instant, the string had turned into a small snake of lava, which coiled itself around Vester's wrist like a pet, a tongue of fire flicking out of its mouth. Billy was fascinated by the sight, but his eyes were drawn back to Vester's face when the fireman said, with strange intensity, "Do you remember what Ivy called Mrs. Russet when you were being Gleaned? When Eva Black was about to kill you to see if you Glimmered?"

Billy thought hard, but couldn't remember anything specific. He supposed that impending death might make a lot of people's memories a bit spotty. He shook his head.

"Ivy called her your Sponsor," said Vester. "Do you know what that means?"

"That Mrs. Russet was in charge of helping me with the tests to see if I'm a Power?" asked Billy.

"Yes, partly," nodded Vester. "But more than that, it meant that she was willing to protect you. A Gleaning is risky. Not everyone comes back. Some people die on the Gleaning table."

"But she said I'd be safe," said Billy, shocked.

"And she meant it," said Vester. "Because when she said she was your Sponsor, she was doing more than volunteering to be your teacher in the world of the Powers. She was saying that if you died and it didn't look like we could bring you back, she would have sacrificed her own life force and passed it to you so that you could live."

"You mean," Billy said, thunderstruck, "she could have died?"

Vester nodded. "She *would* have died. So you could live. And Mrs. Russet, as nice as she can be, doesn't go around volunteering to trade her life for just anyone. She clearly believes that you are important, Billy. That you have some critical part to play in the battle that we're now in. And I tend to agree with her. You've managed to wound a Black, you survived your first Test of Power, you have ridden a Unicorn. And since you came to Powers Island, there have been all manner of strange events."

"Like Fulgora turning into a dragon," said Tempus.

"Not to mention Wolfen showing up, and the war beginning," agreed Vester. "Billy, I think that you are at the center of all this. So Mrs. Russet's message to you was one that only you would understand, and whatever it means, we have to figure it out, and do it quick."

Billy felt like a three hundred pound barbell had just been placed on his shoulders. He had gone from being that kid that no one sat next to at lunch to being the center of a war in a world he still didn't understand.

Ivy seemed to intuit what Billy was feeling. She hugged him. "It's okay, Billy," she said. "We're here. We'll stick by you and help with whatever you need to do." The tendrils that encircled her arms reached out to Billy as well. It felt like he was being hugged and tickled at the same time. It was a nice feeling.

Billy squared his shoulders as well as he could. "What was it she said?" he asked.

"'Go to where you're empty when you should be full, and say the words you've heard me say to the jumper that never quite eats,'" recited Ivy.

They all looked at Billy. He thought. Nothing was coming to him. He thought some more. And even more nothing came to him.

"Go to where you're empty," he mumbled. "Empty, full, jumper." He rolled the words around in his mind. They felt like they should mean something.

And then, suddenly, his head popped up. He wouldn't have been surprised to see a giant light bulb flashing over him.

"What is it, my boy?" asked Tempus. "You know what she was saying?"

"Not all of it," grinned Billy. "But I think I know where we have to go."

"Then, by all means, let's go there," said the Gray Power. "Shall we go by Wind, or travel by Fire?"

"We can use my key," said Vester.

"Bah!" snorted Tempus. "Never again. No home-made Transport Keys for me. Especially not one you've made."

The two looked as though they were about to start bickering once more, but Ivy, ever the peacemaker, broke in. "Boys, boys!" she shouted. Tempus and Vester broke off long enough to look at her.

"Don't you think we should find out where we're going before we decide how we're going to get there?" she asked.

Both Vester and Tempus looked slightly embarrassed. "Quite so," said Tempus, and Vester nodded mute agreement.

Ivy turned to Billy.

"Well," she said, "it looks as though you are to be our guide on this quest. So where are we going?"

Billy grinned for a second, but then his grin faded. He *was* pretty sure where they had to go.

But he was also pretty sure he'd prefer to stay in the pit of a Russian volcano than go there.

# CHAPTER THE FOURTEENTH

*In Which Billy sees Justice Done, and then sees Himself...*

Once Billy had told them where he thought they should go, they decided to travel by Fire, which Vester told Billy was the fastest of the Elemental traveling methods. Though Tempus insisted that Wind was much more comfortable, even he agreed that speed probably counted more than anything in this case.

Billy was nervous, though. Holding hands with Vester, perched at the edge of a slim outcropping that was all that stood between him and a volcano's simmering stomach, he couldn't help but wonder what would happen if Vester's spell went wrong.

"Don't worry," murmured Vester. "As long as we're all holding hands, I can extend my protection to all of you. For a little while, at least."

Billy asked what "a little while" meant, but his words were not heard by the others, because at that moment Vester jumped, pulling Billy, Tempus, and Ivy with him in a human daisy chain, and Billy's words were lost far above them.

Down they plunged, down to the abyss of fire that had already nearly claimed Billy for its own today.

And here I go, jumping in on purpose this time, thought Billy.

He closed his eyes involuntarily. Vester had assured him it would be all right, and Billy believed his friend intellectually, but it was hard for his *body* to believe it wasn't about to be burned to a crisp. Billy felt his muscles clench involuntarily, and he bit his lip. He almost jerked his hand out of Vester's in mid-flight, but realized at the same instant how disastrous that would be, so instead he held the young fireman's hand even harder.

Billy and his friends hit, not with a splash, but with a thick wet burble. This, Billy had been told, was to be expected: after all, they were not jumping into a swimming pool, they were jumping into lava. But he was still surprised when he sank slowly into the lava, as though he was in quicksand, or had somehow fallen into the world's biggest pudding cup. It was hot, but not as hot as it should have been, more like standing under the sun on a summer day.

The four friends, still holding tightly to one another, slowly sank below the lava. And Billy, being shortest, was the first to go under.

As the gooey stuff hit his chin, he looked at Vester with sudden panic. "Do I hold my breath?" he asked. He didn't want to be a mummy. Or did you become a *burnt* mummy if you didn't hold your breath while traveling by fire—Cresting, as Vester had called it?

Vester smiled. "You can if you want to, but it's not a requirement."

"So I won't become a—blurble," said Billy. He said "blurble" because before he could finish his sentence, he sunk below the surface of the lava.

Afterward, if Billy had had to describe what happened to him, the best he could have done would be to say that he kept *hearing* the color red, and kept *seeing* what marshmallows smelled like when being toasted in a campfire. His insides turned out and his outsides turned in. He felt as though he was suddenly everywhere and nowhere at once, just as he imagined an enormous fire would feel: so huge it could devour a forest, yet at the same time so ghostly it couldn't be touched.

Billy felt himself become thin, thinner, thinner. So thin that soon he was only a single chain of atoms long enough to wrap around the world twice. But at the same time he was still aware of who he was, and that Vester was holding his hand.

The red sound grew louder, and suddenly Billy could see a blue pinpoint of light. The blue light grew, then multiplied into several lights, then those several blue lights became even more. They looked somehow familiar to Billy. But before he could figure out what they were, he suddenly found himself standing on solid ground again.

He was in a dark place. What little light there was came from the machine behind him. Billy could hear it whispering its ever-present drone in the background. It was a gas heater. The blue lights that Billy had seen were the brightly burning gas jets that heated the air that would warm the huge building they were in.

Vester, Ivy, and Tempus were there, too.

"Wow," said Ivy. "I'd forgotten what that was like."

Vester grinned at her, then smiled even wider at Billy. "How'd you like Cresting?" he asked.

"Great," said Billy. "It was perfect." And he meant it. Only the ride atop the Unicorn had even come close to what he'd just felt.

"Well," said Tempus, "I would hold off on calling it perfect until you have ridden the Winds. Cresting magma and then being thinned out like taffy and delivered through a gas jet is not my idea of 'perfect,' and that's a fact."

"Everyone likes different things," said Ivy, obviously trying to forestall another argument between the Red Power and the Gray.

Billy looked around. He didn't recognize where they were. He looked at Vester. "I thought you said you could get us there," he said.

"I did," replied the fireman. He stepped to a nearby door and opened it. "But I had to take us through a fire source, and the best one was in the gas jets in the heater in the main heating and air conditioning room."

Billy followed him through the door and quickly saw that Vester had been as good as his word. They were exactly where Billy thought they needed to go.

They were at Preston Hills High School.

He looked up and down the halls. No one was visible.

"Follow me," he hissed, and ran as fast as he could down the hall.

"Why are we here?" asked Ivy.

"I think this is what Mrs. Russet meant," said Billy, huffing with the effort of his run. "She said to go where I'm empty when I should be full. When all this started, when Mrs. Russet first took me to Powers Island, it was from here. It was right after lunch. I didn't eat much. Someone knocked over my lunch tray." He deliberately didn't mention that *he* had been the one to knock over the tray in a crazy attempt to call attention to the bullying Cameron Black had been involved in. That wasn't something he wanted to get into with these people who had somehow been deluded into thinking he was worth spending time with.

"So we're going to the cafeteria?" asked Ivy.

"Do they have those delicious ice cream sandwiches?" asked Tempus. "Or maybe even," he managed to lick his lips as he ran, "some yummy Salisbury steak?"

"No," said Billy.

"No Salisbury steak?" moaned Tempus.

"They have Salisbury steak here some days," Billy reassured his friend. "But we're not going to the cafeteria."

"Then where?" asked Vester.

Before Billy could answer, he stopped running as suddenly as if he'd slammed headfirst into a concrete wall. Just around the corner, he could see Harold Crane and Sarah Brookham, Cameron's assistants in the Torture Brigade. It wasn't that Billy was afraid they were going to stick him in a locker—he thought that was highly unlikely, given his present company. But they *would* see who he was with.

Billy glanced at his friends. Vester looked more or less normal. But Tempus, ablaze in the full-blown vomitous glory of his moving Hawaiian shirt and his pink too-short shorts, was sure to draw attention. Not to mention the young/old Ivy, with her wreathe of writhing plant life serving as her primary clothing. And it wasn't even that they were going to draw attention. But Billy had enough trouble in his life without having it get around that he was part of some strange carnival sideshow.

He backpedaled and motioned for the others to follow him, hoping that he could find an alternate route around the two bullies. Then his stomach lurched as he heard Harold's voice.

"Hey, nimwad." Billy wasn't facing him, but he knew that Harold was addressing him. Slowly, Billy turned back. Sure enough, Harold and Sarah were both looking at him and his friends. Both appeared on the verge of hysterical laughter; the two Torture Brigaders had clearly determined in an instant that these were grown-ups of a sort that they could get away with treating like they treated other kids: meanly.

"Finally running away to join the circus, eh?" asked Harold.

"Yeah," said Sarah. "Finally running away, huh?"

"I can see it now, Bumbling Billy and…uh…." Harold's voice drifted off. The bully clearly couldn't think of a good insult. This was no surprise, since Cameron had always been the brains of the group. And Sarah made Harold look like a NASA scientist in comparison. In fact, Billy was pretty sure that if the two pooled their brain cells, they would have almost mind power to win a tic-tac-toe match against a carrot. Almost.

Having thought of no way to finish his insult, Harold just sneered at Billy's friends. "So doofuses of a feather flock with each other, huh?"

"Yeah," said Sarah. Her jaws were, as always, engaged in an intense battle with a stick of chewing gum.

Billy didn't know how to get around this situation. But matters were taken out of his hands by Tempus, who stepped forward and stuck out his hand. "Friends of Billy's, I presume," he said with a smile.

Billy's eyes rolled in their sockets. Wonderful. As he had suspected, there was always a little farther down to go in the social pit that he was constantly digging for himself.

Harold looked at Tempus's hand like it was a crab's claw covered in snot. Then he laughed. "Dooooofuses!" he said in a singsong voice. Sarah laughed too, her beady little eyes perspiring with the effort of keeping up with Harold's comparatively witty banter.

"Doofus?" asked Tempus. "I must have been on Powers Island too long this time," he murmured. He looked at Billy. "Is doofus a good thing?"

"No," muttered Billy. "It's not."

Vester was gritting his teeth. The fireman started to move forward, but before he could, Tempus held out a hand and stopped him. "No, my friend, I think I can deal with this." He looked back at Harold. "I take it, since there are no other students in the hall, that class is now in session."

Harold took a moment to process that. "Yeah," he said. "What about it?"

"Well, why aren't you in class?" asked Tempus.

"Hah!" Sarah Brookham said. She almost lost her gum in the explosion of breath that passed for her laughter.

"I see," replied Tempus gravely, as though she had just quoted a lengthy scene from one of Shakespeare's more difficult plays. "I used to know some people like you two," he said. "Didn't like to learn, didn't want other people to be happy. No brains at all, just like you two."

"Hey!" said both Harold and Sarah at once. "Who says we got no brains?" continued Harold.

"Well, perhaps you do," conceded Tempus. "But you don't deserve them. So you know what I'm going to do?" He leaned in close to Harold and Sarah, and suddenly a strong wind whipped through the hall. "Since you don't deserve your brains, I think I'm going to blow your brains *out*."

And with that, he clapped his hands. A miniature storm erupted right over Harold and Sarah, complete with thunderclouds and rain. A fierce wind flung the two delinquents into the nearest wall, where they were pinned there by the mini-hurricane Tempus had conjured up, while Billy and his friends stood dry and happy only five feet away.

Within seconds, Harold and Sarah were wetter than any student they had ever dunked in a toilet. Both of them were crying, pleading, *begging* Tempus to stop whatever it was he was doing.

Billy thought it was, quite possibly, the most wonderfully delicious thing he had ever experienced in his entire life.

Tempus just smiled. He clapped his hands again, and the rain clouds disappeared. Now, a stinging Arctic wind blew against the two bullies. Billy could see them grow cold and blue, their clothing drying instantly in the gale winds. Billy thought he could see tiny icicles form in the bullies' clothes, and a few small ones hanging out of Harold's nose.

Another clap of Tempus's hands, and the wind stopped. Billy had a moment to notice—and relish—the fact that Tempus's wind had somehow dried Harold and Sarah completely, with one exception: both of them had large wet spots on their legs that made it look an awful lot like they had just wet their pants.

The two kids, no longer pinned to the wall by Tempus's magic, stared at the old man in horror. Finally, Tempus whispered, "Well, get to class."

Harold and Sarah bolted like rabbits with Taser guns attached to their tails, disappearing around the corner in an instant.

Tempus turned to Billy, a broad smile etched across his weathered old face. "I was never very popular in school," he said, as though in explanation.

Ivy sighed. "You should grow up, Tempus."

"I will when I'm a hundred," he said.

Vester was trying hard not to smile, clearly wanting to be a good role model. He looked at Billy. "Where exactly are we going?" he asked.

Billy pointed. The room was just down the hall, not twenty feet away. "Mrs. Russet's class," he said.

When they entered the classroom, it was empty, as Billy had expected. Mrs. Russet had brought him to Powers Island a long time ago, it seemed, but as before, no time had passed while they were on the island. They had been in the Russian volcano for a bit more than half an hour, though, and that meant that Preston Hills High School was still in the middle of its after-lunch class period. And that, Billy knew, was Mrs. Russet's free period, so there was no one in the room.

Not even her, thought Billy. The thought worried him. Where is Mrs. Russet now? he wondered.

He shook himself free of that thought as best he could. It didn't go anywhere good. And he was doing the best they could to help her by being here right now.

At least, he thought to himself, I *hope* this is where we're supposed to be. He swallowed hard, trying to gulp down his worry.

Vester appeared to share Billy's concern. The fireman was looking all around, not seeing anything of interest. "Now what?" he asked.

Billy hurried to Mrs. Russet's desk. He pulled open a drawer. Nothing. Just pens and pencils, a stapler, some tape. He pulled open another drawer. More of the same.

"It's got to be here," he muttered.

"What does?" asked Tempus. He eyed the papers in Mrs. Russet's desk drawers. "You think she left a note or something?"

"She wouldn't do that," said Ivy. "She wouldn't go to the trouble of leaving a coded message that lead to a note right out in the open." Then she eyed Billy uncertainly. "Would she?"

Billy opened the last drawer. "Ah-ha!" he whisper-shouted triumphantly. He held up his prize to show everyone. "The jumper that never quite eats!" he exclaimed proudly.

Tempus eyed Billy with a decidedly nervous eye. "It's sad when the brain starts to go in one so young," he whispered loudly to Ivy.

"Look, I know it must seem crazy," said Billy, "but this is what she was talking about, I just know it." He put down what he was holding, laying it carefully on Mrs. Russet's desk for everyone to stare at.

It was the ceramic frog. That cute little play-thing that had come alive and seemed to wink at Billy on that very first day, the day when Mrs. Russet had given him and the rest of the class a pop-quiz. The day she had first suspected he might be a Power.

As before, the ceramic figurine held a half-eaten bug in its mouth. "It never quite eats," said Billy, pointing to the insect form.

"Sad, like I said," whispered Tempus again.

"Shush, Tempus," hissed Ivy. She looked at the frog. "I think Billy's right. I can feel something." She closed her eyes. A few of her leafy vines snaked out to touch the frog. "Something familiar about this." Then the vines snaked back to join the rest of the writhing greenery she wore. Her eyes opened. "But I can't figure out what."

They all watched the frog for a long minute. Billy didn't know what to expect, but whatever it was, it wasn't what happened then: absolutely nothing. In a world where everything was suddenly not what it seemed, where flytraps ate zombies and rock-monsters were destroyed by flying Unicorns, Billy didn't think it was unreasonable to expect that the frog would do something. But it didn't. It just sat there, still and cold, and stared at them, and continued not doing anything.

"Boo!" shouted Tempus suddenly. They all jumped.

"Tempus!" snapped Vester.

Tempus shrugged. "I thought it might scare the frog," he explained.

"No," said Vester after a moment of glaring at the older man. "There's more to the riddle. We're at the place where Billy was empty when he should be full, and we've found the jumper that never quite eats. But there's more."

"I have to say the words to it," said Billy. "The words I've heard Mrs. Russet say."

"What words?" asked Ivy.

Billy frowned. "I don't know."

"How can you not know?" asked Tempus. "The riddle said she said whatever it is to you! So how can you not know?"

"She's my teacher," said Billy. "I hear her say around two trillion things a day." He thought for a moment, then looked at the frog, crossed his arms, and said in his best Mrs. Russet impression, "All right everyone, pop quiz!"

The frog didn't do anything.

Billy tried again. "This work is horrible. Everyone gets an 'F'!"

The frog continued not to do anything. The frog, it seemed, had a talent for this.

Billy tried one more time. "Open your history books, class."

This time, the frog did so much nothing that Billy was sure he'd never seen anything do as much nothing as the frog was doing right now.

He sighed. "I don't know what else to say," he said.

Vester looked at the frog carefully, examining it like he probably examined burning buildings before going in. "I think we're on the wrong track," he said. He looked at Billy. "Whatever she said, it was something that *only* you heard. Not something that she said to everyone, but something only you, Billy Jones, would know about."

Billy thought. That certainly cut down on the number of things he had to choose from. The only times he had ever been alone with Mrs. Russet were that first day of school, when he had first seen the frog, and the day she had brought him to Powers Island.

"A magic keyword, maybe," said Ivy.

"What's that?" asked Billy.

"It's like a password for your email or your bank account. Some Powers lock their Imbued Objects so they'll only respond to that word or phrase." She pursed her lips. "I wonder if Lumilla did that. My father...," she began. She tensed a moment, obviously thinking about her father, worried about the danger Veric the Green might be in. Then she seemed to mentally steel herself and continued, "My father does that. He has a secret sentence that only he uses, and a person has to say it to use certain of his most powerful Objects. Sort of like the anteroom, where we had that hot chocolate: you had to know the right word to get through the door."

Billy thought. Ivy's words had triggered something in him. He remembered something, but it wouldn't quite....

Then he snapped his fingers. "She *did* have something she said!" he exclaimed. "It was something she said right before she used her key to take me to Powers Island." He inhaled to say it, then exhaled without a sound.

"What is it?" asked Tempus.

"I don't remember," said Billy sadly. "It was something about rabbits, but," he shrugged. "I had just punched a bully in the nose—more or less—and I thought I was about to get in trouble. So I wasn't really taking notes."

Ivy looked at Vester. "Do you think you can help?" she asked.

Vester stared at Billy. Then slowly nodded. Billy looked from the fireman to the plant woman. "Help how?" he asked.

"Do you remember Fulgora's cloak of fire?" asked Ivy. "The one she wore when sitting with the Council on the Diamond Dais?" Billy nodded. "Do you remember what you saw in it?"

"Memories," said Billy, thinking of the images he had seen in the Red Lady's beautiful cloak. "My memories."

Vester nodded. "It's a power of the Reds. Memories are a part of the Fire that moves us all. It makes us much of what we are. The good memories where we've done what's right warm us in bad times, and the bad memories of times we've harmed others or done something wrong burn us and stop us from being happy."

"So can you help me remember what Mrs. Russet said?" asked Billy.

Vester nodded again. "I think so. Bringing back a memory is hard, and I can't always do it. But we're close to where you heard the words, right?" Billy nodded. "Good. Being close helps."

Vester held out his arm. The lava snake he had conjured up in the volcano wriggled out onto his wrist again. Vester put his hand on Billy's head. "Do you trust me?" he asked.

Billy nodded. "Will it hurt?" he said.

"It shouldn't. Not if I can find the memory quickly."

"And what if you don't find it quickly?" asked Billy.

Vester looked very uncomfortable. "It's like Fulgora's cloak. People can get lost in memory. Some never quite come back from their memories. They become shells, wishing for some perfect moment to happen again. So they try to re-find that moment all their lives, and by doing so they never really live." He looked seriously at Billy, trying to convey the importance of what he was now saying.

"You could get lost in yourself, Billy, and never come out of it. So only you can make this decision; only you can decide whether you think it is worth risking your own life to find out what Mrs. Russet wanted you to know."

Billy smiled as bravely as he could. "Go ahead," he said to Vester. He said it quickly, because he knew that if he thought too much about what Vester had said, he might lose his nerve. "I'm ready as I'll ever be."

Vester nodded gravely. Billy felt something dry writhe across his forehead. It must be the lava-snake. Then, he felt the Fizzle move to his eye. He closed his eye involuntarily, but it was no use: he couldn't shut out the fire. The flame touched him coolly, and Billy felt suddenly like he had exploded into a million pieces.

He found himself in a room. A room the size of a planet. Billy stood at the very center of the room, and all around him, as far as he could see, were things that looked a lot like flat panel television screens, or maybe computer monitors. Some were big, measuring what looked like hundreds of feet across. Some were tiny, so small that an ant could use it to furnish its apartment with. And each screen showed a scene, a billion moving pictures that each replayed some moment in Billy's life. He felt like he was in the largest theater in the world, surrounded on all sides by images of himself.

It was almost overwhelming, the sights and sounds of his whole life crowding in on him at once. Billy started to bow down under the weight of it all.

"I've got you," came an echoing voice. It was Vester, his disembodied words resounding through the vast room of Billy's memories. Billy felt comforted by his friend's presence. "Don't look at the memories too closely," came the fireman's voice. "You're not ready for that yet."

Billy—or whatever part of him was in this huge room—closed his eyes. That helped somewhat, though he could still hear everything going on around him, so many sounds from so many moments of his life.

The sound of a bicycle bell from a day in the park with his father....

The sound of a song in church....

The sound of Blythe's voice, saying, "...going to be at my locker in five minutes. If you learn to talk before then, maybe we can go to class togeth—"

Blythe's voice cut off suddenly, like a plug had been pulled.

"Hey!" Billy shouted inside himself.

"Sorry," said Vester's voice. "I'm trying to help you find a specific memory. Go ahead and open your eyes now so you can see what I'm doing."

Billy's memory-self did that. He saw that most of the infinite screens around him were now blank and silent. Only a relatively small number still held images. And all of them had one thing in common: Mrs. Russet.

Billy saw flashes of her all around. He heard her voice, saying everything she had ever said to him. It was so much less than he had been hearing and seeing only a moment ago, but it was still overwhelming. He could see why people could lose themselves in such a place as this.

Then, out of the mass of noises and sights, he heard them. He heard the words he was trying to hear. He looked at one of the screens, far in the distance, and as he looked towards it the scene came into sharp focus. He found himself suddenly before that scene, moving through a million miles of memory in an instant. He saw Mrs. Russet, leading him to the janitorial closet. He saw her pull out her beehive key for the first time. He saw her lips move. He heard the words.

"Got it," the self that was himself whispered, and as soon as he said that he found himself back in the class again, back in Mrs. Russet's room. Ivy, Tempus, and Vester were all staring at him with a mixture of support and concern on their faces. Billy hardly noticed it, though. Nor did he really pay attention to the lava snake crawling back across Vester's arm and slinking down the neck of his friend's shirt. He didn't want to notice anything, he just wanted to remember what Mrs. Russet had said.

He looked at the frog.

"Buster bumpkin bunny burps," Billy said.

The frog....

... slowly...

... winked.

Billy smiled. He had done it!

But there was no time for him to congratulate himself, because an instant later a voice said, "I wouldn't be too happy if I were you."

Billy's eyes widened. The voice was the last one he had expected to hear.

It was the voice of Mrs. Russet.

# CHAPTER THE FIFTEENTH

*In Which Billy receives Instruction, and is Chased once again...*

Billy felt his eyes bulge like the eyes of a fish. Worse. He felt them bulge like the eyes of a fish with some kind of genetic disease that made its eyes so bulgy that even the other fish made fun of it.

He saw with some satisfaction that he was not the only one trying out for the "World's Most Giantest Eyes" competition: Ivy, Tempus, and Vester all wore the same shocked expression he suspected was on his own face. They wheeled around, looking for Mrs. Russet.

"I say again," said the teacher's voice. "I wouldn't be too happy just now."

"The frog!" said Ivy.

Sure enough, it was the frog. The figurine's mouth was now open, allowing Billy and his friends to see the half-eaten insect inside its mouth. And the frog's mouth was where Mrs. Russet's voice was coming from.

"If you're hearing this, Billy, then it means some very terrible things have happened," said Mrs. Russet's voice. The frog kept its mouth open, but its tongue suddenly snapped out and licked its open eyeball. That didn't make much difference to the sound coming from it, though. Mrs. Russet's voice sounded as clear as though she were standing right there with them.

"I suspected such events might occur, and that's why I prepared Methuselah this way," said Mrs. Russet's voice.

"Who's Methuselah?" asked Billy.

"Methuselah is the name of the frog," answered Mrs. Russet.

Billy's eyes did their fish impression again. "Mrs. Russet!" he shouted happily. "You can hear me! Where are you? What's going on? How can we—?"

"Stop shouting," came his teacher's voice.

Billy did. The frog—Methuselah—lifted one leg and extended it to full length like it was stretching out a kink. Then it licked its other eyeball.

Mrs. Russet continued. "Thank you. Not that it would matter, I suppose, since I can't hear you anyway."

Billy frowned. "Then how did you know—"

"Then how did I know you were shouting?" said Mrs. Russet from wherever she was. "Because I know *you*, young man. You're far too excitable at times."

Billy's face flushed. The world could be ending, he thought, but there's always room for a little bit of criticism in front of my friends.

"But now is neither the time nor the place to discuss that," continued Mrs. Russet's voice as the open-mouthed Methuselah methodically stretched its green limbs. "As I said, if you're hearing this, it's because some very bad things have happened. I suspect that, among other things, it is very likely that I have been abducted, perhaps even worse."

"You believe it likely?" asked Tempus. "What in the world do you mean, Lumilla? Don't you *know* you've been abducted?"

One of Methuselah's sticky eyes rotated to focus on Tempus. "I say likely, Tempus, because I am not talking to you right now."

"What?" asked Billy, Tempus, Ivy, and Vester, all in the same instant.

"This is a pre-recorded message," continued Mrs. Russet's voice.

"Then how do you know what we're saying?" asked Billy.

The frog's eye turned to Billy now. "I told you," said Mrs. Russet's voice sternly. "I know *you*. It's not a leap to figure out what you're going to ask and when, just as it's not too hard to deduce that in the event you are listening to this, you are currently standing in my classroom during fifth period, and Ivy, Vester, and Tempus are all with you, Mr. Jones. Nor is it difficult to deduce that Ivy's left arm needs pruning, Vester has his shirt untucked, and Tempus desperately needs a change of wardrobe."

Billy glanced at his friends. Sure enough, the plants on Ivy's left arm *did* look a bit raggedy than the rest of her outfit. And Vester's shirt *was* untucked. And Tempus most assuredly *could* have used an outfit that didn't showcase his knobby knees and white legs quite so much.

"Now listen carefully," snapped Mrs. Russet. "Methuselah has limited recording time. He's a good frog, but even the best frogs have their limits."

The frog seemed to nod at this, as though agreeing with her. It took a quick bite of the bug in its mouth, then opened its jaws wide again so Mrs. Russet's voice could continue.

"I've likely been abducted. And I'm afraid that if that is the case, I need rescuing," continued the voice. "You will have to find me, and the others who were kidnapped, on Dark Isle."

"How can we find Dark Isle?" asked Ivy incredulously. "We're not Darksiders!"

"Shush, Ivy," snapped Mrs. Russet. "I told you, I don't have much time."

A computer-like voice suddenly broke into the conversation, it too coming from Methuselah's mouth. "Recording time low," it said. "One minute remaining."

"Fiddle-sticks," muttered Mrs. Russet. There was a wet thudding sound like she was pounding on the frog, trying to get it to work better. "Methuselah, some day I swear I'll...." A few more wet smacking noises emerged from the frog's mouth. "All right," continued Mrs. Russet. "I have to talk fast. You need to go back to Powers Island. All of you."

"It'll be crawling with Darksiders," interjected Vester.

"I know there will be Darksiders," said Mrs. Russet at the same time. "Perhaps even zombies. Nevertheless you have to go there. All of you. But—and this is imperative—you cannot give Billy any further Tests of Power. There is, however, something you *do* have to do on Powers Island. There is one place that you can hide in, and I suspect you may find allies there. So as soon as you get to Powers Island, go as quickly as you can to—"

The voice cut off. There was a "beep," then that mechanical voice came again, saying, "Record time depleted. Please see Powers Island Customer Assistance Department if you have any questions or comments."

Tempus frowned at Methuselah, who seemed to shrug as though saying it wasn't his fault. "These things always do croak on you at the worst time," said Tempus. The Gray Power picked up the frog and shook it, clearly hoping that might get Methuselah to divulge a bit more information. All that Methuselah did, however, was kick its legs and pee in the old man's hand.

"Gah!" Tempus shouted in disgust. He dropped the frog and wiped his hand on his moving Hawaiian shirt. Methuselah landed with a thunk back on Mrs. Russet's table, and then glared at Tempus for a split second before taking one more quick munch of the bug it was eternally eating and then turning back to ceramic again, cold and lifeless.

"Wonderful," said Vester. "So we know we have to go to Powers Island, but not *where* on Powers Island. And we also don't know what we're supposed to do when we get there, or how to find this 'secret place' Mrs. Russet was talking about." He plinked the now lifeless Methuselah with a finger. "Thanks a heap, froggy."

"So what do we do?" asked Billy.

"Well," began Tempus.

"I think we just head on over to Powers Island," said Ivy.

"Well," said Tempus again.

"Are you nuts?" responded Vester to Ivy. "Didn't you hear what Mrs. Russet said? Powers Island is going to be enemy territory. Darksiders and zombies everywhere."

"*Well!*" shouted Tempus. Everyone looked at him. "Thank you," he said. Then, a bit more slowly, and in a suddenly quiet voice, he continued, "Wherever we go, I suggest we go there soon. As in, now."

"Why?" asked Ivy.

In answer, Tempus pointed. Billy and his friends all followed the old man's finger to see what he was pointing at. The window. The windows to the class were frosted glass: the kind that allowed light in, but didn't permit anyone to see more than a blurry image of what was on the other side.

Still, in this case, a blurry view was quite enough. The thing passing by the window was humanlike in form, though whether a man or a woman, Billy could not tell. He could, however, make out a pair of distinctively huge eyes atop the head, and noticed a shuffling gait, as though the being didn't really know how to move properly.

"Zombie," he whispered.

"Quite so," agreed Tempus. "It seems that if we don't go to the enemy, the enemy will come to us."

"Maybe it's coincidence, maybe they're looking for something else," said Ivy.

"Not likely," said Vester. "We're being hunted." He pulled out his marble, the red Imbued Object that had transported them from Powers Island to the Russian volcano. Tempus eyed the marble with clear distrust.

"Do you think that's a good idea?" asked the Gray Power.

Outside the class, the zombie had stopped. It was turning slowly right and left, as though trying to smell something.

"Those great greasy eyes," whispered Tempus in disgust.

"What about—" started Billy in a normal voice, but he was cut off by Tempus, Ivy, and Vester all "shush"ing him instantly.

*Billy: Messenger of Powers*, by Michaelbrent Collings * 197

"Sorry," Billy whispered, embarrassed. Then, in a quiet whisper, he said, "What about the eyes?"

"Zombies all have them," whispered Vester, the fireman's eyes intently tracking the zombie's progress as it wondered to and fro. "They can see more than most people, and their night vision is amazing."

"Don't try to play hide and seek in the dark with a zombie," contributed Tempus. "Not that I've tried," he said almost apologetically.

"Why do they have the eyes at all?" asked Billy. They were all talking quietly, but he noticed not a one of his friends was moving in the slightest. Apparently zombies could see better than they heard, though it was clear that no one wanted to talk more loudly than they had to, just in case. Knowing about the zombies' vision was a good fact to have, and Billy filed it away in his mind for quick access should he need it later.

"No one knows exactly why their eyes are so big," whispered the motionless Ivy. "But they all have them. It's as though when the Death Power takes over a dead body, it gives them those eyes to remind everyone that Death is, ultimately, everywhere."

That gave Billy a horrible thought. "You said that zombies are made out of the bodies of dead Powers. What would happen," he gulped quietly, "if someone made a zombie out of a live Power."

All three of his friends grew even more still, if that were possible. "No one has ever managed to do that," said Vester.

"Not that a few people haven't tried," added Tempus. Ivy shuddered.

Outside, the zombie was still moving back and forth, but then finally seemed to decide that whatever it was looking for wasn't there. It shuffled away, and soon was gone from the limited view afforded by the classroom's frosted windows.

Billy and his three friends all visibly relaxed.

"What was that thing doing here?" Billy asked.

"Well, I would guess that either it realized the value of a quality education," began Vester, "or it's looking for you."

Billy felt that chill that was rapidly growing to be an all-too familiar part of his life. He shivered.

"Now, Vester," scolded Ivy. "There's no use scaring him."

Vester turned on Ivy. "Yes, there is. He's got to know, from now on, what's happening and what he's up against."

"But we don't *know* what we're up against," said Ivy.

"Then we have to give him worst-case scenarios until everything is clear," said Vester. Ivy started to say something, but Vester spoke right over her. "The last time this happened, the last time Wolfen started a war, do you know why he got as far as he did?" Without waiting for an answer, Vester continued. "It wasn't because he was the strongest, or the smartest. It was because so many of us insisted that nothing was wrong, that nothing was happening, that the things happening to our friends and…"—he choked up, unable to continue for a moment—"And families…. That the things happening to them weren't really happening, or weren't as bad as they seemed."

He pointed a finger out the window, where the zombie had been. "So if that zombie is here, then it's here for Billy, or for Mrs. Russet's frog, or for some equally evil purpose. And fooling ourselves is just going to get us killed, or worse."

Billy couldn't think of much that would be worse than getting killed, but he got Vester's point. And the point seemed to make sense. It was certain that some kind of attack had been launched, and that the zombies were a big part of it. So to pretend that a zombie was just a random event seemed foolhardy in the extreme.

"If it's looking for me," asked Billy, "then why didn't it look in this room?"

"What?" asked Ivy, looking relieved to be on another topic of conversation.

"Why not come in here?" asked Billy. "If it's at my school, looking for me, wouldn't it have instructions to look in rooms where I might be?"

"Probably not," said Tempus. "Zombies, thankfully, are fairly stupid creatures. They do quite well with certain directed tasks, but don't do well with improvisation. So if one is told to rip out your liver and eat it, for example, he will. But he's not likely to eat your intestines, or your brain. Just exactly what he's told."

"The zombie's going to eat my liver?" asked Billy, horrified.

"No, no," said Ivy placatingly, sending a look at Tempus that was sharp enough to cut diamonds. She patted Billy. "Tempus just means that, if it's looking for you, the only information the zombie probably has is what you look like. Not much more can be fit into what's left of its mind. So it will stay in a defined area—the school, for instance—and keep an eye out for you. But it won't be thorough, and it won't improvise. Just basic tasks." She squeezed him reassuringly. "Which is a huge plus, don't you think?"

"Sure," said Billy dully. "It's good to know that the living dead aren't Ph.D. candidates, as well. Because that would be rotten."

Ivy either didn't catch or just ignored his terrified sarcasm, because she grinned brightly and said, "See? Things are looking up already!"

"Shh!" hissed Vester. They all quieted instantly, as another form shuffled past the classroom windows. It was clearly a zombie, and just as clearly a different one than the monster that had walked by earlier: it was shorter and fatter, and its eyes—even through the glass—were visibly larger.

"How many of those things are out there?" whispered Billy.

Tempus said, "Probably just those two, maybe one or two more. The Darksiders are committed to the idea of enslaving humanity, but they're not going to risk revealing their existence prematurely just to find you. Armies of the undead marching on the world's largest cities will come later, not now."

Again, Billy did not feel particularly heartened by this news.

The second zombie passed by. As soon as it was gone, Vester turned to Billy, Ivy, and Tempus. "Come on," he said. "We've got to get going."

He pulled out his marble, the Object he'd used to Transport them to the volcano earlier.

"No way!" objected Tempus. "I told you, no more trips with amateur keys!"

"C'mon, Tempus, we made it, didn't we?" said Vester indignantly. Ivy closed her eyes in resignation. Billy could see that these two men, though best of friends, were like an old married couple that couldn't help but fight over everything.

"Yes, we made it," Tempus replied. "If by 'made it' you mean 'almost died in agony.'"

"You're being melodramatic," said Vester. "As usual."

"Yes, I agree," snarled Tempus. "But melodrama is appropriate when contemplating the ridiculous, and thinking I'll ever let you Transport me anywhere ever again is just that: ridiculous!"

"Hey, hey!" said Billy. He was surprised that he managed to half-shout at the two older men. They, too, were surprised, as he could see by the looks on their faces. He grew suddenly bashful, almost ashamed of himself for daring such impertinence. "Sorry," he managed. "Just, couldn't we argue about this stuff somewhere else? Somewhere without the undead around every corner?"

"Quite sensible sounding," said Ivy. She glared at Tempus and Vester. "In fact, it's sensible enough that you and I should do it whether *they* do or not, Billy." She held his hand, then walked toward the door. She put her hand on the door handle, then Ivy looked once more at the Red and Gray Powers. "I have a key of my own, and it can get us all to Powers Island just fine. So Billy and I are going, just as Lumilla told us to. If you care to come with us, fine. But," she finished, the strength and immovability of a redwood tree creeping into her normally willowy voice, "leave the silly arguments behind. There's enough to be worried about without worrying that you two will bicker me to death."

Tempus and Vester looked embarrassed and contrite. Billy already knew that the peace wouldn't last, but he hoped his two friends could get along long enough for all of them to find safety.

Ivy turned the knob, and Billy and his friends skulked out of the room. They walked hurriedly along the halls, each of the four adventurers looking in as many directions at once as possible, keeping an eye out for zombies, hall monitors, and any other horrors that might lurk in a high school.

"Where are we going?" Billy asked Ivy as they went. "Why can't we just use the key and go now, from here?"

"My key doesn't work inside buildings," she said. "Where's the closest door out?"

Billy pointed in the direction they were going. "Straight ahead, down some stairs, and there's a door leading out right at the bottom." He looked at his watch. "We better hurry, though. It's only about five minutes until class ends, and there are going to be about two thousand students running around in the halls at that point."

Ivy stepped up the pace. But the group hadn't gone more than a couple feet when Billy heard his name being called.

"Billy? Billy!" It was Blythe, who had just turned a nearby corner and spotted them. She ran up to them, holding a hall pass in one hand and a half-devoured candy bar in the other.

Billy froze in place. He looked around. No zombies. He didn't know what to do. If he stopped to talk, then he and his friends might be caught. If he walked away, then even worse things might happen: like Blythe never talking to him again.

The beautiful girl was next to them in an instant. "Hey," she said. She took two massive bites of her candy bar, making it disappear as though by magic. Billy wondered if there was a special Power that could control calories. If there was, then Blythe was definitely one of those.

"So I was going to be mad at you for ditching me earlier" she said, throwing the candy wrapper into a nearby trash can, "but then I decided not to be. Anger is bad for the complexion. But I do want an explanation."

She seemed to notice the rest of the group for the first time. Billy's spirit sank through the floor. How could he explain this strange menagerie he was wandering around the halls of school with?

Luckily, Blythe provided an explanation for him. She leaned in conspiratorially to Billy. "You know, even though we're allowed to bring our families in costume this year, I hear most students don't do that. And they definitely wait until after classes are over."

"Whah?" Billy managed to say.

Blythe frowned. She pointed over his shoulder. "You know, the dance."

Billy looked at what she was pointing at. There was a sign that said "Halloween Bash—Family and Friends Welcome—Awards for Best Costumes" hanging over the hallway.

"Oh, uh, yeah," he said. "This, uh," he stuttered, pointing at his friends.

"We're his cousins," said Vester. He stepped up and held out his hand for Blythe to shake. "And he invited us to the Halloween—uh—thing."

"So what are you?" asked Blythe.

"Well, I'm a fireman," said Vester.

"Where's your outfit?" shot back the girl.

Vester frowned. "I'm a fireman on his day off."

Blythe frowned too, then apparently decided to accept that. "And you two?" she asked Ivy and Tempus.

"I'm the Happy Green Giant," said Ivy, "You know, like the one that sells peas and green beans on the commercials? And this," she said, pointing at Tempus, who looked like the entire conversation had passed well over his head some time ago, "is Uncle Buck. He's dressed like a tourist. Who is color-blind. And has just come out of a coma. And—"

"Hey!" said Tempus indignantly, apparently just catching up at this moment to what was going on. "What's wrong with my outfit?"

"Nothing," answered Blythe, apparently completely mistaking the question. "You totally look like an ex-coma patient color-blind tourist. I mean, it's not what I would have guessed just looking, but now that I know what the costume is supposed to be, I think you hit it dead-on. Let the judges know at the dance. You're a shoo-in for some award." She looked back at Billy, taking another candy bar from her backpack and starting to eat it in bites that would have made a great white shark envious. "So," she said, suddenly uncharacteristically bashful, "I guess that means you'll be at the dance?"

"Uh, yeah. Definitely," said Billy. He had never been to a dance before, but then, no one had ever cared about whether Billy went to one or not, so missing them had been easy.

*Am I just dreaming?* he thought. *Or did Blythe just sort of ask me to the dance?*

"Cool," said Blythe, and Billy thought she was blushing a little. "Like I said, I was going to be mad at you, but I figured that anyone who can give Cameron a bloody nose deserves at least one free pass."

"Well, it was nice to meet you," said Ivy in a too-bright voice before grabbing Billy's hand in a vise-like grip. "Now, where did you say that thing was that you wanted to show us, cousin Billy?"

Billy allowed his three friends to drag him away from Blythe, then shrugged their hands off and hurried back to her, even as she began to turn away. "Blythe!" he shouted.

She turned around. And, as usual, any sense of what he had wanted to say went right out the window. "Yeah?" she said. He noted that she had finished off the second candy bar and now had a licorice whip in her hands.

*She must have the metabolism of a hummingbird with ADD,* he thought.

"Uh, about Cameron," he said.

"What about that dirt-bag?" asked Blythe. The way she called Cameron a dirt-bag made Billy's heart start knocking even harder in his chest. *She was perfect,* he thought.

He didn't say that, however. What he said was, "Have you seen him around?"

Blythe frowned. "No. Not today. Why?"

Billy shrugged. In truth, he had suspected as much. He was positive that Cameron Black was a Darksider, following in the footsteps of his mother and the strange Power named Wolfen. So it was no surprise that he wasn't here today. He was probably with the other Darksiders, helping to plan the next horror that would be visited on the world of the Powers.

"No reason," answered Billy. Then, over Blythe's shoulder, he saw something. A figure moved into the hall. A lurching, stumbling figure with gray-green skin and two huge eyes. To Billy's horror, the creature immediately spotted him, and behind him, Ivy, Tempus, and Vester.

"RUN!" shouted Ivy.

Billy didn't think. He just grabbed Blythe's hand in his.

"Hey," she began, "what's the big ide—?" But Billy jerked her forward before Blythe could finish her indignant question. He pulled her with him toward his three friends, and they ran for all they were worth.

"What's going on?" asked Blythe. "What the heck is going on, Billy Jones?"

"Later!" he managed. He threw a glance behind him. The zombie had been joined by another one, both of them running leadenly behind Billy and his friends. As he watched, a third zombie, then a fourth, and a fifth, all converged until they were running in a shuffling, greasy group through the halls.

"EEK!" he heard, and looked ahead again just in time to see that Harold and Sarah—who had apparently just been cowering in the corridor after their stormy run-in with Tempus—had just stepped unwittingly into the path of the onrushing Powers.

Ivy, Vester, and Tempus managed to avoid running the junior members of the Torture Brigade over. Billy didn't have as much luck, however. He didn't completely barrel into Harold Crane, but he felt his elbow crack into the bigger boy's ribs as he dodged by. "Sorry!" he shouted without thinking.

Harold screamed like he'd been shot with a gun that was loaded with hornets and piranhas, then dropped to the ground, holding his head in his arms like he was expecting the roof to collapse. Sarah, meanwhile, looked like she was doing her best to actually chew through the wall to get away from Billy and his friends.

"What's with them?" wheezed Blythe, still being pulled along by the strength of Billy's desperate grip.

"Probably had too much caffeine in their energy drinks or something," Billy said lamely. He risked another glimpse back. The team of undead ran right over Harold, leaving the would-be bully sprawled unconscious behind them.

Billy couldn't help but grin. His grin disappeared, though, when he remembered what Tempus had said: it *was* possible that some zombies' touch could kill. Even Harold Crane, the punk-haired bully, didn't deserve that.

Billy had no time to dwell on it, though. Up ahead, Vester had disappeared around a corner, which Billy knew led to the stairway he had told Ivy about. Just a few feet, down the stairs, through a door, and they'd be outside.

"Billy, what's going on?" asked Blythe. She had managed to keep a grip on her licorice whip, and took a bite even as they ran. She appeared quite fine with the idea of running, and Billy's heart thudded a little harder when he noticed that she was still holding his hand as they ran. But how was he supposed to answer her question?

"It's complicated," he finally said. It wasn't a good answer, but it was all he could come up with. And it seemed to satisfy Blythe, because she didn't ask again. Either that, or she just had too much licorice in her mouth to speak right now.

Billy turned the corner that his friends had gone around, and was surprised to see that Tempus was standing there. "Go," said the old man, gesturing for Billy to continue down the stairs.

Billy did so, and a few moments later heard something that sounded like a fierce windstorm behind them.

"What the...?" began Blythe, starting to look over her shoulder.

"Look out!" screamed Billy, trying to divert Blythe's attention from the magic that was going on only a few feet away.

"What?" she screamed back, looking at the stairs in front of them.

"Uh, I thought there was a bug," he managed lamely.

"A bug?" she asked incredulously.

A vomit-colored shape whipped by them at that moment. Tempus. "Storm spell!" he shouted. "It won't hold them for long though!"

Blythe looked at Billy with a look that clearly asked both what was wrong with Billy's "cousin" and if whatever it was, was genetic.

Billy shrugged and did his best to look innocent.

Ahead of them, Tempus was banging through the door, holding it open for Billy and Blythe. Billy crashed through, and had a split-second to see Vester standing nearby, before the fireman swung a heavy hand...right at Blythe.

"No!" yelled Billy. But it was too late. Vester's hand hit Blythe on the top of the head. It was a glancing blow, even Billy could see that it hadn't been a hard impact, but Blythe fell as though she'd had a piano dropped on her.

"What did you do?" screamed Billy.

Vester pushed the younger boy roughly out of the way. "They're not interested in her!" he shouted, lifting Blythe and putting her carefully against the wall. "They want us! You want her to be safe, then the best way to make sure nothing happens to her is to *not* bring her with us!"

Billy looked at the beautiful Blythe, who was still just as lovely as ever, even though there was a half a bite of licorice hanging from her limp mouth. "But what did you do?" he asked.

"Just a Short Circuit spell," explained Vester. "She'll wake up in a few minutes with a headache and no memory of the last five minutes or so."

Billy's stomach sank. He knew that was probably the best thing for Blythe, but it meant she might not even remember seeing him, wouldn't remember asking if he was going to the dance.

"Shoot," was all he could manage. The only other thing he could think to say was a word he had said once about a year ago, and when his mother heard about it, he was grounded for a week. "Shoot," he said again.

"Sorry, Casanova," said Vester with a grin as he turned back to Billy.

"So she won't remember any of what's happening right now?" asked Billy. When Vester shook his head, Billy ran over to Blythe.

"What are you doing?" shouted Vester.

Billy grabbed Blythe's hand. It felt wonderful, warm and full of life. "I just wanted to say," he began, "because I probably won't have the guts to do it when you're awake. But, well…you're really cool, and really pretty, and really nice to me. No one has been really nice to me in a long time, not at school. And," he gulped, amazed at how hard this was. "… and I really hope we can be friends."

There was a thud behind them, and the school door banged open. Five zombies almost fell over themselves in their hurry to pursue Billy and his friends.

"Ivy!" shouted Vester.

Billy looked over. Ivy had already made it outside, he saw, and had run to the edge of the sidewalk, where a small patch of lawn grew. She threw something into the grass. "Come on!" she shouted.

Vester yanked Billy away from Blythe's unconscious form, grabbing Billy by the collar of his shirt and propelling him forward, the two of them following Tempus, who was already running with superhuman speed toward Ivy.

Behind them, the zombies moaned in what Billy swore was a sound of tremendous hunger and need, and followed after the fleeing friends, moving far too quickly for comfort.

Billy looked ahead again, and saw that in front of Ivy, something was growing out of the lawn. It grew rapidly, from seedling to sapling to tree. Soon, what looked like an old oak tree had sprouted before them, thirty feet high. As Billy looked, a great hole opened in the trunk of the tree. Ivy hopped in, followed quickly in by Tempus.

How is that possible? wondered Billy. The tree can't hold both of them inside it. It's not big enough.

Then he almost smacked his forehead. Of course! This was Ivy's Transport key!

"Go, go, go!" Vester was shouting, pushing Billy as fast as his legs could go. The zombies were gaining on them. Closer, closer, gaining on the fireman and on Billy with every step. Their pale, rotten fingers reached out, straining to touch the two fleeing friends. Just one touch was all they would need.

"Hold your breath!" shouted Vester, and he threw Billy into the hole in the tree.

Billy held his breath. He wondered if, as when they had traveled through Vester's Transport spell, the zombies would be able to follow them.

The same jerking sensation that shivered him from head to foot came, and he stumbled as solid ground suddenly appeared below him. A pair of hands grasped him. Tempus's.

Billy looked up, and saw that there was a black hole in midair, through which he could see Vester, as though through a window. The fireman leaped through, landing in front of Billy. Behind him, he could hear Ivy murmur a word or two, and the hole started to close.

But would it close quickly enough? The zombies on the other side of the doorway through time and space reached out, trying to get a handhold on the closing door, trying to follow Billy and his friends.

But the hole closed just in time. Billy wondered if the tree at Preston Heights High School had disappeared as well, or if the gardeners were going to have a mystery on their hands. Regardless, however, he was relieved to see that the zombies hadn't made it through. He couldn't think of anything worse than being pursued by five zombies.

"Phew," Billy whispered, bending over and gasping to catch his breath.

"Not exactly my sentiments," whispered Tempus nearby.

"Why?" asked Billy. But before he had even straightened up, he saw what Tempus was talking about. And immediately wished he hadn't.

"How could we have been so stupid?" asked Ivy.

Vester muttered something under his breath, something that Billy was pretty sure would have gotten him at least two *months'* grounding, with nothing but bread and water to keep him alive if his mother had heard him say it.

But Billy couldn't blame him for the sentiment.

They were in the Accounting Room in the tower on Powers Island, the same place that Billy had appeared each time he had come to the island. Behind the group was the mummy with its "This is what happens when you don't hold your breath" sign. In front of Billy and his friends were the three carnival fortune tellers that would provide the required badges. Behind the fortune tellers were the banks of magical elevators that it seemed could take a person anywhere on the island.

None of that was new.

What *was* new, however, was who else was in the room.

Billy gulped. He knew, now, what was more frightening than being chased by five zombies.

It was being in a room with five hundred of them.

# CHAPTER THE SIXTEENTH

*In Which Billy is uncounted, and Friends say Goodbye...*

The zombies were everywhere. *Everywhere*. They stood so closely to one another that it was almost impossible to see anything *but* zombies. In fact, the only places there were no zombies were three thin paths that lay between the massed bodies of the living corpses, like three woodland trails between tall and frightening trees. Each path lead to one of the three cases that held the fortune-teller-like mannequins—the Counters, as Vester had called them—that provided badges to all the Powers who came to the island. A person would be able to walk to the Counters without having to go through—and be touched by—a zombie, but would not be able to go anywhere else,

Tempus raised his arms with a shout, clearly preparing to cast a spell and go out with a bang that would take as many of the zombies with him as possible.

"Wait!" shouted Vester. He pulled at the old man's arms.

Tempus resisted. "They won't get me that easily!" he shouted. "Not this time!"

"But look! Look!" screamed Vester. "They're not moving! They're not attacking!"

Tempus lowered his arms and looked around. Billy did likewise, forcing himself to move slowly in spite of the panic that threatened to overwhelm him at any moment. He didn't want to make any sudden moves that might trip a reaction from the zombies.

What Vester had said was true. The zombies, hundreds of them, were all looking at Billy and his friends. But none of them was moving.

"What are they waiting for?" asked Ivy.

Vester's eyes closed and he pointed at the three paths between the zombies, the paths that led straight to the Counters. "They're waiting for us to get our badges," he said with a tone that sounded almost resigned to Billy, as though he had lost all hope.

"I don't get it," quavered Billy. The weight of the zombies' stares was almost palpable, bearing down on him like a lead blanket.

"It's the way Powers Island was designed, remember?" asked Vester. "The White King made it so that there would always be an equal number of Darksiders and Dawnwalkers on the island. And the way we know that is because every single person who comes to Powers Island shows up here before anything else. This room is the only way to get onto the island, you can't appear anywhere else without coming here first."

"So?" said Billy, still confused, still terrified. "What does that have to do with why they're not trying to cream us?"

"Because most people can't tell a Dawnwalker from a Darksider just by looking at them," said Ivy, suddenly catching on. "So to keep the count of who's what on the island, the Counters were designed. Then the Council monitors—or used to monitor," she interjected with a sad frown, "how many of each side came through here."

"Simply put," finished Vester, "the zombies are probably under orders to wait until any arriving Powers get their badges, then if they're Dawnwalkers, the zombies will pounce on them."

"Then why don't we just go?" asked Billy. "Just Transport out of here? I know Mrs. Russet said to come here, but she couldn't have known about...." He gestured wildly at the legions of undead that loomed like terrifying gargoyles all around them.

"Remember that are two types of Transport spell," said Vester. "If you use an Imbued Object, then it leaves the door open behind you. With this many zombies, it's certain we still wouldn't be able to get away: the zombies would just follow us to wherever we went and fight us there. And if we do a Transport spell without a key, then it takes a couple seconds to gear up for it. And I'm betting," he said in a whisper, "that these guys are under orders to jump on anyone who tries that."

"So we're goners," Billy said, almost moaning. At this point, he had already faced almost-certain death enough times that he would have expected to be used to it by now, but apparently one never got quite used to one's own impending demise.

In that respect, he realized, the looming threat of death was a lot like talking to girls. He also realized at the same moment that it was a bit odd to be thinking of girls at a time like this, and forced himself back to the more immediate problem: staying alive.

"All of us goners? Not necessarily," said Tempus. The old man was chewing his lip thoughtfully, looking around with an uncharacteristically coherent expression.

"What is it?" asked Vester. "You see some way out for us?"

"Not for all of us," said Tempus with a sad shake of his head. "But perhaps," he added, "for one."

"What do you mean?" asked Ivy. "We can't Transport anyone out of here, any more than we could do it for ourselves."

"I don't think we have to," said Tempus. He thought another moment, then continued. "It's like you said, Ivy, the zombies are waiting for Dawnwalkers. But one of us *isn't* a Dawnwalker."

Billy was confused, until Vester snapped his fingers. "That's right!" he almost shouted. Then he looked at Billy. "You're unDetermined, both as to power and affiliation."

"So what does that mean?"

"It means, my boy, that you're about to be on your own," said Tempus.

"No!" said Billy, almost shouting.

But Ivy and Vester were nodding. "I think he's right," said Ivy. She looked at the three aisles between the zombies, each of them leading right to the fortune tellers that would seal the doom of any Dawnwalker who came to the island. "I think that no matter what Tempus, Vester, and I are about to get caught. But you...." She looked at Billy. "...You they might not get."

"No, it's not true," said Billy desperately. "You don't have to be caught, none of you do. We can all get out of here, we just have to think. And besides, even if I *didn't* get caught, I wouldn't know what to do here! I wouldn't know where to go!"

Vester, Ivy, and Tempus all looked at him with sympathy. Billy felt sick inside, not just at the fact that his friends were talking about sacrificing themselves, but even more so about the fact that in this moment of terror, they seemed to be more concerned about his mere feelings of fear than they were about their own certain capture and possible death.

"What do I do? What *can* I do?" he finally managed in a small voice. None of his friends had an answer for him.

Finally, Ivy stepped forward. She hugged Billy tightly. "We don't know what you can do," she admitted. Billy could see she was crying a little, her green tears once more tracking down her face. He ached for how she must be feeling. To have lost her father and now perhaps to face her own death in the same day. Billy couldn't even imagine the depth of her pain. Even though Billy and his own father didn't have the closest relationship, he didn't know how he would go on without knowing his father was safe.

"We don't know what you can do," Ivy repeated, "but we do know you're special. Lumilla knew it, even Eva Black and Wolfen seemed to know it. Maybe the Unicorn will come again. Maybe something else will happen. But I think that Lumilla knew this would happen. She knew that we would have to be taken by the zombies, and that you would be left here without us. Somehow she knew. Just like I know that whatever you are supposed to do next, *you will find a way to do it.*"

She kissed his cheek, then straightened up and without another word marched quickly down one of the aisles to the nearest of the three Counters.

"Wait!" Billy shouted. He couldn't believe what he was seeing. Was Ivy really going to just give up and go to her slaughter?

Tempus's hand on his shoulder answered that question. "Don't, boy," said the old Gray Power. "It's her way. The way of the Greens. Though there are exceptions to the rule, most Greens will save others' lives, but not fight for them. This is the path Ivy has chosen, and it is her right to choose it."

As he said this, Ivy arrived at one of the Counters. She pressed the button on the side of its case, and the mannequin-like figure dropped a badge into her waiting hand. The instant she took it in her hands the nearest zombies lunged at her. All Billy got was a short glimpse of her before a blanket of zombies came between him and the Green Power, making her impossible to see. There was not a sound, but when the zombies finished their nefarious work and then moved back into their previous positions, Ivy was gone. There was no trace of her left.

Billy's lip started to quiver. Was she gone forever? Had she been eaten? Or just knocked out and Transported somewhere? He had no way of knowing.

Out of the corner of his eye, he saw Vester and Tempus share a meaningful glance. Tempus nodded, as though Vester and he had just shared some silent communication about something terribly important.

"Go to one of the Counters now, Billy. Move as far away from us as you can," whispered Tempus. His voice was unlike Billy had ever heard it before. It was even more chilling than it had been right after Billy's Gleaning, when he and his friends had been trapped under the earth and Tempus had whispered, "He is coming, he is returning, he is returning, he is here," over and over in that strange haunted voice of prophecy. The voice Tempus spoke in now wasn't haunted, it wasn't feeble or scatter-brained.

It was deadly.

Billy hesitated. He felt rooted to the spot. Leave his friends' sides? After what had just happened to Ivy?

"No," he whispered, though he was now almost as frightened at the terrible look on Tempus's and Vester's faces as he was of the zombies around them.

"Ivy did not fight," said Tempus. "It was not her way. But as for me," continued the old man, and Billy could feel the hairs on his neck stand straight up as magical power flowed to Tempus, "They'll find me not to be such easy prey."

"But—" Billy began.

"GO!" shouted Tempus.

Billy went, unable to control his feet as they led him in the one direction that was open to him: down one of the paths between zombies, down one of the thin trails leading to the Counters.

About half the zombies in the room watched him go, their bulbous eyes tracking his movements with a predatory gleam. The other half watched Vester and Tempus, standing motionless as Billy's two friends waited until Billy was practically pressed up against a Counter's case. When he had gone as far as he could, he turned to his friends again.

"What are you going to do?" he asked.

Vester looked at Billy grimly. The lava snake the fireman had conjured earlier emerged from his clothing and wrapped itself loosely around his neck. The Fizzle, which had previously been fairly innocuous looking—or, at least, as innocuous looking as any snake made of fire *can* be—now had a distinctly cobra-like appearance. It hissed sharply, the sound like embers crackling in a bonfire.

"What are we going to do?" said Vester, repeating Billy's query. Then in answer, Vester closed his eyes for a moment, and when he opened them, fire blazed where his eyeballs had been. "We're going down with a fight," he said.

As soon as he said this, the closest zombies apparently decided that this was indeed a hostile enemy, because they suddenly lunged at Vester. But before they could get to him, Tempus clapped his hands together with the sound of thunder. Completely gone was the feeble and silly man, and now a mighty Gray Power of the Wind stood in his place. A turbulent whirlwind knocked the nearest zombies off their feet as Tempus gestured, and the wind that Billy had first seen Tempus dressed in now cloaked his body once more, the dark gray clouds writhing around him, dark and angry.

But even though the first wave of attackers had been knocked down, for every one zombie that fell two more took its place. Billy could also see that even the fallen zombies were shuffling once more to their feet, turning baleful eyes toward his friends.

But Vester had not been idle, either. As soon as Tempus cast his first spell, Vester had grabbed the tail of his Fizzle. In one quick motion he cracked the snake at the nearest zombies, wielding the lava animal like a whip. The snake bit at every creature it touched, and the zombies in range of Vester's attack were forced to fall back or be scorched by the terrible heat of the snake.

Tempus, meanwhile, was still using his power over the air to push zombies away from him, knocking them into walls, into each other, into anything.

For a few moments, the zombies could not seem to get through the defenses of wind and flame that Billy's friends had erected. He heard a sizzling in the air as the lava Fizzle managed to bite several zombies, charring their flesh and causing them to fall back with moans of pain.

But still they came, the Darksiders' horrible troops merciless and unresting. They couldn't be stopped, they couldn't be killed. Slowly, slowly, they pressed ever closer to Billy's friends.

Billy could see that the Gray and Red Powers who were so valiantly fighting were tiring now. He remembered what Vester had said at Fulgora's Challenge: that spells took a lot of energy. And he knew from things that Vester and Tempus had said that neither of them was a top-level Power, not on par with a Councilor or someone with that kind of spell strength at their disposal. So Vester's attacks with the lava snake were slowing, and each of Tempus's winds was a little less strong and threw a couple fewer zombies away from them.

Through all this, Billy pressed himself against the glass case of the Counter, trying to avoid being touched by any of the zombies nearby. But they had no interest in him, and not a one moved toward him. Apparently Vester had been right: until someone was shown to be a Dawnwalker—either by receiving a Dawnwalker badge as Ivy had or by attacking the zombies like Vester and Tempus were doing—the zombies wouldn't attack.

But Vester and Tempus *had* attacked, and they were now paying the price for their courageous stand. The zombies pressed in on Billy's friends, a horrible writhing mass, frightening to behold. As with Ivy, soon he could no longer see Vester or Tempus. But he could hear the struggle continuing long after he could no longer view what was happening.

Then, quite suddenly, there was silence. The deathly silence of the grave. The undead soldiers that had pressed in on Vester and Tempus withdrew into their semi-orderly mass, once again allowing three aisles to the Counters. Billy saw with some satisfaction that many of the zombies moved with less grace than before, their bones broken by Tempus's wind, and even more of them bore the burn marks of Vester's snakebites.

But Billy's friends were no more. Vester and Tempus, like Ivy, were gone.

And Billy was alone.

He looked around. Every zombie in the huge Accounting Room was now focused on him. Watching. Waiting. He experimented a bit by taking a step away from the Counter against which he had been cowering. At this, the zombies drew close to him, and several reached out their hands to within inches of him. Apparently there was no going back.

Billy turned slowly to the Counter. He pressed the button on the side of the glass case, as he had before.

The Counter dropped a badge into the receptacle. Billy picked it up. Once again, "Billy—unDetermined" was all the badge said. Billy stuck it to his shirt, where it magically remained. He had his eyes closed as he did so, more than half expecting the zombies to lunge at him.

As he put on the badge, he felt a strange coolness travel up his leg. Was this what it felt like when a zombie touched you? he wondered. A cool feeling, and then…nothing?

But the cool feeling dissipated as suddenly as it had come, and Billy remained standing. He risked cracking one eye open. The zombies were still all around him. But now they didn't seem to even notice him. They just stood still, looking in all directions, clearly waiting for any new arrivals. As for Billy, however, it was as though he no longer existed in their minds.

Tempus was right, he thought to himself. They don't even really notice me. Because I'm not a Power, and I'm not a Dawnwalker. Not yet, anyway.

But even though he was not in imminent danger of attack, he still didn't see how his situation could be described as anything less than horrid. No spells of his own, no powers to control, no friends to help, and surrounded by a horde of undead soldiers working for what he understood to be the most evil and powerful Black Power of all time.

And to think I ever believed Harold Crane was scary, thought Billy. The thought brought to mind the image of Harold and Sarah, both looking like they had just wet their pants thanks to Tempus's spell. Billy almost smiled. Then he remembered what had just happened to Tempus, and the smile disappeared faster than an ice cube dropped in a fire.

Billy felt like crying, just curling up right there next to the Counter and weeping until he passed out. But he couldn't do that, he knew. He didn't have the luxury of doing something like that. Not after what his friends had just done. They had gone bravely to their fate. Billy would not—could not—just give up after seeing that kind of courage.

He looked around. What could he use in here? What could be done to get out of his current predicament? He remembered his father talking about his job as a paramedic. In one of the few moments in his life where his father had really opened up to Billy, he had told him about being in the middle of an accident scene that had left over a dozen people in various stages of injury. Billy had asked how his father even knew *what* to do first, let alone remembering how to do it. His father had looked at him and said, "In any emergency where life is on the line, you calmly assess the situation. Determine a course of action. Then act on it without hesitation." Well, now Billy knew his own life hung in the balance, and he would have to stay calm and find a way out of here.

As he looked, though, he saw nothing particularly useful, not until...the elevators! He didn't know if they were still working, but imagined they probably would be, to allow the Darksiders who might come around to get from place to place on the island.

But would they work for him? And even if they did, where would he go?

Billy decided to answer those questions later, and just take things one step at a time. He was already drowning in an ocean of problems, so these difficulties just added a teacup more of water to his troubles.

And the first problem became readily apparent: no fewer than fifty zombies stood between him and where he wanted to go. He took a step toward the elevators. Though the zombies didn't make a move to attack him, they didn't get out of his way, either. There was no clear path to where he wanted to go.

Billy looked for some way around, but saw nothing. The only way out of here would be through the zombies. He took a breath, then oh-so-carefully stepped forward. He walked two steps, and then turned sideways to squeeze between two of the undead monsters. There was barely an inch of clearance on either side of him, and he knew that just touching them would knock him unconscious—if he was lucky. He gingerly took another step, moving to another small space between zombies. And another. It was like he was playing a giant game of pickup sticks, only instead of not being allowed to let any sticks move, he wasn't allowed to move himself. And the consequences of losing would be much more severe than any game Billy had ever played.

It seemed to take hours to move the hundred or so feet to the elevators, and Billy's muscles were quivering from the effort of moving so slowly and carefully. But at last he made it. The elevators stood before him, silent and unmoving.

Then, suddenly, Billy heard a "pop."

He looked over, and saw someone stepping through a dark hole that had opened in the room at about the same place Billy and his friends had just appeared. Billy could see through the Transport doorway that had been opened. He glimpsed a dark place with lit torches, a place made of dank stone and chains. If there was an encyclopedia somewhere that had a List of Ten Places You Never Want to Find Yourself, the place Billy saw was definitely near the top.

But he didn't have much time to process the place the newcomer had come from, because most of Billy's attention was on the person himself.

The newcomer spied Billy almost at the same instant Billy saw him.

"You!" snarled Cameron Black.

Cameron started to run toward Billy, the bigger boy's hand outstretched, no doubt preparing to cast some evil spell that would quickly end Billy's existence.

But now the zombies moved, closing in quickly on Cameron. It seemed that he, too, had to go to the Counter before he would be allowed to do anything else. "No," shrieked Cameron. "I'm a Darksider, you idiots!" But it was no use. The zombies herded the bigger boy to a Counter and wouldn't let him near Billy.

Billy, meanwhile, had turned around and was hurriedly stabbing at the elevator call button. He waited a very long time—maybe one millionth of a second—before hitting the button again in a rapid series of stabs that he knew would leave his thumb bruised. He didn't care. He just wanted to get out of here.

"Come on, come on," he whispered.

Cameron had gotten his badge now. "Cameron Black—Darksider," it said.

As soon as he stuck it on his shirt, the zombies started to clear a path for the bigger boy to move to the elevators. "Move, move!" screamed Cameron, unable to get to Billy as fast as he wanted. The Black Power's hand was stretched out again, and Billy said a quick prayer that Cameron couldn't do anything long distance.

BILLY: MESSENGER OF POWERS, BY MICHAELBRENT COLLINGS * 217

Apparently Cameron couldn't, because in spite of how hard his heart was now beating, Billy was grateful to feel that it *was* still beating. He kept stabbing the elevator button.

Cameron was within twenty feet now.

Billy was sure he was breaking all the bones in his thumb. "Please, please, please, please," he said in a wheeze that disturbed him to hear coming from his own mouth.

Fifteen feet.

Ten feet.

Nine....

Eight....

Seven....

DING!

Billy almost fainted with relief—which would have been a very bad strategy under the present circumstances—as the nearest elevator slid open with a musical chime. "Whaddya want?" it asked in a familiar New York accident. It was the same elevator that had taken Billy and Vester to the stadium to see Fulgora's Challenge against Napalm. Without waiting for a reply to its question, the elevator said in a bright Bronx tone, "Hey, it's you! Where's your buddy, the fireman?"

Billy threw himself into the elevator. Behind him, Cameron screamed in rage and then said something under his breath. Billy felt something nameless whip by him, numbing the tip of his ear. Whatever spell Cameron had tried to throw at him, it had just barely missed.

"Close!" screamed Billy. Cameron was raising his hand again, clearly close enough to hit Billy with something awful that would end his adventure right now.

"Where you wanna go?" asked the elevator.

"UP!" was all Billy could think to say.

"You got it!" said the elevator. Cameron said a word, and then moved his arm like he was pitching a fastball right at Billy's head, but at the last second the elevator's doors slid shut. There was a muffled thud outside at almost the same instant.

"Ow!" howled the elevator. "No respect, I tells ya." Billy felt the elevator begin to move upward, and saw as before flashes of the floors they were passing. He felt like kissing the elevator. "Ever since the place got put under new management," the elevator was still saying in its cabbie-like voice, "everything's just the pits."

"Sorry," Billy said automatically, still reveling in the experience of being neither zombie-zapped nor Cameron-creamed.

"Yeah, you're all right," said the elevator. "You and your buddy, what was his name?"

"Vester," said Billy sadly.

"Yeah, he was a good one. Good sense of humor. Not a lot of folks with senses of humor, especially not these days. Here," it continued, "you look pooped. Take a load off." A seat popped out of the side wall, and Billy dropped into it gratefully. He felt like a tire with all the air let out of it, flat and spent.

The elevator was still talking. "Yeah, now it's just nasty people. No politeness, now it's just 'Go here,' and 'Do that,' and 'No, I will *not* take my dead bodies up the stairs.' It's enough to make a grown elevator cry."

"Sorry," said Billy again. This time, he was more talking to himself. He felt very alone once again, the elation over his narrow escape dissipating and a sense of solitude, fear, and desperation taking its place. Vester. Tempus. Ivy. All of them gone. Maybe unconscious wherever they were, maybe worse.

Billy sniffled in spite of himself. He felt hot, stinging tears. Partly they were fear, partly they were shame. He felt embarrassed. Ivy, ever the hopeful pacifist, had gone with dignity to her fate. Vester and Tempus had fought like Roman gladiators, without fear even though there was no hope of victory. And what had Billy done? Cowered and ran.

Billy's mom had told him a lot of times that fighting usually wasn't a good thing, and that sometimes it took more courage to run from a fight than it did to get into one. The way she had told him that, he got the sense that she knew about it from personal experience. As always with his parents, she wouldn't talk about whatever it was in her past that made her believe it so fervently, but Billy believed her.

But at the same time, he didn't see how his mom's philosophy about running away could possibly apply here; he didn't see how running away would be a sign of bravery or wisdom in this case. He hadn't done anything. He had no power. No Unicorn had come to save the day. All he'd done was provide an audience to his friends' defeat.

He sniffled. "Say," said the elevator. "You okay?"

"I don't know," said Billy.

"Here," said the elevator. "Have a hanky." A box popped out of a compartment and Billy took the proffered tissue. He blew his nose loudly. "Don't litter, though," said the elevator, and another compartment popped open, with a little sign above it that said, "Biodegradable Trash Only—No Fizzles or Rock Monsters." Billy tossed his tissue into the trash, then put his head in his hands.

"Hey," said the elevator. "Cheer up, it can't be as bad as it seems. Whatever it is, it just can't be."

"You're right," said Billy. "It isn't as bad as it seems, it's about a million billion trillion times worse."

"Whoa," said the elevator. "That's pretty bad." Billy nodded sadly. "Well, if you want, I can give you some magic that will help, guaranteed."

Billy felt himself brighten somewhat. Perhaps this elevator was more than just a conveyance: maybe it was one of the allies Mrs. Russet's frog-message had spoken of. "Really?" Billy asked. "What magic?"

"The magic," began the elevator, and a drum roll sounded from its speakers, building up the suspense, "of good humor."

"What?" asked Billy, totally confused.

"Did ya hear the one about the two peanuts who were in an alley and got assaulted?" the elevator asked with a braying laugh. "What about the one where the mushroom walks into a restaurant and the manager tells him, 'We don't serve mushrooms here,' and the mushroom says, 'Why not? I'm a fun-guy.' Get it? Fun-guy. Like 'fungi,' like a fancy word for a mushroom. Ah-hahahaha!" The elevator was cackling semi-hysterically at its own jokes, and Billy could actually feel the thing rocking back and forth with laughter.

Billy just sat there dully, not sure how to react. Jokes were definitely not the thing he needed right now. He needed something tougher on his side. Like a deadly poisonous bear made entirely of smaller but also-poisonous bees. Or at least an F-16 fighter jet.

The elevator was still laughing. Then the laughter petered out, and Billy could swear he heard the sound of jolly tears being wiped from an eye. "Whew! Those never go out of style, do they?" asked the elevator.

Then it dinged. Billy jumped at the sudden sound.

"What was that?" he asked.

"We're here," replied the elevator, still wheezing from its fit of laughter. The doors slid open.

"Where's 'here'?" asked Billy, but the view he was presented with as the doors opened gave him his answer.

"You said you just wanted to go up," answered the elevator. "Well, this is as up as I go."

It was the top of the tower. Nearby, Billy could see the river that bisected the tower, though instead of being bordered by beautiful flowers and leaves, now the river was muddy and full of rocks. The tower itself was covered in rubble, evidence of the fight that Ivy had told Billy about. The Darksiders had taken the Dawnwalkers of the Council, but Billy could see that, like Tempus and Vester, the Councilors hadn't gone down without a fight.

Nevertheless, this didn't look like a good place to be. The top of the tower would be open and exposed, nowhere to run to, nowhere to hide if he was found.

"Well?" prompted the elevator, and Billy realized he hadn't moved a muscle.

"Uh," said Billy, unsure. "Couldn't I go somewhere else?"

"Like where?" asked the elevator.

"Um, somewhere to hide?" asked Billy hopefully. A hiding spot would be good. And quick, because he had no way of knowing if Cameron could find out where he'd gone to, or if the bigger boy was hot on his trail.

"Well, sure, I can take you right to some primo hiding places!" said the elevator enthusiastically.

"Great!" said Billy, brightening at the first good news in what felt like forever.

"Of course, you'll have to travel with someone for part of the way," continued the elevator.

"What? Who?" said Billy in a panic.

"Dunno. Some lady just pressed my button, if you know what I mean. Creepy gal, dressed all in black, big nasty bug on her shoulder."

"Mrs. *Black*?" screamed Billy.

"Yeah, that's the one," said the elevator happily. Then in a conspiratorial tone, it said, "Not one of my favorite passengers, I can tell ya."

"But, but," said Billy, sounding like an airplane engine trying to turn over. "But, but, not her. Can't you just ignore her?"

"Nah, rules are rules. I'm an elevator. Someone presses my button, I gotta go. But I can hide you after I pick her up," it said reassuringly.

"But she'll have killed me by then!" moaned Billy.

The elevator was silent for a moment. "That'll definitely make it harder to hide you," it finally said. "But not impossible," it continued. "Like they always say, 'You can always find a good places to shove a corpse.'"

"What? Who says that?" said Billy in a frenzied tone. He was fairly sure he could actually feel his brain melting in a combination of confusion and panic. "Never mind," he said an instant later, before the elevator could go off again on one of its well-intentioned but supremely unhelpful tangents. "I'll just get off here," he managed, and stepped out of the still-open doors.

"All righty then," said the elevator. "It's been a pleasure, kid, as always. Now I'm off to get that Mrs. Black." The elevator shuddered as its doors closed. "Ugh," it said. "Creepy people wearing creepy bug pins, the place has just gone straight to...," then its voice was lost to Billy's hearing as it dropped through the ground of the tower, leaving no trace of its existence behind.

Once again, Billy was alone. He appeared to be in a somewhat better situation now, since there were no zombies around, but he still felt very exposed. In fact, he felt more than exposed. He felt like he was being watched.

He looked behind him, and saw immediately that the elevator had deposited him within a few yards of the Diamond Dais. The podium was still cracked, with the single thin shard of crystal still jutting up from its center.

Billy also saw something else. He saw that his feeling had been correct. He *was* being watched.

The figure was draped across the Black Throne, one leg thrown disdainfully over the arm of the dark pearl chair. The man smiled when he saw Billy, then hopped in an almost chipper way out of the seat. The happy jaunt to his gait, however, was belied by the serpentine look in his eyes, and a grin like a spider inviting a fly into its parlor.

"Hello, Billy," said Wolfen.

# CHAPTER THE SEVENTEENTH

*In Which Billy is Cleansed, and taken Away...*

Billy's tongue felt like a giant rock in his mouth, thick and dry and useless for speech. A sudden feeling of fear had gripped him from his toes to the crown of his head.

Wolfen walked to the edge of the Diamond Dais and jumped lightly to the ground below, seeming almost to float down. His green eyes flashed with a disturbing inner light, as though Wolfen's mind was ablaze with a dark fire.

"Why so quiet?" purred the Power. He approached Billy with a kind of deliberate casualness, appearing to walk in an almost meandering gait that nevertheless moved him closer to Billy with every step.

Run, Billy thought to himself. Run.

But he couldn't move. His feet were planted as firmly on the tower as though he were part of the stone it was made of.

Wolfen was still wearing the black clothing covered by a white coat, the exact same outfit Billy had seen him wearing before, on the day that Wolfen had sworn allegiance to the Council. From what Billy understood, Wolfen's words had to have been true, because the Diamond Dais had turned green when the Power spoke them. Nonetheless, the Council had been attacked, and Wolfen stood before him now, his smile broadening as he contemplated the fear-ridden Billy.

"I must confess," said Wolfen, "you're somewhat less than I expected. The way Lumilla spoke of you, I rather pictured someone a bit more imposing." Wolfen paused, leaning in close to Billy. "At the very least, a bit braver."

Billy felt his lip quiver. He was surprised at how terribly frightened he was. Not that Wolfen wasn't scary. He was. But Billy could somehow feel, in a strangely disconnected way, that his fear was far out of proportion to what it should have been.

Wolfen waved a hand, and Billy's fear doubled in intensity, almost causing him to fall over. Billy clutched at his stomach in raw terror, biting his lip to keep from shouting.

"What you are feeling," said Wolfen in a calm, conversational tone, "is the Dread. It's one of my specialties." The way he said that left Billy with no doubt that Wolfen had other specialties, and that some of them were much, much worse.

Every bad thing that Billy had ever experienced, every frightening moment, every pain from the smallest sliver to the time he had broken his leg in grammar school and had to have surgery, crowded into Billy's mind. It was as though he was made of fear, a writhing snake of horror that would suffocate him in its constrictive grasp.

Billy could feel his heart pounding. Far too hard, far too fast. He could hear his pulse in his eardrums, beating with machine-gun speed and intensity, and knew his heart couldn't keep up like this for much longer: he would literally drop dead of fear.

Wolfen walked slowly around Billy, taking his time, a hawk circling an injured field mouse before dropping in for the final blow. He spoke as he walked, and the words confirmed Billy's suspicions: "If I don't let up soon, Billy, you will simply fall over and be consumed by your greatest fears." He made a small movement, a crook of his finger, and Billy felt the terror ease somewhat. It didn't go away entirely, but his heart slowed from its dangerous speed.

Billy's mouth still felt dry, but he managed to croak out a single word. "Why?" he said.

"Always an interesting question," responded Wolfen. He smiled. "But not to be answered today, I think." He suddenly stopped circling, standing behind Billy. Billy still couldn't move, but he felt the intensity of Wolfen's hateful gaze boring into him. "Instead," continued the evil Power, "I think I will ask the questions, and you will answer them." He leaned toward Billy, and Billy could smell the man's rank breath, rotten and fetid, as though he hadn't brushed his teeth in a million years. "Who are you, Mr. Jones?" asked Wolfen.

"I don't know what you mean," Billy managed to answer through chattering teeth.

"Who are you?" repeated Wolfen. "What is it about you that made Lumilla think you were so special?"

"What have you done with her?" Billy asked.

Immediately, he knew that was the wrong response. His fear redoubled, and he fell to his knees. "I've done as I pleased with her," was Wolfen's cryptic response. "Just as I will do with any Power who crosses me." He stood in front of Billy now, legs wide, fists clenched as though he was restraining himself from physically attacking Billy.

Instead, however, he reached out to Billy. He extended a finger, and Billy was reminded for a moment of the clutching hands of the zombies he had repeatedly escaped from. But this was no zombie reaching for him now, it was something much worse. And Billy couldn't even *move* this time, much less actively flee from the reaching grasp.

Wolfen's claw-like hand moved closer to Billy. The finger was only a centimeter away from Billy's heart, from his chest. Billy braced himself for whatever might come, knowing at the same time that whatever it was, he couldn't possibly prepare for it. It would be devastating, and Wolfen would have no mercy.

But at the last second, something intervened. There was a hiss, and a bright flash of light. Billy had a quick glimpse of a red form. Whatever it was moved too fast to be made out, but it was lithe and angry, and had appeared from somewhere close, before disappearing once again to wherever it had come from.

He had no time to ponder this strange event, though, because at the same time it happened Wolfen cried out in rage and pain. The hand that had only a millisecond before been reaching out to Billy was now clutched against the Darksider's chest. In that same instant, Billy felt himself suddenly free to move again, the icy grip of the Dread gone.

Billy wasted no time, but stood and ran as fast as he could. Behind him, he heard Wolfen whisper, "How?" Then, in a voice that was so full of hate Billy could hardly bear to hear it, the Black Power screamed, "You will be *mine!*"

But Billy didn't turn around to see if Wolfen's expression matched the sound of his voice. He just ran for all he was worth. Billy had never been athletic—just one more reason he had been picked on all his life—but fear of the terrible force behind him lent him strength and fleetness. He felt as though he could have outrun a cheetah.

Unfortunately, he didn't know where he could go. He was just running aimlessly, without a plan of any kind. As far as he knew, there was only the Diamond Dais, the river, and the plant life on the tower. The Diamond Dais was where Wolfen was at, the very place Billy least wanted to go. The river was fast moving, and both sides of it ended in waterfalls that would send Billy plummeting over the side of the tower, thousands of feet to certain death. And the plant life that had once covered much of the tower was now either buried in rubble or dried and withered, offering no place to hide.

Billy heard Wolfen scream again; apparently whatever had just happened had really hurt him. Then Billy heard Wolfen's feet as the Darksider began to run after him.

Billy looked around, still running as fast as he could, but hearing Wolfen right behind him. Rubble and rock were scattered everywhere, some of the pieces quite large, but Billy knew hiding behind a big stone would be futile, since Wolfen could undoubtedly just zap him right through it.

However, seeing the rubble gave Billy an idea. He glanced around and saw what he was looking for, running as quickly as he could to a particularly large stone nearby. He prayed silently as he ran that Wolfen wouldn't guess what Billy was going to do; he remembered Mrs. Russet saying that the most powerful Black Powers could level entire cities, so he was sure that hitting Billy with a crippling Dread—or something even worse—would be no problem for Wolfen. Indeed, Billy suspected that the only reason he wasn't already laid out flat was because Wolfen's concentration had been broken by whatever pain he had just experienced. But that wouldn't last for long, and Billy knew that if he was caught before he could put his idea in motion, if Wolfen so much as laid a finger on him, he would be trapped again, and this time for good.

But Wolfen didn't seem to guess what Billy was planning, apparently blinded by rage that someone—anyone—had dared to escape from him or hurt him in any way.

Billy made it to the stone he had spotted. Now there was nowhere farther to run, he was literally between a rock and a very hard place.

"There's nowhere to go, Billy!" Wolfen screamed triumphantly, now only a few yards behind Billy. His triumph turned to indignation and anger however as he finally realized what Billy was doing. "No!" he screamed.

But it was too late. Billy hurriedly traced the word "Transport" on the rock with his finger, and just as it had done before, a golden doorway—the doorway to the anteroom that was hidden in this stone—opened up.

Billy yanked the door open and stepped through it, slamming it shut behind him. Wolfen's incoherent cry of wrath was instantly cut off. Billy backed away from the doorway as fast as he could, looking around for a chair or something to wedge under the door. But then he realized that the door opened *outward*, so putting a chair under the door handle would be useless. Besides, just as before the only thing to sit on in this cheery room was a collection of colored beanbags. He couldn't even throw anything through the large window that looked out onto the beautiful snow-caked vista outside the room. The glass looked very thick, and he doubted he could muster the power to smash through it with a beanbag and flee out into the dazzling storm of snowflakes beyond.

Billy ran around the bar from which Vester had served him the hot chocolate that had tasted so wonderful at the time. It seemed like a million years had passed since then, a thousand lifetimes in which Billy had experienced so many new things that he bore little resemblance to the boy he had been.

Behind the bar, on a small shelf below it, was a mug that was already full of hot chocolate. Not a "Vester special" this time, but a simple cup of cocoa. That was all Billy had been hoping to find, and he realized that the magic hot chocolate bar would serve the hot chocolate wished by anyone in the room.

Billy hefted the mug. He dumped the chocolate unceremoniously on the floor, then held the empty cup over his head, waiting for the anteroom door to open. When Wolfen came in, Billy would chuck the mug at the evil wizard as hard as he could. Billy knew it was a useless gesture—he never got picked for baseball teams at school precisely because he could throw a ball about as accurately as a paralyzed earthworm—but he was determined to do something.

So he held the mug overhead, and waited.
And waited.
And waited.
And the door....
...finally....
...didn't open.

Billy lowered the cup, frowning. What had just happened? Why wasn't Wolfen barging in here? Then he realized: the doorway to the anteroom was activated by a special key word, a word that Billy had known because Mrs. Russet had told him. But Wolfen, apparently, did *not* know the word. So Billy was safe. For the moment at least.

Billy breathed a sigh of relief. Then new terror flooded him as he felt something scuttle across his foot! Billy screamed and threw himself backward. Unfortunately, there was a wall right behind him so instead of getting away from whatever monster was now attacking, he just managed to bounce gracelessly off the wall and then go down in a pile on the floor, where he saw what had run across his foot.

It was one of the rock Fizzles that cleaned this room. It had a rag in its many dexterous hands (or was that feet?), and was conscientiously and rapidly cleaning the mess Billy had made when he dumped out the cocoa on the floor. Within an instant, the spill was gone, as though it had never been. The Fizzle, though it had no eyes in its tiny rock head, seemed to look at Billy. It shook its top two arms/legs at Billy, clearly communicating the idea of "Be more careful next time!" And as soon as it did, it immediately ran over and scrubbed a bit of cocoa off Billy's shoe, sighing in exasperation.

Then the Fizzle spotted the remains of the cocoa mug, which had fallen to the ground and shattered when Billy fell. The Fizzle seemed to droop a bit, not in depression, but almost as though its low expectations of Billy's ability to keep things tidy had just been fulfilled.

Billy watched, his terror at the thought of Wolfen barging in after him momentarily alleviated, as the rock Fizzle expertly flicked the dirty, cocoa-saturated rag it held. The rag whipped around the rock creature, wrapping itself around the Fizzle like a toga. The move reminded Billy of an expert kung fu fighter throwing nunchuks over his shoulder: clearly this was a kind of Bruce Lee of cleaning.

The Fizzle scuttled over to the pieces of broken mug and began to gather them up in its tiny arms (Billy decided he was just going to call them arms, even though the Fizzle seemed to run on them or use them to grasp things at will). However, even with its many hands, it was too small to get all the pieces gathered up. A shrill whistle came from the Fizzle, and a moment later three more of them appeared from nowhere, emerging from the darkness under the bar.

The newcomers—each subtly different from one another, but cut from similar molds—scuttled over to the Fizzle who was holding some of Billy's mug. They put their heads together, and Billy could hear wordless whisperings, with one of the Fizzles occasionally glancing over its shoulder at Billy. There were no expressions on those tiny stone faces, but each time that happened, Billy felt like the Fizzle in question was saying "How could you?" in exasperated tones.

Finally, all four Fizzles gathered up the last bits of Billy's broken mug. Then they scampered off under the bar, and with four matching "pops," they disappeared, leaving Billy, once more, alone.

This was fine with Billy. He got slowly back to his feet, glancing at the door to the anteroom once more. Still no Wolfen. He looked back at the shelf under the bar, and saw that a new mug of hot chocolate had appeared. Billy took it and sipped it gladly. The liquid, as it had before, tasted absolutely wonderful. It seemed almost like Billy was pouring courage and consolation down his throat, making him feel as though perhaps everything would turn out all right.

He looked around. As before, the pot-bellied stove glowed with cheery warmth, and the window offered a spectacular view of the windswept mountains and the beautifully shimmering snowflakes that were too large to be believed and constantly grouped themselves into shapes and images. Billy watched, in quick succession, a snowflake beaver, a snowflake book, and a snowflake baseball bat appear. Apparently the snowflakes were practicing their "B" words today.

Billy sank down on a bean bag, grateful for a moment alone to think without having to worry about sudden and painful doom falling on him. He had almost forgotten what a moment without threat of death felt like.

He thought about Wolfen. How had the man lied to the Diamond Dais? What was he doing just sitting there alone? Waiting for Billy? That seemed to make no sense, but Billy had to admit to himself that Wolfen hadn't seemed at all surprised by Billy's sudden appearance out of the elevator.

What seemed to make even less sense, however, was Wolfen's failure to keep Billy under the control of the Dread. What had happened when the Black Power reached out? What had caused the bright flash of light? What had saved Billy?

"What saved me?" he said out loud. He did it unconsciously, not expecting any reply, just so deep into his thoughts that his mouth was operating on its own.

But in spite of the fact that he didn't expect one, a reply *did* come. Billy felt a sudden coolness at his leg. It was just like the cool tingling he had felt before, down in the Accounting Room. Vester and Tempus had just been dispatched by the zombies, and Billy had had his eyes closed and felt that strange sensation.

Billy looked down at his foot, for now the cool feeling had traveled there. And he saw what had saved him from Wolfen.

It was Vester's lava Fizzle, the red snake emerging from Billy's pants leg where it had been hiding and then laying in a small coil nearby Billy's feet. Billy remembered Ivy telling him that Fizzles could be let loose if their makers weren't careful. Apparently Vester had allowed this one to go free, either on purpose or because the zombie attack in the Accounting Room had not allowed him to maintain control over the magical creature.

The lava Fizzle flicked a flaming tongue out and in, staring at Billy. Billy looked back at it. The snake's skin, being molten rock, moved back and forth in a shifting pattern that was both beautiful and disconcerting. Its eyes were simply two spots that glowed a bright yellow, like embers about to be cast off at any moment. But even though the Fizzle had been born of lava and the Element of Fire, it didn't burn the hardwood floor below it. Apparently it could control its heat.

Of course, Billy thought. That's why I didn't feel it burning me. That's why it felt cool, like a regular snake would have.

Billy leaned a bit closer to the snake. "You saved me?" he asked. The Fizzle paused a moment, its tongue still flicking, then slowly dipped its head in affirmation. "Why?" asked Billy. But the Fizzle clearly couldn't talk: it just stared at Billy and shook its head back and forth. "Well," said Billy. "Thank you."

The Fizzle grinned and nodded. A clear "you're welcome."

"Do you have a name?" asked Billy. The Fizzle shook its head. "Can I give you one?" Nod. Billy thought. What would he call it? Fire-monster? Snaky? No, those sounded lame, and Billy wanted something cool for the beast that had just saved his life.

"Viper?" he tried. The Fizzle looked vaguely disgusted. "Flame?" Even more disgusted. "What about His Royal Highness Prince Snakeyton the Third?" Billy asked with a grin.

To Billy's surprise, the snake nodded, looking very pleased. Billy laughed. "That's a bit long, though," he said. "How about I just call you Prince?" The snake nodded again, as though accepting this, but it seemed slightly less thrilled over the shortened version of his new name.

"So," Billy said after a moment, "you can't talk." The snake shook its head. "But you did save me. Was that on purpose?" Nod. Billy thought. "You're a Fizzle. Do you know who made you?" Another nod. Billy thought some more. He remembered that Imbued Objects had a piece of their maker's essence inside them. He wondered if it was the same for Fizzles. "Since Vester made you, do you have some of Vester's feelings?" He felt rather silly asking that question, but Prince took it in stride and simply nodded. "So...," Billy began slowly, working it out in his mind as he spoke, "you like me, and don't like Wolfen." The snake nodded, but slowly, as though Billy was almost, but not quite right. "You like me, and *hate* Wolfen?" he tried again. This time, the nod was more vigorous, but still held something back. Billy tried again. "You *love* me, and hate Wolfen?"

This time, the snake nodded enthusiastically. Billy felt warm inside. His parents loved him, he knew that. Or at least, he knew his mom loved him, and suspected it was also true of his father. But he couldn't think of anyone else who had ever expressed that feeling. He'd never met his grandparents—all of them had died before Billy was born—and none of his schoolmates had ever shown him any particular affection. So knowing that Prince loved him, and that that meant that *Vester* had come to love him, even in the short period they had had to interact, meant a great deal to Billy.

He stood quickly, suddenly resolved to fix things. He was going to find his friends. He was going to find Dark Isle, and he was going to free them.

He looked at the anteroom door. There was no way out there: he didn't know if Wolfen was still waiting for him, or if Cameron or Eva Black might be lurking outside the door, but he couldn't risk that. Not until he had some way to fight them, some weapon or something that would even the odds.

Billy spent a few moments looking around the room. He looked behind the pot-bellied stove, to see if perhaps there was another door leading out. He tapped the walls and the floor, listening to hear if there were perhaps hollow spaces that might hold a hidden doorway or even just something he could maybe break through to make his escape. But everything was solid and firm.

He looked at Prince. "Do you know a way out?" Snakes didn't have shoulders, at least as far as Billy knew, but he could swear that the Fizzle shrugged. Billy continued looking, but didn't have much hope. It appeared as though he was going to have to go back out the way he had come in.

At least I can wait a while here, he thought. Maybe they'll be gone when I come out.

Then on the heels of that he thought, Fat chance.

A moment later, another thought popped, unbidden and most certainly unwelcome, into his head. It consisted of only two words, but those words were more than enough to send him rocketing around the room, looking—frantically this time—for a way out. The words were these: Mrs. Black.

She was a Councilor, he realized. She probably knew the keyword for the anteroom, even if Wolfen didn't. And he knew that she had been in the tower, because the elevator had told him so. Surely Cameron would tell his mother that Billy had been in the Accounting Room, and just as surely Mrs. Black would be able to track him down, get into the anteroom, and then turn him over to Wolfen.

Billy's sense of urgency increased as he thought all of this. He didn't have hours, or perhaps even minutes. How can I get out? he thought desperately. How can I get out?

Prince followed him around as Billy looked helplessly for some sign of an exit, but other than providing companionship he didn't give much help.

Billy looked at the huge glass window. The snowflakes outside had arranged suddenly into a chillingly accurate rendition of Wolfen's face, then into an equally frightening version of Mrs. Black's cold features. Billy ran at the glass, thinking he might be able to just smash through it himself. But it was no use. The glass—if it even was glass, and not some kind of magical substance that couldn't be broken—resisted him easily, and once more Billy found himself bouncing to the floor like a rubber ball. His shoulder ached.

"Ow," he moaned. Still on the floor, he looked around again. "How do I get out?" he said. Prince hissed. "Sorry, how do *we* get out?"

He looked out the window again. There *had* to be a way to break it. But then his attention was arrested once more by the snowflakes outside. They had made a new shape. At first Billy didn't recognize it, but then suddenly he realized what it was: a cocoa mug. Billy watched as, slowly, in a glimmer of bright color, the snowflake mug tipped, and Billy could actually see snowflake cocoa spilling out before scattering into separate pieces in the storm.

He couldn't look away from the sight. Somehow, he felt, the snowflakes weren't just making a random shape this time. It was like they had done when they had formed a large hand waving goodbye the last time he had left the anteroom. They were, not talking exactly, but communicating somehow.

They're trying to help me find a way out, he realized.

"But how does a mug of cocoa get me out?" he asked.

In answer, the snowflakes repeated their pantomime, the icy doilies whirling together to once more make the shape of a mug, which once more spilled out.

Billy thought. He looked at Prince. The Fizzle looked thoroughly puzzled.

Then, suddenly, Billy knew.

He hurried to the bar. As he had expected, there was cocoa waiting for him once more. But not just one mug. This time, the entire space beneath the bar was chock full of steaming cups of cocoa. The smell was delicious, but Billy had no intention of drinking them.

He put a hand on the floor. "Get on," he told Prince. The lava snake obliged, curling up on Billy's wrist. As soon as the snake was safely in place, Billy used his other arm to sweep every single mug under the bar out onto the floor. They landed in a wet, sloppy shatter that immediately drenched everything—including Billy—in wonderful-smelling chocolate that was littered with shards of broken cups.

A moment later, a Fizzle—the same one who had cleaned up Billy's first spill—ran out from under the bar. It screamed a tiny, high-pitched scream when it saw the mess. A moment later, a dozen or so other Fizzles appeared, holding rags and tiny mops. They began scrubbing at the mess.

Billy looked under the bar again. More cocoa had appeared, in answer to his silent request. He swept that onto the floor as well, the cleaner Fizzles jumping out of the way of the new torrent of spills and cocoa disaster. Billy wished more cocoa into existence and did it again. And again. A dozen more Fizzles appeared, then two dozen, then hordes of the tiny rock creatures were all around, trying in vain to keep up with Billy as he spilled cocoa as fast as he could.

Soon the room was awash in hot chocolate and panicky Fizzles. Some of them were actually crying in frustration, grinding little sobs with dust-tears that ran down their faces.

"I'm not stopping," said Billy, sending another round of cocoa clattering to the floor. "I'm going to do this forever, until I drop."

The cleaners all gasped in horror. They all stopped moving, clearly paralyzed by such a callous, psychopathic disregard for neatness.

Then, one of the Fizzles nearby raised its tiny mop. It shouted a high-pitched scream that sounded amazingly like a bugle calling to arms. "Attack," it seemed to say.

And that's just what the rock Fizzles did. Billy saw instantly that the Fizzles' didn't just twirl rags with the skill of a martial artist, they actually *knew* some kind of magical karate. All of them dropped into what Billy could only assume were fighting stances. Then, with a synchronized "Key-yah!" the Fizzles attacked. The room was instantly filled with Fizzles that jump-kicked; with Fizzles that ran at Billy while carving intricate and dangerous-looking, though tiny, figure eights with their mops; and with Fizzles that did cartwheels and flips as though they had seen one too many kung fu movies.

They swarmed at Billy, and soon there were dozens if not hundreds of the rock janitors punching and kicking at Billy's feet, pushing him bodily away from the bar. Billy's feet slipped on several of the creatures as he stepped backward, and he went down—for the third time—to the ground. This time, however, it wasn't only floor he fell on. It was Fizzles. They grabbed him tightly, holding his arms, holding his feet, holding his pants and his shirt, even holding his hair.

Billy struggled for a moment, but it was no use. The Fizzles had him held fast. The first Fizzle, who Billy had come to think of as something of a leader, crawled onto Billy's chest and looked at him. Billy could feel the triumph in the Fizzle's stance.

"It doesn't matter," Billy said. "You can't hold me here forever, and as soon as you let me up, I'm going to go back at it again." The Fizzles all gasped once more, and Billy added the coup-de-grace. "As long as I'm in this room," he said as belligerently as he could, "I will make…a…*mess*."

Another gasp. The leader Fizzle jumped down off Billy's chest, and he could hear a buzzing sound as the Fizzles around him conferred. Then, suddenly, he was hoisted bodily in the air, hundreds of Fizzles moving under him to support his weight, like ants lifting a grasshopper.

At the same time, Billy heard something. The door to the anteroom! It was out of sight on the other side of the bar, but Billy could hear it opening. It was Mrs. Black, or even worse, Wolfen, it had to be!

But the Fizzles paid no heed to the sound. They simply continued marching him toward the bar, still holding him firm. They walked with him right under the shelf.

"Where are you, Mr. Jones?" came the voice of Mrs. Black.

But Billy had no chance to answer, because at that moment, the Fizzles holding him all gave a shiver, and with a small "pop" Billy suddenly found himself somewhere else.

# CHAPTER THE EIGHTEENTH

*In Which Billy is Unexpected, and meets Someone New…*

Billy let out his breath. Holding it whenever Transporting was quickly becoming second nature to him. He managed to look at his wrist, and verified that Prince was still coiled coolly around it before the Fizzles holding his hair yanked on it so that Billy's head snapped back and all he could see was a ceiling.

And what a ceiling! It was white, and that was all. That may not have sounded like much to anyone not actually there, but Billy had never in his life seen anything quite so white. It would have made a super-model ashamed of the color of her artificially brightened teeth, and a polar bear would have looked black if standing in front of it. It was so clean and spotless that it actually glowed, reflecting every bit of light in the room as brightly and perfectly as a mirror.

Below him, the Fizzles that Billy now thought of as the Kung Fu Cleaners were holding a whispered conference of some kind. Apparently they decided that in this place Billy was no longer a threat to the world's cleanliness, and so they dumped him unceremoniously on the ground before skittering away. The leader of the Kung Fu Cleaners, the Fizzle who had berated Billy for spilling his cocoa in the first place, cast a last threatening look at Billy, then ran off as well.

Billy rose slowly to his feet. He had been dropped on the floor in some form or other four times in the last few minutes, and his body was starting to feel the effects. He suspected that he would resemble a grape this time tomorrow, puffy and round and a beautiful shade of deep purple from head to toe.

He looked around and took in his surroundings. It was an awesome sight. There were Kung Fu Cleaners everywhere. Not just the hundreds that had grabbed Billy, but thousands, perhaps *hundreds* of thousands. And each one was actively cleaning something: dishes, cups, silverware. Fizzles were loading dirty clothes into what looked like a washing machine the size of a house. Fizzles were putting even more sopping wet laundry into a dryer that was equally as big.

One Fizzle, Billy saw, was busily sorting socks into two mountainous piles, one of which had a sign that said "Left Socks Here," while the other had a sign proclaiming "Right Socks Here." This seemed to Billy to be not only a bit excessive, but actually ridiculous, because dozens of other Fizzles were hurriedly crawling around, on top of, and through the two piles, finding paired socks and throwing them into a bin the size of a dump truck.

But beyond all that, beyond the sorting and the cleaning and the polishing, beyond the hundreds of thousands of Fizzles and their hundreds of thousands of tasks, the thing that was first and most noticeable was that the whole place gleamed. Everything was pure, spotlessly white. The laundry machines, the neat stacks of clean plates, the floors. The place he was in was so large and so full of cleaning appliances that Billy couldn't see any walls, but he suspected they, too, were that same brilliant white.

Something tapped his foot. It was another Kung Fu Cleaner, the Fizzle tapping on Billy's sneaker with its mop as it cleaned the floor. Billy obligingly lifted his foot, and the Fizzle ran under it, mopping for all it was worth, continuing on in a perfectly straight line until it disappeared from Billy's view.

"Where are we?" he asked Prince. The snake hissed, and licked itself like a cat. Cleaning itself. "Well I *know* we're in someplace clean," said Billy. "That's not much help."

As he spoke to Prince, a thought struck him. Fizzles, he now knew, carried something of the personality of their makers with them. So what kind of person would create Fizzles who knew karate and were concerned with cleanliness to the point of it being a psychiatric disorder?

A moment later, he had his answer as a spot of color appeared in his view. The color was brown, a brown coat worn by a bent and wizened old man who limped slowly, leaning on a cane held in each hand, into the area where Billy stood.

"More bleach!" bellowed the old man to the Fizzles who were washing clothes. He grabbed a sock out of the sock pile. The sock, like the floor and ceiling, was so dazzlingly white it almost hurt Billy's eyes. But the old man apparently did not agree like what he saw. "You call this clean?" he grumped, throwing the sock back into the pile with a disgusted look. "It's like a pig wore it to a pig sock hop in a mud pool and had pig mudshakes which it spilled on its muddy socks."

Now, quite suddenly, the man spotted Billy. He frowned. "You," he finally said, "are filthy."

Billy didn't know quite how to respond to that. On one hand, he knew he was sweaty and drenched with hot chocolate. On the other hand, considering what he'd just been through, he thought he probably looked rather spiffy. At least, he did as long as you defined "spiffy" as "not dead."

The old man didn't wait for a reply, though, and snapped his fingers imperiously. Several hundred Kung Fu Cleaners swarmed toward the man, who was clearly their master. The man pointed at Billy. "How did he get here? Who is he?"

The assembled Fizzles looked at each other as though waiting for someone to step up and start talking first. "Well?" asked the old man, waving his cane in what Billy guessed was supposed to be a threatening motion. Unfortunately, any sense of threat was mitigated by the fact that as soon as the cane left the ground, the old man toppled to the floor.

Billy rushed forward to help the old fellow up. "Are you okay, sir?" asked Billy.

"Certainly I'm okay," snapped the old man, yanking his arm out of Billy's grip. This caused him to fall again. Billy helped him up, and this time the old man let him do it, even going so far as to pull Billy with him as he hobbled along on his inspection tour. As they walked, Billy could see that the old man wore one of the required badges—the ones that called out a person's name and affiliation with either the Darksiders or Dawnwalkers. Unfortunately, the old man's cloak was so voluminous that the badge was always mostly covered in folds of dark cloth, so this strange old man's identity remained a mystery to Billy.

And even if the badge *had* been visible, Billy didn't know if he could have spared enough attention to read it. The old man was moving at a surprising pace, pounding along on two feet and two canes as he inspected his domain. The old man constantly called out directions to the cleaning rock Fizzles, sternly reprimanding them for the "untidiness," "uncleanliness," and "downright filthosity" of the area. Billy wasn't even sure that "filthosity" was a word, but he *was* fairly certain that he had found the person in charge of cleaning, not just the anteroom, but much of Powers Island.

His suspicions were confirmed as he passed a chute, out of which half-eaten hot dogs from Powers Stadium were falling, landing in a bin the size of a garbage truck, all of them screaming piteously about the fact that they would never be eaten.

"Quiet!" roared the old man as he passed them. He handed Billy his canes, which Billy took automatically, then climbed with surprising nimbleness up the side of the container that held the hot dogs. He leaned far over the side, his cloak riding up to reveal the old man's white legs and long white underwear, his behind stuck high in the air. Billy looked away, embarrassed. He didn't know if there was some social rule against looking at the legs of hundred-year-old men, or watching their bony behinds stuck up in the air, but if there wasn't there should have been.

The old man finally hoisted himself back over the side of the bin and clambered down holding a pair of half-eaten hot dogs.

"My prayers have been answered!" shouted one ecstatic frankfurter.

"Praise be to the Powers!" chorused the other.

"Eat me first!" said the first.

"No, eat *me* first!" countered the second. This spawned a short argument.

"He doesn't want you first, you indigestible pig's foot!" screamed one in miniature rage.

"Well, if you think he'd eat a hot dog made of chicken lips like you, you're sadly mistaken!" yelled the other.

The old man quickly settled the argument, however, by squishing both of the partially eaten hot dogs into his mouth at the same time. His cheeks bulged like a fat squirrel's, and tears ran down his cheeks, but he managed to chew and swallow the entire mass.

Billy felt slightly ill, both at the fact that the hot dogs were what car commercials tastefully called "pre-owned," and at the fact that he was pretty sure he could hear moans of satisfaction still coming from the old man's throat as the hot dogs went down.

"Well, don't just stand there," crabbed the old man, grabbing his canes from Billy and resuming his walk.

Billy looked down at Prince, hoping for some clue that would help him to know what he should do next. The lava snake appeared to be asleep, however, leaving Billy alone to hurry after the old man.

"Where are we going?" asked Billy.

"Where do you want to go?" responded the old man.

"Uh, I don't really know," Billy finally managed.

"Then it doesn't really matter, does it?" answered the old man. "And you never answered my question."

"What question?" answered Billy, thoroughly confused.

"What kind of bleach do you think you're using?" asked the man, adding greatly to Billy's confusion before he realized that the old man was talking to one of his Fizzles. The Fizzle spoke in its high-pitched voice, a sound that was almost unintelligible to Billy—though he got an impression that the Kung Fu Cleaner was begging for mercy—but which the old man apparently understood quite well. "Humph," he said in reply to the Fizzle. "You know what I think about the generic brands. Well, what's your name?"

Billy stood there for a long moment before he realized that this last sentence had in fact been addressed to him. "Billy," he managed. "Billy, uh, Jones."

"Well, Billy Uhjones," said the old man. "I'm Rumpelstiltskin." He threw open his robe to show Billy his name tag, and sure enough, it said "Rumpelstiltskin" on it. But to Billy's surprise, that was all it said. There was no indication of the man's power, or of whether he was a Darksider or a Dawnwalker. Billy was almost shocked; he had thought he was the only one on Powers Island who was unDetermined.

Maybe we're not on Powers Island, Billy thought, maybe this is somewhere else.

But as soon as that thought came, he dismissed it. If they weren't on the island, the old man wouldn't have had a name tag in the first place, and Billy's own tag would have disappeared in a puff of smoke and flame, the same as it had done each time he left the island.

"Yup, Rumpelstiltskin's the name," continued the doddering old man, "but my friends call me Terry."

"Okay, Terry, I—" began Billy.

"Who said we were friends?" asked the man. Billy was floored. He couldn't keep up with this guy's train of thought. Or was it trains? Certainly the man seemed to be going in all directions at once, and Billy wasn't quite sure how to follow along. "Now," continued the old man, "if your name was Billy *Jones*, for instance, then maybe we'd be friends. But I make it a practice not to consort with *Uh*joneses. They tend to be a bit sneaky. Small feet, you know." Then he cast a long look at Billy. "No offense," he added. "Your feet look fine."

"But," Billy finally managed when Rumpelstiltskin stopped talking long enough to take a breath, "I *am* Billy Jones."

"Nonsense," said Rumpelstiltskin—or Terry, as his friends called him. He whacked a Fizzle who was mopping the floor too slowly. "I've met Billy Uhjones, and you look just like him. I met him just recently, in fact, seems like only a few minutes ago."

"That was *me*," said Billy in exasperation.

"See?" crowed Rumpelstiltskin in triumph. "You admit it! You're Billy Uhjones all right."

"But I—" started Billy, then sighed and dropped his head in defeat. "Never mind," he mumbled.

"I never do," said Rumpelstiltskin. He grabbed a pair of paper towels from a nearby dispenser and started using one of them to clean the other.

Billy stood silently for a moment, then said, "Excuse me." He didn't want to stand here waiting for this lunatic to come to his senses. His friends still needed him, and he had no idea if Wolfen or Eva or Cameron would pop in here at any second, looking for blood.

"Why?" asked Rumpelstiltskin, looking up from his cleaning. "What did you do?" When he saw Billy, he said, "Who are you, anyway?"

"I *told* you," said Billy, muffling a scream of exasperation that was desperately trying to escape. The only thing that kept him from letting it out was the fact that his mother had always told him to respect his elders, and Billy suspected that this guy was as elder as they came. "*I'm Billy Jones*," he finished semi-calmly, though his teeth did grit together when he said it.

"Billy *Jones*?" asked Rumpelstiltskin in delight. He dropped his two paper towels to the floor, where a Kung Fu Cleaner immediately grabbed them and deposited them in a nearby trash can. "Well, why didn't you say so?" He hugged the very surprised Billy. "I'm Rumpelstiltskin!"

"Thanks, er, good to meet you, Rumpelstiltskin," Billy finally managed when the man let go of his embrace long enough for Billy to snatch a quick breath of air.

"Well, she told me you might be coming, and she certainly was right, that's true," said Rumpelstiltskin.

"Who told you that? Who's 'she'?" asked Billy with a sinking feeling. Rumpelstiltskin seemed harmless enough, but if Eva Black had been the one who warned him that Billy might be coming, Billy knew he could expect no mercy. He shook his wrist, trying to wake Prince up. But the lava snake just batted its ember eyes once, then tightened its curled body a bit and went back to sleep.

Great, thought Billy, I have a snake made of fire who wants to watch out for me, but has to go and hibernate when I need him.

"Who told me what?" asked Rumpelstiltskin, confused.

Billy was tempted to let the matter drop and just run away, but he again had no idea where he would go. He didn't even know where he *was*, not really, so the idea of escaping seemed a bit ludicrous. Besides, he wanted to end this exasperating conversation if possible, and Rumpelstiltskin had seemed almost lucid a moment ago when mentioning that someone had told him of Billy's coming.

"Who told you I was coming?" asked Billy. Then, to cover all his bases, he added, "My name is Billy Jones, and you said someone said I was coming, and I want to know who."

"Ah, quite right," said the man. "Well, the prophecies of the Book of Earth certainly mentioned this as a possibility." His eyes went to that far-off place he seemed to live in. "That's probably where she got the idea in the first place." He frowned. "And here I thought she was so smart. Cheater."

"*Who* is a cheater?" Billy demanded, his frustration rising to hitherto unknown heights.

"My wife, of course," said Rumpelstiltskin.

"Who's your wife?" asked Billy.

Rumpelstiltskin frowned. "I don't know," he said, and for a moment his eyes grew sad. "She was something important, though." Then he brightened, and snapped his fingers. "I know," he exclaimed, "she was a Brown Councilor." Then he frowned once again. "If only I knew what that was."

Billy almost fell over right there. "Mrs. Russet?" said Billy, stunned. "Mrs. Russet is your *wife*?"

"Who's Mrs. Russet?" asked Rumpelstiltskin.

"You said she was your wife," answered Billy. And he thought, Mrs. Russet is this kook's *wife*?

"I'm not a kook," said Terry indignantly. Billy's ears reddened as he realized that in his surprise he must have spoken aloud. Then Rumpelstiltskin's expression changed. "Actually, on second thought, I guess I am a kook. That's what everyone always calls me, anyway." He focused back on Billy and applauded. "Well done, my boy! Hit the nail right on the head." Then he leaned in close to Billy, teetering on the very edge of his balance, his canes at forty five degree angles from the floor. "Did you know you were an Object of Prophecy?" he asked.

"I had heard that," said Billy, still off-balance by the revelation that Mrs. Russet had a husband, though apparently Rumpelstiltskin himself could not remember her name. Mrs. Russet was a *teacher*, for crying out loud. He had never imagined her with a husband. Rather, he had always figured that she went to a house that looked like a dungeon and ate students who hadn't done their homework before curling up for a nice night's sleep in a coffin or something. And even more unsettling was the fact that Mrs. Russet, the most no-nonsense and probably smartest person he had ever met, was married to a guy who spent time sorting left and right socks and obsessively using paper towels to clean other paper towels.

"Good," said Rumpelstiltskin Russet, grinning at Billy with a smile full of teeth that badly needed braces. "Have you heard the prophecies?"

"I think I've heard some of them," said Billy, trying to remember some of the things that Mrs. Russet had read out of the Book of the Earth. "Something about the world ending, and a diamond splitting in half."

"Bah," said Rumpelstiltskin with a dismissive wave of his cane. "Those are the boring ones. I like the one that goes like this:

*"There was once a messenger true*
*Who both came and went through the blue.*
*He used a big blade,*
*And the dead were waylaid,*
*And he felt like he'd soon have to poo."*

Billy gawked. "That's from the Book of the Earth?" he finally managed. "A limerick?"

Rumpelstiltskin cackled. "What, you don't think the Earthessence has a sense of humor? Have you ever seen the Scandinavian coastline? All those fjords? Who thinks of that stuff?" he then asked with another laugh.

"I don't know," said Billy absently. Assuming that Rumpelstiltskin was actually quoting a real passage from the Book of the Earth—a huge assumption, considering that this guy was clearly in need of a good psychiatrist and some serious medication—Billy wondered what this new part of the prophecy meant.

"Do you have to go to the bathroom?" asked Rumpelstiltskin suddenly.

Billy was surprised by this sudden turn to the conversation, but before he could say anything, he realized that yes, indeed, he *did* have to go. "Actually, yes," he said.

"See?" Rumpelstiltskin cackled in victory. "The prophecies are already coming true! You have to poo!" And then he danced a little jig, kicking up his legs as best he could.

Billy decided that he would ignore Rumpelstiltskin—and the last line of the limerick—for now. But the rest of he poem might help him figure out what to do next. "The dead" could clearly be some kind of reference to the zombie hordes that had taken control of Powers Island, but what did the poem mean when it talked about a blade? A magic sword? An Imbued spear? An enchanted butter knife? And what did it mean that the messenger "came and went through the blue?"

"Do you know what it means?" he finally asked Rumpelstiltskin, almost instantly regretting it.

"I most certainly do! And I can explain everything!" proclaimed the Brown Power. Then he frowned. "You'll just have to remind me what it is we were talking about first."

Billy shook his head in defeat. There was no getting anywhere with this man. But that thought led to another.

"How did I get here?" he asked.

"My Fizzles brought you, of course," said Rumpelstiltskin. "They must have decided you were too big a mess to be handled 'offsite,' as it were." He eyed Billy's clothing again. "And I must say, they were right."

"And where are we?" asked Billy, relieved to have finally gotten something resembling a straight answer from the man.

"The Cleaning Room," answered Rumpelstiltskin, as though the answer needed no further explanation. Billy decided to let that one go as well.

"Does Eva Black know how to get here? Or Wolfen?" he asked.

"That harpy?" said Rumpelstiltskin with a snarl. He shook both his canes this time, clearly upset by the very mention of Mrs. Black's name. "She doesn't care about menial things like cleaning. Never mind that without me and my friends, the whole of Powers Island would look like the city dump in Newark, New Jersey. Never mind that without us, we'd be buried in used cocoa mugs and hot dog wrappers up to our—"

"And what about Wolfen?" Billy interrupted, determined to keep this conversation on track.

"Wolfen?" asked the man, looking confused. "Isn't he dead already?"

"No!" said Billy. "Don't you know anything about what's going on on Powers Island? With the Darksiders? With...," he slowed, then in a softer voice, said, "With your wife?"

Rumpelstiltskin's countenance changed. The tiny old man seemed to shrink in on himself, like a candle flame about to puff out of existence. "My wife," he said. Then suddenly, as fast as he had wilted, he seemed somehow stronger and taller. "I know she's been taken captive. And I know that some very bad things are going to happen to her soon, if they haven't already." Then he grinned and returned to his demented self once more.

Billy was aghast. "You mean you *know*?" he said, totally shocked. "And you're not doing anything about it?"

BILLY: MESSENGER OF POWERS, BY MICHAELBRENT COLLINGS * 243

Rumpelstiltskin looked at Billy with rheumy eyes that shone with half-hidden tears. "My boy," he said. "I can't do much. I've done what I could, just waiting for you."

"Me?" Billy was now even more confused. "Why me?"

"Because," said Rumpelstiltskin, his eyes now shining with tears of a different kind, tears of hope and longing, "you are the Messenger. You are the one who is of all Powers. If anyone can save us all, you can."

"Then help me," pleaded Billy.

Rumpelstiltskin shook his head. "I can't leave here," he said.

"Why?" asked Billy.

The tired and scared-looking old man gazed all around. The work of cleaning went on on all sides, continuous and unwavering as the existence of the sun. "I can't leave," he whispered. He looked back at Billy. "Who will watch my babies?" he asked, gesturing at all the Fizzles. Then, in an even more melancholy tone, he said, "Who will do the cleaning?"

Billy wanted to say something else. It was incomprehensible to him that this man was unwilling to leave the Cleaning Room to go after his wife, even if he didn't remember who she was; to try to save the woman he had married. Billy knew that if his mother was in trouble, his father would move heaven and earth to save her. His father, though often distant, was a peace-loving man, whose job as a paramedic was devoted to saving others. Nonetheless, Billy knew that if his mom was being hurt, those people responsible would have to watch out, because his father would come after them, and would be relentless.

But Billy didn't say anything else to try and convince Rumpelstiltskin "Terry" Russet to come with him. The man was very sick, it was clear. A sad and broken man who didn't have the strength to leave his sanctuary. Billy knew he should have felt angry, but all he could muster was pity.

"Is there any way you can help me?" Billy asked. "Anything at all?"

"I don't know," said Rumpelstiltskin. "What do you want me to do?"

Billy thought. "I need to get to Dark Island," he finally said. "That's where my friends are being held."

"Well, if that's the case, I can give you a nice rope to hang yourself with," said Rumpelstiltskin. "It'd be quicker and less painful than going after the Darksiders in their stronghold."

"Look," said Billy, surprised at the strength and determination he heard in his voice. "I'm going to find a way to Dark Isle, with or without your help. So if you've got anything to say that might help me, say it now. Because I'm going."

And he meant it. Even though he didn't even really know where he was, he *would* find a way. He *would* find Dark Isle. He *would* save his friends. No matter what.

Apparently, Rumpelstiltskin saw something in Billy's face that made him believe his words. The old man thought for a long while, then finally said, "There may be a way. But," he added with a grimace, "I don't think you'll like it."

Looking at the expression on Terry's face, Billy had no doubt that the old man was right. He wasn't going to like it, whatever "it" was.

But he had no other choice.

# CHAPTER THE NINETEENTH

*In Which Billy is given a Plan, and travels the Earth...*

When Billy heard the old man's idea, his response was short and to the point. "What?!" he screamed. "Are you crazy?"

"Not exactly," was all Rumpelstiltskin could manage. "At least, I don't think so. But then," he added, "I don't know any crazy people who think they *are* crazy, so me not thinking I'm crazy doesn't mean that I'm not really crazy, does it?"

Billy tried to follow the convolutions of Rumpelstiltskin's sentence, got halfway through it, got lost, started over, got lost again, and finally decided to give the whole thing up as a bad job and go back to his original question. "What?" he asked again, though slightly less loudly this time.

"I know it doesn't sound very nice, but I really think it's the only way," said the old man.

Billy didn't like it. In the whole history of bad ideas, he supposed this had to be near the top.

"Attack a zombie?" Billy asked, hoping without much hope that he had heard the old man incorrectly.

"No, no, not attack a zombie," said Rumpelstiltskin with an exasperated tone. He looked away from Billy for a moment, yelling, "Hey, don't put those forks that way! They all have to point east! East, I tell you!" The rock Fizzles he spoke to rapidly began reorganizing a pile of forks that went nearly to the ceiling.

Rumpelstiltskin looked back at Billy. "I never said to attack a zombie. I think doing that would be a terrible idea. Terrible, like the invention of dirt." The old man shuddered at the mere thought of such stuff. "I said you should just shake hands with one."

"Okay," said Billy slowly. "So I just walk up to the nearest zombie that I find, say hi, ask him his name, introduce myself, and shake hands. Maybe ask if we can go to a movie or something, or if he wants to come over to my place to play video games."

"You have video games at your house?" asked Rumpelstiltskin. "Lucky!"

"No, I don't have any video games!" yelled Billy. Prince, still curled on his arm, came suddenly awake and hissed at Billy, clearly letting his friend know that he was trying to sleep and would appreciate a bit of quiet. "I don't have any video games," Billy continued in a softer voice. "I just—"

"Well, if you don't have any video games," interrupted Rumpelstiltskin, "why would you bother asking a zombie to play with you? Besides," he added with a roll of his eyes, "you'll be unconscious the second you touch it. Can't play video games when you're passed out, can you?" He rolled his eyes again, as though frustrated that he had been put in charge of a kid who clearly had a lower than normal IQ.

"I *know* I'll be unconscious," Billy half-snarled. His mother's words about being respectful to elders kept coming back to him, but somehow he felt it difficult to concentrate on that during any conversations with Rumpelstiltskin. He took a deep breath, composing himself, then continued, speaking slowly and clearly. "Try to understand. I don't want to be unconscious. I think unconsciousness would not help me much. I think it would mostly leave me helpless. I think that would be bad."

"I agree with everything you said," said Rumpelstiltskin. His brow wrinkled. "At least, I think I did. What was the middle part again? Right after you said 'I.'"

Billy growled, the strange sound coming unbidden from his throat. Rumpelstiltskin looked surprised at the sound. He felt his stomach. "Was that you making that noise, or me?"

Billy let the growl turn into a scream of frustration. "Help me! Please!" he shouted. Then, because he suspected that continuing to talk to Rumpelstiltskin would just result in there being two insane people in here—as opposed to just one—he started to look for a way out of the room. He'd be better off on his own, he decided.

"Whatcha lookin' for?" asked Rumpelstiltskin.

"A way out," replied Billy. He started walking in a random direction, trying to move away from Mrs. Russet's crazy husband. He kept a lookout for a door or an elevator or some other method—magical or otherwise—of exiting this place.

"Wait, wait!" shouted Rumpelstiltskin, hobbling after Billy. "If that's all you need, I can help you with it, no problem!" Billy waited for a moment, looking at the old man with a combination of exasperation and hope.

Rumpelstiltskin fumbled in the folds of his cloak, almost falling over several times as he did so, his two canes clutched in one of his hands while the other went in and out of huge pockets, searching for something. Finally, he said, "Ah-ha!" and pulled out a sponge.

And then he promptly threw the sponge at Billy.

Billy, stunned, didn't move a muscle. The sponge bounced off his head, landing on the floor with a wet "splooge" sound. Billy blinked rapidly. He suddenly couldn't think straight. It felt as though the sponge had been the last overload that finally blew his brain into crackling bits of malfunctioning machinery.

He looked down at the sponge. It seemed to sway back and forth in front of him, whirling around like some kind of insane ballet dancer who had had one too many caffeinated drinks.

Billy blinked and frowned. What had Rumpelstiltskin done to him? The old man came close, and Billy saw with some surprise that the old man now appeared to be much taller, and much younger. Merely old, instead of ancient. Rumpelstiltskin still held his canes, but they were at his sides, as though he didn't need them.

Rumpelstiltskin leaned down and picked the sponge off the floor, putting it wetly back into his robes. Then, in a strong voice completely unlike what he had sounded like only a moment before, Rumpelstiltskin said, "Sorry about that. But sometimes it takes magic to make us understand things."

Billy stood transfixed. The man in front of him was still the same Rumpelstiltskin that Billy had been speaking to, but he was at the same time a completely different person. As Billy watched, Rumpelstiltskin's image seemed to flicker. For a moment, Billy saw him as he had first seen him: bent and feeble. Then he saw the young, strong version of the man for a second. Then he saw both of them at once, like a pair of photographs that had faded into one another.

"We have to move quickly. The spell won't last long," said Rumpelstiltskin. "And I can only muster the strength to do this once in a great while."

"What are you doing, Rumpelstiltskin?" asked Billy.

The old man who was two men at once looked at him sharply. "Call me Terry," he said. Terry waved one of his canes, and Billy felt something move behind him. He glanced around, and saw that a stone chair had erupted from the ground at his back. Then he felt a strong hand on his chest as Terry pushed him into the chair.

This younger, more focused, and suddenly very intense version of the man Billy had been talking to looked at Billy closely. "I don't have time to explain," he said quickly. "But I need you to understand something. My wife believes that you are the Messenger, the one who will destroy the world of the Powers as we know it, and who will herald the return of the White King." Terry put a hand on Billy's arm. "I don't know you well enough to know of myself whether you are the Messenger or not," continued Terry in that suddenly strong voice. "But I have faith my wife is right. And you have to have faith, too, Billy. Believe in yourself. You have powers that no one save the White King himself can understand. And you have friends, something that no Power can take from you, not even the Power of Death itself."

With that, Terry stood straight, holding his hand over his heart as he recited:

*"Through fires of fate and storms that save*
*Through winter's gate and water's grave*
*Shall come the One, once lost, now found*
*Seen by the Son whose love abounds.*

*A sword, a spear, and armor strong*
*A shield to wear, and dagger long*
*To fell the Dark and bring the Light*
*To call the spark that ends the night.*

*And through it all, one twist of fate:*
*A child whose call will seem too late*
*But though the Dark seems once to win*
*The child will spark the light again."*

The hairs on Billy's neck and arms stood up straight as Terry spoke the strange poem. It was as though the words were electric, burning themselves into Billy's mind. Somehow, though he didn't understand much of them, he felt comforted. He felt as though the writer had written the words for him and him alone; a message sent through time and space, to find him now, at this moment, when he most needed courage.

The stone chair below Billy grew suddenly warm, as though it, too, had felt itself buoyed up by the verses.

Billy looked at Terry. The man still stood tall, but as Billy watched, he started to wither and bend. Terry grimaced. "I can't hold on much longer, boy," he said, and Billy heard the tremor of age return to the Power's voice. But Terry then straightened again, as though forcing himself to remain young and strong for just a moment longer. "You are the Messenger," he told Billy again. "You speak for the White King. Speak your Message, and you will prevail."

Then, just as suddenly as he had come, the hale and hearty version of Terry disappeared, leaving behind the tiny, hunched man who tottered on his canes. Rumpelstiltskin looked around as though confused, then seemed to notice Billy for the first time.

"Ah!" he said happily. "You're all ready then?"

"No, I—" began Billy.

"Good!" said Rumpelstiltskin. He laughed. "Remember, don't get off the chair, or you'll end up buried."

Then, before Billy could say anything else, Rumpelstiltskin waved his canes like a pair of conductor's batons. As soon as he did, the stone chair leapt downward, dragging Billy with it as it plunged into the earth. Billy shut his eyes automatically, then opened them a second later. Then closed them again so as to avoid being violently sick.

What made him feel so instantly queasy was the sight of dirt, rock, mud, and the various other things that made up the earth. All of it. The entire planet. Billy understood that, in the same way that through the magical spell called Cresting, a Power of Fire could travel through the flames of the earth, so now he was experiencing travel as Brown Powers did it: through the earth itself. He knew Rumpelstiltskin/Terry was a Brown Power—clearly shown by his robe and by the fact that all his Fizzles were made of rock—and he knew also that Rumpelstiltskin—or Terry—was doing this to him now.

He could see the different layers of the earth flashing by at tremendous speeds as he whipped through the planet. Before, when Cresting, he had felt light and ethereal, like a flame. This was a different feeling. Traveling by the Element of Earth was something that had great weight and strength. The millions of tons that made up the planet all seemed to press in on Billy, falling to rest upon his head, shoulders, and lap. The weight was crushing, petrifying.

And yet, Billy found that he could stand it. He was one with Earth, and so he both felt of its great weight, and also partook of its tremendous strength. He was like a mountain, its very mass making it vast and strong. He was like a cliff, steep and impregnable. For a moment, Billy wished he could face every bully he had ever known. He felt invincible, eternal. He was Earth, and Earth would never fade.

All around him, he began to make out tiny details of his path through the Earthessence. He saw plain rocks and pebbles, and dirt and mud. He also saw beautiful geodes: great purple, red, and orange crystals the size of redwoods, sitting in silent wisdom in caverns untouched by human hands. The crystals glowed with inner power, the Earthessence pulsing through them like a living thing.

Billy knew that any geologist who saw such things would have wept at their sheer beauty and magnitude. But for him, bonded now to the earth as he traveled, it was like viewing a part of his own body. He watched as crystal caverns came and went, he saw the plates upon which the continents floated shifting restlessly in their beds, he felt raw diamonds the size of cars pass by and through him. And it was all a part of who he now was.

Then, suddenly, the granite chair upon which he sat lurched to one side. Billy was brought back to himself as he suddenly realized what was really happening to him: Terry had hatched a crazy plan to get Billy to Dark Isle, and the first part of it had been set in motion.

There was a great rushing noise, the sound of an earthquake, the cacophony of a landslide, and Billy felt himself emerging from the depths of the earth. He felt himself moving toward the outward crust of the planet. There were no more crystal caves now, no more diamonds, no more of the deep and secret things of the earth. Now there was only stone, and rock, and dirt.

Then, with a final whoosh, Billy found himself outside. He was still sitting on the chair, but he was no longer inside the earth. Indeed, now it seemed as though he had gone to the opposite extreme: he was sitting on top of the highest peak on the highest mountain he had ever heard of.

Billy's breath was taken away by the sight, and he was utterly transfixed by the raw, unspoiled view of what seemed to be the entire world set out below him. It was so beautiful that Billy hardly noticed that it was so cold his breath was freezing in his lungs, or that there was hardly enough air to sustain him for more than a few moments.

He suddenly understood what drove men and women to climb mountains, to swim under icebergs, to drive themselves to the limits of human existence. He felt the exuberance of being among a select few who had ever seen a beautiful scene of nature, untouched by humanity, innocent and unspoiled as Eden must have been.

A fizzling, sizzling noise drew his attention away from the sweeping vista before him. As it had every time he left Powers Island, Billy's name tag disappeared with a puff of smoke. Billy felt strangely naked without it, as though he had suddenly lost a bit of himself. Whether this meant he was becoming a Power, or merely that he was finally getting comfortable with the idea that Powers actually existed, he couldn't tell. But it was with some sadness that he watched the "Billy" badge disappear.

His sadness didn't last long, however, as less than a second later Billy's chair jerked again. Once more he felt himself drawn deep into the ground, below the slowly undulating masses of stone that held all of civilization upon them, and that contained the remnants of all civilizations that had gone before. More crystals, more diamonds, more stones and rocks and caverns and great stony halls passed before Billy's eyes.

Then, looming ahead of him, he saw a sudden dark spot, like a place where there was no earth, no water, no air, no fire, no life, no death, no nothing. Only void. And Billy realized that this must be the place that separated Powers Island from the rest of reality, the place that kept it secret from prying eyes, and changed the flow of time so that an hour on Powers Island would be as but a twinkling of an eye in the real world.

He passed through the void, like a man trying to jump over the Grand Canyon, his chair of stone the only thing keeping him grounded in any kind of reality. Billy felt like, had he not been sitting on that chair, he would have puffed out of existence like a candle flame and simply ceased to exist.

But then he landed, once more finding himself surrounded by the Earthessence, once more traveling through rarefied halls of beauty and perfect symmetry as he traveled the earth's lengths. And soon he once more heard the whooshing noise, the cascade of sound that signified the end of a trip through Earth. He gripped the edge of his chair, willing it to keep on going, to keep on traveling. He knew where it was headed, and it was not someplace he wanted to be.

Unfortunately, Billy was not in charge of where the stone chair would take him. And so it was that he found himself coming up through the earth, which parted like liquid before him, then slammed shut behind him as he traveled upward. The rushing noise all around him grew and grew until Billy felt sure that the earth itself was about to crack. And then, just at the moment when he felt he couldn't bear it any more, the instant he felt himself going mad with the enormity of his travels, all was silent.

Billy looked around.

He didn't have much time to take in his surroundings, because an instant after he arrived, he found himself sprawled on the floor as the stone chair withdrew into the ground again, leaving him behind and alone.

Or rather, not alone. Because Billy was surrounded.

Even though he knew where he had been headed, because Rumpelstiltskin had told him, he was still disheartened. Part of him had hoped—perhaps foolishly—that Rumpelstiltskin would have changed his mind and sent Billy somewhere else. Somewhere slightly more pleasant, like the inside of an ant hill or directly in the path of a major earthquake.

But no, true to his word Rumpelstiltskin had sent Billy exactly where he didn't want to be: to a place where he was surrounded by zombies, to a place where a Darksider could show up at any moment, to a location where he was closer to Wolfen and his evil army than he cared to be.

He was back in the Accounting Room.

Little appeared to have changed. The place was still so full of zombies that any movement was highly restricted. As before, the zombies were packed so tightly it was like being in the center of a can of undead sardines. As before, the only gaps in the solid mass of rotten bodies were three paths that led to the three cases that held the three Counters.

Billy stood in one of the paths. His badge was gone, and per the rules of Powers Island, he had returned to the Accounting Room to be Counted and Determined. No one, he knew, could get onto the island without coming here first. And so the zombies waited to pick off any Dawnwalker who might appear in a vain hope that Powers Island would be a place of refuge in the war that had so suddenly broken out in their midst.

The zombies nearest Billy turned to stare at him, waiting for him to make a move. He couldn't pass by them to get to the elevators without going to the Counters first. He also knew that if he attacked them—as Vester and Tempus had done—his end would come swiftly and without mercy.

He could do as he had done before, and go to the Counters to get his "Billy—unDetermined" badge and then get to the bank of elevators beyond the zombies. But he didn't see much advantage to that. It wouldn't help him to get any closer to saving his friends, and there was even the possibility that after his first escape from this room, the zombies might have been told that they were to treat a "Billy—unDetermined" badge just the same as a Dawnwalker badge: attack and destroy on sight.

Billy felt his very limited options pressing in on him. He knew he didn't have long to choose a course and act, though. As before, at any second a Darksider might happen along. And though the zombies were none too bright, a Darksider—even one who didn't know

Billy—would surely be interested in why this boy was just standing there, instead of moving forward to be Counted.

Even worse, perhaps, was the possibility that a Dawnwalker would appear near Billy, and that he would be caught in the magical crossfire that could erupt between zombies and a Power.

No, he didn't have much time. He didn't have many options. And he needed to get to Dark Isle and save his friends as soon as possible.

If they're even alive, he thought. He tried to stop that depressing possibility from entering his mind, but no matter how much he shouted it down, it kept coming back.

What was it that Rumpelstiltskin had said about his wife? Ah, yes, it was, "I know she's been taken captive. And I know that some very bad things are going to happen to her soon, if they haven't already."

So who was to say that all his friends hadn't already been destroyed by Wolfen's army? Billy would be the first to admit that he wasn't the best history student in Mrs. Russet's class, but even he knew that in times of war the prisoners often didn't last long in their prisons.

Maybe I should just go home, Billy thought. Maybe I can get to the elevators, and maybe one of them will know how I can get home. Maybe I can just forget about it, forget about them and go back to living my life the way I did before Mrs. Russet first brought me here.

The thought was tempting. It was almost upsetting, in fact, how much Billy wanted to just go home and go back to the way things had been before. But as he thought this, he suddenly felt as though the world was closing in on him. He felt trapped, imprisoned. Locked in a tiny cell that allowed barely enough room to breathe in. The feeling was oddly familiar.

Then, with a startled jerk, Billy realized why the feeling was familiar.

I'm stuffed in a locker again, he thought. Only this time I've put myself there.

And it was true. Each time he had ever been put into a locker, the worst part wasn't the physical act of being shoved inside. The worst part was when Cameron—or Harold, or Sarah, or whoever was tormenting him that day—said, "Stay here. Don't tell." It was the worst part because Billy's tormentors were not just taking his freedom for a moment, they were stealing it forever, because they knew that, come what may, Billy would obey them. Because they knew Billy was afraid of them, and that Billy would never go against his fear.

But he was different now. He wasn't the same Billy who had meekly submitted to every indignity. He wasn't the same Billy who had cowered away from the merest hint of any conflict. No. He wasn't that boy.

"I am the Messenger," he said aloud to himself. And he was almost startled. Part of the reason he was startled was just because his voice sounded so out of place in this room that had become something of a mass grave. But mostly he was surprised because he actually believed what he had said.

"I am the Messenger," he said again. Then he turned to the nearest zombie.

As he did so, Terry's words came to him. Not the meandering crazy-talk that *Rumpelstiltskin* had spoken for most of their conversation. Rather, Billy remembered when *Terry* had been strong and tall, when his mind had seemed whole and coherent. "You are the Messenger," Terry had told Billy. "You speak for the White King. Speak your Message, and you will prevail."

Remembering these words, Billy again felt the hairs on his neck and arms stand on end. Somehow, he knew that Terry's words were true, just as he had known that Terry's poem was truth. Whether it was some Element or some other force, Billy knew he had heard Truth. Not mere truth in the sense that it is true that two plus two equal four, but Truth in the sense that there were some things that were woven inextricably into the fabric of the universe, engraved on every atom of existence. Billy had heard Truth in Terry's poem, and he could not deny it.

And, knowing this, he also knew that he had to act on what he knew.

He walked to the nearest zombie. He stood directly in front of it so that the zombie's huge, faceted eyes were focused only on him. Billy was disconcerted to see that this particular zombie was wearing the tattered remnants of the uniform of a fast food restaurant that Billy knew quite well.

That explains why they never got my order right, he thought crazily, his mind obviously trying to hide from the thought of what Billy had set himself to do.

Billy cleared his throat noisily.

Yup, he thought at the same time. Crazy must be a contagious disease, because I've definitely caught it.

At the noise, the zombie moved its neck slightly, adjusting its gaze downward to look more directly at Billy, but other than that it showed no sign it was aware of Billy's presence. Nor would it, Billy knew, unless Billy tried to attack it or to escape. Then, the zombies would close in on him quickly.

But Billy planned neither to attack nor to attempt an escape. Instead, he hitched himself up, standing as tall as he could—which wasn't very tall at all—and then he spoke. His voice cracked as he did so, breaking the dignity he had hoped to achieve, but even with that, he was proud of the fact that not only did he manage to get the words out, but he did so without wetting his pants.

"I am the Messenger," he said. "I speak for the White King. And I bear a message for Wolfen."

At these words, every single zombie in the room turned their dead, huge eyes on Billy. They moved in unison, so perfectly synchronized that they seemed to be attached somehow. But at the same time, there was no rustling of clothing, no murmurs, no noise at all. The movement of hundreds of zombies brought no sound, only the deep silence of the tomb.

Billy resisted the urge to shrink back under the force of the many undead eyes that now focused exclusively on him. In fact, to his surprise, he felt braver than he had just a moment before. He spoke again, and this time his voice did not crack. It was deeper, more confident.

"I bear a message for Wolfen," he repeated. Then, with his newfound strength, with a look so powerful and dignified that he felt like his own mother might not have recognized him in that instant, Billy continued. "The White King will speak, and I will be his mouthpiece."

The zombies looked at one another in confusion. Clearly this was outside the range of instructions they had been given. Tempus had said that zombies were good for simple tasks, and here Billy was obviously pushing them beyond their capacity to act.

Billy walked closer to the zombie he had been talking to. "Do not look away from me, foul creature!" he shouted. The words surprised even him. For a moment, it felt as though Billy was not himself, that he was merely observing his body, which was being controlled by someone infinitely wiser, stronger, and better than Billy himself could ever be.

The zombie jerked its gaze back to Billy, and to his surprise, Billy thought he saw something totally unexpected in the zombie's weird gaze: fear.

Billy, still strangely disconnected from his own actions, seized on that fear and used it like a weapon. "Yes, fear me," he said in a voice no longer entirely his own. He was no longer Billy. Or rather, he *was* Billy, but Billy had very suddenly become something new and greater than he had been only moments before.

He had become the Messenger.

An almost audible hum could be sensed through the room, as power built within its walls.

Billy pointed a finger at the zombie, then repeated the words, "Fear me, and tremble, for I am the Messenger. I am the one come to prepare the way for the White King's return. I am the one who will destroy the world."

He leaned in close to the zombie, finger still pointing at the undead creature.

"Take me to Wolfen," he said, his voice cold and menacing.

And with that, he reached out and grabbed the zombie's hand in his own.

Instantly, a cold pulse flashed through Billy's body. His heart skipped a beat, then sped up.

Then it stopped.

Darkness closed all around Billy.

He sank to the ground.

His eyes closed.

And the darkness claimed him.

# CHAPTER THE TWENTIETH

*In Which Billy is Surprised who he sees, and Becomes what he Is...*

When he opened his eyes, Billy had a sudden understanding of what anvils must feel like. He felt as though a large sledgehammer was pounding white-hot nails into his skull, then those nails were being removed and some kind of strong acid was being poured through the holes and directly into his brain.

"Uhng," he said. It was the best he could do at the time, and he was actually proud of it. Though not exactly scintillating conversation, it beat out his first impulse—to throw up and immediately pass out again—by a mile.

"Uhng," Billy said again. Then, to make sure he drove the point home to any listeners, he said it two more times, adding the word "oog" to the last one, just to show he was more than a one-trick wonder.

After this short but heartfelt monologue, Billy dared to crack open one eye. This resulted in a whole new deluge of acid-brain-pouring, so he closed it again. He tried opening the other eye, which had similar results, and so he closed that one as well.

After a moment, he reasoned that maybe the trick was to open both eyes at once, sort of like diving right into the deep end of a swimming pool. He tried this, and quickly discovered that when the swimming pool was full of brain-melting acid, diving into the deep end was probably a bad idea.

In spite of the pain, however, he managed to keep his eyes open, blinking through a haze of tears and trying to make out where he was. At first, all he could see was a dark blur. However, after only a few minutes his sight cleared up to the point where he could see a slightly *less* dark blur.

Progress, he thought. At this pace, I'll have the vision of a tree bat in only a few short years.

"Billy," said a voice.

Billy's head whipped toward the sound so fast he thought his neck might snap.

"Ivy?" he whispered.

"Oh, it *is* you," came the voice. It was rich with happy tears, but sounded strangely muffled.

Billy smiled. He didn't know where he was, but he was among friends. Or at least, he was among friend. And if Ivy was close by, things couldn't be all that bad, could they?

"Ivy, what's going on? Are you all right?" said Billy. He was still blinking madly, trying to get his eyes to remember that he was in charge and that he preferred them to function at all times.

"Oh, Billy, it's been terrible," said Ivy. Billy could hear his friend sniffle. "My father, and Vester, and Tempus, and Mrs. Russet," she began.

"What about them?" Billy almost shouted. "Where are they? Where are *we*?"

As he said this, his vision slowly started to resolve. He saw that he was in a cell of some kind. It was cubical, about ten feet to a side, but instead of being made of bars and concrete, the ceiling, floor, and walls were all made of what looked like thick glass. And as far as he could see, there was no entry or exit anywhere. Just a perfect, unbroken cube. He wondered how he was going to keep breathing, since the place certainly looked airtight. But then he realized that living long enough to run out of air was probably a best-case scenario anyway, and just let go of that line of thought.

As he looked around, he saw that he wasn't alone. There were other cubes. Thousands of them, it seemed, all stacked on top of each other in a mountain of transparent cells. Billy's own holding cell was about ten cubes above the ground. He could see straight below him to the mass of other glass cells underneath his. They were all full, all the cubes he could see. Each one held a single person in it. Some of the people slept, others paced back and forth in their tiny compartments. Some were screaming in fear, others moaning with dreadful resignation to their fates.

He looked up, and realized he couldn't see the sky: row upon row of other cells were stacked above his, and the mass of bodies above him obscured his view. He couldn't even tell how many rows of cells there *were* above him. There were enough that they all blurred together at some point. The weight of the cells and the people in them seemed to press down on Billy, making him feel claustrophobic as no trip through the depths of the earth had managed to do. He felt like he had been stuffed in the world's most awful locker.

Billy looked to his left and right now, trying to spot Ivy among the hive of Dawnwalkers who were imprisoned in this magical jail of sorts. At last, he spotted the Green Power, and gasped at her appearance. Ivy was still clothed in her plants, but those plants were completely wilted, if not dead. Scattered brown and yellow leaves littered the floor of her transparent cell, and the rest of the vines that still wrapped themselves around her looked brittle and pale. She was slumped against the wall of her cell, a cube that was only about twenty feet away from Billy's.

"Ivy," he said again, "what's going on? Where are we?"

"We're in—" she began, but a voice interrupted her.

"You're in Wolfen's power," said the voice. "More than that, you don't need to know."

Billy whipped around in time to see a dark hole appear behind him. And out of the hole stepped the owner of the voice, that low, too-sweet voice that contemplated death as a delicacy.

Mrs. Black smiled, her almost happy bearing belied by the animalistic leer in her eyes and the predatory twist of her mouth. "So, my boy, we work so hard to catch you, when all we really had to do was wait for you to catch yourself." Mrs. Black smiled daintily. "I must confess I'm somewhat disappointed," she said. "I had hoped to have some...*alone* time with you."

Billy gulped. He glanced toward Ivy, and saw that his friend was pressed against the wall of her cell that was closest to Billy, a look of concern on her face. The plants she wore apparently weren't completely lifeless, because they twitched and writhed with brittle scrapings, echoing their mistress's fear.

Billy looked back at Mrs. Black, surprised to see that she hadn't conjured up some kind of enchanted firearm or at the very least a pointy stick to jab him with.

Mrs. Black seemed to understand the look on his face, because her smile drooped a fraction. "Don't worry, we've decided not to touch you. Not yet, at any rate." Then her shark's grin returned suddenly. She waved a hand, and Billy felt terror course through him. The Dread. He gasped, and immediately doubled over as Mrs. Black leaned in close. "Lucky for me," she said, "there are a lot of things I can do without actually touching you at all."

Another wave, and the fear Billy felt increased, almost immobilizing him in its terrible grip. Silent tears poured down Billy's face. He felt something warm at his heart, and looked down. Bent double, he could see down the loose neck of his t-shirt, and he spotted Prince in there. The fire snake Fizzle had encircled itself around Billy's torso, and was now pressing its head against Billy's chest, near his heart. It was Prince that was giving Billy the feeling of warmth, and with it some measure of resistance to Mrs. Black's spell of Dread.

Billy blinked back his tears, not wanting to give Mrs. Black the satisfaction of seeing him cry. But he still couldn't move.

"No!" shouted Ivy, her hands banging uselessly against her glass cell.

Mrs. Black looked at the Green Power and laughed. "Does this bother you, Ivy my dear?" Another dark laugh, then Mrs. Black continued, "Too bad the prison cancels out the Dawnwalkers' Powers, isn't it?"

"If you hurt him, so help me, I'll—" began Ivy, her small fists curled at her sides.

"You'll what?" interrupted Mrs. Black. She prodded Billy with her toe as she spoke, as though he were a cockroach that was lying on its back, and she was checking him for life before wadding him up in tissue and then dropping him down the toilet. "I know your type, little Ivy. Ever the peace-maker, ever the pacifist." Mrs. Black's prodding turned almost into a kick. But Billy hardly noticed. Indeed, he would have been glad to have something to focus on other than the bad memories and terrible feelings of fear and inadequacy that accompanied the Dread. "You're all about peace and love," continued Mrs. Black to Ivy. "But when push comes to shove, those things don't even mean enough to you to be willing to fight to keep them, do they?"

The warmth at Billy's bosom increased, and he managed to rise slowly to his feet.

"That's it, Billy," shouted Ivy. "Don't let her beat you! Don't let her get you down!"

"Silence!" snarled Mrs. Black. She waved a dismissive hand at Ivy, and instantly most of Ivy's plants went from brown or gray to deep black. The flowers and vines around her died instantly, and Ivy winced as though this had caused her some kind of physical pain.

That would make sense, Billy realized in the midst of his misery. If the Powers put their own essences into their spells, that would mean that killing Ivy's plants would result in some pain to her personally.

Mrs. Black smiled and laughed at Ivy's pain. "Sorry," she said in mock pity. "That looked like it hurt." Then Mrs. Black grinned sarcastically. "But look on the bright side, Ivy." She gestured at Ivy's glass vault. "You're the only plant I know with her own personal greenhouse."

Then Mrs. Black gasped in clear amazement as Billy, his forehead sweating from the effort, somehow managed to stand. His shoulders were drooping from the almost physical weight of the Dread, but he struggled to his feet anyway, buoyed up by Prince's help and by an inner strength he hadn't known he possessed.

Mrs. Black waved again, and Billy winced as the terror he felt redoubled. But he wouldn't let the fear rule him, wouldn't let himself be pushed down again. He gritted his teeth, and managed to grind out the words, "Don't you think…Wolfen will…be angry if…you kill me?"

Mrs. Black curled her lip derisively, but then waved a hand once more, and Billy could feel the Dread dissipate and leave him. Mrs. Black looked at him as though re-appraising something she had already dismissed as being of no value. "Well, well," she whispered. "Perhaps you are more than what you seemed, Mr. Jones."

"That's right, Eva," shouted Ivy from her cell. "He's the Messenger! Lumilla knew it, and you know it, and Wolfen must know it, too!"

Billy quietly wished for Ivy to shut up. His friend was in the Darksiders' power, and he knew that her triumphant words would not go unnoticed or unpunished. He knew that she must be desperate, jailed as she was, helpless and at the mercy of the merciless, and so was grasping at Billy's ability to withstand the Dread as a kind of victory by proxy. But he didn't think now was a good time or place for her to go flaunting her small triumph.

Mrs. Black's expression darkened, and Billy knew he was right. Ivy, too, seemed to sense that she had crossed some kind of line, for she grew suddenly silent, and moved as far from Mrs. Black as she could.

To Billy's surprise, Mrs. Black didn't lash out at the captive Green Power. Instead, she just smiled. The smile, though, was more chilling than any threat could have been. "Don't worry, my dear," whispered Eva Black. "Your time will come. Just as it will come for Lumilla, and Vester, and any of the rest of your friends who dare stand against Wolfen." She looked at Billy and added pointedly, "Wolfen the White, the *true* Messenger and King."

Ivy shrunk back, but in spite of the threat in Mrs. Black's words, Billy's heart leapt in his chest. His friends were still alive! They had to be!

"Where are they?" he yelled without thinking.

"Who?" asked Mrs. Black innocently. Then she waved her hands expansively. "Perhaps they are here, in the prison. Perhaps they are somewhere else on Dark Isle. I'm quite sure I don't know."

Billy was positive Mrs. Black was lying, but he also knew that he wasn't likely to get a straight answer out of her. She approached, and Billy took a step backward in spite of himself.

"What?" purred Mrs. Black. "Afraid? But I thought you were the Messenger. Surely the White King would let no harm come to you." She said it mockingly, her words like honey-coated poison.

As she spoke, she reached out and grabbed Billy, her icy fingers wrapping around his pale wrist. As soon as she did, a searing pain etched itself into Billy's arm. He looked at where Mrs. Black was touching him and saw that the skin around where she was grabbing had turned an ugly gray, the color of death. The gray color pushed its way up Billy's arm, and he gasped.

He felt Prince move under his shirt, and knew the Fizzle was about to strike at Eva.

Not now, Billy thought. Not now, Prince, now is not the time.

He didn't know how he knew that, but he somehow sensed it was true. Now was not the time for the Fizzle to strike. There would come a time to do battle, but the time was not now.

Either Prince sensed Billy's thoughts somehow, or the snake decided on its own to lay low for a time, because Billy felt the serpent flatten out against his skin and suddenly stop moving.

"Come," said Mrs. Black. She touched her ever-present scarab broach, and Billy knew enough to hold his breath. "My minions in the Accounting Room told me you wanted to talk to Wolfen," she said, and Billy felt that familiar yanking as he was Transported from his cell to somewhere else. "And I guarantee you," she said as they arrived in their new destination, "Wolfen wants to talk to you, too." She laughed, that dark, evil laugh of hers. "Talk, and maybe other things. Things that are much more...fun."

A dark crackle of electricity marked her words, and a second later, before Billy had a chance to really realize where they were, a clap of thunder struck close nearby. It was so loud that Billy felt like his ears were going to explode. He winced, and then opened his eyes.

"Never will those who wage war tire of deception," said Mrs. Black. Then, a moment later, she added, "For mine is the kingdom, and the power, and the glory."

Billy didn't know what she was talking about. But he did know that what he saw terrified him. He had seen Dark Isle once before, on the wings of the Unicorn when the magical creature spirited him away from his first Test of Power. But that had been a view from afar. He had glimpsed the rocky cliffs, the black and shark-infested waters that surrounded the island, the forbidding rocks and sand. He had not, however, stood upon its highest peak, as he did now.

Behind him, and far below, he could hear the crash of water. He risked a look, and saw that the peak on which he stood ended only a few scant feet behind them, falling away in a vertical line that ended in the angry ocean that surrounded the island.

Then he looked back to the middle of the island. To the horribly gleaming majesty of the newest addition to Dark Isle: the prison.

Billy had himself been inside the prison only moments before, and had felt burdened by its enormity. Looking at it from the outside he felt absolutely crushed by it, even though he was no longer captive in those crystal cubes. The prison was as huge as he had suspected, a gleaming mountain of glass blocks that had been carefully stacked, as though some evil toddler had used the island as its playground. Only instead of the colorful letters and pictures of a child's playthings, each of these blocks held a single isolated soul inside it.

Billy felt completely discouraged. He knew that Powers Stadium had held over a hundred thousand people in it, and that half of them had been Dawnwalkers. Vester had also told him during Napalm's Challenge of the lovely Fulgora that that was almost all the Powers on the whole earth. And if that was true, and if Billy's eyes weren't lying, probably most of the Dawnwalkers were already here, incarcerated in this crystalline prison.

Mrs. Black's hand traced itself along his shoulders, almost playfully. "Beautiful, isn't it?" she asked. "Twenty years in the making, a plan so perfect that all would happen in a single day. A plan that would stage an attack and, in one single moment, both begin and end the war."

Billy looked away from the terrible sight of all the imprisoned Dawnwalkers. He peered around Dark Isle, trying to find something that would lift his spirits. But there was nothing. The entire island was still forbidding, dead and gray. It was nothing but cliff after cliff, each peak separated by a tiny valley or just a series of paths carved into the naked rock. Periodically, the stark bareness of the place was broken up by a river or a lake. All of the bodies of water seemed gray and angry, however. Not a single one was at peace: all the rivers were rapids, all the lakes were tempestuous and stormy. Most of the water drained through the angry rivers and led eventually to the black sea around Dark Isle, to the deadly rocks and the circling sharks.

Billy could also make out people in the island: Darksiders who were hurrying from place to place, working at some chore or other.

No doubt they were carrying out some kind of nefarious plot to expand the war to encompass the whole earth.

There were also zombies. Even at the distances involved, he could clearly make out their mottled skin and those huge, fly-like eyes that all of them had. And not just a few of them, either, there were thousands of them, crawling like death-bearing ants over an anthill.

Mrs. Black's fingers pushed at Billy's cheek, forcing his gaze back to the huge prison where his friends were probably all imprisoned. "Beautiful," she repeated.

"What's going to happen to them?" asked Billy.

"They will be...re-educated," said Mrs. Black. "You'd be surprised how many people change their minds given the right incentive."

"Not my friends," said Billy.

Mrs. Black laughed. "No?" she asked. "Well, you might be right about that, Mr. Jones. Tempus, he already went through this once, and the old gray fool could never be turned." Her lips curled in disgust. "Some people just don't know what's good for them."

Billy didn't respond, still looking for some way to get out of his predicament. He saw none. Even if he could run, where would he go? Perhaps he could lose himself in the cliffs for a time, but he suspected that the Darksiders would be able to track him. Maybe he could try swimming away, but then he would be at the mercy of the rapids, and eventually would find himself in the deadly ocean, among the waves and the hungry sharks.

Billy shivered. Mrs. Black smiled. "You see, there is no hope for any that would stand against us." She looked at Billy. "In fact, that's why we're here. So you can see that."

Mrs. Black suddenly took Billy's hands in hers. Her touch now felt surprisingly gentle, almost caring. "I wanted you to see the lies you've been told."

"Lies?" asked Billy. "What lies?"

"The lies that you have believed, because you have never known truth," said a new voice.

Mrs. Black straightened up instantly, smoothing her dress self-consciously as Wolfen appeared beside them. The dark master joined them in looking over Dark Isle. His long hair, now loose and hanging to the middle of his back, whipped around his head in the strong winds that ruled on this peak. The salt-and-pepper hair looked like some kind of evil halo around him.

Wolfen, too, touched Billy's shoulder in a way that was more familiar than Billy liked. He almost preferred it when Wolfen and

Mrs. Black were trying to kill him: at least he knew how to react in that case. This new friendliness disconcerted him.

"I've never been told any lies," Billy managed, more to say something than because he had any idea of what Mrs. Black and Wolfen were going on about.

Wolfen laughed. "My boy," he said, "you've been told nothing *but* lies since you first were introduced into our world."

Billy was confused. "What are you talking about?" he demanded.

"The War of the Powers, the Messenger, my role in it all," said Wolfen. "All of it. None of what you have been told by the Dawnwalkers is true."

"Yes it is," Billy said. "It was in the Book of the Earth."

"Was it?" asked Wolfen. "Did you *see* any of what they told you was written in the book? Or did you just hear it second hand from the Dawnwalkers? And from Lumilla, who appeared to read from the Book of the Earth, but never actually let anyone else see it?" And Billy, thinking back, had to admit to himself that he *had* never actually seen anything that Mrs. Russet had read from the book.

"So?" he asked. "That doesn't make it a lie."

"No, it doesn't," agreed Wolfen good-naturedly. "But it doesn't make it true, either."

"At least they never tried to kill me," said Billy.

"No?" said Wolfen. Mrs. Black laughed, appearing genuinely amused at Billy's statement. "Who brought you to the Test of Five? Who suggested that you be killed in the first place? Mrs. Russet. Who wrapped you in weeds when you wanted to leave? Ivy the Green. Who took you to a volcano where you almost died? Vester."

"Who actually killed me during the test?" retorted Billy. "Mrs. Black. And who attacked me on the top of the tower? You did, Wolfen."

Mrs. Black winced as though Billy's words had cut her deeply. "Billy," she said, "I was bound by the laws of our people to kill you. But I didn't want you there in the first place. I was doing everything I could to convince you to leave. I thought the Test of Five was too dangerous, and I wanted you to have no part of it. So I tried to scare you away. And it would have worked, too, if it hadn't been for Ivy and Lumilla keeping you pinned there."

"And I wasn't attacking you when you arrived on top of the tower," said Wolfen.

"You were!" shouted Billy. "You cast the Dread on me!"

"Only to stop you from running, from hurting yourself," insisted Wolfen. He knelt before Billy, hands still on the boy's shoulders, and looked earnestly into Billy's eyes. "I wanted to stop you and ask you to join us."

Wolfen turned to look at the crystal prison that covered so much of the island. "They didn't want me to say anything," said Wolfen. "And who can blame them for wanting me to remain silent! After all, it was the Dawnwalkers who stole our birthright from us."

"What?" asked Billy. He had expected to be taken away by Mrs. Black and killed or tortured. What was going on? Why were they talking to him like this?

"It's true, Billy," said Wolfen. "There *was* a War of the Powers. But the Darksiders didn't start it. It was the Dawnwalkers, trying to stop us from taking our rightful place."

"What place is that?" asked Billy. He still didn't believe what Wolfen was saying, but he had to admit he was curious. He had never heard this side of the story before.

"We wanted to help humanity," said Wolfen.

"By ruling them?" challenged Billy.

"Yes, by ruling them," said Wolfen. Again Billy was surprised. He had expected a denial of this charge. But Wolfen was admitting it.

"Think, Billy," said Mrs. Black. "What is the world like? Evil at every doorstep. The nations constantly in turmoil. People dying in senseless wars everywhere. Children suffering at the hands of people thousands of miles away from them. The earth itself in danger of being snuffed out by the ravages of humanity. Why would anyone want that?"

"And yet," said Wolfen, "that is precisely the status quo that the Dawnwalkers seek to protect. That is the way they want things to go on. And always they are there, behind the scenes, working their magic so that they are always comfortable, happy, content. Humanity suffers because they are left to themselves, and to the whims of uncaring Powers who will not lift a finger to save them."

Billy opened his mouth to say something. But nothing was coming. He felt Wolfen's words seeping into him, like water into wood. Wolfen's eyes bored into his, burning the words he said into Billy's mind, which was starting to feel confused and weak. Could Wolfen be telling the truth? Vester had himself said that the Dawnwalkers believed that their control over the Elements should only be used by and for the Powers, hadn't he? And Tempus had shown little compunction about terrorizing Howard and Sarah, though Billy had to admit he too had enjoyed the moment.

Could the *Dawnwalkers* be the evil ones?

As though sensing his thoughts, Wolfen said, "We're not what you think, Billy. We're not evil."

"I don't believe you," said Billy. But the words were more a whisper than anything. He clung to his belief in his friends, but his grip on that belief seemed to be weakening.

"Don't just take our word for it, Billy," said Mrs. Black. She waved a hand expansively, taking in the whole of Dark Isle. "Look, and see for yourself."

And suddenly, Billy found he could see all parts of Dark Isle. It was like the Close-Up spell in Powers Stadium, allowing him to see anything and everything he wished. "What the…?" said Billy.

"Death sees all things, Billy," said Mrs. Black gently. "It is the thing with the truest vision, and through it we can see reality as it is."

Billy cast his now far-reaching gaze around the island. He could suddenly see that the Darksiders were not, in fact, moving around like people engaged in evil deeds. There were young and old, fat and thin, short and tall, beautiful and plain people. There were doctors, and police officers, and gas repair people, and people in business attire, and some in pajamas. Just normal folks. Nor were they holding dead cats or cutting up chickens while chanting strange-sounding incantations. Instead, most of them seemed like they were on a vacation, chatting with one another in small, close-knit groups that moved from place to place. True, they were moving around in close-knit groups that had to move out of the way to avoid a zombie from time to time, but other than that it looked like any of the little cliques that Billy saw moving around the halls of Preston Hills High School.

Most of the people, Billy saw, were smiling. Many of them were laughing. Some wore scowls and frowns, too, but no more so than you would expect to see on any street in the world.

"Do you see, Billy?" came Wolfen's voice. "Do you see us, not as you have been *told* we are, but as we *truly* are?"

"No," was all Billy could say. "I don't believe you," he repeated once again. But the words were weak. They were beginning to lose their meaning.

"Then look, see one more thing," said Mrs. Black beside him. Suddenly, Billy's all-seeing gaze was moved without his control. It zipped through the peaks and valleys of Dark Isle, soaring above it like an eagle, passing lightly among the throngs of Darksiders who walked its paths. And finally, his view came to rest upon one person.

Billy gasped. He rubbed his eyes in disbelief. It couldn't be.

But it was.

Blythe Forrest, the most beautiful girl in school, the only girl to be nice to him since as long as he could remember, the closest thing he'd ever had to a friend his own age, was walking with a group of other young people along one of the paths that crisscrossed Dark Isle. She was laughing with them, not a care in the world, it seemed. One of the kids in the group punched her good-naturedly in the arm, and she laughed even harder, apparently enjoying whatever joke she was the butt of.

"You see?" said Mrs. Black. Billy felt her hand on his neck. "You like her, don't you? You think she's a good person, right? Then why not the other Darksiders like her?"

"She's," Billy stammered, "she's not. She can't be.... She just...." His voice disappeared like a sigh in the night, petering out to silence. He felt his breath hitching in his throat, felt his head spinning. Blythe, a Darksider?

Billy tried to look away, but found that he couldn't. As with the first time he had seen her, she was beautiful, mysterious, captivating to him in a way he had never before felt. But now, looking at her was not mere fun, it was tinged with a deep fear.

What if Wolfen and Mrs. Black are right? he thought again. I never heard any other side of the story. Maybe Mrs. Russet, and Ivy, and Tempus, and Vester...maybe they were wrong. Maybe they *deserve* to be in prison.

He wrenched his eyes away from Blythe Forrest and looked back at the stack of glass cells that housed the Dawnwalkers. It sparkled in the sky, catching the sunlight and turning the scene into something almost beautiful.

Billy felt something tugging inside him. This was a moment of choice, he realized. When he went back to the Accounting Room on Powers Island—if he ever did so—would his "Billy—unDetermined" badge now say "Billy—Dawnwalker"? Or would it proclaim that he was a Darksider.

For a moment, Billy didn't know. And for a moment, he honestly didn't know what he even *wanted* it to say.

Below him, far away, Blythe laughed again.

How can she be happy if this is a bad place? Billy thought. How can the one person who was nice to me be evil?

He thought about staying on Dark Isle. Staying with Blythe. Being, as he had said he wanted to be, her friend.

Being a Darksider.

That tugging feeling deep inside Billy teemed and writhed, like a living creature that dwelt inside his heart and was only now awakening. But would it be a creature of the Dawn, or one of the Dark?

Billy took one more long look at Blythe.

"Stay," whispered Wolfen.

The creature in Billy's heart opened its eyes, and Billy suddenly saw what he was.

"No!" he shouted. He shook Wolfen's hands from his shoulders, shrugged away from Mrs. Black's matronly touch on his neck. Suddenly, Blythe disappeared from his view and he found himself back on the rock again, high above Dark Isle, Wolfen in front of him and Mrs. Black behind. "You're lying!" he screamed at Wolfen. "You weren't trying to save me on top of the tower, you were trying to stop me, to hurt me. Good people don't hurt other people to help them!"

"Billy," began Wolfen, his voice the embodiment of calm reason. "Think this through. Look at it from our point of view."

"No," insisted Billy. "I won't. Your point of view is wrong. It's not what I believe. It's not what I *am*."

"What you are?" said Mrs. Black, the mocking tone returning to her voice now. "Just what are you, Mr. Jones? A no-Power *human*? A boy with no friends at school, a boy with no future in life, a boy with—"

"Stop!" Billy shouted. "If that was all I was, you wouldn't be wasting your time up here with me like this. Neither of you would be." He looked into Wolfen's eyes, returning the dark master's gaze steadfastly. "But that's not all I am. I am the Messenger. I speak for the White King." He glanced back at Mrs. Black, who was looking at him with a mixture of surprise and disgust on her face. "And you would do well to remember that, witch."

Billy saw Mrs. Black's expression change to one of searing hatred and rage. "You...*dare*?" she snarled. Her cheeks went white, her lips pale, all the blood seeming to rush from her face as she drew herself up to her full height.

Billy thought for a moment that she was going to hit him. But she didn't. She stood as still as marble, as silent as a gravestone. But that wasn't all she was doing, he knew. He could feel the air around him start to crackle with energy. Nearby him, Wolfen sighed, as though resigned to what was going to happen.

"Hear this, false messenger," said Mrs. Black at last. "Hear this, false speaker. None shall dare to challenge the Dark and live."

With that, a small insect rose from behind Mrs. Black. It fluttered around her hair for a moment, then flapped its way over to

Billy. It was a bug, he saw, a large gray moth. It flew before him in lazy patterns, its wings a blur. Then suddenly it was as though Billy could see the insect in slow motion, every detail of the moth clear to him.

It was a moth, but not alive. It was in the shape of an insect, but was only a mockery of such a thing. Instead of a body with pliant wings, it was made entirely of tiny bones, of minute skeletons that created a lacework of grays and blacks. The back of the moth's bone-wings were patterned strangely, in the shape of a skull. Billy couldn't help but shudder at the sight of the strange creature. Even though it was tiny, he could sense the power coming off of it in waves.

"The Death's Head Moth," said Mrs. Black. "One of my own little contributions to the artistry of the Dark." The moth continued to fly slowly in front of Billy, as though showing off for him. "Do you want to know what it does?"

Billy didn't. He looked around for an escape from the doom he could feel coming toward him. But there was nothing. Wolfen was on one side, Mrs. Black on the other. And on the other side there was nothing but a steep fall to a deep ocean full of deadly sea life.

"It is a Harbinger," said Mrs. Black. "It foretells doom. Your doom, Billy Jones." She licked her lips in that disconcerting way of hers. "But don't worry. You won't be gone. You'll be dead, but will remain under the power of the Dark."

Billy didn't understand what she was saying. He didn't know what would happen if the Death's Head Moth touched him, and he didn't want to find out. However, it appeared that he didn't have a choice in the matter, because the moth at that instant swooped in toward him. Billy ducked away from it, which made Mrs. Black laugh. At the same time, he felt Wolfen's hands close around his arms, holding him tightly in place.

The moth fluttered lazily before him, wheeling about for another chance to land on Billy and do its evil work. It swooped straight at Billy's right eye, and Billy could only scream.

There was a flash, a sizzling sound. Then he heard Wolfen swear behind him, and saw that Prince had chosen its moment to fight. The Fizzle had erupted from its hiding place in Billy's shirt, and caught the Death Head's Moth in its flaming jaws at the last second.

Mrs. Black shrieked as though in pain, and clutched at her eye like she had been stabbed there. Wolfen's grip loosened at that moment. "Eva!" shouted the dark master.

BILLY: MESSENGER OF POWERS, BY MICHAELBRENT COLLINGS * 271

Billy hurled himself away from the fracas, moving in the only direction left to him: towards the edge of the cliff. He moved instinctively, without thinking about it, but as soon as he had taken only a few steps, he looked behind him.

Prince was on the craggy ground behind him, the lava Fizzle working its jaws back and forth as it tried to get a death-drip on the moth. The bone insect was fluttering its skeletal wings, trapped in Prince's mouth. The Fizzle grew brighter as it chewed, and Billy could feel heat rolling off it in waves as Prince tried to snuff the Death's Head Moth out of existence. Mrs. Black screamed again, and sank down to her knees, still clutching at her eye.

The moth struggled to get away, but Prince just clamped down tighter and tighter, and grew brighter and brighter as its heat intensified. Soon Billy could barely look at the Fizzle, which was now a white-hot line of heat on the ground.

Then, slowly, the heat faded. The Fizzle let its fire dim. Billy was elated. Prince had done it! The snake had saved him again! The Death's Head Moth lay unmoving in its mouth, crushed and broken.

But Billy's elation was short-lived. He squinted, barely able to believe his eyes, as the crushed bones that made up the moth's body slowly re-formed and knit themselves back together again. Worse, Prince was no longer moving.

"Fool!" shouted Mrs. Black, still on her knees, clutching at her eye with one shaking hand. "You can't kill Death!" She laughed then, an insane laugh that sent shivers up and down Billy's spine.

Billy looked back at Prince. The Fizzle was writhing. It had seemed as though the snake had caught the moth, but now Billy could see that it was the other way around: Prince was trying to get *away*, but couldn't. The Death's Head Moth flapped its wings again, beating them around the lava snake's eyes. Billy could see Prince's ember-eyes blinking, fading, dimming like coals left too long in a fire-pit.

"Prince!" he shouted.

The snake twisted and jerked, but could not pull itself away from the fearful creature of death that Mrs. Black had conjured up. It rolled its fire-lit eyes toward Billy. Run, it seemed to be saying with its look. "No," Billy said. "I won't leave you."

Run, Prince's eyes continued to say. Run now.

But Billy couldn't—wouldn't—leave his friend. He moved toward where the snake and the moth were struggling, and reached out to grab the insect, to pull it away from Prince. But before he could, Prince's tail flashed out. It hit Billy's shin like a flaming whip, and Billy winced in pain as he was burned right through his pants.

Prince opened its jaws, and a dreadful keening wail issued from its mouth. It quivered rapidly now, and its color dimmed from yellow to orange to deep red.

It was still looking at Billy, though. Looking with eyes that now seemed to be covered by a white coating, like it was wearing a veil. Run, fool, run! said the snake's look.

The moth had settled down onto Prince body, now, and was walking along the length of the Fizzle. Wherever it touched, Prince's body turned to gray. Soon, Prince was more gray than red.

And then, with a final shudder, the snake whipped about once again. There was a crackle, and a smell like sulfur, and then the Fizzle was motionless. It still remained, but no fire was in it. Instead, it was now only a gray carcass. Then, to Billy's horror, the body seemed to transform. The Fizzle's gray skin resolved into thousands of tiny thread-like shapes. The eyes opened once again.

"Prince?" said Billy in an uncertain voice. But the Fizzle looked at him now without any love. Its eyes, once bright friendly embers, were now emotionless pits of darkness. The lines on its body shifted and hardened, and Billy suddenly realized what had happened.

"Prince," he said again. But he knew it was no use. Prince, his friend, was gone. In its place was only a long serpent made of the same tiny bones as the Death's Head Moth that flapped near its head. It was a newly born servant of Death.

The new Death Fizzle hissed at Billy. Then, with the dry rasp of bone scraping across stone, the snake crawled to Mrs. Black and wound itself tightly around her ankle.

Mrs. Black, though still holding her eye in pain, laughed at Billy's expression. "They all leave, don't they?" she taunted. "All your friends. They leave you alone to face your fate." She grunted, and pulled her hand away from her eye.

Billy almost screamed at what he saw there, but bit back his terror, knowing he had to keep his wits about him if he was to survive.

Wolfen helped Mrs. Black to her feet, then both the Darksiders turned their terrifying gazes on Billy full force. Billy stepped back, trying to move as far as he could from them, but suddenly he felt his heels hanging over nothing. He had come to the edge of the cliff.

He chanced a glance behind him, and saw nothing. Only a long fall to an angry surf and treacherous rocks. As though they could sense that a meal was nearby, the circling sharks below drew in close, swimming restlessly.

"Nowhere to go," said Wolfen. His voice was only a whisper, but it hit Billy like a hammer. Because there *was* nowhere to go. His friends were imprisoned, or worse. He had no powers of his own. He had no one to help him.

Then, unbidden, the words that Terry had spoken came to him mind:

*"Through fires of fate and storms that save*
*Through winter's gate and water's grave*
*Shall come the One, once lost, now found*
*Seen by the Son whose love abounds.*

*A sword, a spear, and armor strong*
*A shield to wear, and dagger long*
*To fell the Dark and bring the Light*
*To call the spark that ends the night.*

*And through it all, one twist of fate:*
*A child whose call will seem too late*
*But though the Dark seems once to win*
*The child will spark the light again."*

Billy looked below him. The sharks still waited, the sea still clearly hungered for him.

"Water's grave," Billy whispered. Then he looked at the Darksiders as they stepped confidently toward him. "You can't have me," he said.

"What?" said Mrs. Black, stopping for a moment in surprise.

"You can't have me," said Billy again. "I know what you want. You want to make me yours. But you can't. Because I'm not yours."

He looked down again. Gulped.

"You are!" shouted Mrs. Black, her voice almost hysterical with frenzied rage. "You're ours because all things come to us in time. All things come to Death!" And on her ankle, what used to be Prince hissed angry agreement.

Billy just smiled. "Not me," he said, surprised at the calm that he suddenly felt. "I'm not yours. I am the Messenger. I am not here to be your servant, but to destroy your world." The words came as though from a great distance, like he was hearing someone else say them. But he felt their truth, even more so than he had before, when braving the touch of the zombies. "I am no one's servant. I am the Messenger, and I answer only to the White King."

"You...will...be...*mine*!" shouted Wolfen, and lunged at Billy.

But before he could take more than a single step, Billy smiled. The truth of what he had said coursed through him like a cool stream through a desert. He looked at Wolfen without fear. He gazed at Mrs. Black with sudden pity.

"I am not yours," he whispered. And he knew it was true. He was Billy, the Messenger, servant of the White King, and ender of the world.

And with that thought in his mind, Billy jumped from the cliff.

# CHAPTER THE TWENTY-FIRST

*In Which Billy is Eaten, and hears the Music of the deep...*

Billy discovered something very surprising in the next instant: falling to certain death, either by splattering oneself all over pointy rocks, or by drowning in raging surf, or by being eaten by ravenous sharks, is not as fun as it sounds.

He was totally sure—positive in fact—at the moment he had jumped from the cliff that it had been the right thing to do. But falling rapidly toward a three-way doom had done amazing things—bad things—to his self-confidence. He supposed that this was probably normal: anyone in his position probably would have self-confidence issues.

Or, at least, he *would* have supposed all this if he had been thinking about the subject somewhere else. Somewhere slightly safer. In a magical palace made entirely of pillows where everything was wrapped in a foot of three-ply toilet paper, for instance.

But Billy wasn't falling to such a wonderful place. No, he was falling, falling, falling, to the raging sea below. He seemed to recall something about the fact that a person could be killed if jumping into water from too high. The surface tension—the power of the water's surface holding itself together—could make the water feel like concrete.

Luckily, there was no real surface tension, because the ocean below was so very turbulent that the water felt only as hard as dropping headfirst onto a pile of cardboard boxes, instead of onto a garage floor. But it still hurt when Billy slammed into the water with a huge splash. The breath was knocked out of him, and he gasped in a lungful of water as he plummeted downward below the ocean's surface.

He coughed and hacked, trying to resist the urge to inhale. He clawed at the water, pulling manically, trying to swim to the air above. But before he could do so, he realized he was not alone.

The sharks.

They were huge, with gaping jaws full of teeth like broken bottles, dark eyes, and a decidedly unhappy look on their faces. Worse, they were everywhere, thick gray bodies swimming powerfully all around Billy, eyes on the lookout for prey.

Billy tried to calm down, not an easy task when one finds oneself twenty feet underwater in a stormy sea surrounded by man-eating sharks just off the rocky coast of an island devoted entirely to dark magic. But he did succeed to some extent. His panicked thrashing went to a mere manic swimming, and he managed to stop the coughing attack that had threatened to drown him. He thought as he did so that he noticed two or three of the sharks notice *him*, but decided to concentrate on that later.

First things first, he thought. Air now, sharks later.

So Billy pulled himself upward as quickly as he could, his lungs burning from lack of oxygen, and only barely managed to break the surface before his body decided to inhale whether he wanted it to or not. He gasped a huge drought of air. It smelled of brine and salt, but to him it was sweeter than anything he'd ever smelled before.

Unfortunately, he had only a short moment to savor the experience before a wave crashed over his head, pushing him downward once more. He fought his way up again, coughing and spluttering, and did his best to look around.

That turned out to be a bad move. He would have preferred ignorance. He found himself now in the middle of a trio of twenty-foot-high rocks, which jutted out of the water like a witch's teeth. The rocks funneled the surf toward Billy, and the pounding waves threatened to crush him at any moment against one of the rocks or against the cliff face at his back. It was stormy, too, a contained thunderhead seeming to hang directly above Billy, lightning flashing from it periodically with a crash and a boom.

Worst of all though was that Billy had been right about what he thought he saw below: the sharks *had* noticed him. He couldn't see much, but he could make out several dark shapes in the water, gray forms that were larger than a man. They circled around him as Billy desperately tried to remain afloat, and more and more of the shapes joined the hunting party until Billy felt like he was in the eye of a hurricane made of sharks.

Soon, the huge bony fishes grew bolder, venturing closer and closer to Billy. Several gray-black fins broke the surface of the water nearby as the sharks played a nasty game of cat-and-mouse with him. Only he was a mouse without a hole, caught out in the open with nowhere to run.

Another wave crashed down on Billy, casting him under in a spray of surf and salt. When Billy came up again, he saw that the sharks had scattered for a moment. Apparently they didn't like being on the surface in such turbulent weather. But soon they closed in again, circling him confidently.

One of the shark's fins appeared nearby, slicing through the ocean like a razor blade. It was headed right toward Billy! Billy wanted to shriek in terror, but couldn't. It was all he could do to get any air into his body, what with the constant pounding of the waves, and he couldn't waste any of it, not even to scream.

The fin streaked toward him, then veered away at the last second, so close that Billy could actually feel the wake of the shark's passage. Another fin emerged, and another, two more sharks now converging on him. This time, the sharks came even closer. Billy could feel the flicking of one of the shark's tails on his leg as the two sea hunters swam by. The touch was slight, just a graze, but Billy could feel the naked power of the shark's muscles.

Billy looked around wildly for some avenue of escape. He looked at the nearby rocks to see if he could climb onto one of them, but they had been polished to a sheen by the smoothing action of the surf. He glanced at the cliff face behind him, but could see no caves to hide in, no handholds to lock onto. He even looked skyward in the hopes of seeing the Unicorn, but saw only dark angry clouds.

He felt something at his side, and looked down to see that this time, one of the sharks had actually bumped its head into Billy's side. It felt like he had been walloped with a rubber-coated jackhammer, though Billy knew that the shark was only playing with him, not trying to hurt him in any way.

At least, not yet, Billy thought.

But he also knew that the situation couldn't last long. The sharks had gone from being unaware of his presence to circling him warily, to doing reconnaissance in order to find out if he posed any kind of threat. Billy was no threat, he knew, and he figured that the sharks probably knew it as well by now. So it was only a matter of moments before one of the sharks tried to get a free Billy sample before the full Billy feast began.

Indeed, as soon as he thought this, he saw another of those frightening fins cutting through the water, heading straight toward him. This one was coming faster than the others had, too, and Billy thought he could see the jaws gaping open wide, ready to take a chunk out of him.

I hope I give you heartburn, was all Billy could manage to think under the circumstances.

But the shark apparently wasn't worried about gastrointestinal distress. It continued picking up speed, moving toward Billy faster and faster. The beast was huge, and it got huger looking as it came closer. Billy tried to flee, using sort of a frenzied doggy-paddle, but he knew it was hopeless. The shark must be coming at him at about thirty miles per hour. Billy was moving at a speed of maybe thirty *feet* per hour. There was no hope of outrunning the hungry predator.

He looked back. The shark was almost on top of him. Only twenty feet away now. And then ten, and then five. Billy closed his eyes, resigned to the end, just hoping that it wouldn't hurt and that he would, in fact, give the shark not only heartburn, but preferably also some kind of explosive diarrhea.

But the end didn't come. The expected bite didn't happen. Billy cracked open an eye. The surf still pounded, the waves still rolled. But all the sharks were suddenly, mysteriously absent.

Billy wanted to shout and clap for a moment, but he quelled the urge. For one thing, he still needed his hands to swim in the deadly surf. For another, recent experience had taught him that if one bad thing had exited the scene, it was most likely because something worse was waiting in the wings.

And sure enough, Billy had done little more than notice the lack of Billy-eating sea-life when the water suddenly *disappeared* from under him. It was a strange sensation, water literally dropping away from below like some great plug had been pulled on the ocean's bottom. A moment later, however, just as Billy began to fall downward, he felt the water rise up below him again. He heard a huge noise at the same time, something terrifying but somehow familiar, a sound like a cross between a saxophone and a river barge's foghorn.

The rapidly rising water pummeled him to one side, hurling him into something rough. Whatever it was felt like thick braided ropes. Billy had an instant to notice that the ropes were suddenly all around him; that he was in the center of some kind of container that was over ten feet to a side.

The container lifted up all around him, and then started to close overhead.

Water started rushing in as the rope-like strands began to press closer to Billy, and he saw the container continue to close above his head. At the same time, he heard that sound again, louder this time, coming from all around him. That sound that was part melody, part roar.

And this time, Billy recognized it. Worse, knowing what the sound was made him suddenly realize exactly what kind of a container he was in. The ropes that were not ropes clamped down around him, pushing him downward. He felt his feet touch something rough and strong, and as soon as they did the object slammed into Billy, clamping him tightly from the waist down. Billy couldn't move, couldn't get free now no matter how hard he strained.

Again, the blast of noise issued forth from all around him, one last time as the "ceiling" closed over Billy's head. Now it was dark. He could hear water rushing all around him. It was all terrifying, but not nearly as terrifying as the mere fact of where he was.

Billy had been swallowed by a whale.

Some great leviathan of the deep had been called forth somehow, had risen up and swallowed Billy whole as he treaded water on the surface. No doubt whatever person had been controlling his fate of late had seen Billy about to get torn to bits by sharks, decided that would be far too nice a thing to have happen to him, and had called up something that could instead swallow him in one piece and then slowly digest him over a period of a few days.

The sound came again, the whale's call coming up from what Billy now knew was the huge beast's throat. But it sounded different now, more familiar.

We must be completely underwater now, he thought. That's why the sound is different. We're under the ocean.

The thing that now held Billy firm moved slowly, like a thick rubber blanket with a mind of its own.

It's the tongue, Billy realized. The whale's tongue, holding me trapped.

His heart started beating rapidly, and Billy was pretty sure he was about to do one of two things: either have a heart attack...or have several of them.

The tongue shifted again, moving Billy around like a particularly juicy piece of prime rib.

Baby back Billy ribs, thought Billy insanely. Then he went back to his pitiful prayer that the thing now eating him would have some kind of horrific intestinal disorder that would cause it to explode. Preferably while the whale was right in front of the girl whale it liked during the Whale Undersea Formal Dance.

But then Billy realized something odd: the tongue, though not allowing him to move around as he wished, wasn't moving him deeper into the monster's throat, either. In fact, every time the tongue adjusted, Billy got a bit more comfortable.

Not only that, but though Billy could hear water rushing by at a tremendous pace right outside the whale's mouth, the mouth itself now had no water in it. Like the whale had sectioned off a section of itself solely for the purpose of carrying Billy.

But why would it do that? Billy thought.

He felt around him as best he could. Most of what he felt was that ropey substance. It was thick and rough, like the kind of ropes you would see in a western movie, usually hung around some poor sap's neck.

Billy realized he didn't much care for that comparison, and pushed it out of his thoughts as much as possible. He was still curious, however, what the thick, itchy substance all around him could be. Then he had a flash, remembering a lesson from biology class.

It's baleen, he thought.

That had to be it. The ropey substance was actually made of the same thing as hair or fingernails, and some whales used it when eating. The baleen hung like Venetian blinds from those whales' upper jaws. The whales would scoop up huge amounts of their preferred food, usually a kind of tiny shrimp called krill, swallowing vast amounts of water at the same time. They would then press their tongues up to force the water out, and the krill would get caught in the baleen, allowing the whales to then swallow the tiny creatures in one huge mass.

But it's not eating me, thought Billy. Why not? And what's it going to do instead?

It was now clear to Billy that the whale had no intention of actually consuming him. The water could still be heard outside the whale's mouth, moving quickly as the behemoth swam swiftly through the ocean's depths. But Billy had no way of knowing where the whale was ultimately headed, or what it planned to do with him when it got there.

Billy, as he had that first day of Mrs. Russet's class when faced with the terror of a pop quiz, tried to relax as his mother had shown him how to do. He closed his eyes, even though it was already pitch-black in the whale's craw. He breathed in and out as slowly as he could, trying to control his heart rate and his breathing. He focused on the pink and red sparks that he could see behind his eyelids, imagining them to be stars whirling through a tiny universe in his mind.

The song of the whale jerked him out of his self-induced trance. The sound was incredibly loud in the whale's mouth, so concentrating on anything else was out of the question. The whale sang loudly and long, a meandering tune that would have been quite lovely and calming if it weren't for the fact that Billy was right in the middle of it.

The whale song stopped abruptly, but then Billy heard more. Not from this whale, though. He heard a different whale, seeming to respond to the musical communication of the one that now held Billy. He wondered for a moment if the other whale wanted to know why Billy's whale was talking with its mouth full. Or maybe Billy's presence made his whale sound as though it was wearing some kind of whale retainer for its whale overbite.

Regardless, the second whale's singing was joined by the sounds of a third whale. And then another, and then even more. Soon, Billy couldn't distinguish among the many rich sound waves he heard, which were only slightly muffled by the fact that he was currently inside something's mouth. But it was clear that, where there had only been a single whale before, now Billy was at the center of come kind of Whale Convention.

The songs continued, with Billy's eardrums being blasted periodically as the whale in which he rode would burst forth in its own conversational song. It seemed to go on forever, for days and days. Billy knew that couldn't be possible: there couldn't be more than a few hours' worth of air in here with him, at most.

That thought, of course, gave him even more to worry about.

Wouldn't it be ironic, he thought, to suffocate while completely dry in the middle of the ocean?

His subconscious must have been trying to tell him something with that internal question, because soon after he thought about suffocating, his fingers and toes started to tingle. The air around him took on a stale flavor, oddly acidic and nasty. Billy started gasping, and even though it was pitch dark where he was, he swore that a black ring started pushing in on the edges of his vision.

I'm out of air, he realized. Or at least out of oxygen.

Soon, Billy's fingers and toes were numb, and the tingling had moved up to his arms. He got very light-headed, and simultaneously felt as though his head might pop like a balloon at any moment. It also got very hard to concentrate on anything in particular. A haze of thoughts whirled through his mind, calling up images and memories without rhyme or reason:

Seeing Vester emerging from the wall of fire in the Hall of Convergence.

Feeling the wind on his face as he rode the Unicorn.

Blythe's hand in his as he told her he liked her and hoped they could be friends.

Blythe's laughing face as she walked along the paths of Dark Isle.

His mother, singing Happy Birthday.

Himself, holding a shining object aloft, then crashing it to the ground with a sound like thunder.

Billy shook his head, trying to clear away the cobwebs in his mind. What had that last image been? He couldn't remember that ever happening before. Yet he had seen himself in it, as though it had already occurred. What was the shining object? Why would he hit the ground with it?

He tried to focus on the image, but his mind was now too muddled from lack of air. Billy's eyes started to flutter.

I don't like tapioca pudding, he thought, his mind now firing completely randomly. It makes goldfish dress in poodle sweaters.

And on that note of wisdom, Billy's eyes closed, and the thick black ring that had been pushing in at the edges of his vision now overwhelmed him. Billy went limp, thinking about tapioca pudding and hearing the songs of whales all around as he fell blissfully into unconsciousness.

# CHAPTER THE TWENTY-SECOND

*In Which Billy finds help in a Most Unusual Place, and Bargains for the future...*

When Billy returned to consciousness, he didn't know where he was. But the fact that he *had* in fact returned to consciousness at all seemed to be a good sign, since he had fully expected that never to happen again.

He thought about sitting up to see where he was, but then decided to just lay where he was for a minute. Wherever he was about to find himself, it felt cozy and dry, so why ruin the moment? He let himself ease back into full alertness, allowing himself to slowly come back to reality. If the word even meant anything any more.

Finally, he opened his eyes.

A blue fish was hanging in the air directly in front of him.

Billy closed his eyes.

He opened them again.

The fish was still there.

Billy hadn't really expected that. He had more or less figured that the fish was just an illusion his over-extended mind had coughed up. Sort of like a psychic hairball. But no, the fish was still there, hanging in the dry air right in front of Billy's gaze. It was a beautiful blue fish, about the size of Billy's hand, with wide white eyes on either side of its head, and a long thin nose—or was it snout?—that ended in a tiny mouth framed with delicate teeth.

The fish continued to hang there, looking at Billy. He noticed that the fish's gills were flapping like they were caught in some kind of breeze.

Something else floated into Billy's view, something yellow and far too close for comfort. Billy batted it away with his hand, and to his surprise realized that what had just drifted over his eyes was his own hair. But it wasn't curly. It was straight now.

Straight? How can my hair be straight? thought Billy. Did the whale style my hair while it was eating me? It must have, because the only time my hair is straight is when it's....

The end of that thought sent Billy bolt upright. A shock of pain sizzled through his head at the movement, but Billy barely noticed as he looked around himself.

The only time his hair was straight, was when it was wet. And as Billy looked around, he realized that the fish hadn't been hanging in midair in front of him...it had been swimming.

Billy was still in the ocean.

The soft thing he had been resting on was the muscular body of a giant clam, six feet in diameter, its huge shell open at the middle so that Billy felt like he was laying on some kind of strange bed with a gigantic curved headboard behind him. The fish he had seen when he first awoke was floating in the water before him, still looking at him with apparent curiosity.

Billy felt at his neck, half-expecting to find he had grown gills there. But there were none. So how was he breathing? he wondered.

Then he suddenly realized: he wasn't.

No air was going into or out from his mouth or his nose. It was like he was holding his breath. But there was no discomfort, no burning in his lungs as there should have been. He just simply wasn't breathing.

Maybe I *am* dead, after all, he thought. And then he wondered if this was Heaven. If it was, his Sunday School teacher had gotten a few things wrong over the years.

He glanced about again, and saw that the giant clam was sitting in the middle of the seabed. All around it were huge blooming flowers of coral, like orchids and lilies in the sea. Brightly colored fishes flitted all around the coral, darting in and out of gaps in the reef like they were playing the world's largest and fastest game of hide and seek. What looked like tiny shrimp sat astride some of the fishes, preening and cleaning them as they swam.

There was a creaking sound, and Billy suddenly jumped to his feet and pushed off the clam's muscular body as the clamshell slowly pulled itself shut, encasing the clam in a six-foot shell of solid armor. Billy now found himself hanging lightly a few feet above the floor of the ocean. He looked up, expecting to see the water's surface not too far overhead: after all, it was so bright that he knew the sun must not have too much water between it and himself. But to Billy's surprise, he saw that the light all around was being supplied by a thick ceiling of jellyfish, hundreds of thousands of them, which floated about a few hundred feet above him. Their long, trailing tentacles dangled below them like an upside-down jungle. The jellyfish glowed a pale blue, and their tentacles themselves flashed quickly in all the colors of the rainbow. It was entrancing, beautiful, unreal.

Billy's admiring gaze was interrupted, however, by the blue fish he had first seen when he awoke. It swam up in front of Billy's face, then made a motion with its head. It swam a few feet away, then swam toward him again and made that same motion once again.

"Do you want…?" Billy began, then stopped. His voice was coming out, but it sounded different. Again, he realized that as he spoke, no breath was coming out of his mouth. It was trapped within him somewhere. And so the noise he was making did not come from air passing through his voice box. It came from somewhere else within his body, just as the song of a whale must do. And like the whales, Billy's voice now had a sonorous lilt to it, the hint of music unsung.

"Do you want," he tried again, "me to follow you?" he asked the blue fish, which was still watching Billy.

The fish rolled its eyes. Apparently, no matter where you were, the sign for "Well, duh," was the same. It swam a few feet ahead of Billy, then turned its head to wait.

Billy had never been much of a swimmer. His best swimming had been done when he had accidentally been invited to a pool party in fourth grade, and everyone there had decided that he would make a great ball in a pickup game of pool volleyball. And even then, he had mostly just done something that could hardly be described as swimming. More like a kind of desperate flopping. So he had no idea how he could possibly keep up with the swiftly swimming fish.

But to his surprise, when Billy reached out to paddle toward the fish, the movement was fluid and practiced. It was as though he had been transformed into an Olympic swimmer. But more than that, because with one kick he shot forward ten feet, moving at a pace impossible for any human to achieve.

The blue fish didn't give Billy time to ponder this newest magical development, though, as it shot away full speed. Billy swam after it, easily keeping pace, feeling like he could even swim faster if necessary. He was amazed, and felt for the first time in his life as though he could have been picked first for a game of underwater Marco Polo or some other poolside game.

But where are we going? he wondered.

He asked the question aloud to the blue fish, but the fish seemed not to hear the query, apparently intent on just getting to where it was going. Soon, however, Billy spied a large crack in the coral that was piled like a living mountain beside and all around him. The blue fish sped directly at it. Billy was worried for a moment that he wouldn't be able to make it through the fissure, since the gap seemed a bit too slim for him to squeeze through. But as he swam toward it, the crack opened wider, the coral on all sides pulling itself away to allow enough room for him to pass through easily.

Billy swam through the doorway that had been created, and then found himself somewhere he was quite sure no other human had ever been. He was inside a coral mountain. He knew that coral reefs were created by the skeletons of dead coral, piled high in interlocking pieces, solid through and through and tough as rock. But this coral reef was different. It was hollow.

And it was beautiful. The place Billy now found himself was like a great hall in some amazing palace. Rubies, diamonds, and emeralds the size of a person's head were inset all over the coralline walls. The walls themselves glowed with the same slowly strobing inner light as the jellyfish had displayed, rendering the inside of the mountain into an ever-moving exhibit of all the colors of the spectrum.

The blue fish was still swimming ahead of Billy, so he had little time to take in all the beauty around him. But he did glimpse that there were numerous window-like holes in the coral mountain, allowing him to view the open ocean outside. He saw enormous shapes outside the mountain, lumbering forms that moved with surprising fluidity and delicacy through the sea.

The whales, he realized. *The whales who brought me here. They're still nearby.*

As if in answer to his thought, Billy heard whale song echoing in through one of the windows to this undersea palace. The music was more beautiful than it had seemed before, touching Billy's heart deeply with the otherworldly perfection of its graceful melody.

He ripped his eyes away from the scene outside with difficulty, and realized that the blue fish was gone. He looked around the vast empty space for it, but couldn't spot it anywhere.

As Billy looked around in confusion, the whales rumbled forth another stanza of music.

"They like you," said a voice. "It's why you're alive."

Billy turned to the voice, and though he didn't gasp—he still wasn't breathing as far as he knew—his eyes bulged out of their sockets at what he saw.

It was a mermaid.

At least, he thought that's what it was. But where most mermaids—or at least, all the ones he'd heard of in stories—had tails like a fish, complete with fins and scales, this one's tail was quite different. The fins were there, but instead of scales, the mermaid's tail seemed to be made of millions of tiny pieces of coral, all hooked together in an intricate maze of color and life. Some of the coral glowed, some of it shot forth tiny tentacles to grab at particles of microscopic food, some of it spread forth long leafy arms, then just as quickly withdrew them.

Nor was that the most interesting thing about the mermaid. Her eyes held that distinction. The eyes had no pupils, and the irises were deepest blue. They were the color of a pure glacier floating in the Arctic Ocean, a blue so deep and true that it spoke of the very Essence of all that was Water. The color of the Blue Element in its rawest form, swift and powerful as all the waves of all the seas.

The mermaid smiled, and her teeth were pointed as a shark's, spiny and shining like razors. But in spite of her alien appearance, she was quite beautiful. She was beautiful in the way that a tidal pool could be beautiful, or in the way that a manta ray could be beautiful: entrancing, but with more than a hint of danger within it.

Her skin was a light green, the color of seaweed, as was her hair, which hung down about her in a pale green mane that covered her from neck to belly. She had arms, muscular and strong, which waved lazily back and forth in the tiny currents here in the sea palace.

"Who likes me?" Billy finally managed to say.

"The whales," answered the mermaid. Like Billy's, her voice was tinged with that hint of song, that music that Billy was rapidly coming to expect as a part of the deep blue around him. "I don't usually save air-breathers. Those that I see are usually already gone, drowned in the depths of Blue. And those who aren't, I let be for Blue to take. But the whales spoke for you."

"They spoke for me?" asked Billy, confusion clear in his tone. "What do you mean?"

"Artemaeus spoke for you," said the mermaid. She nodded, and Billy looked over his shoulder to see the huge head of a great blue whale poking in through one of the windows in the coral palace. It met Billy's gaze stolidly with its own, and then slowly dipped its head.

Billy's mouth gaped open. It was the whale he had seen in the wall! The one he had seen in the Hall of Convergence, where one wall was water and the other was fire. The whale he had seen with Mrs. Russet when on his way to the Test of Five.

"Ar...Artemaeus?" he stammered. The whale dipped its head again, then pulled away from the window and swam quickly off, disappearing from Billy's view in an instant. "Where did he go?" said Billy.

"Not far," responded the mermaid. "Tell me, what is your name?"

"Billy Jones," responded Billy. Then, almost hearing his mom's voice in his head giving him a mini-lecture on manners, he said, "It's a pleasure to meet you. And what's your name?"

The mermaid smiled that beautiful and sharp smile, clearly amused by him. "I have no name," she said. "I had one once, but gave it up to become what I am. So now I have no name but Blue, because Blue is me, and I am Blue."

Billy wasn't sure he really followed what she was saying. "Your name is Blue?" he asked, confused.

The mermaid laughed again. The sound was like raindrops on a roof: soothing, yet energetic. "No, I have no name," she said again. "But if you wish to call me Blue, I will not object."

"Okay, Blue," said Billy uncertainly. He looked around. "You saved me?"

"Yes," said Blue simply. "Though I prefer air-breathers not to enter my domain, Artemaeus is one of the old ones of the deep. He is wise, and he said you were special, Billy Jones. So he saved you from the sharks, and then sang to me and asked me to let you be here with us in the deep."

She turned suddenly at that, and began swimming away.

"Wait!" shouted Billy. "What do I do now?"

The mermaid turned back to him, those blue eyes of hers bright and piercing. "Whatever you wish. Swim. Eat. Play. Be happy, for you are a visitor to the Earthsea, a guest of Blue."

"But wait," Billy said again as Blue turned once more to leave. "I can't just stay here! I have friends. They need my help."

"I can help you assist them if you wish," said Blue. "I haven't anything else to do today. What ocean are they in?"

"They're not in an ocean," said Billy. "They're on Dark Isle. Trapped by the Darksiders."

"Not in the ocean?" said Blue quizzically. "Then why would I help them?"

"Because they're my friends," said Billy.

"Ahhh," sighed Blue, as if in sudden understanding. "Your friends are other air-breathers."

"Yes," said Billy. "They're Powers, they're on Dark Isle, and they've been captured by—"

A curt wave of Blue's hand cut him off. "None of that matters," she said. "Blue does not concern herself with things of the world above."

"But what if Artemaeus speaks for one of my friends, as well?" asked Billy.

"Would he?" said Blue.

"He might. I think he knows Lumilla Russet."

Blue shrugged, the movement barely visible through the floating mane of green hair that surrounded her like an aura. She opened her mouth, and sang. It was like the whale song Billy had heard, but shorter, and livelier. It sounded more…direct, somehow, as though the whales put poetry into their words, and Blue cared only about simple sentences and direct questions.

Soon, an answering call came. Billy saw that it was Artemaeus, the huge blue whale's head once again poking into the coral palace. The whale sang back to Blue, then disappeared into the open sea once more.

"Well?" asked Billy.

Blue shrugged. "He said that he does know Lumilla Russet, but he has no particular desire to help her. She's rather rude to him at times."

"But she's like that to everyone," said Billy.

"All the more reason to leave her to her fate," said Blue in a wise tone of voice.

Billy was desperate now, knowing that this strange creature was his only hope to help his friends. But he couldn't think of a way to persuade her. She was simply too alien-seeming, too disconnected from the things that made him happy and were important to him.

He decided to try a new tack. "Blue?" he said.

"Yes, Billy?" came her strange, lilting response.

"You said I can do whatever I want down here."

"Yes, you are a guest of Blue," she agreed.

"Well, what do *you* do down here? What do *you* like?" he asked.

She smiled. "I catch fish, and I ride the currents, and overlook my domain. I swim with the sharks, and tear into flesh; and I sleep with the jellyfish, and light up the sea. I drift with the unborn eggs of fish in the tides, and I watch the oldest whales go to their graveyard to die. I am Blue, and I see those things."

"But what do you *like*?" Billy tried again. "I mean, do you read, or watch movies, or—"

"Oh, Billy," Blue laughed. "You *are* funny. I can see why Artemaeus likes you." Then she stopped laughing. "None of those things you say are things of Blue. They are things of Brown, or Gray, or Red. These things have no place in my world."

"But, but," Billy sputtered. Blue was now moving away, clearly bored by this conversation and ready to leave. She was no longer listening to Billy. He looked about, seeking some hint, some clue as to what to do next. But all he saw was the beautiful palace all around, with its coral, its diamonds and emeralds and plenteous treasures...

"Treasure," murmured Billy.

Though he whispered it only to himself, the word had an effect on Blue. She stopped moving, immediately straightening up. She didn't turn to face him again, but she did speak. "Treasure?" she said.

"Treasure," Billy repeated. Blue turned to him. He pointed at the giant gems that were scattered all around this beautiful place. "Diamonds, emeralds, rubies. Those are all things of the Earth—of the Brown—aren't they? But you keep them near you. So *some* things about the other Elements are of interest to you, right?"

Blue seemed to carefully contemplate his question. At last she said, "I would perhaps debate with you whether these things you call treasure are truly of the Brown, for so many of them find their final resting places in the Blue. But yes, we do like treasure." Her eyes closed lazily as she spoke, as though she was thinking of some particular memory, something that brought both pleasure and pain at the thought of it.

Then her eyes snapped open. "Do you have treasure?" she asked suddenly. "If you do, perhaps something could be arranged for your friends."

Billy's heart leapt, then stopped leaping just as quickly. What fourteen year old kid had treasure? The nearest he could come was....

"You can have my watch," he said. He looked down at the birthday present his parents had gifted him with and saw, to his surprise, that it was cracked and destroyed.

Blue swam over and grabbed his arm, none too gently. "Ow!" Billy howled, but Blue didn't seem to pay any attention to this. "Broken," she said. "It's been crushed by the depths. It's no treasure."

"Crushed?" repeated Billy, still surprised to see that his birthday gift had lasted such a short time. "What do you mean it was crushed by the depths?"

Blue looked at him like he'd just asked her if she was sure that one plus one *really* equaled two. "You are thousands of feet below

BILLY: MESSENGER OF POWERS, BY MICHAELBRENT COLLINGS * 291

the water's surface, Billy. No air-breather, not even a machine from the air-breather's world, can come to this place without suffering destruction. The water is heavy here, and so it will crush and destroy the things of the air."

"Then how come I haven't been crushed, too?"

"Because I changed you," said Blue. "That was what was needed when Artemaeus brought me to you. You had no oxygen left in your body, and no way to fashion any, so I changed you."

"You changed me?" asked Billy incredulously. "How?"

"I made you more efficient. You don't need air as much now, you can hold your breath for a very long time. And your organs are tougher, able to withstand the depths all around us. You are part of us now, Billy, one of the Blue. Just as am I, just as is Artemaeus." Blue touched him as she said this, and her touch was electrifying, like sticking a knife in a light socket. She was concentrated Element, Billy realized. Somewhat like a Fizzle, only much, much stronger. Then she grabbed the wrist with the watch again. "At any rate, this is no treasure."

"Well," said Billy desperately, "what kind of treasure *do* you want?" He thought of Mrs. Russet and her incredible powers; of the diamonds the size of cars that he had seen while traveling the Earthessence on Rumpelstiltskin's stone chair. Surely arranging for one of those to be given to this weird creature wouldn't be a problem, not if he could rescue Mrs. Russet first. "I could get you diamonds."

Blue smirked. She waved at the palace of coral and gemstones all around. "I have enough of such things already."

"Gold?"

"There are mountains of it, already buried in coffers and safes on ships that have met their end in the Blue," she said dismissively. "All these things of which you speak are of little interest to us. They fall to us, and we use them as we will. But if there were no more of it, we would not miss it at all." She bent down and plucked a slowly-moving sea slug from the floor at her feet. It was gorgeous, a tiny animal striped with red, fuchsia, magenta, white, yellow. The colors were so bright they seemed unreal. Blue allowed the animal to crawl on her hands as she said, "If there were no gems in our world, no gold in our sea, we would have the beauty of our own selves. We are not wanting of anything from the world above."

"Not *anything*?" asked Billy. He didn't know what else to do.

Blue put the sea slug back down, where it continued to crawl slowly around. When she straightened up to look at Billy, there was a sly look in her eyes that he didn't like. "Perhaps there might be *one* thing, Billy Jones," she said.

"What?" he asked quickly. He knew he sounded over-anxious, but didn't care. Anything this creature could give him to help him stop the Darksiders and retrieve his friends was desperately needed. She was his only hope, and the cunning look on her face suddenly told him that she knew it.

"Come with me," she answered, and swam to one end of the great hall in the coral palace.

Billy swam after her, still amazed at how fast he could go. When Blue came to one end of the hall, another doorway opened in the coral, magically pulling back to allow her to go through it. Billy followed, and found himself in a much darker, murkier place than he had been in before. What little light there was here was supplied by a trio of glowing white lobsters, crawling on the craggy walls and ceilings. The room itself was almost bare. The walls were coral, just as the great hall had been, but all the coral here was bleached the same color: a clean, simple white.

The floor was covered in sand, and the sand, too, was purest white. And etched on that sand was a picture of sorts. It was as though a master artist had come down here to work and realized he left his paints at home. So rather than go back and not do anything, he had simply drawn in the sand.

"Swim softly here, Billy Jones," warned Blue. "The sand is soft, and currents will fade its outlines." She pointed at the floor over which they both now floated. "Do you see what it is?"

Billy looked closely. It was clear that whatever this was, it had once been an intricate sand drawing, now faded by generations. "Who did this?" he asked as he looked.

Blue shook her head. "I do not know. I do not remember. My memory fades before that time. It has been here as long as I have been Blue, and as long as Blue has been me."

Billy slowly maneuvered himself so that he was floating face down, his eyes only inches above the sand drawing. "It looks," he said at last, "like some kind of sword or something."

"Yes," Blue breathed. Billy looked at her in surprise. She sounded really excited. More excited than he would expect over him simply being able to tell what the picture was.

"So what about it?" he asked.

Now it was Blue's turn to look a bit nervous, as though unsure how to say this. "It is mine," she said.

"But it's a sword. Aren't swords for air-breathers?" Billy asked.

"Yes, they are, but that one is mine. I don't know how I know, but I do know it. The sword is a thing of Blue. And I want it." Blue's voice was almost trancelike, detached, like she was speaking from somewhere so deep inside herself that Billy wasn't sure if she was even seeing him right now.

"I don't know where it is," said Billy.

"No, you don't," said Blue, snapping out of her reverie. Then, without any kind of preamble, she said, "What are you?"

And Billy answered as in a tone that was as quick and frank as her question had been. "The Messenger," he said simply. He was surprised how much he was starting to think of himself as that, even though he still had no idea what it meant to be the Messenger.

Blue nodded. "I thought as much. Artemaeus certainly seems to think so."

"He does?" said Billy in surprise.

But Blue wasn't really listening to him now. "The Messenger can find my sword," she said, then focused on Billy. "You can find my sword, and return it to Blue," she announced with finality.

"I, I don't...," began Billy, totally confused. His role in this magical world was as fluid as the water he now floated in, currents of change around every moment. The Messenger could get Blue her sword?

Then a chilly thought swept through him. He remembered that several of the Prophecies about the Messenger and the White King had mentioned a sword:

*A sword, a spear, and armor strong*
*A shield to wear, and dagger long*
*To fell the Dark and bring the Light*
*To call the spark that ends the night.*

And also, in Rumpelstiltskin's silly-seeming limerick prophecy:

*He used a big blade,*
*And the dead were waylaid,*

"Is this sword," he said, gesturing at the sand picture below them, "the sword of the White King?"

"It is," said Blue, "and it is not. It was mine, then his, and now his, but to be mine."

"But, I think the White King needs it to fight the Darksiders," stammered Billy.

Again, Blue made that dismissive gesture of hers. "Air-breather problems. They have nothing to do with me here; they cannot touch the deep. They cannot touch Blue. And," she added, with an intense look that Billy didn't like at all, "I *want* the sword." She stared at the sand picture for a very long time, then looked back at Billy. "What is it you want me to do?" she asked.

"Save my friends," he answered immediately.

"What friends?" she asked. "And where are they?"

"Vester, Ivy, Tempus, and Mrs. Russet are my friends," he said. "And they're on Dark Isle."

Blue pursed her lips, thinking. "Dark Isle moves about," she said, almost to herself. "It's how it avoids being found by the Dawnwalkers or by the world of mortals. Finding it could be difficult."

Billy watched her as she said this. It looked like she was figuring something out in her mind. Then, at last, she looked up at Billy.

"I will trade you," she said. "I will give you the lives of your friends and free them from Dark Isle, if you will promise to return the sword to me."

"But I don't even know what the sword *is*," Billy protested. "I don't know what it is, or where it is, or anything. How do you even know I'll ever find it?"

"If you are the Messenger, then you will find the sword. It is your destiny," said Blue.

"But then I'll need it for the White King," said Billy.

Blue shrugged. "This is the bargain. You may remain here with me and mine in the deep, and be happy. Or you may return to the world of the air-breathers, and I will free your friends, and you will promise me the sword when you find it."

Billy didn't know what to do. He knew he didn't want his friends hurt, but he sensed that the sword Blue wanted possession of was something very important to the return of the White King. Something that might change the course of this current War of the Powers.

Then again, he thought, if I don't save my friends, there won't even *be* a War of the Powers. Because near as I can tell, the Darksiders have already won.

Billy would have taken a deep breath if he had been breathing. But he wasn't, so he didn't. Instead, he just looked at Blue as evenly as he could, and simply said, "Done."

He held out his hand to shake and seal the deal. Blue just smiled and turned on her tail—literally—and swam toward a new door that was opening in the coral.

*Billy: Messenger of Powers*, by Michaelbrent Collings

"Come," she said. "Dark Isle has moved again and is close by. Now is the time to act."

Billy hurried after her, his supernaturally fast strokes letting him keep pace with this strange creature. They swam out into the open sea, and as they did Blue plucked an outcropping of rock from the sea floor. It was long and flat on one end, and coiled in upon itself on the other. It looked, Billy thought, like a cross between a gong and a tuba. And as it turned out, he wasn't far off. Blue snapped another rock off another nearby outcropping and used the second piece to hit the first rock on its flat end.

A clear, bell-like tone rang out. It rattled Billy's teeth in their sockets, and he knew it must be heard for miles around.

"What are you doing?" he managed to ask when the sound petered out.

"Warning the deep," she said.

"Of what?" he asked.

Without ceasing to swim or slowing her pace, Blue looked at him. "Do you think that freeing your friends on Dark Isle is something that can be easily done?" she asked. "It is going to require great magic, great movement of the deep. I am warning all those around the island to get away, lest they be caught by the violence and destroyed."

Billy gulped. Blue was still lovely as she had been, but now that subtly-sensed danger he had felt in her was surfacing. She was part of the water itself, it was certain, and just as water could be beautiful, so also it could be deadly. He was now seeing the dangerous part of Blue. And it frightened him.

On they swam. Blue used a few more ocean rocks to sound her alarm periodically, each time causing Billy's teeth to come a bit looser in his head.

*I better not eat any apples any time soon*, he thought. *My teeth'll pop right out if I do.*

At last, they arrived at what looked like the base of a tall mountain, which stretched up high before them, disappearing above the surface of the ocean hundreds of feet above.

"We're here," Blue announced. She began to swim upward, and Billy realized that what he was looking at was not the base of a mountain, it was Dark Isle itself.

Billy thought about warning her of the sharks, but then realized that he hadn't seen *any* sea life at all for the last half an hour or so. And besides, he realized, Blue was probably not the kind of creature that would be scared of sharks, not even special forces sharks armed with bazookas and tuna nets.

Billy swam up beside Blue. As they neared the surface of the ocean, she moved closer to the undersea rock face of the island. She pointed, and Billy's mouth opened wide. "What is *that*?" he asked.

"Your ride and your protection," answered Blue.

It looked like a starfish. But where most starfish had five thick legs and were about the size of Billy's hand, this one had several dozen legs and was the size of a Toyota. Each of its legs was studded with powerful suckers, and Billy could tell just by looking at the creature that whatever it grabbed onto wouldn't get out unless the starfish let it get out.

Without further warning, Blue shoved Billy at the starfish. Two of the creature's legs immediately lanced out and gripped Billy around the arms and shoulders. As he had suspected, the grip was like iron. He kicked and shouted, but it was to no avail. The starfish had him held fast.

He looked at Blue. "We had a deal!" he cried.

"And we still do," she said. "The star is part of it." Then the mermaid nodded to the starfish. The creature wrapped more of its arms around Billy, hugging him tightly to it, then began using the rest of its prehensile arms to climb.

The starfish moved rapidly, its sucker feet enabling it to grasp and hold onto anything. Soon, both it and Billy were fifty feet above the turbulent water, dripping as they ascended the highest peak of Dark Isle. Billy managed to look down, and could see Blue, still below the surface of the water, apparently waiting for Billy to get to some predetermined spot.

But then he lost sight of her as the starfish continued to pull him up. Up, up, up they went, until finally they crested the very peak where Wolfen and Mrs. Black had tried to convince Billy that they were on his side, and that he should join them.

The starfish mostly let go of him then, though it still clung tightly to his ankle with one of its serpentine legs. Billy could see the island once more. Nothing much had changed, though he could see that Blue had been right: the island itself had moved. The sky here, wherever "here" was, was now a slightly different color, as was the water around the island. They could be on the other side of the earth from where they started, for all Billy knew.

But other than that, the rest of the island was as it had been. Darksiders walking about, doing their chores or meeting with one another. Thousands of zombies lurching about doing the menial tasks of the island. And a glimmering, terrifying castle of transparent cubicle cells looming over the whole of it.

How is Blue going to save all of them? Billy wondered.

He felt something tugging at his leg. It was the starfish, one of its rubbery legs curling more tightly about Billy's. He could also see that the starfish's other legs were gripping the rock below it with all their might.

What's going to happen? Billy asked himself. For clearly something *was* going to happen. And whatever it was, it was going to be big.

# CHAPTER THE TWENTY-THIRD

*In Which Billy sees what he has Done, and realizes the Price...*

It started with a sound.

Not a large sound.

But in spite of the fact that it was a small sound, it was piercing. All around the island, wherever Billy could see, the Darksiders stopped walking or talking, and looked at one another as if to say, "Did you hear that?"

The sound came again. Louder this time.

It sounded like a waterfall, Billy thought. Or maybe like pounding surf crashing on a beach at night.

He looked over the cliff to the ocean below and saw that he was wrong. It wasn't like waves crashing onto a beach. It was quite the opposite, in fact. The water all around Dark Isle was drawing away, exposing the stone foundation of the island, withdrawing more and more until Dark Isle could be seen from its top to the very lowest point where it joined itself to the ocean floor.

Billy tried to position himself so he could see more of what was happening, but the starfish wouldn't let him. Indeed, it clung tighter to Billy, and pulled the him with closer to it.

"Hey, I want to see," he protested. But apparently the starfish either didn't hear or didn't care. Either way, Billy once again found himself cocooned in the starfish's strong grasp, with only his head free to move. The starfish flattened out as much as possible, using its arms to wiggle into every crack and cranny in the ground below them, holding as tight as it could.

Billy was upset for a moment, wanting to see what was going on, but soon realized he needn't have worried about not seeing. Indeed, he wished he *couldn't* see.

The rushing sound stopped. All was silence. Billy thought he could have heard a pin dropped on the far side of Dark Isle. Then, he once again heard the noise of rushing water. This time, though, it was from much farther away. He craned his neck in the starfish's grasp, trying to see what was happening, and realized that all the water around Dark Isle hadn't *disappeared*. It had just moved away, stacking impossibly on top of itself like sand dunes on the beach. Now the entire island was ringed by an unbroken circle of water that loomed higher than the peak upon which Billy was being held.

On the very crest of the water that circled the island, Billy thought he could see a tiny figure: Blue, arms high in the air, clearly sustaining this magical water surge.

No, not surge, Billy thought. Tidal wave.

Sure enough, an instant later Blue dropped her upraised arms. The circle of water collapsed inward, a violent implosion that brought all the pent-up water crashing down on Dark Island.

Billy could see the water forming into the shapes of sea creatures as it slammed into the cliffs and plowed through the valleys of Dark Isle. He saw sharks and seahorses of surf, whales and walruses of water, all of them sweeping over the island like a tsunami.

And then the water hit the prison. At first, the giant wave just exploded into diamond slivers of surf as it impacted the strong structure. But then another surge of water came, and another. And Billy screamed, because whatever Blue was doing, she wasn't freeing his friends. She was letting mayhem loose on the island.

With a sound like shearing windows, the prison began to fragment. Crystalline cubes separated from one another and plunged into the water all around them. Most of the cubes themselves began to fragment, allowing those inside to push their way out.

Any freedom the imprisoned Powers might have felt, however, was in most cases swiftly stolen from them as wave after wave churned over the island. There was a crash, and one of the highest of those waves actually crashed over the peak that Billy was on. He now saw why the starfish was there, as its firm grasp was the only thing that kept Billy from being washed off the cliff by the wave's force.

Billy screamed in spite of the starfish's sustaining grip, terrified at the dark cascade of water sweeping over him, and more terrified at the thought of what havoc was being wrought on the lower parts of the island. He closed his eyes against the thrashing surf, and when he could open his eyes again, he saw that Dark Isle…was gone. Covered in water, only a few of its highest peaks still in evidence. It was like the city of Atlantis, now lost forever below the ocean's angry tides.

There was no trace of the prison.
There was no trace of the Dawnwalkers.
There was no trace of the Darksiders.

There was no trace of Blythe.

Billy began to cry.

"Why so sad, Billy Jones?" asked Blue. Billy looked over and saw that she was floating lazily in a nearby wave as it rolled over what had just moments before been thin air between mountainous peaks which were now buried.

"You lied!" he shouted, half-blinded by a combination of tears, rage, and sorrow.

Blue looked genuinely surprised and perhaps even a little hurt by this statement. "I never told an untruth of any kind, Billy Jones," she said. Her voice, now in the air, had lost that musical tone it held while underwater, and her eyes were not as blue. But Billy could still sense the power radiating from this alien creature.

"But you said you would save the Dawnwalkers," he protested.

"No," she said firmly. "I said that I would save your *friends*. Vester, Ivy, Tempus, and Mrs. Russet are the people you named."

"And you didn't even do that!" he shouted, rocking back and forth furiously, trying to get free of the starfish that still clung to him so tightly. "You just buried Dark Isle underwater forever and destroyed the prison."

"Not forever," she answered. "The waters will subside in time, just as they always do. In and out, out and in. The deep becomes shallow and the shallow deep. It is the way of the sea, and not long shall pass before this island rises once more."

"Who cares about that?" screamed Billy. He pulled one arm free and began using it to try to peel the sucker arms of the starfish away from the rest of him. He didn't have much success. "I wanted my friends, and they're gone. They were *in* that prison, don't you understand that?"

"Of course I do," said Blue. And now she sounded a bit irritated, perhaps even angry. "And they are safe."

"Then where—" began Billy. But before he could finish his words, he heard a sound. The rushing water again. He turned to look, fully expecting to see some further devastation or destruction.

Instead, he saw a great wave, formed in the shape of giant seahorses, rolling over the water toward where Billy lay. And each foam seahorse bore someone on its back:

Vester, the fireman looking thoroughly uncomfortable around all this water.

Ivy, her eyes bright and shining, holding her hands high up to take in as much sunlight as possible, the black and withered plants that plaited her body turning green and lively once more.

Tempus, his knobby knees knocking together, his moving Hawaiian shirt flapping in the tempest, shouting "Giddap!" for all he was worth.

And, on the last seahorse, Mrs. Russet. She alone was not moving. She was unconscious, draped over the back of one of the watery seahorses.

Vester was the first one to see Billy in front of them. "Billy!" he shouted happily, waving one hand, then immediately re-clutching at the seahorse, clearly worried about losing his grip and falling into the water.

Ivy and Tempus both saw him then, and shouted and laughed with joy. The starfish let Billy go as his friends approached. Soon Vester, Ivy, and Tempus all held Billy in a huge group hug on top of the mountain. Their seahorses all dissolved into foam and disappeared as each of Billy's friends stepped off. At last, only Mrs. Russet's steed remained, water flowing through it in salty currents, as it waited for them to notice its burden.

It snorted, and Billy tore himself away from the happy reunion long enough to say, "Mrs. Russet?"

Vester hurried over to the seahorse, and tenderly took Mrs. Russet's limp form from the seahorse's back. That seahorse, too, disappeared in a shower of sea foam as Vester turned back to the group of friends.

He lay Mrs. Russet down tenderly—or as tenderly as he could considering her bed was the wet, cracked ground of this mountain peak. "What happened to her?" Billy asked in a quiet voice.

"We don't know," said Ivy. "She wasn't with us in the prison. Or at least, none of us saw her there."

"Bah," said Tempus, his familiar combination of gruffness and absent-mindedness a welcome treat to Billy's ears. "They wouldn't dare put the likes of her in something like our measly 'prison.' Why, Lumilla could have escaped that thing with both eyes closed and one leg tied behind her back. No, they weren't even going to *try* 're-educating' her, of that I'm sure."

"Then why did they keep her alive?" asked Billy.

Before the friends could answer, Billy heard Blue speak his name. He turned, and saw her still there in the ocean, her head poking out of the water. He also noticed that, just as she had said, the ocean level was already dropping back to its former place. Soon Dark Isle would be above water again. Who knew how many Darksiders or Dawnwalkers had survived the tidal wave, but whatever Darksiders were left were sure to return. They had limited time here.

But that didn't matter to Blue, Billy knew. "Remember," she said. "Remember our deal."

"I will," Billy said. He felt both grateful for his friends' lives and sick at heart that the deal he had struck had been followed in such a way that countless others might have been lost.

"The sword," said Blue. "When you find it, it is mine."

"It's yours," Billy agreed. Blue did not, he knew, have any interests but her own at heart. She had met the letter of their deal, but had violated its spirit. But in spite of that, Billy would keep his word. "As soon as I find it."

Blue nodded, and her eyes became even deeper blue for a moment. Billy felt an arc of power pass between them, sealing the deal. The promise made had magic behind it, he knew, and he could not break it, even if he wanted to.

Blue nodded again, and then with a flick of her coralline tail she disappeared below the surf.

Billy turned back to his friends and saw them staring at him oddly.

"What?" he asked.

"Uh...," began Tempus, the old Gray Power clearly unsure how to say this. "What was...what was that all about, Billy?"

"She saved you," was all Billy could think to say. "She was the one who saved you all."

The confusion on Tempus's, Vester's, and Ivy's faces didn't go away. In fact, their confusion appeared to grow even worse. "How could that...thing...have saved us?" asked Ivy.

"I don't know," admitted Billy. "But she did."

"And how do you even know it was a 'she'?" asked Vester, the fireman's face still visibly concerned.

Billy rolled his eyes in the universal "Well, duh," he had recently seen a small fish do. "You can tell it's a girl by looking at her, Vester."

Vester blinked, confused. "You can tell a girl dolphin from a boy dolphin?"

Dolphin? thought Billy. Then, out loud, he said, "What the heck are you talking about?"

"You," said Ivy. "We rode up here, found you with a big starfish, and then we got Mrs. Russet down, and then there was this dolphin in the ocean."

"And you were clicking at it," said Tempus.

"Clicking at it?" said Billy dumbly.

"Clicking at it," affirmed Tempus. "And it clicked back at you, and then it swam away."

"But it wasn't a dolphin," said Billy. Why hadn't his friends seen Blue as she was? "It was a mermaid."

Ivy, Tempus, and Vester all looked at one another for a moment. Then the three burst out laughing.

Billy felt himself get a bit upset. "What's so funny?" he asked.

"There's no such thing as mermaids," said Ivy with a weary giggle. Billy could see now that much of his friends' apparent humor wasn't really directed at him: they were just happy to be alive after their captivity and the tidal wave, so they were letting that happiness out in semi-appropriate bursts of laughter. But it still stung Billy.

"How can you say that?" he asked. "How can you say there are no mermaids, or that the Unicorn wasn't real, or anything else? You all live in a world where rock giants box, and there's a magic room for hot chocolate, and hot dogs want to be eaten. So why not a mermaid? Why not a Unicorn? Why not believe in me?"

Hot tears started to drip down his cheeks. He was ashamed of himself; he had cried twice now in less than a few minutes. But he didn't try to hide the tears or even wipe them away. Let them make fun if they wanted. He knew he wasn't really crying about their apparent lack of faith in him, anyway. Not really. He was crying about Blythe being a Darksider, and about the huge wave that had washed everyone away, and about the fact that he was hungry, and tired, and had no idea what to do next. He was crying about the fact that only a few short months ago he had thought the end of the world was being stuffed in a locker, and now he knew that the end of the world might actually mean the world literally coming to an end. He was crying because Mrs. Russet, the first teacher who had ever taken much interest in him, was lying here, unconscious on a cliff on Dark Isle.

He was, in short, crying for himself. For the world he had once had, and should have enjoyed, that was gone forever. The world where he had not been the Messenger, just Billy.

Now he wiped away his tears, sniffling and trying to get himself back under control. Tempus laid a bony hand on his shoulder and Ivy said, "We're sorry, Billy. We didn't mean anything." Now she began to cry, too. "I think it was just because we've been in there so long."

"What do you mean?" asked Billy. "How long has it been?"

"My boy," said Tempus, "it's been several weeks since we last saw you at the Accounting Room."

Billy's jaw gaped open like a bass fish. "How is that possible?" he asked. "I just left you guys a little while ago…." But then he realized that he had no idea how long he had been unconscious when the zombies had touched him, or how long he had been asleep after blacking out in the mouth of the whale.

But weeks?

He shook off the thought. It didn't matter now. What mattered now was getting off Dark Isle, and figuring out what to do next.

"What now?" asked Tempus, apparently thinking along the same lines as Billy.

"I don't know," said Vester in response. The fireman looked haggard and worn, and Billy's friend had the beginnings of a beard on his sweat- and sea-drenched face. He looked like he had lost a few pounds, too, and Billy wondered if the Dawnwalkers would have simply been allowed to dwindle and die in their cages if Billy—and Blue—had not intervened.

"I think we should get out of here," said Ivy.

"That goes without saying," said Tempus shortly. "But where *to*, my dear? I mean, it's one thing to say, 'I think we should get out of here,' and it's quite another thing to have a plan, a method, a—"

A noise sounded close by, and all of them looked over to see a gnarled, motley green hand reach up from somewhere below the edge of the cliff. The hand pulled, and it was immediately followed by an equally motley arm. Then a head with two huge eyes peered up at them. A zombie!

"I really think," Ivy said again, "we should get out of here. Like, now."

There was another sound, a crunching and crackling, as another zombie started to pull itself up onto the small plateau where Billy and his friends now stood. Clearly a few the zombies had been less affected by the tidal wave than had the living inhabitants of the island. Soon, a half-dozen or so of the creatures stood nearby, looking at Billy and his four friends with their faceted, insectile eyes.

"What are they going to do?" whispered Ivy.

"I don't know," whispered Tempus. "But don't let them give you a hug, no matter how friendly they seem."

Vester rolled his eyes. "I don't think they know what they're supposed to do."

Sure enough, the zombies continued just looking at the group, and Billy thought Vester was probably right. Still, it was uncomfortable being so close to such nasty creatures.

"Can we just get out of here?" whispered Billy.

"Don't know," said Vester. "They took away all my fire when they put me in that dratted prison box, so I'm pretty much useless until I get my hands on a lighter or I find a spark somewhere."

"Same boat I'm in," said Ivy. "All I have left is my blouse-plants," she said, gesturing at the vines that were wrapped around her. "And I'm too tired to do much more than maintain my current state of apparel. Certainly can't fight off any zombies like this."

"That leaves you, Tempus," said Vester. "Can you blow these jokers off the cliff or something?"

"Well," harrumphed Tempus. "You see, Vester? You see? Another reason why air is far superior to fire. Air is always around, so I don't rely on a lighter or any kind of sparking device to maintain control over *my* Element."

With that, the old man turned to look squarely at the zombies, which in turn regarded him with something that Billy might have described as a bemused expression…if the undead soldiers could be capable of something so light and unimposing as a "bemused expression."

Tempus rolled up the sleeves of his Hawaiian shirt so high that his bony shoulders stuck out of them. As before, his shirt was animated, seeming to show an image of a real Hawaiian shoreline. And now, as Billy watched Tempus prepare to cast some kind of really devastating spell, he could see that the Hawaiian coast on the shirt was now being hit by a typhoon.

Tempus clapped his hands together with the sound of thunder. Then, he screamed, "Putrid creatures of the grave, begone!" He pointed his fingers at the monsters, and Billy fully expected shards of hard air to shoot out of his fingernails and skewer the undead soldiers before sending them over the cliff side to their re-deaths.

Instead, there was a small breeze, and the zombies looked at each other in what, again, would have been bemusement if zombies could be capable of that kind of an expression.

Tempus tried again. Once more, there was a tiny ripple of air, and then nothing.

Tempus looked at his fingers like he was looking down the barrels of loaded shotguns that must have misfired, trying to figure out what had gone wrong.

"Huh," he said. Then, with an apologetic shrug, continued, "I guess that fight in the Accounting Room and my time in the magic-canceling field of my cell must have dampened my spells."

"Ya think?" said Ivy sarcastically.

The zombies, meanwhile, had apparently decided that, ineffectual though his attack had been, Tempus—and by extension, everyone else on the top of the cliff—was guilty of some kind of crime against the Darksiders. So they immediately began to step forward, reaching out their hands to touch Billy and his friends. Soon, Billy,

Vester, Ivy, and Tempus were all standing back to back in a rough square, Mrs. Russet at the middle, trying to keep her safe.

It was hopeless, Billy knew. Two Powers who were out of power, one who thought he was a superhero in exile but who couldn't generate enough wind to blow his nose, and the unconscious Mrs. Russet. At their best, all of them but Mrs. Russet might have fallen prey to half a dozen zombies. And they were far from being at their best.

Billy felt Ivy's hand, reaching for his, clutching him reassuringly for a moment. "You tried," she whispered. "No matter how this turns out, you tried your best."

"I'll remember that," he whispered back sourly. Somehow, just having tried his best didn't seem to count for much right at the moment.

As the six zombies slowly approached, there were scrabbling noises as more zombies clambered up onto the top of the mountain, crowding in close to Billy and his friends. It was only a matter of time before the zombies touched them, and all would be lost once more. Because as Blue had said, the waters would recede, and there would be nothing then to stop the Darksiders from reconverging on this place, finding Billy and his friends, and incarcerating them anew.

Suddenly, though, the zombies stopped. Those nearest to Billy looked terribly confused, though Billy couldn't see anything that might confuse them. They held their hands to their faces, as though inspecting them. And then, with a whoosh of air, the zombies just... exploded. The turned into piles of ash in an instant, and the next second the ash itself disintegrated. Billy winced at the sudden, tremendous heat he could feel.

"To arms!" he heard someone say, and looked up in the sky.

It was Fulgora! The beautiful Red Lady, the Red Councilor, the woman whom Vester had saved, and the person Vester loved. She was riding what looked like a burning tiger, soaring through the air on crimson wings of flame. She held up her hands, and more of the zombies near to Billy and his friends turned to ash and then vanished in a puff of smoke.

"Fulgora!" shouted Vester. Then, abashed, he said, "I mean, My Lady!"

But Fulgora paid no attention to his shout. She was intent on the zombies that had made it to the top of the mountains. "Venomous fiends!" she shouted, and with one hand clenched in the flaming fur of the tiger, she used the other to hurl bolt after bolt of fire at the zombies on the mountain. Each one that was hit burned instantly to ash, as though it was made of kindling and kerosene.

Soon, the mesa was cleared of the undead. Fulgora's fiery mount dropped toward Billy and his friends, and as it touched down it turned into a sheet of flame that wrapped itself around the beautiful woman like a bright dress.

"How did you get here?" asked Ivy, clearly amazed at the Red Lady's sudden appearance.

"I've been looking for you for weeks," she responded. "After...." She paused a moment, then went on. "After what happened to me during Napalm's Challenge, I went to my home to see if I could find out *how* it happened. Then I returned to Powers Island, only to discover that the Darksiders had attacked."

"But how did you escape the zombies? And how did you *find* us?" asked Ivy again.

Fulgora looked at Ivy with a look that clearly conveyed the fact that the answer to both questions should have been obvious. "I am not just any Power. I am the Red Councilor." Then Fulgora looked at Mrs. Russet's still form. "What's wrong with her?" she asked.

Vester couldn't speak. Billy saw that his friend was still lovestruck, and completely unable to communicate when Fulgora was near. "Uhhh...," said Vester.

Fulgora looked at him for a moment, clearly waiting for something a bit more conclusive to be said. "Uhhh...," Vester repeated.

Fulgora looked a bit disgusted. She turned to Billy. "You," she said, "unDetermined one. What has happened here?"

"Uhhh...," Billy said. He wasn't love struck, he just didn't know what to say. It seemed like a really broad question, and he just wasn't sure what the proper place to begin his answer might be.

Fulgora rolled her eyes. "Men," she muttered, and turned to Ivy. "Ivy, what's wrong with Lumilla?"

"Well," said Ivy, wringing her hands, "I don't know. She wasn't being kept with us. But I think," she held her hands even tighter, the tendrils that clung to her winding tightly around her as well, mirroring her concern. "I think that she might have been tortured."

"Tortured?" said Billy. "But there's not a mark on her."

"There are some tortures that leave marks we can see, and others that leave no marks but are far, far worse," said Fulgora. Tempus nodded in agreement, his hands unconsciously dropping to feel at his own battle-scars under the folds of his Hawaiian shirt.

Ivy nodded. "I suspect that someone has used the Dread on her for far too long."

Fulgora touched Mrs. Russet's cheek. "She's cold," said the Red Lady, seeming by those words to agree with Ivy's assessment.

"What does that mean?" Billy asked Tempus.

"It could mean anything," Tempus began in a falsely jovial and carefree tone. "It could mean they just went skiing with her and she didn't have her long underwear on. Or maybe they took her swimming and the pool wasn't heated. Or maybe...." The Gray Power stopped, and Billy could see now that the old fellow was trying hard not to let tears come.

"It means that they wanted her to talk, to tell them something," said Vester. "And she wouldn't. So they kept at her with the Dread, until she couldn't take any more. And after a while, there was nothing left of her but fear. Nothing left to hang onto."

"So what are you saying?" said Billy. "That she's gone? That she's dead?"

"No," said Fulgora. "Death is a natural part of Life. It comes to us all in time. What is here," she said, motioning at Mrs. Russet's motionless form, "is much worse. It's not death, it's not life. It's an existence that is bounded on all sides by bars of fear and chains of terror. It is literally a personal hell."

"What do we do?" asked Billy.

"There is nothing *to* be done," said Lumilla. Then she touched her dress of fire. She peeled away a thin slice of it, and the fire writhed and reformed in her hands, quickly hardening into the shape of a slim rapier. She brought the weapon high over her head, directly over Mrs. Russet's unmoving shape. "The only thing that is left for her is mercy."

# CHAPTER THE TWENTY-FOURTH

*In Which Billy braves the Dread, and Falls...*

Billy acted without thinking.

He threw himself at Fulgora, locking his arms around her waist and driving her to the ground. At the same time, he shouted, "Are you *nuts*?"

Luckily, the Red Lady was a petite woman and unprepared for Billy's outburst, and so even Billy's small frame was enough to knock her down. They hit the craggy rock of the cliff top with a bone-jarring thud, and Billy felt his breath jerk loose from his lungs in a whoosh.

Fulgora was on her feet almost instantly, shoving Billy to one side and breathing like a wounded rhino. She wasn't hurt, he could see at a glance. She was just angry. White rage gripped her beautiful face, draining it of blood and turning her pale. Only her lips remained red, pressed tight against half-bared teeth.

Her fire-sword was still in her hand, and she held it in a guard position, as though preparing for Billy to attack her—or preparing herself to attack him. Even so, Billy didn't flinch. He was too amazed at what had just almost happened to be afraid.

"Are you nuts?" he asked again. "You're going to kill her? Because she's under a *spell*?" He looked around at Ivy, Vester, and Tempus, who all stood frozen in their places. "What kind of people are you? What kind of world is this?"

"Be careful, child," said Fulgora quietly, in a voice tinged with danger and menace. "You do not know of what you speak." She paused, then added, "And you clearly don't understand to *whom* you are speaking."

"I totally don't," Billy agreed. "But I know that killing Mrs. Russet is *not* going to happen." He clambered fairly awkwardly to his feet, then moved himself to a position between Fulgora and the unconscious Mrs. Russet. He drew himself up to his full height—all five foot nothing of him—and then stared at the Red Lady as intensely as he could. "You're not going to touch Mrs. Russet," he said. Then, as though explaining his reasoning, he added, "She's my teacher."

Fulgora's eyes flashed, and once again Billy was faced by a Red Power with actual flame in her eyes. The sight almost made his knees start knocking together, but he stood his ground. Even though he'd probably daydreamed of having Mrs. Russet assassinated on more than one occasion—usually when she was handing out homework assignments or returning graded history tests—he was not about to let this crazy woman attack his Sponsor in the world of the Powers.

Fulgora took a step forward. Billy didn't know what she was planning to do, but he was pretty sure it involved him being moved very forcefully out of the way, and perhaps some kind of spontaneous combustion of his spleen or something. Still, he just gritted his chattering teeth together and did his best not to wet his pants as he crossed his arms in what he hoped was a determined-looking way.

Before Fulgora could move too far toward him, however, a form interposed itself. It was Vester. "My Lady," the fireman said. "Please. He's just a boy."

Fulgora didn't seem to notice Vester at first. Then she looked at him, apparently seeing who he was for the first time. "You were the one who rescued me, aren't you?" she asked.

After seeing how the fireman felt about Fulgora, Billy fully expected Vester to literally explode in amorous excitement at being recognized by his lady love. To Billy's surprise, however, Vester's expression didn't change from the pleading look he wore. "Yes, my Lady," was his only reply.

Fulgora stared at him for a long moment, fire still flashing in her eyes, the flaming rapier gripped in her palm. At last, however, she nodded curtly. "I am in your debt," she said. "Your request shall be honored." Then she looked over Vester's shoulder, staring down at Mrs. Russet's still form. "But you know that you show her no kindness by stopping me."

"Perhaps not," agreed Vester reluctantly.

"Foolish," said Fulgora, but her tone was no longer angry. She walked to the edge of the cliff and sat down well apart from Billy and his group of friends, staring out over the sea, which continued to grow lower and lower, baring more and more of Dark Isle. Almost instantly, Fulgora seemed to withdraw into herself, as though she were no longer aware of Billy, the other Powers, or anything else around her.

Billy watched for a second, then saw Vester's shoulders droop. The fireman exhaled nervously, then turned to Billy. He was wearing a jittery half-hysterical smile, the kind of smile you might see on someone who had miraculously survived a major earthquake. "You are very brave and," he said, glancing at Fulgora, "very lucky."

"Was she really going to do it?" Billy whispered. "Was she really going to...?" Billy gestured at Mrs. Russet, unable to even speak the dreadful thought aloud.

Vester hesitated. He looked at Ivy and Tempus. Neither the Green nor the Gray Power seemed willing or able to offer any guidance. So he looked back at Billy and simply said, "Yes."

Billy was even more shocked now than he had been when Fulgora first drew her sword. "What kind of person—what kind of *monster*...?" he began, then looked at Vester incredulously. "And you *like* her?"

Vester suddenly looked supremely surprised. This was odd, Billy thought, because Vester's infatuation for Fulgora was so blatant it would be obvious to anyone with a pulse and more than two brain cells to rub together. Even the zombies probably knew about it, and talked about it at zombie slumber parties, or whatever it was that zombies did on their time off. But still, Vester clearly believed he had been hiding his emotions very well. The fireman looked at Ivy and Tempus, his mouth a round "O" of surprise.

"I don't," he said, "I mean, you know, I never—"

"Forget it," said Ivy with a wave of her hand. "Everyone knows."

Vester blushed a deep red, and Billy could swear he actually saw small curls of embarrassed smoke come out of the Red Power's shirt. As fascinated as he was by Vester's obliviousness, however, Billy still wanted an answer to his question. "How can you like someone like that?" he asked again.

Vester looked back at Fulgora, who still sat in a trance, apparently no longer aware of or interested in anything that happened around her. "She's not like you and me," he finally said.

"No kidding," said Billy sarcastically. He was surprised at the venom in his voice, but the emotion he had pent up over the last hours was now bubbling to the surface. All his fear, his guilt, his anger, it was all coming out. "I mean, sure, who hasn't whacked a teacher from time to time, but really—"

"Billy, be quiet," said Ivy suddenly, interrupting him before he could really work up a good head of steam. Billy turned to her, surprised. "Vester is right," said Ivy. "Fulgora *is* different. She was born in a place very different from where you or I came from. She has spent a short amount of time in what you call the 'normal' world—as when Vester met her—but she has never really lived there."

"What do you mean?" asked Billy.

"Just as Powers Island is a land apart, so also there are other places," replied Ivy. "Fulgora is from one of them. It is a land of war, and warriors. A place called the Underworld of Flame, where the cities are built on the very magma flows that heat the earth itself."

"It's not a very hospitable place," interjected Tempus.

Ivy went on as though she hadn't heard. "Fulgora is a Princess of those people, and has been trained in the art of war from her birth."

"Then if they're so tough, such warriors, why aren't they fighting with the Dawnwalkers?" asked Billy.

"They don't like to get involved," said Vester. "Even though Fulgora is herself a Dawnwalker, her people have resisted following her into this battle."

"Well regardless of all that," said Billy, "does the fact that she's a warrior princess mean that she can just go around killing people?"

"No, it means that she has seen suffering, because she has seen war," said Tempus. The old man knelt slowly beside Mrs. Russet's quiet form, gently holding her hand. "And she believes that there are some pains that are so great, it is mercy to end them…any way you can."

Billy swallowed. "No," he said. "We're not giving up on her."

Ivy touched Billy. "We're not saying to give up," she said. "But if Lumilla is locked into the Dread…." Ivy shuddered. "No one lasts long if that's where they are, and the end is always terrible."

"Where they are?" said Billy, mostly to himself. Then he looked at Vester, sudden hope in his eyes as he remembered his own brief interaction with the Dread. "The Dread is like someone's worst fears, right?" he said.

Vester nodded. "That's a very basic explanation, but yes, that's what it is at heart. So?"

"So someone's fears come from things that have happened to them," Billy said. Vester, Ivy, and Tempus all looked at him blankly. "Don't you get it?" Billy was so excited now that his words jumbled all over themselves as they raced to get out. "Fear is just bad memories, things we've learned and things we're worried about happening again. *Memories*." He looked at Vester. "And you and Fulgora can go into those memories. Just like you did with me. So you can go in and you can help Mrs. Russet find whatever it is that's scaring her, and get rid of it."

Vester shook his head slowly. "Billy, I never went into your memories. I guided *you* into them. This," he said, indicating Mrs. Russet, "is totally different. She's not here anymore. I can't help her go inside herself to fix whatever's wrong. She's *already* inside herself. She's stuck somewhere in there, reliving some awful moment or moments, over and over again."

"Then if Mrs. Russet can't do it herself, one of us can go in there," said Billy urgently. He was unwilling to just roll over and let Mrs. Russet disappear into an oblivion of despair.

Vester was still shaking his head. "Billy, I know this is hard for you—it's hard for all of us—but it doesn't work that way."

"Why not?" Billy demanded. "Why doesn't it? You guys are Red Powers. You can see into people's memories. Why not hers?" He was trying to control the frustration and helplessness that threatened to overwhelm him at any moment. I'm the Messenger, he thought. Messengers don't give up. They deliver their Message.

Then he thought, But what if the Message *is* to give up? What if the Message is that the world is really ending, and this is how it starts?

Shut up, he thought back at himself.

"What you and I did together in seeing your memories was incredibly difficult, Billy," said Vester. "And that was when I was guiding *you* through your own memories. I don't think I have the power necessary to guide you—or anyone else—through someone else's mind. Not only that, but the process itself could actually destroy your teacher." He paused, clearly trying to find the right words to explain to the young boy what going into Mrs. Russet's mind would be like, finally saying, "Can you imagine having someone else invade your head during a nightmare? It wouldn't be pleasant, I think. For either of you."

Billy wanted to keep arguing. But he didn't know what more to say. He just stood there, clenching and unclenching his fists in mute frustration. Nearby, he was aware of Ivy and Tempus taking turns looking from him to Vester to Mrs. Russet, their eyes sad.

Don't give up! he wanted to shout at them. She's not gone, so how can we give up? All he could manage, though, was, "We have to do something."

"I'll take him in," said Fulgora suddenly. Billy looked over at the Red Lady in amazement. She had gotten to her feet and was now looking at him steadily, her expression strange.

"What?" said Billy, caught off-guard by her sudden re-entry into the conversation.

"I can take someone else into Mrs. Russet's mind," she said. "I'll take you."

Ivy, Tempus, and Vester all erupted into an avalanche of protests at the same moment. "No!" and "Too dangerous!" and "Impossible!" were only a few of the words that Billy heard as his friends voiced their opposition to this new plan.

But Fulgora only looked impassively at him, as though none of the others existed. "If you truly want to bring her back," she said, "then I'll help you try." Billy's three friends were still shouting down the idea, and Fulgora now turned on them. "Silence," she commanded in an eerily soft voice.

As one, the three other Powers on the plateau immediately shut their mouths. Fulgora, though young and slight in frame, was clearly someone that they respected. Billy suddenly realized anew what it meant to be a Councilor: it meant you were one of the top six rulers and one of the strongest people in the entire world of the Powers. He felt awkward all of a sudden, as though he had been called out of class to go to the principal's office and discovered that the President of the United States was waiting for him there.

Fulgora misread his expression. "Afraid?" she asked. "There's nothing to be ashamed of in that. Even the greatest warriors fear."

"I'm not afraid," Billy said quickly. Too quickly, in fact, for he realized that he *was* afraid. What would Mrs. Russet's vast room of memories look like? His own had been almost overwhelming. How much worse could hers be, with so many more memories contained in it, and all of it under the hold of the Dread?

"Of course you are afraid," said Fulgora. Her burning eyes seared into him. "Either that, or a fool. And I think you are not a fool, Billy Jones. Though perhaps a bit impatient and intemperate at times." This last she said with something that almost approached a smile, which nearly sent Billy into surprised shock.

"My Lady," said Vester haltingly, his tone low. "Billy is just a boy. And no one who has ever tried to pull someone out of the Dread has ever returned."

"He's not much younger than you or me," replied Fulgora. "Besides, boys have lived and died for causes—and for friends—before. Don't sell him short because he has fewer years than you."

She was still looking at Billy, her eyes ablaze. Billy could almost feel her walking through the corridors of his *own* mind, fingering through his experiences, his feelings. He closed his eyes for a moment, fighting off the feeling, then opened them and looked back at her with as much courage as he could muster. "Tell me what to do," he said.

"Billy," said Ivy, pleading in her voice.

But before he could say anything else, Fulgora nodded. She touched her cloak of flame, peeling away part of it, the fire pliant and moldable in her hands. In an instant she held her fiery rapier once again. She put two hands on the hilt, and the blade separated into two distinct swords, one in each hand. She touched the sharp tip of one blade to Mrs. Russet's forehead. The other she brought swiftly up to where its point hung only inches in front of Billy's eyes.

"Tell you what to do?" she said. Then smiled a tight smile. "No one knows."

And with that, she jabbed her blade at Billy. Just as he had done when Vester had taken him into his own memories, Billy once more felt the touch of cool flames, and then felt himself explode from the inside out. He closed his eyes, and when he opened them, everyone was gone.

He was alone, which he had expected, but the place he found himself was completely *un*expected. "Where am I?" he wondered aloud.

In answer, he heard a high-pitched screaming that echoed around the halls of the vast place he was now in. The noise was terrible, haunting and fearful. Billy thought it sounded a lot like the kind of noise a scary ghost would make if something had scared *it*. He clapped his hands over his ears, wincing, and waited for what seemed like infinity years plus one until the shrieking stopped. Or rather, didn't stop, but eased off until it was merely an eerie whine in the background, constant and unnerving.

Billy took his hands from his ears, slowly, ready to muffle them again if the sound should return to its previous levels. It didn't, though, and he was able to look around and try to figure out where he had found himself.

It was a library. That in itself surprised him. This was nothing like the world-sized room full of television-like screens that had housed his own memories. Instead, it was a world-sized book collection. There were books everywhere, housed mostly in shelves so tall they looked like they might topple over at any time, but the books were also on the floors, some desks and tables, any surface that would hold them. The shelves themselves had ladders next to them, ladders that went up and up and up until they disappeared in what looked like a cloudy night sky. And all the way up were books, books, books. The only places where there were no books on the shelves were at the ends of some of them, where low-wattage light bulbs were strung, providing a dim light that cast dark shadows throughout the huge space.

He realized that the books must be what Mrs. Russet's memories were housed in. It made sense: she was older, she was a history teacher. Exactly the kind of person that would see herself in a book, rather than on an electronic screen.

But where to start? How could he pull her out of the Dread? How could he find her at all in the vastness of her mind?

"Hello?" he said. He was hoping to hear Fulgora's voice, just as he had heard Vester's on his previous trip through Memory. But only silence greeted him. "Fulgora?" he shouted. Nothing. This time he was on his own. The thought scared him more than a little, and he truly realized for the first time what a dangerous thing he had volunteered to try.

For lack of anything better to do, and as much to get his mind off the danger he was in as for any other reason, Billy walked over to a nearby book. It was a huge, dusty tome almost the size of Billy himself. It was propped up against one of the shelves, its thick leather color dark and mottled, reminding Billy strangely of the skin of the zombies.

He reached out a hand to pull open the huge cover, but before he could, the book fell over. The sound was huge and echoing in the chilling vastness of the library. And as it fell, that strange banshee scream returned for an instant. Billy jumped in fright at the weird sound. He looked around, and realized that the light bulbs of the library were all flickering, as though their power was being interrupted somehow.

As before, the ghost-wail slowly ebbed and faded, though still echoing at the edges of his hearing. Once more, Billy reached out to the huge book that now lay flat on the ground before him. He touched the cover, and the screaming started again. He tried to ignore it, to just pull open the cover of the book so that he could see inside, but the harder he tried the louder came the screaming. The lights flickered again, and as Billy continued trying to open the great book, they began to spark and then go out, extinguishing one by one.

Soon, the library was in near-darkness. But still Billy pulled at the cover of the great book. It wasn't just the ghost noises that were making it difficult, either: the book itself seemed to be resisting his pull, growing slippery and slimy as an eel. It also seemed heavier somehow, like it was drawing extra mass from the air around it.

There was a sudden click, and Billy felt something move under his hands. He looked at the book, and saw that a dingy padlock and

BILLY: MESSENGER OF POWERS, BY MICHAELBRENT COLLINGS * 317

an equally tarnished looking hasp had sprung into existence on the side of the book. With a snap, the hasp shut of its own accord. The padlock slammed closed with finality, locking the contents of the huge book away from Billy's eyes.

He let go of the book now. This one was sealed, maybe forever, and couldn't be opened. As before, once he stopped touching the book, the frightening scream that echoed through Mrs. Russet's library of memories slowly faded into a whispering cry.

Billy went to another book. This one was smaller, though still not something he would want to lug around in his backpack. He touched it, and immediately the same things happened. The scream returned, the cover grew clammy and heavy and cold, almost writhing under his fingers. Then another lock appeared, another click sounded, another book of memory was closed to him.

This time, however, he was aware that as he pulled on the book there was more going on than before. More light bulbs seemed to be going dark, but not only that, the entire library itself seemed to be changing. Before, it had started out as something that reminded him of a school library: metal shelves and stacks of books on fairly new-looking furniture. But the more books he touched, the more dingy and grotesque the library seemed. Cobwebs sprang into existence between the shelves. The dim light bulbs turned into foul-smelling hurricane lamps that flickered eerily. The shelves themselves grew warped and rusted, and as Billy moved deeper into the library, more and more of them looked like they were made of wood, and very old.

He continued moving, though, occasionally reaching out to touch some book or other, to see what would happen. Each time, the screaming started, the cover would writhe, and the book would end up locked.

Now, the library he was in bore no resemblance to the place Billy had been in only moments before. The hurricane lamps had been replaced by candles that were propped in holders that looked like they had been fashioned from the skeletal remains of small birds and animals. The shelves themselves were a sick-looking yellow, and curved at the edges. With a start and a shudder, he realized that they were made of what looked like huge bones, lashed together with tendons and strung in huge lines that reached to the sky above.

The books themselves were more forbidding as well. They were clearly older, more neglected. Most of them looked like they were falling apart, and many of them were covered in strange symbols that Billy didn't understand but which nonetheless made him shudder in sudden fear.

But no matter how awful the surroundings, no matter how decrepit the volumes of paper, he couldn't open a single book. All were sealed away from his eyes, their locks appearing the instant he tried to read any of them.

Billy remembered what Vester had said before he had come here: that Mrs. Russet was stuck inside herself, reliving some memory over and over. Billy had figured that her memories were recorded in these books, but how could he find the right one? And how could he open it to look once he *did* find it?

He looked around. The library was now a completely terrifying place, cold and dank, like something out of a nightmare.

Of course, he thought. This is *her* nightmare. This is what Mrs. Russet's mind looks like when it's under the Dread. He shivered, and realized that his hands and feet were getting very cold.

It's taking me, too, he thought. He hadn't thought of that. But now he was living in Mrs. Russet's mind. And so if her mind was being shaped by the Dread, it made sense that he would be infected by that terrible power as well.

"Mrs. Russet!" he shouted, feeling panic start to well up inside him. The candles flickered in the eye sockets of the skulls they sat in, like horrifying jack-o-lanterns in a Halloween gone terribly, terribly wrong. "Mrs. Russet!" he shouted once more. In fact, it was more of a scream this time.

Billy started to run aimlessly, shouting his teacher's name over and over, feeling his own sense of self and purpose start to recede under the gloomy influence of this terrible place. Soon, he became aware that he was shouting Mrs. Russet's name repeatedly, but couldn't remember why he was saying that, or what he was doing here. He felt like he was in the belly of some great dark beast, waiting for his turn to be digested.

"Mrs. Russet!" he screamed again, no longer sure what he was saying, just saying the only words that his growing terror would allow. "Mrs. Russet!"

And suddenly, he heard something. The banshee screaming was following him like a shadow now, cloaking everything he heard in a shroud of fearful sound. But underneath that noise was something else. Something less actively terrorizing, but perhaps even more hopeless.

Billy had forgotten his mission. He had forgotten what he was doing here, or who he was here for. He knew only fear now. But he also knew that this new sound was something different in this nightmare world, and anything different had to be a step up. So he listened as best he could, trying to find the source of the noise.

He turned left down one bone-aisle of books and skeletal light, then right down another. The sound of weeping and woe grew louder. Another left, then straight for a long time. Right. The rows were endless, each darker and drearier than the last, the wind-wail of ghostly howls clinging to him with every step.

Then Billy turned again, and abruptly came face to face with something. Something unexpected in this nightmare place of hidden Memory. Something he could barely even identify in his state of almost mindless panic.

What is that? he thought. What is it? What is it?

Then, after a long while, came an answer: Ah, yes, I know what that is. It's a woman.

And so it was. She was young, very young, perhaps twenty years old, maybe less. And she was the source of the endless howling that Billy had followed—and that had haunted him—for what seemed like forever.

He couldn't see much of her face, because it was buried in her hands. But she was slim, not too tall. She wore a rather old-fashioned dress and blouse, with black shoes that were the kind Billy's mother would have called "no-nonsense." She was crying, huge, body-wracking sobs that shivered her from top to bottom. The cries bounced off the horrid shelves of the library, growing louder and louder as they echoed, and becoming the terrible ghost-screams that had hounded Billy in this place.

With the crying, however, the screaming and wailing that had so pervaded Billy's world seemed to withdraw a bit. And as it went, Billy started to feel more like himself again. He still didn't remember exactly where he was, or even what he was doing there, but he at least had a sense that he was supposed to be doing *something* in this ghastly place.

He looked around, lost and frightened, but could find no clues in his surroundings. Just bone and leather, candles and paper. No clues, no solace.

Billy turned back to the crying woman. "Hey," he said softly. "Are you okay?"

Clearly she wasn't okay, he could already see that, but he for some reason felt like it was important to help her. To stop her from crying.

The woman looked up. Her face was as young as he had thought it would be. Unlined, uncreased, the face of someone who hasn't yet experienced much of life.

"Who are you?" asked the woman.

"I...I'm Billy," answered Billy. He wasn't at all sure that was the right answer, but it was what came to him out of the fog he was trying to find his way through right now.

I'm losing myself, thought Billy. Just like Vester warned.

Then on the heels of that thought came another: Who's Vester?

But then Billy's thoughts were drawn back to the woman. She grabbed the hem of her skirt, and used it to dab at her eyes. Billy saw that under the skirt were several layers of petticoats.

"Oh," said the woman, with that stuff-nosed voice that always accompanies too much crying. "I don't know why I'm crying. It's just that it's all so terrible." And with that, she went into a new round of howling sobs.

Billy patted her uncertainly on the shoulder. "What is?" he asked. She didn't answer, just continued crying, so he tried again. "Can I help you?" he asked.

The question stopped the woman's sobs dead, like some kind of emotional light switch had been flipped to "off" position in her head. "I don't think so," she said in a shattered, haunted whisper. "No one can."

She looked down, and Billy's eyes followed hers. He saw that before her, sitting on a table made of what looked like a huge ribcage with a slab of unevenly carved granite atop it, was an open book.

An open book? he thought. There *are* no open books here. Not here, not in the Dread.

Once more, with this thought came the sense that he didn't really know where these ideas were coming from. Light was beginning to glimmer at the edges of his mind, but still there was too much shadow, too many cobwebs, too much...Dread.

Billy shook his head and looked at the open book again. It was small, barely the size of a paperback, but with a worn spine that allowed it to sit flat, open to a page about a third of the way through. The other two thirds of the book were sealed with a grisly string of tendon and gristle that wrapped from within the book and bound that last part tightly shut.

But as Billy looked closer, he saw that the book had no words. Just empty, blank paper stared up at him and the woman. She didn't seem to realize it, though, focusing all her attention on the open page.

"It's blank," he said.

"I know," she answered. This sent her into a new round of wailing. "He's gone," she said in a hitching voice between sobs. "He's gone, he's gone, he's gone."

"Who?" asked Billy, growing more and more confused.

"I don't know," answered the woman. "Don't you see, he's gone!" And she fell to the ground, clutching at herself and saying "he's gone" over and over again.

Billy didn't know what to do. He wanted to comfort this strange woman, wanted to help her. But he didn't know what he could do. He looked at the open book again. Clearly, this was the source of her woes. Maybe he could close it, and get her mind on something else.

But when he tried to do that, he couldn't. It was as though the book was super-glued to the macabre table below it, unmovable.

This is the open book in the locked library of Mrs. Russet's mind, thought Billy. He didn't know exactly who "Mrs. Russet" was, any more than he had known who "Vester" was. But the thought seemed to make him feel better. It was like he was putting together a jigsaw puzzle in a dark room. All he could do was feel a piece, then touch the rough edges of the other pieces until two clicked together. The picture wasn't visible to him at all, but he could feel the puzzle coming together, bit by bit.

The Dread is a re-lived terror, he thought. This is the library of Mrs. Russet's mind. The books are all shut, except this one. And this one is the one the woman weeps over.

This is the book of her fear, he realized. And as this thought came to him, so also did the understanding of what he was doing here, and who this mentally and emotionally crippled woman must be.

"Mrs. Russet," he whispered. He knew it was so, that it must be so, even though he didn't understand the how or the why of it all. This woman, young as she was, broken as she appeared, was somehow also his old, implacable, and above all tough history teacher.

And with that realization came the understanding that whatever was in the open book before him, only Mrs. Russet could read it. Because it was her fear, and hers alone.

But then how can I help her? thought Billy.

He knelt down beside the crying girl. "Lumilla," he whispered. It felt strange to call his teacher by her first name, even in her present form. But it would have been even stranger to call her "Mrs. Russet."

Besides, it seemed to have been the right choice, because Lumilla's crying diminished noticeably as he said her name. "Lumilla," he said again, as calmly and softly as he could. He touched her shoulder again.

"That name," said Lumilla, confused. "That name is familiar."

"It's you," said Billy. "You're Lumilla."

Her tear-streaked face looked up at him, the barest hint of hope glimmering out of her eyes. "How do you know?" she asked.

Billy hesitated. This wasn't Mrs. Russet, not the way he knew her. So he didn't think she would understand their relationship, not really. Instead of trying to explain it, therefore, he simply shrugged and smiled and said, "Because we're friends."

"We are?" she looked around as she said this, as though afraid that it might not be true. Billy couldn't blame her. Almost worse than being alone in this terrible place would be having a friend, and then having that friend taken away.

"Yes," he said soothingly. "We're friends. And I'm not going anywhere. I'm here to help."

"But how can you help?" she asked, and started weeping again, though more quietly than before. "How can you help when he's gone?"

"Who?" asked Billy.

As before, Lumilla didn't answer. But this time she stood up and pointed at the book, the empty book that was two-thirds sealed.

"Lumilla," he said, "I can't read it."

"Don't read," she whispered, and grabbed his hand suddenly. "*Feel.*" And with that, she forced his fingers to touch the pages of the book.

Billy had already touched the book, when he had tried to close it. This time, however, touching it at the same time as Lumilla did, he got a sense of what was there. Not a total picture, not the details, but a gist of what she saw in the pages of her fear. It was like he was seeing a movie trailer in his head, just the high points of the story, just the parts that mattered most.

Lumilla, young. Beautiful, not broken. Bold. Discovering the Power that she was.

She went from her family. She went on a journey. Finding evil and darkness in the world of the Powers. But also finding light.

She found someone. A man. "My name is Terry," the man said.

"Really?" said Lumilla with a charming giggle. "I've always thought that was a funny name."

The man smiled. He was strong and tall, with big arms and the kind of presence that made people feel trusted and safe. "Actually, that's just what my friends call me. And if you think my nickname is strange, you should hear what my *real* name is."

Lumilla laughed.

And then it was later. Lumilla and Terry were walking in a park. A magical place, with flowers that danced on their stems in the moonlight. There was a pond, and instead of ducks or geese, the water itself formed into living shapes that ebbed and flowed into and out of existence. The couple walked, and talked, and laughed, and planned for the future they would have, the future they would enjoy together.

Then things moved again, still onward in time. The man was being dressed in a brown cloak. The threads of history marched along the fabric. He sat on a brown throne on the Diamond Dais. Lumilla stood behind him, beaming with pride.

They held hands.

They walked in their magical park. They planned a family.

And then, fire and destruction.

The War of the Powers. Talks of a family ceased. Terry and Lumilla, still young, found themselves ripped from happiness and thrust into chaos.

A sudden jump in time. Terry and Lumilla were fighting side by side, calling up the Earthessence to crush the armies of Darksiders that threatened humanity. The battle was fierce, but the tide was turning slowly in favor of the Dawnwalkers, led by Terry and Lumilla, standing side by side in an unbreakable chain of Power and love.

Then, out of nowhere, a presence. Wolfen. His eyes harsh and angry, his face younger but already gnarled and marked by the clawlike grip of anger and hate. His salt-and-pepper hair only black now, but still long and thick.

He appeared beside Terry. Terry raised his hand, calling up columns from the earth, creating a rock prison around Wolfen. But the Black Power only laughed, and the rocks themselves withered and died before him.

Lumilla saw what was happening, the danger her husband was in. She screamed. She tried to get to him, but the crushing armies of the Dark were everywhere. Fire, Wind, Water, Earth, Life, and Death surged all around in a wall of disorder.

Terry fought. But Wolfen was too powerful. The Dark Master laughed. And touched Terry.

There was a flash of black light, if such a thing were possible.

Another jump in the story of Lumilla's and Mrs. Russet's fearful memory. The War of the Powers was over. Wolfen was vanquished.

Lumilla went to her husband. Terry was on a bed on Powers Island, recovering with countless other wounded and weary warriors of the Dawnwalkers.

Lumilla touched his hand.

"Do I know you?" Terry asked.

And then, before her eyes, he shriveled and shrunk. He became Rumpelstiltskin. He touched her hand. "It's dirty," he said. "You should clean that."

"Come away with me," said Lumilla. "Come back to the world, come back to our special park, walk with me, talk with me."

Rumpelstiltskin shook his head and looked around. "With all this mess?" he said, and laughed that crazy laugh that Billy had later heard when spirited away by the rock Fizzles that would come to clean Powers Island.

Lumilla wept. She was given the Brown Robe. She held the scepter of Power, and read the Book of the Earth. She grew, and aged.

And was alone.

Billy suddenly found himself back in the library again. Lumilla was crying. "He's gone," she was saying again, over and over, as she had before.

Billy was shocked, heartbroken. He had never suspected that Mrs. Russet could have such tragedy in her past. Not the strong, almost impervious-seeming teacher that ruled both her class and the Brown Throne with such an iron hand.

But then, he thought, maybe that's how she became so strong. Because she had to be. Maybe that's what makes anyone strong.

He looked at the crying woman. This was her memory. This was her Dread, the one moment in her life that had become her world, the sum of her existence.

"It's not true," he whispered to her.

"He's gone," she answered.

"It's not true," he said again. "You're more than this. You're more than this one moment. It never broke you. You're strong, and wise, and good." Without thinking, Billy hugged Lumilla, clutching her to him as his own mother must have held him when he was a baby. He rocked her, and thought of Rumpelstiltskin. "He still loves you, Terry is still in there somewhere," he said.

Lumilla shook her head, the weeping quieter and somehow more intense than it had been. "He's gone," she said again. She was locked in that thought, it was clear.

Billy remembered something. He held Lumilla's face in his hands, forcing her to look at him. "He's not gone," he said. "I saw him. I saw Terry."

"You saw Rumpelstiltskin," said Lumilla firmly.

"Mostly," agreed Billy. "But then, at the end of our meeting, he changed." Lumilla said nothing, but gazed at him with hope. This was what he could give her, Billy realized. He couldn't change her own memory, but perhaps he could make it less important by giving her a piece of his own memories. He let himself think of the funny old man who had eaten half-finished talking hot dogs. He remembered the laughter and the light in the man's eyes as he gleefully recited a borderline dirty limerick. He thought of the look in Terry's eyes when he talked of his wife, who had "cheated" by reading the Prophecies in the Book of the Earth.

Billy couldn't help but smile at the memories. He hadn't realized until now what a bright spirit Rumpelstiltskin was. Do we all have that brightness, he wondered, even when it isn't seen by others?

Do I have it?

Billy smiled still wider at that thought. "He remembers you," he said to Lumilla. "He's not the same. Wolfen's spell hurt him, hurt him badly. But he's not gone. There's still part of him that is there, that remembers and loves you."

"Just a shadow," whispered Lumilla. "Just a shadow of what was. The rest of him—the best of him—is gone."

"No," said Billy sternly. As he spoke, he continued to look in Lumilla's eyes. And he realized that they were changing somehow, their color dimming a bit. Her skin, too, was different. A bit more wrinkled.

She's becoming Mrs. Russet again, he realized.

And he continued talking, guiding her past the prison of her fears as best he could. "He's a shadow, maybe, but there are only shadows when the real thing is close at hand. You can't have a shadow with no substance nearby. He's there, somewhere. He's sick, but he's there."

"How do you know?" said Lumilla. She looked like she was in her forties now, showing the signs of the burdens that had been placed on her at a time when she was far, far too young.

"Because I saw him. I saw Terry," said Billy.

"Rumpelstiltskin," said Lumilla firmly, and Billy saw her start to grow younger again, as though she were spinning back to her time of greatest woe.

"No!" he almost shouted. The sound echoed through the dismal library. "I saw *Terry*. He sent me through the earth. He came up with the plan that eventually got me to Dark Isle," said Billy. Then, with urgency, he said, "Don't you see? *He helped me rescue you.*"

Lumilla stared at Billy. He could see her, willing to hope, wishing to believe.

Her face grew aged. Her face wrinkled.

She smiled.

"Hello, Mr. Jones," she said.

Billy smiled back. "Hello, Mrs. Russet."

He had never thought he would be so glad to see a teacher.

She stood, once more the Brown Councilor. She was, in fact, even wearing her Brown Cloak, and holding the crystal staff that she had used to defend them against the blue dragon, Serba.

Billy stood with her. He hadn't realized how much he had come to rely on his teacher. But having her back, after so long apart, he felt for the first time as though everything might actually work out in the end.

Then his eyes fell upon the book. The book of Mrs. Russet's memory, her Dread. As he watched, it changed. The un-sealed portion of the book separated itself from the rest. It grew bright, as though glowing from an inner light. The brightness increased in intensity until it shone like a small sun, blinding Billy.

Then the light dimmed, and when Billy could see again, he realized that the library had changed. Gone was the dungeon-like place with its skeletal candle-holders and horrid shelves. Gone were the books that looked like they were covered in skin. Gone were the sounds of banshees and ghosts in the night. It was still a library, but perfectly clean and bright. The books were no longer locked, but stood open on the shelves, each framed individually in a beautiful nook of crystal that glowed from within.

This was a place where anyone looking for light and knowledge could come, and be edified and illuminated.

He looked at the place where there had been a table made of ribs and stone, expecting it to have changed as well. But to his surprise, it hadn't. It was still a terrifying piece of furniture, and though the memory of Mrs. Russet's loss had separated itself and disappeared into the rest of the library of light, the sealed portion of that fearful book still hunched like a tumor on the table.

"What is that?" Billy asked Mrs. Russet.

Her face showed uncharacteristic fear as she looked at the book. "I don't know," she said. "Something that I once knew, but not any more."

"It's not your Dread?" he asked.

She shook her head slowly. "No. Not my Dread. But something terrible, I think, and something that I will one day have to face." Her face scrunched up, as though she were willing herself to remember something terribly difficult. "A baby," she said almost to herself. "A baby was stolen from its family. And…." She struggled to remember for a moment longer, then shook her head again. "I can't see any more." She looked at the table for a long moment, then took Billy's hand suddenly.

"Come," she said.

"Where?" asked Billy.

"Back," Mrs. Russet said simply. She waved her crystal staff, and before them the ground rippled and swayed like liquid. It rolled up in a huge wave, then solidified into a long, winding staircase of white marble that led up, up, up, to the very heights of Mrs. Russet's library.

"Come," she said, and pulled Billy with her. They climbed the marble stairs. It went forever, it seemed, one stair after another. They ascended to the highest shelves of Memory, and beyond, into the cloudy night sky that was the only ceiling above the library.

And still up they climbed. Now the misty clouds were thick around them, the white marble of the staircase dim and slick under their feet. Billy was relying totally on Mrs. Russet to guide him as the cloud closed in around them. It condensed on his face like perspiration, and he had to continually wipe at his eyes to be able to see.

Then one time he looked down, and realized that the library was gone. Mrs. Russet's Memories lay behind them.

"Where are we going?" he asked. But before Mrs. Russet—now only a dim form in the mist—could answer, he suddenly slipped on the stairs.

He pinwheeled his arms, struggling for balance, trying to maintain a hold of Mrs. Russet's hand. But he couldn't. The mist was everywhere, making everything slippery. He lost his grip and fell screaming through the mist, dropping into an eternity of free-falling dusk.

And when he hit the ground, it was with a crushing impact that made Billy feel like he had been squashed under the heel of a giant.

"Oof," he said.

He slowly opened his eyes...and saw Ivy. The Green Power smiled at him.

"You're back."

# CHAPTER THE TWENTY-FIFTH

*In Which Billy sees the Armies return, and Old Enemies come to call...*

Billy and Mrs. Russet were soon helped to their feet by Vester, Ivy, and Tempus, all of whom were overjoyed to see them returned. None of them could believe what had happened, and they were effusive in their words of praise and surprise at Billy's accomplishment.

"No one has ever done that," said Ivy. "Once again, you've shown yourself to be quite a surprise," said Vester. And Tempus, for his part, just kept murmuring, "I say, quite remarkable, I say, quite remarkable," over and over in an amusingly befuddled way.

Only Fulgora was silent. Hers was the first hand out to help Billy up, though, and as she did so he again saw that trace of a smile on her lips. He realized, too, for the first time that under her cloak she was still wearing her red armor, the same suit of mail and red steel that she had worn at the time of Napalm's challenge. Indeed, looking back, he realized that she had always had it on, every time he saw her. Even at their first meeting, when he first saw her on the Red Throne, he remembered now, she had been wearing her outfit of war. This drove home to him some of what Ivy, Vester, and Tempus had alluded to: this was not only a Red Power, she was a creature of war.

So Billy felt a flush of pride at the mere fact that Fulgora was helping him stand: he read in her assistance that she now accepted him. He had taken a test of bravery, and he could see that he had passed it. She gripped his hand firmly, then moved away to allow Billy's three friends to hug and, in Ivy's case, kiss him, each saying how happy they were at his return.

Mrs. Russet was there too, and each of the Powers—even Fulgora—welcomed her back as well. But for Mrs. Russet there were no kisses, no hugs. The other Powers were all friendly, courteous, and kind to her, but Billy realized for the first time that Mrs. Russet truly occupied a separate station from the rest. Maybe it was her position as a Councilor, maybe it was her great powers, or perhaps it was merely that she was clearly one of the smartest and most able people in the world. But now, having seen what could send Mrs. Russet into a tailspin of Dread, Billy noticed her isolation. So when Ivy, Tempus, and Vester were all done, he walked to her as well, intending to hug her and tell her how pleased he was to have her back, and how much she had been missed.

To his surprise, though, he found when he faced her that he just couldn't do it. Students and teachers just didn't hug and declare devotion and affection, even if it was there. It would be like a mule hugging a rabbit: sure, they could be friends, and perhaps even walk on the same road together, but actually hugging would just be too weird to contemplate.

Mrs. Russet seemed to understand this unwritten rule of the universe as well, so she didn't seem disappointed that Billy didn't do more than shake her hand and mumble a quick, "Glad you're okay." But she *did* hold onto his hand for a long while. She didn't hold it in a strange way, it just seemed like a natural extension of his handshake. It went on for a few moments, and at the end, Mrs. Russet smiled, a quick tilt of a smile, and mouthed "Thank you."

Billy blushed, and smiled back. They looked at one another for a long time, teacher and student, Sponsor and unDetermined, friend and friend.

Then Mrs. Russet turned to everyone and asked them to tell her what had happened since their captivity. Vester and Fulgora both immediately protested that surely this wasn't the time or place for story telling, and Billy couldn't help but notice how pleased Vester was when Fulgora agreed with him. But Mrs. Russet just said, "Bah. There is always time to know what has happened. The study of the past is the preparation for the future."

So Vester, Ivy, and Tempus all told what had happened to them. There wasn't much to tell, really: just long periods of confinement in their crystal prison cells, with only a few times that each had been let out for a short period of questioning at the hands of some lower-ranked Darksider.

Mrs. Russet also had little to tell: she had been questioned, it was true, but the questioning and the force of the Elemental torture at the hands of Black Powers had been so fierce that she couldn't remember much of it. Only fear and pain. "And that," she said, "is not a fit conversation to have with such young—though strong and able—people present." She did however mention that Mrs. Eva Black had played more than a small role in the horrible ordeal. She even could remember seeing Mrs. Black's son Cameron at a few of the sessions, and said almost casually that the boy had grown in power and stature among the Darksiders, and was already a trusted lieutenant in their army.

When Mrs. Russet turned to Fulgora, asking where she had passed her time in the weeks since she had turned into a dragon at her Challenge and then disappeared from the volcano, the Red Lady again declined to answer in detail. She said that much of her time had been spent finding Dark Isle, but more than that she refused to disclose. And clearly no one, not even Mrs. Russet, thought it very wise to press the Red warrior princess too far or too hard on the subject.

At last they came to Billy. Mrs. Russet shook her hand before he started, and thrones of stone came up from the earth. "I suspect that this will be a longer tale," she said as each person in the company took a seat. To Billy's surprise, the chairs were not hard and uncomfortable as he thought they would have been. Instead, they seemed to be covered in some kind of clean mud: it didn't come off on their clothing, but still seemed to mold itself to the contours of each person's body. Billy's chair was, in fact, the most comfortable thing he had ever sat on.

Slowly at first, then with more confidence, he told them some of what had happened. He omitted some things, but gave them the high points. For instance, he told them of his rescue by Rumpelstiltskin, but didn't mention Prince at all. He wanted to brag about the fire snake's bravery, but couldn't bring himself to talk about it, for that tale ended in the bright Fizzle's conversion to Mrs. Black's plaything through the power of the Death's Head Moth.

Other things, things he did mention, were greeted with surprise to the point of disbelief. The whole story with the sharks, and his rescue by Artemaeus the whale, and the encounter with the mermaid Blue in particular were hard for them to understand. None of them, not even Mrs. Russet, had ever heard of such things happening before. But unlike the others, Mrs. Russet didn't say she didn't believe in mermaids. She just narrowed her eyes as though thinking hard about something, and asked Billy to continue.

And he did, though when he told of the dark outcome his deal had had, he almost started crying. He still couldn't believe that his agreement with Blue had ended in both the Darksiders and the Dawnwalkers being almost completely destroyed.

"It's okay, Billy," said Ivy, the Green Power of Life always acting as the comforter, trying to build people up from despair. "You couldn't have known."

"She's right," said Vester. "All you have been guilty of was being braver and brighter than anyone I have ever met."

Tempus, still in a bit of shock over all that had happened, continued saying "I say, quite remarkable, I say, quite remarkable."

And Fulgora, still looking like she was ready to gallop off to war at any moment, merely nodded gravely at Billy and said, "Your choices were the choices of any good warrior whose friends are prisoners." High praise indeed.

But none of it seemed to matter that much to Billy. Too much of Dark Isle all around them was still covered in water for him to forget the devastating result of a bargain misunderstood. He felt himself—again—crying. He sniffled and tried to hide the tears from the others.

Ivy stood and walked to him, holding his hands down as he tried to bury his face and hide from his friends' gazes. "Don't look away, Billy," she said. "Don't try to hide the fact that you weep even over lost enemies. It's what makes you a true servant of Life, and greater praise I cannot think to give."

"She speaks truth, in her way," said someone else at that moment, and Billy immediately recognized the sing-song lilt in the voice and the sound of rushing waters. He looked over, and sure enough, there was Blue. The mermaid was sitting atop the crest of a huge water spout that had risen out of the ocean below and now stood as high as the cliff where Billy and his friends now were.

Billy had very mixed feelings upon seeing the strange mermaid. He looked around, and saw that this time his friends saw her as well, and from their shocked expressions, he knew that she was not appearing to them as a dolphin, but apparently had decided this time to show herself as she really was. His first reaction was a feeling of some happiness, coupled with a desire to say, "See? I told you!" to all his friends who had not believed that a mermaid could be real.

But that's not what he said. Instead, he turned his face away from the mermaid, and said, "Go away, Blue. I hate you."

He could sense rather than see her surprise. "Why hate Blue?" she asked.

"Because of what you did," said Billy, gesturing around him at the waste of Dark Isle.

"Ahh," said Blue. "Because of our understanding. So many feel this way of the deep, of Blue. They travel her, and use her for sport and gain, but when some find that there is a price to her presence, they bellow and wail. But such have always been the ways of Blue. She takes little that is not freely offered, though many do not realize the realities of their offerings. But she is deep, and terrible, and true. She is Blue."

The Powers atop the cliff were amazed at this strange coralline creature, and none of them could say anything. But Billy could. "Shut up," he said. "I don't want to hear you talk like that. You killed all those people." Now some of his friends—especially Ivy—did speak, murmuring quiet assent at his words.

"And would you not have done the same?" said Blue to all of them. "Were you not at the very steps of a war to end all wars, a war to end the other side? Were you not already engaged in destruction, with what I brought as its ultimate end? But," she continued before anyone could argue with her, "so that you may know that you know little of Blue...."

And with that, the mermaid raised her arms. The sea that now covered and surrounded what was left of Dark Isle started to bubble all around them. Billy felt a thrill of fear. What was Blue up to now? He barely knew her, but knew enough to worry about her strange and alien ways.

"Artemaeus, Artemaeus, Old One of the deep," sang Blue as the water bubbled and broiled with whatever was happening below. "Come to me, my friend, my companion of ages and eons."

She raised her arms even higher, like a conductor of the world's greatest and largest symphony orchestra, and now the source of the bubbling could be seen.

Whales. First hundreds, then thousands, and then what seemed like tens of thousands. The leviathans surfaced with a spouting of water and air, surrounding the island like smaller living islands as far as the eye could see.

At the front of the great expanse of whalekind was Artemaeus. The great blue whale looked at Billy with its enormous eyes. And as it had before, it dipped its head at Billy in a slow and ponderous bow, and Billy stood from his granite chair and bowed somberly back.

"What is this?" demanded Fulgora. As always, she was almost imperious, the warrior princess speaking as though she had an army at her back, ready to enforce anything she said. "Have you returned to wreak havoc on us with your forces, to kill the leftovers?"

Blue looked at the Red Lady with an almost savage expression. "Blue speaks not to you, young Fire, youthful Flame. Blue speaks to Billy, to the Deal-Maker, the Messenger, the Seeker to be and the Ender of Worlds."

Billy felt a thrill at her words. What was she talking about? Seeker to be?

Before he could think too long on it, though, Blue continued. "True it is and true it will be that you, young Billy, did not expect Blue to do as she did. But true it is and true it will be that we had a deal, and there was no provision about how each of us would fulfill its terms." The mermaid crossed her arms across the mane of green hair that still almost completely covered her upper body. "Still it is and still it may be that Blue will need you, and you will need Blue. And so I think that perhaps you should be given a token of trust."

She held up her hands again. As one, the thousands of whales all opened their mouths. And as soon as they did, Billy and the Powers near him were all on their feet in shock. For each whale held a single person in its mouth, resting on its tongue. Each person was unmoving, but Billy could see that they were breathing. They were merely asleep, or in some kind of magic trance.

"What's happening?" Billy asked Mrs. Russet. It was a bit ridiculous to expect her to have answers to everything, he knew. But he did expect it, and she didn't disappoint him.

"It's the Dawnwalkers," she said. "All of the ones who were imprisoned on Dark Isle."

Tempus was almost dancing with glee, and a puff of wind launched him ten feet in the air as he laughed. "Phoebus, and Nebia, and Trachton," he said, pointing out several of the sleeping Powers, people who were clearly his friends. "And Grayson and Lamika and Berzeb...and Ralph!" He clapped his hands in delight.

"And...Daddy!" screamed Ivy. Billy looked where she was pointing, and saw that it was true: Veric the Green, Councilor of the Throne of Life, was in one of the whales, asleep on a whale's tongue and a bed of green seaweed.

The other Powers were too astounded to speak. They all had their mouths open wide enough that Billy was a bit worried that the edges of their mouths might meet together in the back and the tops of their heads would fall off.

Vester was the first to say something after Tempus's and Ivy's outbursts. "All of them?" he asked, clearly not believing his eyes. "Alive?"

"True, true as Blue," sang the mermaid. "And unexpected as the treasures of the deep."

"But why?" managed Ivy.

"As I said, and as I am," responded Blue, "it is because Blue wishes to show her signs of solidarity and tokens of trust with Billy Jones. Besides," she added, with an element of glee like sun kissing the waves of a summer beach, "Artemaeus likes Billy, and as one of the Oldest of the Old Ones, he carries much sway."

"Then," said Vester in a strangely quiet voice, "we've won."

Fulgora glanced at Vester when he said this, and Billy saw in her eyes that she approved of his grasp of the underlying realities of the fantastic event now unfolding. "Spoken as a strategist," she remarked with an actual *smile*, and again Billy thought he saw tendrils of pleased smoke curling up from the fireman's clothing.

"What?" said Ivy. "What do you mean by that?"

Fulgora gestured around them, at the whales holding their sleeping passengers. But she allowed Vester to answer, nodding at him to explain himself. "Well," said Vester, the big fireman wearing an expression that was two parts pride and three parts love-struck devotion, "if all the Dawnwalkers are still alive, but there's no army of Darksiders, then…"

"Great Powers of Element and Wind!" cried Tempus. "He's right!" And the wind power again shot into the air, this time going even higher than before, and dancing what looked like a leprechaun's jig on the way down, his knobby knees knocking together as he bobbled in glee.

For a moment, all were silent, and then what Billy could only describe as pandemonium erupted on the cliff. The Powers were all shaking hands and thumping shoulders, hugs and kisses all around. Only Ivy seemed a bit reserved, and Billy could tell that, though she was pleased at the lives saved, she was also saddened by the loss of so many others. She was a creature of Life, and could feel no other way.

But before long, Blue spoke again. Billy looked, and saw that the mermaid's eyes were somber and deep as she spoke. This was not the chaos of the waves, or the uncertainty of the surf. She was speaking with the profundity of the deep, the farthest reaches of Water and the Blue. "But remember, air-breathers, Powers of land," she interjected. "Remember that Blue takes little which is not freely given. And though Artemaeus may like our young friend, and though Blue may seek him as an ally, still she must be true to who she is, to the evenhanded luck of the deep."

And with that, she once again raised her hands, and once again the sees boiled and bubbled with underwater presences. "Come to me, come to me," sang Blue. But this time her tone was less melodious, and harsher. The sharp points of her teeth could be seen clearly as she spoke this new refrain. "Come, Gelgash, and bring your bounty with you."

This time the creatures that surfaced were not whales. They were, instead, what Billy could only think of as the darker creatures of the sea: sharks and giant squids, slimy octopods and seven foot eels, and more than a few creatures that Billy couldn't even name.

And clinging to the backs of each creature was a water-logged, soggy-faced, and very angry looking person.

"The Darksiders," said Vester with an angry hiss that reminded Billy sadly of his friend Prince. And Fulgora suddenly held a rapier of fire in one hand, and a spear of flame in the other.

"Just so, young Flame, you speak true to Blue," said the mermaid in reply to the fireman. "The Deep is capricious, and can be violent. But she will not tip the scales so one-sidedly, not now at any rate."

The Darksiders glowered at the Powers on the cliff. Billy looked around them and couldn't see Wolfen anywhere—the powerful Dark Master must have escaped somehow. But he did see with a start and more than a little fear that Mrs. Black and Cameron were riding on a pair of twin killer whales—apparently some of the only whales that did not ally themselves with Artemaeus, though still clearly servants of Blue.

As they passed, Billy could see Cameron mouth something, and point at him. But surprise lit the other boy's face when nothing happened. He shook his finger like it was a broken remote control, and tried again, but again nothing happened.

Blue noticed the motion as well, and crooked a finger. Immediately, both Mrs. Black's and Cameron's killer whales dipped under the water, dunking the two people under for a moment. When they came back up, spluttering and even more angry seeming, Blue gazed at them warningly. "Your powers will not work at this time, not while you travel at Blue's pleasure, and live only by her leave."

The mermaid turned to Billy again, her eyes still strange, her manner unworldly. Billy realized how alien the sea was, and how fearful, though he had to admit that Blue herself was also beautiful and alluring in a strange and frightening way.

"Then we strike now!" cried Fulgora, and Billy saw the flames writhe around her. But again Blue crooked a finger, and this time a small wave erupted out of the water spout on which she rode. It struck Fulgora with a sizzle, and immediately her fire withered to a spark.

"Not here, not now," said Blue. "Blue has restored what she has taken, but will not allow you to take advantage of her mercies either."

Fulgora glared, but had been thoroughly drenched by the sudden rush of water. Her armor sizzled with contained fury, but it was clear to Billy that here, in the midst of her territory and at the seat of her power, Blue could not be challenged.

"What now?" Billy asked. Blue turned to him, and just as he had to Artemaeus the whale, Billy bowed. It wasn't a calculated thing, just a reaction that he somehow had built into his genes. Both the mermaid and Artemaeus were Old Ones of the deep, and he knew that they were used to—and merited—his respect.

Blue's eyes lightened a bit. "Truly acted, Billy Jones," she whispered. "And so you may first choose, and perhaps we will see if you act truly again."

"What do you mean?" asked Billy. He didn't like how everyone was looking at him all of a sudden, and once again longed for the good ol' days, when Salisbury steak and a closed locker door had been his two greatest fears.

"Blue will not permit the fight to be here," said the mermaid. "But she is wise, and deep, and knows the struggle will continue. So she will take one group one way, and one group another."

There was a long pause. "And?" Billy finally prompted, since he wasn't sure what the heck Blue was talking about at this point and was fairly certain no one else was either.

"And you may choose for the Walkers of the Dawn," said Blue. "You may choose where Blue shall put them and wake them from their slumber of the deep. And you may choose first, and send them where you wish."

"Hey, no fair!" screamed Cameron from his killer whale nearby. "How come he gets to choose first?"

Blue frowned, and just looked at Mrs. Black, who blanched and hissed something to Cameron that Billy didn't catch completely, but which sounded suspiciously like "Shut up, Cam, or you're grounded and won't get to be in charge of the zombies ever again." Cameron shut his mouth, but glared at Billy with murderous eyes, clearly hoping that he would soon get his chance to repay Billy for his bloody nose.

Blue looked back at Billy. "And so?" she asked. "What will Blue do? Where shall Artemaeus take your army?"

"They're not my army," was all Billy could say. He looked at Mrs. Russet, Vester, Ivy, and Tempus for their input.

"No!" shouted Blue. "This is not for them to help, it is for you to decide. Where shall Artemaeus take your army?" she repeated.

"Powers Island," Billy mumbled. He wasn't at all sure that was the right thing to say, but he thought he saw Mrs. Russet smile nearby.

"Very well, you have again acted truly," said Blue with approval. She raised a hand, and just as quickly as the whales had appeared they were gone, apparently already on their way to deliver the Dawnwalkers to Powers Island.

"But how will they get there?" asked Billy. "Doesn't everyone have to go through the Accounting Room to get onto Powers Island?" When Blue just looked at him blankly, he glanced at Mrs. Russet for support. "It's the rules, right? Everyone who goes to Powers Island has to appear in the Accounting Room first, so that there will always be an even number of Dawnwalkers and Darksiders."

Blue laughed, a smile glittering in her sea-colored eyes. "Powers may fly in a way that is constrained, but Blue has her own ways, and she has taught them to Artemaeus. The whales will leave your friends on the shores of the isle, and they will be there waiting for you should you choose to follow. And as for the balance...." The mermaid glanced at the amassed armies of the Darksiders. "I think that those who kept it have not kept it honorably; have not kept the terms of their agreements, so should not be trusted to do so now."

With that, the mermaid now turned her gaze directly to Mrs. Black. "And you?" she asked. Billy was somewhat heartened to hear that Blue's voice grew noticeably colder when she spoke to the Councilor of Death. "Where would you have me take you, servant of Dark?" the mermaid asked.

Mrs. Black thought for a moment. "The City of the Sky," she finally said.

For the first time, Billy saw Blue look a bit unsure. "That is beyond Blue's realm, and beyond her reach," said the mermaid. Her eyes grew cold and gray as an arctic sea as she spoke, and the sea air seemed to turn dismal and dark.

Mrs. Black's thin lips curled in derision. "So you are not omnipotent after all," she said. Blue cocked a finger angrily, and Mrs. Black hastened to add, "though you are very powerful, I concede that." Blue lowered her hand slowly, though Billy could still sea turbulent menace in the mermaid's eyes.

Mrs. Black was silent a moment, thinking. "We have nowhere better to go than here," she finally said. "Will Dark Isle be returned from the sea soon?" she asked.

Blue nodded. "Already the tides recede, and the island returns," she said.

"Then," answered Mrs. Black, "can our army just wait until that happens and then go back to Dark Isle?"

"As you wish," said Blue. She turned back to Billy and her friends. "The Siders of the Dark have claimed this place as their own again, and Blue has promised to take them where they ask. It would be best for you all to leave, thinks Blue, before that should happen, lest you be at their mercy."

Fulgora looked like she was about to protest, and Billy was more than a little worried that the Red Lady might just hurl herself bodily at the assembled Darksiders and take them all on at once. But Vester put a hand on her shoulder, and whispered, "My Lady." Fulgora clenched her fists, but nodded and turned her back on Mrs. Black and the water-drenched hosts of Darksiders.

"Come then," said the Red Lady. She looked around at the assemblage on the cliff. "We are to battle."

Billy looked at Mrs. Russet, waiting for his teacher and Sponsor to speak, wondering if she agreed. And apparently she did. For she sighed and nodded. She looked at Blue and bowed curtly, then clapped her hands together. The granite chairs that had sprung up for Billy and his friends to sit on trembled, and changed subtly. Billy realized that they were now the same kind of chair that Terry had used to take him on his trip through the earth.

"Oh, no," said Tempus, eyeing the chairs suspiciously. "You know I hate to travel by Earth, Lumilla."

"Sit down, Tempus," snapped the Brown Councilor. "All of you, sit."

The group did so, Billy settling into his chair and feeling more than a little proud that he wasn't particularly nervous.

*One trip and I'm already an old hand at this,* he thought with a smile.

Billy looked at Blue. The mermaid was watching him closely. "Fare thee well," said the sea creature. "And remember our bargain, Billy Jones. The sword is mine."

Billy nodded. He was no longer angry at Blue. She was weird and strange, but he could now see that she operated under some kind of rules and moral code, alien though they might be.

"Thank you, Blue," he said.

She nodded.

Mrs. Russet clapped again, and the seats began to rumble. "To Powers Island," she said.

"To the final battle!" Fulgora screamed. And to Billy's dismay, no one corrected her as the seats sank into the cliff.

# CHAPTER THE TWENTY-SIXTH

*In Which Billy Sees a Squooosh, and the End Begins...*

As before, the trip through the earth was beautiful. The crystalline caves and Volvo-sized diamonds spun past them as they traveled through the world. The only difference this time was that Billy was traveling with his friends. All of the Powers seemed to take the trip well, except Tempus. The old Gray Power clutched at the sides of his granite chair and insisted on saying things like "Too fast, too fast!" and "Watch out for the crystals!" and "We're all going to die!" at odd intervals. Apparently the Wind wasn't so comfortable when buried in the Earth.

But still, the trip went quickly, and before Billy realized it they were passing through the dark void that marked the separation between Powers Island and the rest of the world. It was different this time, he realized: the void was not quite so black and forbidding. In fact, rainbow spectrums of color could be glimpsed in the darkness, sparkling like deep jewels, as though something was being born within the emptiness.

And then they were through, and the chairs pushed them up, up, up, until suddenly normal light flowed into Billy's eyes and he saw that they were back in the Accounting Room once more.

Unfortunately, so were the zombies. Or perhaps they had never left at all, simply waiting there for their Darksider masters to return. But regardless of the reason, Billy once again faced dozens of the undead.

Apparently the small army had been given new instructions, to destroy everyone and anyone who might appear in the room without waiting for them to be Counted and receive their identity badges, because as one the fiends moved toward Billy and his friends. Their huge bulbous eyes glinted dully in the light of the Accounting Room, and Billy shrank back against Vester, who was standing nearest to him. Had they all traveled such a hard road and suffered so much, only to be rendered unconscious and taken right back to Dark Isle again?

But Billy had failed to reckon with an important fact: the zombies *had* taken his friends before. But that had been when neither Fulgora nor Mrs. Russet had been among them. And here, for the first time, he got a glimpse not just of how wise and knowing Mrs. Russet could be, but also how dangerous.

Fulgora gave a sharp battle cry and lanced out with the twin swords of fire that were once more in her hands, skewering the two closest zombies. The undead warriors puffed into ash immediately and then disintegrated under the force of her Element. Before this had even happened, though, Fulgora was already whirling on to the next soldiers, and two more were dispatched.

But that was nothing to what Mrs. Russet did. She watched Fulgora's deadly dance for a few moments, then sighed. "Children," she said in resignation. She leaned down and picked up a small pebble from the ground at their feet, and it slowly lengthened into the crystal staff that Billy now guessed Mrs. Russet used to focus and amplify her power. As soon as the staff had grown to its full size, she said, "Fulgora, withdraw."

The Red Lady did so immediately, whirling about after impaling and destroying two more zombies, then rushing back to rejoin the group of Powers with Billy at its center. The zombies followed as she did so, soon tightly surrounding the friends.

"Uh, Lumilla," said Ivy as the creatures drew near. "Now would be a good time."

"I know my dear," said Mrs. Russet.

"So could you get on with it?" asked Ivy nervously as fatal fingers slowly reached out to touch her and the others.

"Certainly," said Mrs. Russet. A cold smile was on her face now. "I just wanted to enjoy the moment a bit." And with that, she stamped the foot of her scepter down, tattooing a quick two-hit drum beat on the floor.

And nothing happened.

The zombies grew closer. Only inches away.

"Mrs. Russet? You going to do something?" squeaked Billy.

That cold smile Mrs. Russet was wearing grew a bit. "Still enjoying the moment," she said. And then, with a rumble and a shock of movement, the floor under the zombies suddenly disappeared. Or rather, it moved upward in a sudden eruption, and with a thud and a rather disturbing "squooosh" that Billy knew would be a featured attraction in his nightmares for years to come, the zombies were all squashed between the ceiling and the floor that had suddenly risen up to meet it like a huge metal press.

Or zombie press, thought Billy.

Thankfully, the part of the floor that had just moved stayed where it was, so he was spared the sight of squoooshed zombie flesh. Now the room was considerably smaller, only a loose pocket around where he and his friends stood, and a small trio of halls leading to the three mannequin-like Counters and then to the elevators beyond.

"Cut it a bit close, didn't you old girl?" asked Tempus, though Billy could tell the Gray Power wasn't at all upset, and had in fact probably rather enjoyed the zombies' mode of passing.

Mrs. Russet's eyes were still cold, but some warmth flowed back to her face. "I did," she said. "But anyone who has been tortured at the hands of the Darksiders gains an appreciation for life's black moments of comedy, don't you think?"

"Quite so, quite so," rumbled Tempus with a chuckle. Then he went to a Counter and collected his badge. The others followed suit, and soon only Billy was left. He was fairly nervous and excited: here he was, joined with the leaders of the Dawnwalkers, preparing for battle with the Darksiders. He had just witnessed if not actually helped with a mass squooshing by the Dawnwalkers' leaders. *He* was now a Dawnwalker. He could at last be Determined.

So his hand was almost shaking as he reached out to touch the button on the side of the mannequin's case. The badge fluttered into its slot. He picked it up....

And his expression fell. "Billy—unDetermined" was all the badge said.

He put the badge on, slowly, and Vester must have seen and understood Billy's disappointed expression. The fireman moved closer to him, then kicked the Counter case as though it was a soda machine that had given him orange when he wanted lemon-lime. "Do these things ever get it wrong?" he asked over his shoulder.

"Never," answered Mrs. Russet. She appeared perplexed as well.

"But surely after all he's done, he's earned the right to be called a Dawnwalker," said Ivy.

"I would agree," said Mrs. Russet. "But apparently there is something about Billy—something deep and hidden—that will not permit this to happen. Just one more mystery about our young Messenger."

Billy was still crestfallen, but he put his badge on and moved to join his friends in front of the elevators. Vester's arm on his shoulder helped him feel somewhat better, as did the realization that Mrs. Russet had called him "Billy." Not "Mr. Jones" or "you lazy excuse for a history student" or "hey you I told you no sleeping in class." Just "Billy." He didn't want to make a big deal of it, since he wasn't sure she had even realized she did it, but he felt warm inside.

She called me Billy, he thought. And smiled. "What now?" he asked as he joined his friends.

Mrs. Russet pressed one of the elevator call buttons, and a door opened almost immediately. "We go up," she said.

The group stepped into the elevator, and Billy was more than a little surprised that no jokes or offers of candy or anything else came out of the elevator as they did so. What was wrong with it?

Then the elevator did speak. "Floor?" it said morosely.

"Top," said Mrs. Russet.

"Yeah, whatever." With a start, Billy realized that this elevator had a New York accent. It was the same elevator that had taken Billy to Powers Stadium and then later to the top of the tower. But where before it had been friendly and joking, now it was bellicose and moody.

"What's wrong?" Billy asked, touching the elevator walls.

"They don't like me to talk," said the elevator dismally. "Just take you to your floor and be done with it."

"Well it's different now," said Billy.

"Actually, Billy," interjected Tempus with a whisper, "it might be better this way. Some of these elevators talk entirely too much and make entirely too little sense."

Billy ignored the old Gray Power, particularly since he knew that the same could be said of Tempus. "Come on," he said to the elevator. "How about a joke?"

"No way," was all the elevator said, and then it shut up and refused to talk any more.

Billy was sad, but couldn't blame the device. It must be terrible to shuttle Darksiders around all day long. If he had to take Mrs. Black and Cameron around all the time…he shuddered at the thought.

He turned to Mrs. Russet instead. "Why are we going to the top?" he asked her.

"Elementary strategic positioning," answered Fulgora without waiting. "Secure the high ground first, if at all possible the greatest defensible position, then reconnoiter and strategize based on the available resources and the dictates of the battlefield."

Billy looked blankly at her, and Vester simplified: "It's always better to start a fight when you're already on top," he said.

Billy still didn't really understand, but he was quiet until the elevator lurched to a halt and opened. "We're here," it said. "Now get out."

Billy and the others did, and as they exited he heard Ivy gasp.

That's right, thought Billy, she hasn't been up here since before the first attack ended. She hasn't seen what it looks like now.

And with that thought, he was reminded forcefully of the fact that last time he had come up here, Wolfen had been waiting for him, staring at the crystal shard that still pierced the center of the Diamond Dais. But when Billy looked around, he saw with relief that the Dark Master was nowhere to be seen.

I wonder where he is? thought Billy. Then realized he'd probably rather not know.

Mrs. Russet, meanwhile, stamped her crystal staff again, and the stone floor of the tower top started to ripple and sway. Soon, there was a castle battlement and walls that had surrounded the Diamond Dais, an impromptu pillbox of sorts, solid and at least somewhat sheltered from any attacks. Mrs. Russet motioned them inside, walking toward the Diamond Dais, and once again the stone steps appeared before her and she was able to walk up them to the podium. Fulgora followed, and the two women sat on the Brown and Red Thrones, seeming to find great comfort in their return to these seats of Power.

"What happens now?" asked Vester. He stood close to the edge of the Dais, head respectfully down.

"Ivy," said Mrs. Russet, "take a vine down to the beach. See if you can find your father. If you do, rouse him and bring him back here. If not, return and report on how many of our forces *are* here."

Ivy's face lit up at the mention of her father. She held out a hand, and one of the many thick vines that still lay all over the top of the tower writhed toward her. It sprouted a hand-like set of branches as it did, and they grasped her and pulled her quickly away, taking her over the top of the tower in an instant. It would have seemed odd to Billy before, but now after his time of exposure to the Powers, all he thought was, That's cool.

"What do we—?" began Vester, but Fulgora held up a silencing hand.

"Wait a moment," she said. "Starting a campaign is much easier when you begin with adequate information resources, so let us see if Veric returns with information that can be of use."

And sure enough, a few minutes later the vine that had disappeared with Ivy in its grasp returned, this time holding both Ivy and Veric. The Green Councilor was clearly ecstatic to be holding his daughter, though he seemed a bit sleepy and somewhat unsure of his surroundings.

The tree branch deposited Ivy next to Vester, Tempus, and Billy beside the Diamond Dais, then carried Veric the Green to his Throne of Life. The man sank into it with a sigh of happiness, and Billy could see the tendrils that coated the Throne whipping out to caress and touch the man with healing fingers.

"I'm sorry to interrupt your massage," Mrs. Russet said. "But we could use some information."

"What?" asked Veric, clearly still trying to shake off the magic sleep that Blue had put him and all the other Dawnwalkers under. "Ah, yes," he said, visibly pulling himself up in his seat. "Ivy told me some of what happened. Just the gist, mind you, but enough." He looked straight at Billy. "Thank you, young man. From what I've heard, we all owe you our lives."

"Thanks and commendations later," said Fulgora sharply. Ivy glared at her and patted Billy as though to say, "It's okay, *I* think you deserve a medal." But Billy wasn't upset at all. Truth to tell, he would only have been embarrassed to have the Green Councilor gushing about him.

"Well then, what is the first order of business, Red Warrior?" asked Veric with a hint of a smile.

Fulgora didn't even notice it. "Troop count. Billy chose extremely wisely in asking to have us all brought here. The time slowing on Powers Island means we will have some time to prepare before the Darksiders return and attack: they will have to gather, and marshal their forces, choose a plan and execute it, and the time they spend doing that will be multiplied ten-fold for us. But the attack is sure to come, and we must prepare immediately if we are to stage a proper resistance. So what are our resources?"

Veric thought for a moment. "I would say that there were ten or perhaps fifteen thousand Dawnwalkers asleep on the beach when I left with my daughter. Hard to guess the exact number, but I'd wager that's about right."

"Only ten or fifteen?" asked Billy, surprised. Then he clapped a hand over his mouth, remembering that Fulgora and the other Councilors hadn't liked it in the past when people spoke out of turn from off the Diamond Dais. But apparently that rule no longer applied to him—at least for the time being. Perhaps he had earned their respect and gratitude to the point where he would be permitted to speak. Or perhaps the rules were just different when war was imminent. But either way, no one on the Diamond Dais told him to be silent or keep it down in an imperious tone. Instead, Fulgora actually answered him with a tone of respect.

"It is a mark of the genius of Wolfen's plans," she said. "They attacked us on a day of their own choosing, and were able to capture all the Dawnwalkers on the island, and track and imprison a great many more who had Projected themselves there to watch my Challenge. Probably about ten or fifteen thousand, as Veric has said. A masterful move that both imprisoned a great portion of our people, and likely also sent all the rest into a panic. They're probably hiding throughout the world now, broken into useless groups and just trying to avoid being hunted down by the well-organized Darksider troops." She frowned then, looking at Veric as she said, "Your news is not good. The Darksiders, if they muster in force, will have three times our numbers."

"At least," agreed Veric.

"And don't forget the zombies," added Vester. Fulgora looked at him and nodded, clearly coming to appreciate the fireman's comments.

Finally, thought Billy. One thing he had come to know about Vester was that the man didn't talk all the time, but whenever he did, it was always something that was worth listening to.

"But I thought...." Ivy looked confused. "Didn't Lumilla just take care of that downstairs for us?" she asked.

"I took care of a few, but I suspect that there will be more...."

"Actually, I don't think so," said Billy. Mrs. Russet, Fulgora, and Veric all looked at him. He felt like an ant under a magnifying glance, and half expected to puff into smoke at any moment. "Uhhh," he stuttered, "I mean, that is, you know, when Blue washed away Dark Isle, it looked like the zombies were all on it...."

"And *they* didn't get saved by the sharks or the whales!" shouted Tempus happily. He shook Billy's hand quickly in sharp up and down pumps as though the old man had decided to run for Congress but only had two days to shake as many hands and kiss as many babies as he could before the election. "Way to go, my boy, way to go!"

Again, Billy's only response was a small dollop of pride that was completely overwhelmed by a huge helping of embarrassment.

"He's right," said Fulgora, and for a moment Billy was worried that now *she* was going to start in on him. But no, the warrior was still a warrior. "This is a tactical coup," she said. "They still outnumber us, but with the undead at their side we would have stood no chance."

"Still," said Veric, "if they outnumber us by three hundred percent, that is something to fear."

"True," responded Mrs. Russet. "But we have two things in our favor. First, as Fulgora already pointed out, the nature of Powers Island means that time is literally on our side. We will have time to marshal ourselves and prepare bulwarks and defenses against the inevitable attack."

"And second?" asked Veric. The Councilor of Life was clearly a smart man, but just as clearly his ways were not the ways of war.

Mrs. Russet looked around to see if anyone else knew what the second advantage would be. And once again, Vester was the one to guess. "Bottleneck," he said.

"Bottleneck?" asked Billy. As he said it, he got the feeling that Tempus was a bit miffed that Billy had beaten him to the question.

"Excellent," said Fulgora, now clearly understanding what Mrs. Russet and Vester had known. "They have fifty thousand to our ten or fifteen thousand, but even so, they can only come through three at a time."

"How come?" asked Billy, then he blushed as he immediately figured it out. Everyone had to come through the Accounting Room before they could appear elsewhere on the island. So even though the Darksiders could appear en masse if they wished, they would still be forced to go through the Accounting Room in small groups before emerging to fight.

"Exactly," said Fulgora, seeing Billy come to understand this concept. "We can prepare for them there, and perhaps hold their entire army off with only a small force of our own." She nodded, her eyes looking upward at nothing in particular, no doubt planning strategies and troop supply lines in her head. "This might be an easy victory after all."

"Somehow I doubt that," said Mrs. Russet dryly.

And Billy had to agree. He knew somehow that this wasn't going to be simple or easy in any way. And he also had the dread suspicion that, whatever happened, he was going to see Wolfen and the Black family again.

Fulgora touched her throne, and a fire-red slate appeared on her lap. She withdrew some kind of a pen from her armor and started writing, complex equations that appeared on the slate in figures of fire as she made calculations in preparation for the upcoming battle.

Mrs. Russet saw what she was doing, nodded, and said, "I assume that this means you will assent to being the battle commander?" she asked with only the barest hint of amused sarcasm.

"Obviously," said Fulgora without looking up. Then she did look up, glancing quickly at Vester. "You will assist me," she said in a no-nonsense tone that brooked no dissent.

Not that Vester was even going to think about dissent, Billy thought. Indeed, he noted that Vester appeared ready to explode—perhaps literally—with joy at the thought.

"All right then," said Mrs. Russet. She looked at the Green Councilor. "Veric, go find Dismus the Gray Councilor and bring him back here." Then she looked at the others in the company in turn. "Ivy, you go to the beach and start waking people up. Tempus, as soon as they're awake, I want a count of how many of each Power we have. Organize them into troops of fifty."

"Who should be in charge of each troop?" asked Tempus, and Billy was surprised to hear how un-flighty and focused the man suddenly sounded. The Gray Power had unsuspected depths to him, apparently.

"I leave that to your discretion, old friend," said Mrs. Russet. "Organize them in a hierarchy you deem appropriate, then return with a roster of troops and the leaders in charge."

Both Ivy and Tempus nodded, and soon were gone, Ivy being carried over the edge of the tower by one of the vines, and Tempus whipping off in a puff of air that propelled him like a knobby-kneed superhero into the sky. Veric followed suit, and a moment later Fulgora told Vester to come with her, and the two walked away, heads together, having what sounded like a friendly argument over some calculation Fulgora had made.

In moments, only Billy was left. He looked at Mrs. Russet, wondering what—if anything—she would want him to do. She was sitting on the other side of the Diamond Dais, so the shaft of crystal that bisected the podium stood between them. Billy could see her through the tall, thin shard of diamond, but the prismatic refractions of the crystal made it seem like there were hundreds of Mrs. Russets looking intently at him.

"Billy," she finally said, "I would like you to do something for me."

"What?" he squeaked. He really couldn't think of anything he *could* do. He had no powers that he was aware of—other than an apparent power to get into lots of trouble—and certainly did not have any kind of special knowledge that would help in preparing for the coming onslaught. So what could he do?

"I want you to tell me everything," replied Mrs. Russet. Billy's look apparently told her loud and clear that he had no idea what she was talking about, because she added, "I know that you were giving us the short version of what's happened to you while we were on Dark Isle," she said. "I would like the long version now." She motioned, and stairs flowed up in front of Billy. He walked up them, grateful that he was no longer being required to climb awkwardly up to the top of the high podium without assistance. She motioned again, and the stairs followed him as he approached Mrs. Russet, forming into a smaller version of the stone Brown Throne upon which she sat.

Mrs. Russet motioned for him to sit. Billy did. "Why do you want to hear more?" he asked. "Why didn't you want to hear it before?"

Mrs. Russet seemed to think hard before answering. "Because what you said," she finally replied, "was enough at the time. But since then I have been thinking, and what I have thought is that you seem to be at the center of everything. And I think that you will be the key to the coming battle."

"What?" Billy asked, incredulous. "I know I've been at the center of stuff, but that's just been luck—bad luck—and I don't see how I can contribute to what's going to—"

Mrs. Russet waved off his protestations. "Billy, I'm not talking about whether you are a Power, or the Messenger, or anything like that. I'm talking about the fact that you are an extraordinary boy—no, an extraordinary young man. Without apparent benefit of any power over Element, you have managed to become a central piece in the game we now play."

"Game?" Billy said almost angrily. He didn't meant to say it, but the fact that Mrs. Russet called all of what had happened up to now a game almost cut him. Such suffering and pain as had been felt by so many was no game. None at all.

"Forgive me, Billy, I meant no offense," said Mrs. Russet. "I just meant that great events have been afoot, and you have been one of the greatest parts of them. No, don't be modest," she said as Billy started again to protest. "You have saved all of us by virtue of your courage and wit, and I think that whether you are a Power or not, whether you are indeed the Messenger that was prophesied or not, you are definitely an asset to our cause. And so," she finished, "I would like to learn from you."

"Learn…from *me*?" Billy asked, not really believing such a thing could be possible.

Mrs. Russet nodded seriously, as though speaking to a colleague instead of a very unsure fourteen year old. "Yes, Billy, learn from you. You have done much, and I want to know all about it."

"But I still don't understand," he said.

Mrs. Russet sighed. "In truth, sometimes I don't either," she said with a half-laugh. "But still we go on, finding our way around like we're in a dark room looking for light to guide us. And sometimes we find that light in the most unusual places." She leaned in close to Billy, holding her crystal staff for support. "So tell me what you have done, Billy Jones, and perhaps we shall be enlightened together."

And Billy did. He told her everything, from start to finish, this time leaving nothing out of his account. They were interrupted periodically by Fulgora and Vester wanting to ask Mrs. Russet's opinion about some battle strategy, and by the reports of Tempus and the return of Veric with Dismus, the Gray Councilor. But through all this, she treated them as mere distractions, listening intently to Billy's story as though nothing else mattered.

When he was done at last, after what seemed like two years of talking, she leaned back on her throne. They were alone once more, the others all gone on various errands, preparing Powers Island for battle. No one knew how long they had before the Darksiders started to appear in the Accounting Room, so some of the strongest Powers among the Dawnwalkers—Napalm and the British bobby Bellestus whom Billy had seen in the Accounting Room when he first came to Powers Island—had been sent there as quickly as possible, both to warn the rest of the Dawnwalkers when the attack began, and to try to hold off the Darksiders where they could be most easily contained. Billy understood that it would be critical for the Darksiders to be held to that room; if they broke free, all would likely be lost, because they would be able to simply overwhelm the Dawnwalkers by sheer force of numbers.

"Well," said Mrs. Russet when Billy's tale was done, "you have told me much, Billy."

"Like what?" he asked. He didn't feel like he had said too terribly much of value, but was glad to hear she at least didn't feel like he had wasted her time.

Mrs. Russet smiled. "Much," was all she would say. Then she stood, putting her hands to the small of her back and stretching. "Ahh, these old bones shouldn't sit so long," she said at last.

That triggered something in Billy. "Mrs. Russet?" he said.

"Yes, Billy?"

"When I was...in you. That is, in your memory, you seemed younger."

"Yes," she said with a twinkle in her eyes. "I *was* younger once. Go back far enough, I was even a baby at one point, if you can believe it."

"But, you seemed much, *much* younger during the last War of the Powers. And Vester said that was only about twenty years ago. So...."

"So what happened?" asked Mrs. Russet. Billy nodded. She grew quiet for a moment, then said, "As you probably guessed, Terry was the Brown Councilor before me. And then after...." she paused, and Billy almost thought that he could see a tear in one eye.

Impossible, he thought. Teachers don't even have tear ducts, do they?

Mrs. Russet cleared her throat, getting herself under control. "After what happened to him, I was made the Brown Councilor. And I have spent much time here, so like Tempus and some others, I have aged beyond what most would think of as my years in the 'normal' world."

Billy nodded. He had suspected as much. But still, that led to another, totally disturbing thought. "So," he said haltingly, "so you'll die."

"Oh, goodness gracious, Mr. Jones. We *all* die, don't you know?"

"But you'll die sooner," said Billy. He didn't like that thought. Not at all. People like Mrs. Russet shouldn't die. They should just stay old forever and teach students until the sun burned out.

"No, I won't die 'sooner,'" she disagreed. "I'll die exactly when I should. As will you, as do we all, sooner or later." She could clearly see, though, that Billy still didn't like this idea. So she leaned even closer toward him, taking one of his young hands in her old weathered one. "Don't you see, Billy? It's not about how long we live in the eyes of strangers, or how great we look to them. It's the *way* we live, and how we look in the eyes of those we love." Her eyes grew misty again. "And believe me," she said quietly, "I know."

Then she straightened, helping Billy to his feet. She also stood up and, seeming almost embarrassed, said, "Now let's go. We've got a battle to prepare for."

# CHAPTER THE TWENTY-SEVENTH

*In Which Billy helps Prepare, and Darkness Comes...*

Within only a few hours, Ivy and Veric had managed to rouse most of the Dawnwalkers, and Tempus had them organized into groups according to the Element each Power commanded, their experience with the Darksiders, and a host of other criteria. Billy was amazed to hear the old man report his doings to Fulgora, shocked at the level of detail that Tempus was able to provide apparently by memory only.

Fulgora, for her part, immediately began issuing orders to the captains that had been called to preside over the groups of the Powers. The final count was a little over twelve thousand: less than a quarter the number of Darksiders that they expected. Fulgora was clearly disgusted to find out that over four thousand of the Dawnwalkers were Green Powers. At first Billy didn't understand why this would upset her, but after asking Vester a few questions under his breath he quickly got the idea that the Green Powers were essentially useless in a fight. They were better as medics, helping the wounded to recover quickly.

"And in a fair, evenly-matched fight, that's great," said Vester. "You can keep a battle going longer if your wounded are able to return quickly to the front lines. But this...." He shook his head. "This doesn't sound like it's going to be a fair fight. So after you take out the Greens, all we have less than ten thousand people against an army five times that size."

"Who are the rest of the people?" asked Billy. "I mean, are there some of every Element on both sides?"

Vester frowned. "Well," he said, "we have a pretty fair mix of Grays, Browns, and some Reds. Most Blues tend to ally themselves with the Darksiders—the chaos in their natures gives itself easily to ideas of submitting others to their will. And the Death Powers are almost all in the Darksider camp."

"There aren't *any* Black Powers with the Dawnwalkers?" Billy asked. He had expected that there wouldn't be many, mostly based off his experiences with Mrs. Black and Cameron. But he had thought that surely *some* of each Element would be on each side.

Vester just shook his head. "No, the Black Powers are all Darksiders, save perhaps one or two. A Black Power in the Dawnwalker army is just about as rare as a Green Power with the Darksiders."

Billy thought fleetingly of Blythe Forrest. He wondered what she was doing now. Was she preparing for battle with the other Darksiders? He didn't remember seeing her among the sharks and the other sea creatures who had carried the Darksiders around Dark Isle, but there had been so many of them that he couldn't have seen more than a small fraction. She could easily have been there. She could easily have spotted him.

Does she hate me? he wondered. And his heart seemed to shrink a little inside him at the thought.

To keep himself from thinking about such things, he asked Vester, "But aren't the Black Powers the fighters?"

Vester nodded. "Yes. They're the ones who train from infancy to cause mayhem. There are some other Powers who also train that way—like Fulgora's people, for instance. But mostly the Black Powers are the destructive forces in our world. They're also the only ones that carry their Element in their own natures." When Billy looked askance at him, Vester continued, "The other Powers need their Element to work with: a Brown needs some Earth nearby, a Red needs a fire or some other access to Flame. The Blacks don't need that kind of assistance. That's why they can just conjure up their spells—the Dread for instance—from within themselves. It also makes them very hard to catch and contain. If you cut me off from Flame, like they did in the crystal prison on Dark Isle, then I'm fairly useless. But put a Black in chains, and he or she can conjure up their Element from within, and still escape."

"Then," asked Billy, "how can we hope to win? Or even just survive?"

"We're putting a lot of hope on the fact that the Darksiders have to come through the Accounting Room," answered the fireman.

"Where do you want the giants working on the battlements?" someone asked the fireman suddenly. In the short time since Tempus had organized the Dawnwalkers, many of them had already begun working on the things the island would need in order to prepare for the coming battle. Fulgora was the prime battle leader, the general of the impromptu forces, marshalling them quickly and efficiently. But all of Billy's friends seemed to have found themselves quickly in charge of various tasks. Mrs. Russet was constantly discussing the battle and the island's defenses with Fulgora, as well as having hurried conferences with other Dawnwalkers whom she would send on some errand or other. Veric and Ivy were busy preparing what Billy understood was the equivalent of a Powers field hospital. Tempus was flitting about, vacillating between his usual absent-mindedness and that unusual level of concentration that Billy had seen him bring to bear recently, the Gray Power flying in and out—literally—with critical messages from all over the island as the preparations got underway.

Vester, for his part, appeared now to be a permanent fixture at Fulgora's side, and Billy was happy to see that the Red Lady was constantly asking the fireman for his opinion on various matters, and even deferring to his judgment completely when she was already involved in one thing and someone else came with another matter that needed attention.

So when Vester said, "Have the rock giants fortify the east side of the island, near the Caves of Wind," it wasn't the first time Billy had heard the fireman issue such an order. Still, Billy was surprised to hear the assurance in his friend's voice. He sounded like a natural-born general.

Vester noticed Billy's look. He shrugged, embarrassed. "Fulgora says I have 'strategic talent.'" He shrugged again. "I don't know what that means, but she put me in charge of finalizing the island's defenses about half an hour ago."

"But if the Darksiders have to come through the Accounting Room just three at a time," said Billy, "then there's no way the fight will spill over to the rest of the island, right?"

Vester didn't answer for a long moment. Then, when he did, it was with the air of someone who had thought hard about how to express something difficult. "The great thing about magic is that there is always something new to surprise you. But the problem with magic is that there is always something new to surprise you." He paused as though to drive his point home, then said, "We'll plan the best we can, but we can't only plan for what we hope will happen. We also have to plan for our worst fears."

Vester looked grim. He glanced around, making sure that Fulgora didn't need him right at the moment, then put his hands on Billy's shoulders. "Billy," he said, "I'm going to level with you: we're in a bad situation here. We're doing everything we can, but still...." He looked at Billy seriously. "This isn't really your fight."

"What do you mean?" asked Billy, guessing what Vester was about to say, and almost surprised at the sinking feeling that accompanied his suspicion.

"Meaning that if you want to go home, no one will blame you," answered Vester, confirming Billy's guess.

"No way!" Billy shouted. He said it loudly enough that several of the nearby Powers looked up from their various tasks for a moment before turning back to what they were doing.

"Hear me out, Billy," said Vester. "I know you probably feel like you want to be here. But this isn't some game. This is going to be a brutal, ugly fight. And there's no assurance that any of us is going to come out of it in the end. My dad didn't. So if you want to leave, then I've already spoken to Lumilla about it, and she said she'd arrange for Transport for you any time you wanted it."

Billy thought how to respond to his friend for a long time. Then, deciding that the short answer would be best, he simply said, "You're nuts."

Vester grinned. "Fulgora said you would say that."

"Really?" asked Billy, more than a little surprised. He knew he had gained some measure of respect in the Red Lady's eyes, but it was still a bit of a shock to hear that she had apparently been talking about him with Vester. "She did?"

"Well, no, actually what she really said was, 'Billy Jones is a warrior spirit, and my fires will turn to ice before he allows us to take him away before the confrontation,'" answered Vester.

"Well, she's right," Billy said.

Vester smiled. But the smile was a bit subdued. "Okay, Billy. But remember what I've said. This isn't going to be a fun thing. And if you ever change your mind, just say the word." He clapped a big, callused hand on Billy's shoulder.

Billy hesitated. He bit his lip for a second, as though chewing on it would magically help him know the best way to say what he wanted to.

"What is it?" asked Vester.

"Well," said Billy, "I'm not going anywhere until this is over. I mean, I'll stick around and help in any way I can. But if things *are* so bad...why doesn't everyone just leave? Why don't the Dawnwalkers all just leave and hide?" He smiled what was meant to be a reassuringly unserious smile, which he knew probably looked more like the smile of a dog which has just found out that the bone it's been chewing on and enjoying actually used to be a favorite cousin's leg. "You know," he continued. "He who fights and runs away...."

Vester thought long and hard about how to answer Billy. "Usually that would be good advice."

"But?" prompted Billy.

"But we have nowhere else to go," admitted the fireman. "There's a whole world out there, but this is the only place we're organized at all. For better or for worse, the Dawnwalkers have spent the last twenty years assuming that the Truce was in force, the Treaty of the Powers unbroken. So we have no system, no reserve forces, no preparations for protection at all."

"That's what I'm saying," said Billy. "Why can't we all go somewhere else and hide and *get* some preparations?"

"Because the Darksiders are *already* organized," said Vester. "So if we leave here, it's going to be an army of fifty thousand, against nothing but hundreds of small pockets of resistance. It won't be a battle, it'll be a thousand tiny slaughters, and there's only one way that can end."

Billy's expression fell. Vester tried to smile in a reassuring way, and Billy suddenly knew exactly what *his* "reassuring" smile had looked like just a minute ago.

Forget the dog's cousin's bone, thought Billy. Vester looks like a dog who just found out his dinner kibbles were actually made of his immediate family.

"But that's not going to happen. No slaughters here," Vester said a little too brightly. Then he grew almost pensive, and in a voice that made Billy feel like he was almost speaking against his will, he added, "Besides, we might have a surprise or two up our sleeves."

"What do you mean?" asked Billy.

"Something Fulgora's been cooking up," answered Vester. "It's part of what she was doing while all of us were stuck on Dark Isle."

"What is it?" asked Billy, intrigued.

Vester shook his head. "Sorry, I shouldn't have said anything. Fulgora made me swear secrecy."

"Come on, Vester."

"Nope," the fireman shook his head. He clearly wanted to tell Billy, but just as clearly was somewhat proud that he had been taken into the Red Lady's confidence enough to be trusted with private information.

"Come on," said Vester, changing the subject. "What say you and I go and watch rock giants building some walls?"

And so they did. Billy traveled over much of Powers Island in the coming days, usually at Vester's or Mrs. Russet's side as one or the other of them traveled somewhere to check on preparations.

Rock giants were indeed building huge battlements on one side of the island, great walls that looked like they grew out of the living rocks of the mountain range close to them. Billy thought the enormous rock Fizzles were amazing to watch, the huge craggy forms plucking up rocks the size of houses as though they were light as cotton candy, then plunking them down on the ground in enormous piles. Vester told him, however, that these would be a last line of defense in the event that the Darksiders somehow broke through the Accounting Room defenses and overran the island. The Dawnwalkers would fall back slowly, trying to resist over every foot of land on the island, and then would finally take refuge in the mountainous battlements, and lose themselves long enough to flee, to Transport to somewhere else...where they would then be most likely hunted for the rest of their very short lives.

After Vester shared this with Billy, the huge walls didn't seem quite so neat anymore.

But day and night, hour by hour, Billy never saw any let up. The Red Powers on the island placed burning pyres every couple hundred feet, which Billy understood from watching Fulgora's Challenge in Powers Stadium would be the equivalent of ammo dumps: they would allow the Red Powers on the island easy access to the flames they would need to cast their attack spells. Brown Powers were everywhere, carving roads out of the bedrock of the island with their bare hands, preparing for supply routes and roads that might be needed in the event of a slow fallback. The Grays patrolled the skies, flying about like man-sized insects, and cultivated rain clouds that could be brought to bear against attackers, slowing them down and giving time for counter-attacks to be launched. And the Green Powers cultivated enormous gardens that grew from seed to vine to flower to fruit in seconds, laying up vast quantities of foodstuffs that would be needed in the event of long term fighting or if there should be any kind of a siege.

Billy was fascinated by all of it. The rock giants building their walls, fire Fizzles of various sizes patrolling the island like walking bombs, gusts of wind being used to move huge bales of supplies from place to place. But as interesting as it was, there was also a disquieting sense of desperation to it, and Billy slowly began to understand something:

It wasn't just Vester. *None* of the Dawnwalkers expected to win.

Even with the bottleneck giving them a clear tactical advantage, even with the extra time they gained because of the way the minutes passed on Powers Island, even with the knowledge that they were fighting for a good cause, Billy could sense an undercurrent of hopelessness. Everyone was going through the motions, but Billy sensed they were doing it mostly because people don't willingly walk to their deaths, even when those deaths are all but certain.

So this is what they felt like at the Alamo, thought Billy on more than one occasion.

But he didn't mention it aloud, though the feeling weighed heavily on him. Vester seemed to know Billy's thoughts, and occasionally would say something clearly meant to cheer Billy up. "Don't worry, we'll be fine," the fireman was continually saying. But Billy knew that whenever a grown-up said that, it meant that they were really worried about the opposite being true.

Only Fulgora seemed to both grasp and fully accept the likelihood of their fates. Once, Billy overheard a short Red Power break down in front of her, crying about the fact that it was hopeless and they were all doomed. Fulgora slapped the man sharply. "We're doomed from the day we're born. We begin dying the moment we start our lives," she said bitingly. "Whether it be here, or in our beds in a hundred years, the place and the time matter nothing. All that *does* matter is how we face Doom when he comes for us, whether we choose to look him in the eye and spit at him, or crawl in the sand like worms. He will take us either way, but one way we at least have our dignity."

"But, I don't want to die," said the babbling Power.

"Nor do I," said Fulgora. "But we can't always have everything we want, can we?"

Strangely, though her words were the most pessimistic of any of Billy's friends, he was more comforted by her honesty than by the too-chipper tone Ivy always got in her voice when he came near, or by Tempus's insistence on listing his favorite restaurants and then telling Billy he was going to take him to one of them on each of Billy's birthdays for the rest of his life.

Fulgora knows it's hopeless, Billy thought. And she doesn't care. Because it's not the winning that matters, it's the fight.

This thought was oddly calming. He didn't have any powers to his name. He didn't know what Message he was supposed to provide, if any. He couldn't do much of anything to help his friends get ready for battle.

But he would fight, just the same. And when it happened, the fight would be all that mattered. The result would be almost an afterthought.

So Billy toured the island with his friends, occasionally helping in a non-Power-like way, digging with his bare hands or laboriously carrying buckets of Green-grown fruits from place to place. It made him feel good to contribute, even in this small manner, and his friends seemed to appreciate it, too. Occasionally in the days that passed he thought of his parents. He wished he could see them again. If he did, he would thank them once more for his birthday watch, and then thank them once more for every other gift they had ever given him. He would let them know that he loved them. Especially his father, whom he was coming to appreciate more and more in the days on the island. Not all fights are physical battles, he realized. Some people fight to put food on their families' tables, and to make a better tomorrow. So his father was a warrior just as much as any of the people around Billy now, and just as much deserving of his respect. Because even though his father was not his friend, he had always provided for and protected his family to the best of his ability.

So I will tell him, Billy said to himself. When I get back, I'll tell him I understand, and thank him for being who he is, and teaching me to be the good man I will one day become.

But the words sounded hollow in his mind, just as Tempus's birthday plans for the next hundred years had sounded.

The fight, Billy thought again. Win or lose is not important. Not right now, anyway. What's important is picking our battles, picking the right battle, and standing for it to the end.

And so Billy passed his days, knowing himself to be a lone un-Determined boy on an island of Powers, until one day several weeks after they had come back to the island. He was sitting on the ground near the Diamond Dais, listening to Mrs. Russet and Fulgora argue over the fine points of warfare. Mrs. Russet kept pulling the Book of the Earth out of the ground and reading obscure historical passages about So-and-So's army, or the Battle of This-or-That. Fulgora, for her part, kept screaming about how Mrs. Russet's methods were historically accurate but no longer the cutting edge of warfare. And Vester and Ivy kept trying to get between the two strong-willed Councilors and keep the peace, and repeatedly being threatened with combustion or having the ground swallow them for their troubles.

He heard all of it, but Billy had to admit to himself wasn't really giving the argument much attention. Rather, he was staring at the crystal shard in the middle of the Diamond Dais. It was twilight, and the last pale rays of sunlight on the island lightly kissed the shard, shattering into thousands of tiny rainbows before disappearing as the sun dipped below the ocean and night claimed the island. Billy watched the lights disappear from the shard, watched it grow dark as the rest of the sky, and felt himself almost dozing, as though hypnotized by the light display he had seen, and lulled into sleep by the approaching darkness.

Then Billy heard a noise. It was muffled but powerful, like a nuclear explosion a thousand miles underwater. The noise repeated itself, and this time the entire tower pulsed. It didn't quake on its moorings, nothing like the day that the zombies had attacked, but Billy jerked into complete wakefulness as he felt the tremor roll through the tall edifice.

"What was that?" asked Ivy.

Everyone on the tower top grew silent and still as a statue. They all listened, waiting for the noise to repeat, but it didn't.

Still, another noise *was* heard: the noise of one of the elevators sliding up through the floor of the tower top and whispering open. The elevators had improved in temperament over the past weeks as they realized that the Darksiders were no longer in charge of the island. But then they had apparently heard some Dawnwalkers talking about everyone's impending doom and had immediately gotten quiet again. Billy had tried to jolly a few of them out of their gloom, but finally had stopped when one of them said point blank to Billy, "Look, you seem nice enough and all, but if you're all going to get wiped out in the next few days, it's probably best that we not get too personal with you guys, all right?"

"Uh, sure," said Billy.

"Good," said the elevator. "That's why we're not even calling anyone by their names any more, to avoid attachment."

"What?" asked Billy, still dumbfounded that even the elevators thought the Darksiders' triumph was a foregone conclusion.

"Like you, for instance," replied the elevator. "We all know your name is Billy Jones, but what we call you amongst ourselves is Boy Number 3583Q."

"3583Q?" Billy repeated.

"Yeah," said the elevator in the closest thing to a cheery tone that Billy had heard from them since the Darksiders had first assumed control of the island. "You know, like rats."

"Rats?" Billy said, his head spinning.

"Like with scientists," clarified the elevator. "I mean, no one wants to take 'Fluffy' out and inject him with something that might make him lose all his fur or something. But you can give White Rat Number 3583Q a shot of whatever and not feel bad about it at all."

Thankfully, the doors of the elevator had opened at that point and Billy had been able to get out without going any farther along on that particular line of discussion. But the conversation had stuck with him, and he had avoided the elevators since then.

Now, however, the elevator that was opening at the top of the tower had his complete attention. Three Powers—Napalm, Bellestus, and another Red Power—staggered out of the elevator. These three, Billy knew, had been in the Accounting Room, serving on guard duty. Now, something was clearly very wrong with them. Fulgora was on her feet in an instant, rushing to them in a flash of red armor. All three of the arriving Powers looked like they might fall over at any second.

"What happened?" she demanded.

"They...they came," wheezed Bellestus in a frightened English accent, his bobby's uniform smudged and dirty. His eyes bugged out of his head with fear, exhaustion clear on his face.

"What do you mean they came?" demanded Fulgora. She shook Bellestus, but the Gray Power's eyes closed and he either fell asleep in exhaustion from overuse of his powers, or fell unconscious because of something more malignant.

The low, intrusive thud happened again. Fulgora whipped around to Napalm, who was holding up the remaining Red Power, an old woman who Billy knew was named Ursula. "What happened, Napalm?" she demanded. "Is the attack under way? Are they storming the Accounting Room?" Without waiting for answer, she whirled to Vester and snapped, "Call up the special forces squad we prepared for the bottleneck defense."

Vester whirled immediately to comply, but Napalm weakly said, "Wait."

Vester stopped. Fulgora wasn't happy. "We can't wait. We have to act. If the Darksiders have come, we have to get everyone we can into the Accounting Room to stop them."

"That's just it," said Napalm. He weaved on his feet as though he too was about to pass out. But at the last second he managed to steady himself. "They came into the Accounting Room, and we were waiting."

"How many of them arrived in the room?" demanded Fulgora. "And why did you abandon your posts?"

"Only three came through," said Napalm. "And we didn't abandon our posts."

"What do you mean? What are you saying?" screamed Fulgora, almost enraged at the fact that she wasn't getting answers as fast as she wanted them.

"Take it easy, Fulgora," murmured Mrs. Russet. "We need speed, not panic."

"I don't panic," said Fulgora. But she closed her mouth and let Mrs. Russet continue the talk with the other Red.

"There were only three Darksiders?" asked Mrs. Russet.

Napalm nodded. As he did so, Ursula, the other Red Power that Billy thought looked like a barracuda with tennis shoes on—spoke. "Only three. But that was enough." She shuddered. "It was Wolfen. Wolfen, and Eva Black, and her son."

"And they fought you?" prompted Mrs. Russet.

"No," said the tall Red woman. "No, there was no fight." She laughed to herself, and Billy could see terror in Ursula's eyes. "They just appeared, and before we could say a word they had us at their feet, cowering."

"The Dread," said Mrs. Russet quietly.

"More than that," replied Napalm. "More than just Dread. This was something worse."

"But you got away," said Mrs. Russet.

Again Ursula shook her head. "We didn't get away. They let us go," she said.

"Why?" said Mrs. Russet.

Napalm wrung his hands and looked up at the night sky. He suddenly looked to Billy like a little boy about to ask his parents not to turn the lights out at bed time, because the monster under the bed might eat him. "They let us go because they wanted us to tell you something," he said.

"What?" demanded Mrs. Russet.

Billy felt his insides curl in on themselves. He could sense that something terrible was coming.

"They wanted us to tell you that…that…," began Napalm. But before he finished his thought, he screamed. The scream was long and horrible, seeming to go on forever before he finally fell to the ground and was still.

Billy couldn't be sure, but he thought Napalm was dead.

Then Billy found out that the Red Power wasn't dead. It was much worse. With a shudder, Napalm's body twitched as though it was being electrified. At the same time, all the lights—torches mostly—that had illuminated the area on top of the tower flickered and went out. The Diamond Dais glowed with an inner light, but the illumination was dim, allowing Billy to see little.

Still, what he saw was enough. Enough and too much. The Red Power who had once been strong enough to Challenge Fulgora continued twitching and convulsing. Then, in the dim light, Billy could see Napalm's skin…*changing*. It looked like it had liquefied, crawling over itself in a flowing pattern, while still managing to cling to the underlying musculature. Then the skin solidified, and Billy could see it was now a latticework. A lace pattern he had seen before. Napalm was gone, and the body that now climbed slowly to its feet was a creature made of tiny bones. As it stood, a small form flickered up from its shoulder.

The Death's Head Moth, Billy realized. It must have come up with Napalm and the others, and done this to him.

Billy tensed, ready to run if the deadly insect should swoop toward him, but the infernal creature just landed on what had been Napalm. The new-born creature of Dark looked at them all impassively, the power of speech gone from Napalm—or what had once been Napalm—in his new, horrifying state.

Everyone was silent for a moment, dumbstruck by what they had just seen.

"What is this?" whispered Fulgora finally.

"I don't know," answered Mrs. Russet quietly. She was looking around them, and Billy could see how tense she was. Then a chill wind whipped up. Lightning ripped through the night sky, illuminating the top of the tower. Billy and the others were standing in the pillbox that Mrs. Russet had constructed, but suddenly a flash of lightning crashed into the structure, reducing it instantly to an ashlike dust that rained down on their heads.

The lightning continued, and in a sudden brief flash of strobing light, Billy could see something. Something terrible, something awful, something impossible. One moment the top of the tower was dark and mostly deserted, just Billy, Mrs. Russet, Fulgora, Vester, Ivy, the two unconscious Powers who were left from the Accounting Room, and the new Death's Head Power that had once been Napalm. No one else.

Then the lightning came. It flashed, and then darkness fell. An instant later there was another illuminating flash, and this time Billy and his friends were no longer alone.

Darksiders were among them. Everywhere. The Dark Powers had just appeared among the Dawnwalkers on the tower, in the time it took for the lightning to erupt across the sky and then disappear again.

And, at their head, close enough to Billy that he could smell the Power's fetid breath when he spoke, was Wolfen. And right behind him stood Eva Black and her son Cameron, both of them glaring murderously at Billy.

The Dark Master looked at the bone-body of Napalm. "Sorry about him," he said, "but if there's one thing I can't stand, it's a messenger who doesn't know how to deliver the messages I want him to deliver." He said this last while looking directly at Billy, a wicked smile playing across his lips.

"How did you get here?" whispered Vester. "You didn't come through the Accounting Room. How did you get here?"

"Well, see, that's the thing I wanted your three friends to tell you," said Wolfen with an amused grin. He looked to Billy like a fox who has just been asked by the chickens if he'd like to come in for some chamomile tea and a scone.

He leaned in to Billy, and lightning tore through the sky again. It made the Darksiders appear like ghosts, bright white in the flashing light, and then disappearing into nebulous black forms among them.

Billy could not see Wolfen's eyes in the darkness, but he felt them on him. Burning him. The Dark Master spoke, and his voice was filled with the terrible threat of death and mayhem. And worse, with a sound that made it clear how much he would enjoy those things when they came.

"The thing I wanted them to tell you was this," said Wolfen. He paused, then said quietly, "We don't need to come through the Accounting Room any more. We can come through anywhere we want."

And with that, a huge fireball ripped through the night sky, an explosion from somewhere in the middle of Powers Island. Then another and another. Wolfen laughed, and the lightning flashed again, this time illuminating white teeth that looked like those of a predator, spittle thick on the man's lips.

Wolfen raised his arms, and when he spoke again it was with a voice of thunder, a sound that Billy immediately knew could be heard on the whole of the island. He spoke only a single word, just two syllables in that thunderous scream. But it was the single most terrifying word that Billy had ever heard.

"Attack!"

# CHAPTER THE TWENTY-EIGHTH

*In Which Billy does battle, and a star Falls...*

The Darksiders around them all erupted into action, but before they had more than an instant to move, Fulgora responded to Wolfen's battle cry with one of her own.

"Destroy them!" she shrieked, and whirled her bright sword of fire. A sheet of flame erupted in front of Billy and his friends, momentarily separating and protecting him from the nearest Darksiders.

Even with the sheet of flame between them, however, Billy saw Wolfen move. The Dark Master clenched his fist as though he were holding an invisible baseball, and hurled it at Billy. Something visibly punched a hole through the flames, which seemed to literally curl and blacken around the void created by Wolfen's spell, and an instant later Billy felt something hit him in the chest. It was something cold and painful, slamming into Billy like a frozen shotgun blast.

The force of the magical attack shoved Billy backward, hurtling him toward the edge of the tower near where the tower's river disappeared over the edge in a spray of watery mist that dissipated in the many thousand foot drop over the side. Billy felt himself being slammed to the edge the deadly precipice, but couldn't manage to care about it. His chest was spasming like he had been shocked with a defibrillator, and he was trying to scream in pain, but couldn't do it. He coughed, trying to catch his breath. He was drowning in agony, and still hurtling toward the edge of the tower.

I'm a goner, he managed to think. He was peripherally aware that fighting had broken out, but was not aware of much else. His whole universe had contracted to only the pain in his chest, the hitching breath in his lungs that just wouldn't come out no matter how badly he wanted it to.

Back, back, back he hurtled. The edge of the tower was only yards away. Then feet. Then inches. And then, in a tightly curled ball of pain, Billy fell off the edge of the tower and plummeted downward.

It was a measure of his suffering that he barely noticed the fact that gravity had grabbed him tightly and was now yanking him downward at a horrific velocity.

How fast can you be going before you die of sheer speed? he wondered fleetingly. But then he grabbed his chest and doubled up in midair as another surge of pain hit him like a mallet in the sternum. He cried out, but the sound was muffled by the wind whipping past him in his descent to oblivion.

Billy's ears were popping continuously, altitude changes squeezing them and then letting them go as his eardrums tried to keep up with what was happening. His eyes were tightly squeezed shut, tears flowing across his face and then being left behind to fall on their own.

He felt mist on his face, and heard a crackle of electricity, and realized that he was now falling through the cloud cover that encircled the tall tower. But he didn't care. His whole world was pain now. *He* was pain. He tightened into a fetal position, trying to concentrate, to will the pain out of him. It was probably hopeless, but as he devolved into a writhing ball of chilled agony, it was all he could think to do.

Get out of me, he thought. Get out of me!

But the pain grew worse, intensifying until the mallet that had been pounding at him now became a white-hot sword, skewering his heart and leaving him breathless. Thick roiling darkness curled in around the edges of his consciousness, and he realized that he was not going to make it long enough to die from his fall: whatever spell Wolfen had cast was going to kill him before he had that chance.

No! Billy thought to himself. It won't end like this!

He concentrated, slowing his breathing as he tried to cast out the pain, the destructive agony that coiled like an angry serpent in his heart. He focused on the pain, trying to wall it off from himself, trying to isolate it and cut it out with his mind.

Billy was acting on instinct now, some animal part of him taking over without thought or plan. He was just a reactive beast, calling on some instinctual response to whatever was happening. And like a bear that can ignore hunger pains over the long winter months of hibernation, like a frog that could sleep below the ice for months without oxygen, Billy gradually became able to function without the part of his spirit that was in pain. The pain was still there, but suddenly it was like it was in another room in the house of his body.

*This is not my Message*, came the thought into his mind. *My Message is not of pain, but of hope.*

And with the thought, Billy thought he could feel a ball of pure white light exploding in his mind, a diamond of hope that refracted radiant happiness all around. And when the light dimmed, the pain that Wolfen had inflicted on him was gone.

What just happened? he thought. What is happening to *me*?

But then he realized that he had bigger things to worry about. The fact that Wolfen's power over him had somehow been broken didn't changed the fact that he was still falling. And very quickly, too.

He fell the rest of the way through the cloud bank, and when he emerged the entirety of Powers Island was spread below him. And it was on fire. Billy could see explosions everywhere, conflagrations running out of control among the hills and forested mountains of the island. The snowy parts he had noticed on his first flights over the island looked half-melted, scorched by the battles going on all around.

He could make out rock giants, thudding huge heavy steps back and forth as the enormous Fizzles swept clubs of stone at tight-knit groups of Darksiders. One of the giants struck, and Billy could almost hear the sound of the club pulverizing everything below it. Then the rock giant looked up, and screamed a scream like an avalanche, and vibrated rapidly. It became, as had Prince, as had Napalm, a creature of skeletal Death. And now the Death's Head Giant swept a club that had become an enormous bone, and when it struck, it struck groups of Dawnwalkers who had until a moment before huddled safely at its feet.

Everywhere on the island, Billy could see that the battle was being lost. The Darksiders were rampant. Huge malignant blobs of darkness kept exploding into existence as Death Powers cast spells of mayhem, leaving unconscious Dawnwalkers in their wake at every turn. Waves rushed over the defensive battlements that had been created on the island, called up by a group of Blue Powers who had aligned themselves with the Darksiders.

And Billy was still falling.

Well, he thought, at least I'll go out with a view.

Then, suddenly, his fall slowed and stopped. He felt strong hands grip him around his midsection, jerking him to a halt.

"See?" said a familiar voice in his ear. "Travel by Wind is the way to go! You think you can get this kind of view traveling by Earth? No! But still Lumilla insists on doing it. And Vester! Don't even get me started on Cresting! Travel through Fire indeed!"

Billy almost laughed. Tempus had saved him! The Gray Power had caught him, snatching him away from certain death. But still, not even the battle all around them could stop the old wizard from complaining good-naturedly. For a moment, in spite of everything going on around him, Billy felt like all was suddenly right with the world.

And then all was suddenly wrong again as a bolt of lightning sizzled out of the clouds above, missing Billy and Tempus by mere inches. Then another, and another, each one making the hairs on Billy's body stand on end, each one accompanied by a deafening clap that alone was almost enough to knock them out of the air.

"Drat! Drat and double drat!" hollered Tempus, his old bony hands digging into Billy's skin as the Gray Power yanked him left and right, taking evasive action from the bolts of lightning that were following them like heat-seeking missiles.

"What's happening?" screamed Billy through the maelstrom.

"Some dratted Darksider!" yelled Tempus, yanking them left through the air as a streak of lightning sliced open the sky where they had both been only a moment before. "Some Red Power is attacking!"

Another streak of lightning sheared close by, and Billy actually felt his arm hairs singe with the heat of its passage.

"Gotta set us down!" hollered Tempus.

"But we have to get to the top of the tower! Mrs. Russet, Vester, the others all need us!" shouted Billy.

"They can take care of themselves, boy!" yelled Tempus in return, and this time he took Billy on a sickening loop through the air as three separate lightning strikes tried to shoot them out of the sky. "Gotta get us grounded!"

Tempus re-adjusted his grip around Billy, then closed his eyes for a moment, and Billy felt the soft pad of air that had been pushing them to and fro suddenly disappear. He and Tempus dropped like rocks to the ground below. Falling, falling, then stopping suddenly for a moment as Tempus slowed them, then falling again as he let his power cede. Billy wondered what on earth the old man was trying to accomplish, but then realized that the erratic pattern of stops and starts would make them incredibly difficult targets to hit.

About one hundred feet above the ground, Tempus concentrated again, and they shot off to the right, skimming over the intense skirmishes that were blazing all over the island. Billy could see Dawnwalkers everywhere, usually huddled in small groups under the baleful gaze of advancing Darksiders.

The island is lost, he thought. Then, in the part of him that was buried deep, in the part that had fought off Wolfen's spell and that somehow was part of him yet not part of him, came another thought: All is not lost, but shall yet be found.

But still, Billy couldn't see how that would be possible.

Then, he saw something bright and shining, like a star hurtling to earth. It fell straight downward, right beside and parallel to the tower, sending off puffs of smoke and sparks of flame. Billy watched it for a moment, wondering what it could be. Then he realized what he was seeing, and he felt himself begin to panic.

Fulgora, he thought. Not Fulgora!

It was one thing to plummet to his own death, but he could now see that somehow the Red Lady, too, had fallen from the heights of the tower. She was spinning wildly in the air, a free fall that could have only one possible end, a bright shining ember that would descend to earth and, as all embers do, disappear forever.

"Tempus, it's Fulgora!" he screamed.

"I know, boy!" shouted the old Gray Power.

"Save her!" screamed Billy.

"Can't," said Tempus, in a voice that was strangled with grief. "I've got barely enough power to keep just us up."

"Save her!" Billy shouted again, unwilling to believe that he was about to witness the death of a friend.

"I can't, I can't!" said Tempus, and Billy could hear the tears in the old man's voice.

Fulgora fell and fell, her brightness shining in the night. Billy could see some of the fighters below him looking at the sight, their battle momentarily on hold as they watched the falling of a star from the heights of power.

No, no, no! thought Billy. She can't! She can't fall!

But Fulgora *was* falling, the forces that gripped her deaf to Billy's wishes, pulling her to her doom.

Then Fulgora's panicked movements slowed. Like a parachute jumper adjusting to perform an aerial stunt, the Red Lady managed to right herself in the air. She was only a few hundred feet above the ground, and still falling, but suddenly something appeared around the burning halo of her body. Something sprouted from her like a crimson vine, then uncurled itself.

Wings! thought Billy. She's becoming the dragon!

And sure enough, the wings beat down in a furious updraft of hot air. This time, however, Fulgora did not completely transform. Only the wings grew from her shoulders, only part of a dragon came from within her. But it was enough to slow her fall, allowing her to drift at a manageable speed to the base of the tower.

"Tempus!" shouted Billy.

"I know!" hollered the old man, and indeed he did seem to know what Billy had been about to say, for he was already banking to go to where Fulgora would land. Billy and the old man arrived just as she touched down, her huge wings pumping in a flash of red light, sparks shooting off her armor like sunspots. Then, in another flash of red, the wings disappeared as they had come, wrapping themselves into their tight curls, and then disappearing into her body.

Tempus let go of Billy, and Billy ran to Fulgora. He almost hugged her, but before he did he could sense the oven-like heat coming off her and changed his mind. He didn't care to get burned by a hug.

Fulgora was looking around herself, blinking as though waking from a dream. One entire side of her head was a huge bruise, an ugly purple and yellow, and one of her arms hung limply at her side. It looked like she had dislocated a shoulder during the fighting. "What happened?" she asked.

"You fell," said Billy breathlessly. "You fell, but you became the dragon—part of a dragon, anyway—and you…you flew down and landed safely."

"What?" said Fulgora, still dazed-looking. "Impossible."

Tempus was wheezing nearby, his hands on his knees, clearly winded by the effort of catching Billy and the ensuing aeronautical acrobatics. "It's true," he managed. "What Billy said is true." He straightened. "I thought you would have believed it possible by now," he managed between gasps.

"What's that supposed to mean?" snapped Fulgora, and Billy was almost relieved to hear her do so: she was coming back to herself, assuming the personality he had come to appreciate in recent days.

"Well," answered Tempus, "I just assumed…I thought that was probably what you were doing all that time when you were gone and we were imprisoned on Dark Isle. I mean," he paused a moment, still trying to catch his breath, "I figured you were off with your people, trying to find out how you turned into a dragon."

"No," said Fulgora, a far-away look in her eyes. "As I said before, I *did* go to my people, and tried to find out for a short time, but never did. Nothing like that had ever happened before, and I got nowhere in my search."

"Then what *were* you doing while we were incarcerated?" asked Tempus.

Billy was surprised. Explosions were still going on all around them, the island was on the verge of collapse, and who knew what was happening on the top of the tower. But apparently Tempus really wanted to know. "Well?" he asked.

Fulgora's eyes narrowed. She didn't answer him, but looked up toward the top of the tower. "He cast me down," she said angrily.

"What?" asked Billy, now even more confused than ever.

Fulgora swung to look at him, anger blazing in her face. "Wolfen. He hit me with some spell, and I only managed to put up a shield in time to block most of it." Billy grabbed his chest in sympathy, suspecting that she had been hit with the same devastating attack he had. But Fulgora didn't notice the movement, now in her own world of indignant anger that someone—anyone—would dare attack her.

"Well," said Tempus almost conversationally, still apparently oblivious to the noise around them, "what did you expect?" He looked at her witheringly. "What kind of special privilege do you think *you* had?" He spat to one side, clearly disgusted with Fulgora. "Especially considering how useful you've been," he added sarcastically.

Billy was shocked. This was totally unlike Tempus. What did the old man think he was doing? Forget about the fact that Billy was pretty sure Fulgora could wipe him out without even thinking about it, but there was a *war* going on. And Tempus suddenly wanted to insult the Dawnwalkers' general and get into some petty argument?

But Fulgora obviously didn't care that there was a war going on either. She drew herself up in the face of Tempus's derision and said, "You *dare*? You dare insult Fulgora the Red Lady, Councilor of Fire and Princess of the Underworld of Flame?"

"Princess, Shmincess," said Tempus derisively. Billy looked back and forth between his two friends, his head whipping this direction and that with the speed of a marble in a blender. "Don't wave your credentials at me, 'Red Lady,'" Tempus continued, bowing in mock courtesy. "Results are what matter."

"You wish to see results?" she whispered. "Results?"

And with that, she turned on her heel and walked away. One of the bonfires that had been set around the island was nearby, and she strode straight toward it.

Billy looked at Tempus in horror as she went, and was shocked to see that, far from looking angry, the old man was grinning. He winked at Billy, and chuckled quietly.

Fulgora, meanwhile, had almost reached the fire when a group of three Darksiders sprung from a patch of nearby shadows. They all hurled their spells at her, but Fulgora was suddenly holding a shield of flame, and the spells bounced off it back at the Darksiders, rendering them all immobile and crying in the darkness, obviously gripped by some form of Dread.

Then, with a last angry backwards glance at Tempus—and Billy noticed that the old man put on an angry face when Fulgora looked back—the Red Lady stepped into the bonfire. There was a great crackling of logs popping in flame, and suddenly she was gone.

Billy wheeled on Tempus. "What the heck are you doing?" he demanded. "You risk getting turned into a toasted Pop Tart by baiting her, and then you keep doing it until she runs away? She's our *general*, for crying out loud! How long are we going to last without her?"

Tempus grinned again, then grew somber. "The battle was lost," he said. "I was flying over the island doing recon—that's how I came to be nearby when you were falling, thank goodness—and I know. We've lost, completely and utterly."

"So you got rid of our battle leader?" said Billy incredulously.

"Not got rid of," said Tempus, a twinkle in his eye. "Just encouraged her to bring reinforcements."

And with that, there was a bright eruption of flame from the bonfire that Fulgora had just disappeared into, and just as suddenly as the Red Lady had gone, she was back again. Only this time, she was not walking. She was riding.

Billy gasped. Fulgora was astride a huge lion of fire. The red animal growled, and flame shot from its mouth. "Meet Volcano," she said, and patted the huge beast.

"What's going on?" asked Billy under his breath.

Tempus grinned, visibly pleased with himself. "I knew that if she went back to her home, they'd see what had been done to their Princess. They usually don't get involved in the affairs of the Powers—though heaven knows we've asked them to often enough—but I knew if they saw Fulgora all roughed up the way she was, they'd take it rather personally...."

"They?" asked Billy. "Who is 'they'?" Tempus didn't answer, but just grabbed Billy suddenly and whipped him into the air. They went up about a hundred feet, Billy writhing in the old man's grasp. "Who's 'they'?" he demanded again. "What's going on?"

"Relax," said Tempus quietly. "I think you're going to want to see this."

Then, before either of them could say anything else, Fulgora, still on her fire lion below them, raised a flaming sword in her one good arm. "Warriors of the Underworld, now is the time to avenge your Princess!"

And with a great rending blast, a huge wave of heat rolled over the island. Tempus went up even higher, allowing more of a view of Powers Island, and as he did so, Billy gasped. He knew from watching the defensive preparations that there were about a thousand bonfires scattered over Powers Island, and from what he could see now, every one of them had grown white-hot. A tongue of flame shot up from each one, a thousand blazing columns of fire that Billy could feel raising the temperature everywhere around them.

And then, figures stepped out of the infernos. They were all dressed in red armor, like Fulgora. And like Fulgora, each was astride some beast of flame. There were war-horses with saddles of ruby fire, giant red bears whose riders roared with the same ferocity as their steeds, huge wolves of flame that bared teeth that looked like the white-hot fires of a welding torch, and even some giant crimson eagles that rose on the updrafts of the bonfires and carried their armed riders into the air.

The riders all held swords, and spears, and shields. And every one of them saluted toward Fulgora.

"See?" said Tempus in a decidedly self-satisfied voice.

At the same moment, Fulgora raised her eyes and spotted the flying pair. "And don't go thinking you goaded me into this, you old Gray manipulator!" she shouted. "I've been planning to bring these reinforcements for weeks, and Vester and I have been working on the appropriate time to bring them into the battle since we got here!"

Tempus's eyes bugged out of their sockets. "When did you have time to go to your home and get them ready?" he shouted.

"What do you think I was doing the whole time you were in prison?" answered the Red Lady, Princess of the Underworld of Flame, and smiled grimly. "What is a general without an army ready to do battle at her call?"

In spite of the dire circumstances, Billy almost laughed out loud at the befuddled expression that took the place of Tempus's satisfied smile.

Fulgora raised her arm, and a lightning bolt arced down from the sky to touch her sword, ringing it with blue flame. Then she slashed her sword downward, breaking the connection between earth and sky, and a sound like a sonic boom rolled over Powers Island. Billy could see an avalanche begin on the snowy summits to the west.

And at the sound, the warriors of fire screamed as one, and attacked the Darksiders.

The battle erupted in earnest now. It had been slowing as the Dawnwalkers' forces were forced toward an inevitable defeat, but now that the red fighters had joined them, the battle raged anew.

Billy and Tempus hung above it all in the sky. Occasionally Tempus would swoop down and Billy would grab a rock or a discarded brick from the ground, then they would go up again and Billy would take careful aim and drop his crude bomb, aiming for the head of a Darksider. "Bombs away!" Tempus would scream, laughing manically as he played the part of a B-17 in this strange war.

The mirth was short-lived, however. Because as they watched, Billy could see that even with the influx of force and skill the Fulgora's warriors brought, the battle was still being lost. The Darksiders still had too many people on their side. Their forces were still too well-organized. And worst of all, the Darksiders' own troops were being continually augmented by the Death's Head Moths that Billy could see flitting about the island. Whatever they touched turned into that hideous latticework of tiny bones he had seen before, and whatever they touched turned instantly into an agent of the Darksiders. Billy gasped as he saw one red fighter astride a huge angry tiger of fire attack a group of Darksiders, scattering them in panic. Then the red warrior suddenly writhed, and both he and his steed were turned to bone as they stood there. What had once been a red warrior now wheeled on his friends, attacking them with a spear that had been transformed to a huge dead tooth in his hands.

We're losing, Billy thought. We're still losing.

He thought about what might be happening on the top of the tower, where he had left Mrs. Russet, Vester, and Ivy behind with the host of Darksiders, but he knew that there was no way he and Tempus could fly up there. The clouds were full of lightning being pulled down by Red Powers on both sides, and to fly upwards would be suicide. So he pushed the thought of his friends out of his mind, and he and Tempus did their best to do their small part in the battle by casting their pitiful bombs of brick and stone.

Billy dropped one rock on the head of one of the Darksiders' monsters of bone, trying to forget that it had until recently been a Dawnwalker, and was thrilled to see the gruesome puzzle of skeletons that made up its head explode into a million tiny pieces. But his smile fled as the pieces then reassembled themselves in midair, and reset themselves on the Death's Head's shoulders again. The monster went forth and continued its attack, undeterred by Billy's direct hit.

Still, Billy clung to a hope that the battle could be won. The red warriors were now aware of the Death's Head Moths, and were taking care to avoid them, burning the tiny insects out of the sky. The battle began to turn again, a fluid beast that could be won or lost at any time by any side.

Billy and Tempus, now near the beach of Powers Island, swooped down to grab another rock. And as they did, Billy saw something in the dark waves that were pounding up to the rocky shores nearby. The waves hissed and burbled, and Billy felt a thrill of hope.

Artemaeus! he thought. The whale had saved him and his friends before, so maybe he had come again in this hour of desperate need. Billy didn't know what a bunch of whales could do, but he had sensed the age, wisdom, and power of Artemaeus, and knew that such a force would find some way to help.

Then, a moment later, he realized it wasn't Artemaeus. Nor was it Blue, the mermaid of the deep.

The forms broke through the surf, their dark shapes barely visible in the night. They slogged out of the water, their bodies shining as moonlight and the fires of battle refracted off their wet bodies and revealed without a doubt what new force had arrived at the island.

Oh, no, Billy thought.

# CHAPTER THE TWENTY-NINTH

*In Which Billy sees two new Armies, and finally speaks the Message...*

But how? was Billy's first thought. How can it be possible?

He knew magic changed many of the rules, but he also had come to understand that though the rules of magic were different, still they did exist. But *this*...this seemed to go against all the rules.

Not only that, it just seemed downright unfair.

It was zombies. Thousands of them. Their insectile eyes glistened like dark oozing sores, and their mottled skin looked even more hideous when illuminated in the fires of war.

Above him, Billy heard Tempus gasp, and felt the Gray Power lurch for a moment, surprise clearly gripping him as well.

And below, the creatures of the Dark moved up the beach in that horrible lurching gait that Billy had come to know and fear. They climbed out of the sea, and then up the beachhead in knots of tens and twenties, and as soon as they had scaled the beach they broke into smaller groups, the evil new army exploding like a dark nova. The undead forces quickly reached the fringes of the battle and began extending their deadly touch to the Dawnwalkers all around them.

How? Billy thought again. They were washed off Dark Isle. Washed into the sea.

And then he realized: *they were washed into the sea.* They were already creatures of Death, and didn't need air. So they had been merely pushed out, and sunk to the depths. And just as several of them had managed to clamber up and attack Billy and his friends when they were stuck on Dark Isle, what would stop the rest of the creatures from simply walking back onto Dark Isle as well, and then being deployed as an encircling army by Wolfen and his followers? Or even just walking straight to Powers Island?

Either way, the horrible creatures were here now, and once again the tide of the battle turned against the forces of the Dawn.

The red warriors and the Dawnwalkers had already been harried by the Darksiders. They had had their numbers stolen by the Death's Head Moths. And now they were having their remaining numbers culled by the devastating touch of the zombies.

Not only that, but Billy could feel Tempus losing steam above him. The old man was drifting lower and lower with each bombing run, and having more and more trouble avoiding the lightning strikes that were hurled from above and the Death attacks thrown from below. On one occasion, Billy saw a black-garbed Black Power hurl one of Death's terrible spells at them, and could feel it barely miss him. Tempus cried out and almost dropped Billy, but then managed to grab onto him again. "It's all right, just a scratch," the old man yelled. But Billy could hear the quaver in Tempus's voice, and knew that their attacks, pitiful and unhelpful as they might be, had drawn attention. They couldn't continue on much longer.

The two dropped down for another rock, and once again scored a bulls-eye: a zombie crumpled to the ground. But once again, the victory was temporary, as the creature slowly stood and continued its relentless pursuit of the Dawnwalkers' forces.

"Can't keep this up," wheezed Tempus. His flight was now disturbingly wobbly, and Billy knew that they would be going down soon.

"Head toward the tower!" shouted Billy. He didn't know how he could be of any help once he got there—the only real help he'd given was because of Tempus's powers, and not any qualities of his own—but he knew he wanted to end things as close to his friends as possible. And Vester, Ivy, and Mrs. Russet were still—he hoped—fighting on the top of the tower. So the tower was where he should be.

Tempus banked, pulling Billy and himself wearily to the center of Powers Island. And as they passed over the island Billy could see that not only had the battle turned, it was now all but lost. The Darksiders' forces appeared almost untouched, while the Dawnwalkers were running away, disappearing as they Transported off the island, or just huddling in magically-exhausted groups, awaiting destruction.

Tempus dipped toward the ground, and once more Billy grabbed a rock from below. They were near the tower now, flying around the base of the huge structure. The fighting was at its most intense here, since the remaining Dawnwalkers who had any fight left in them had withdrawn into a circle around the tower, the giant edifice providing some cover at their backs. But it also allowed for no further retreat.

Billy could see Fulgora, her red lion weary and dim, the light snuffing out of it like a candle flame whose wick has burned out within it. But the Red Lady herself looked as angrily determined to fight to the end as ever.

Billy passed his rock bomb from hand to hand, looking for the best place to drop it, knowing that this would be the last one. Then he and Tempus would fall to earth, to fight and probably die in a lost cause.

But at least I'll be with friends, thought Billy. At least I won't be alone.

The thought was oddly comforting. His whole life, he had longed for friends, for people who would stand by him in the halls and invite him to the events of their lives.

Now, he had found such friends, and more. People who would stand by him in the battles of Power, and would invite him to stand with them and face doom together.

As he thought this, Billy spotted a Darksider that looked like a good candidate for a rock on the head. It was a man who was threatening a small knot of Dawnwalker kids who looked like they were about Billy's age. Billy pointed them out, and Tempus nodded and swung in for their final bombing run.

Billy hefted his rock, taking careful aim....

And then he almost dropped it. Not purposefully—had he dropped it in that instant he would have missed his target by a mile—but in surprise.

Because the rock moved.

Billy yelped in shock as he looked down and saw that the rock was staring at him. Its two craggy eyes were glaring at him as if to say, "I was just sitting there, doing my own thing, and you go and grab me! Who do you think you are?"

Then, even more surprising, Billy felt the rock sprout small arms and legs. Then more arms and legs. And then still more arms and legs.

"What the...?" began Billy.

Then the creature kicked Billy in the hand. Billy yelped again, this time in pain, and dropped the tiny monster. And as it fell, Billy realized what it was. Because as it fell, the creature yelled out what sounded a lot like "Banzai!" in a tiny, high-pitched voice.

It was a Kung Fu Cleaner. In fact, Billy now realized it was the leader of the Kung Fu Cleaners: the one who had first appeared when Billy had spilled hot chocolate in the anteroom in a desperate attempt to escape Wolfen.

The tiny Fizzle hit the rocky ground below with a tiny puff of dust, landing on a cliff on the side of a short mountain. And where he fell, Billy saw something unusual.

"Down!" he yelled at Tempus.

"But what about—" began the Gray Power.

"DOWN!" hollered Billy, in a tone that brooked no argument.

Tempus shrugged and took them down, dropping them lightly within inches of where the tiny Fizzle had fallen. The Fizzle was still there, waiting as the rock ground near it—and near Billy and Tempus—bubbled and rolled like a wave on the beach. A blob of rock rose up, and then started to take shape. It grew arms, then legs, then a head. Features started to appear, as though the stone was being sculpted by an invisible artist, a work of art created without hands.

And then the artist finished its work, and the figure became clear.

"Rumpelstiltskin!" shouted Billy in delight.

And so it was. The bent, withered old man had come from the depths of his cleaning room at last, and now surveyed the island.

"What's going on?" Tempus was saying. "Who is this?"

Billy ignored him, watching the new arrival. Rumpelstiltskin seemed not to have noticed Billy yet. The old man just reached down and picked up the Kung Fu Cleaner that Billy had mistakenly grabbed, and put it on his shoulder like a bizarre parrot.

"My, my, my," said Rumpelstiltskin. Now he noticed Billy. "Don't I know you?" he asked.

"It's me, Billy," said Billy.

"No, you're not Billy," said the tiny old man. "I know Billy, and you're nothing like him. He was surrounded by Fizzles."

Billy rolled his eyes. The last thing he wanted to get into was a discussion like that again. "Forget it," he said. "What are you doing here?" And then he paused before adding, "Are you here to try to help Mrs. Russet?"

"Help Mrs. Russet?" said Rumpelstiltskin quizzically. "Who in the world is Mrs. Russet, and why would she need helping?"

Billy's heart fell. He had hoped, somehow, that Terry had in fact come. But Terry wasn't here, only Rumpelstiltskin.

The ancient man was now looking around the island. "What in the name of all Powers is going on?" he asked.

"A battle," began Billy, but he couldn't say more than that. It was over, the war was over, Wolfen had won. And he stood here talking to an insane old man on a cliff. He wasn't even going to end things at his friends' sides, and be with them when doom came for them all.

"A battle, eh?" said Terry. He leaned his head to one side, toward the Fizzle on his shoulder, and whispered, "I'm sorry I didn't believe you, Pip."

The Kung Fu Cleaner squeaked, clearly saying something along the lines of "Don't worry about it."

Rumpelstiltskin then said, "A battle, eh?" again. Then he cocked his head to one side and said, "Didn't someone just say that?"

"You did," said Billy in a tired, frustrated voice.

"Who is this?" asked Tempus, who had been following all this with confusion on his face.

"It's—" Billy began, but that was as far as he got before he heard a loud, wordless scream. He whirled to see Rumpelstiltskin hopping up and down in rage.

"Look at this!" hollered the wrinkled old man. "Look at what they're doing!" He whirled on Billy. "Are you responsible for this?" he demanded.

Billy had no idea what Rumpelstiltskin was blathering on about. But he blurted out the first thing that came to mind. "The Darksiders did it," he said.

"The Darksiders?" said Rumpelstiltskin. "The Darksiders did it?" His eyes narrowed. "I might have known," he growled.

"What are you talking about?" asked Tempus, the old man clearly tired of being left in the dark by what was going on.

"What am I talking about?" said Rumpelstiltskin. "What am I *talking* about?" He waved his arms, taking in the whole of Powers Island. "*Who is going to clean up this mess?*" he screamed.

Then he turned, and to Billy's surprise, he grabbed the Kung Fu Cleaner off his shoulder and hurled it off the mountain with all his might. "Go get 'em!" yelled Rumpelstiltskin.

Billy buried his face in his hands. Perfect, he thought. The Dawnwalkers are all but conquered, Wolfen is at the brink of winning it all, and what do we have left on our side? One crazy ex-Councilor with his attack Fizzle.

Then, he heard Tempus say, "Oh my." The words were soft, but Billy heard the surprise in them. "Oh my," said the Gray Power once more, and Billy looked up.

As soon as he did, his jaw dropped open like he had suddenly lost all control over the muscles in his face.

The Fizzle had hit the ground running, and gone immediately for the nearest Darksider, the one who had been menacing the

Dawnwalker kids that Billy had seen earlier. The Fizzle threw itself onto the Dark Power's body with a tiny attack cry, pummeling the man with a variety of karate kicks using every single one of its many legs. Billy saw immediately, however, that the Darksider was merely annoyed by this. A single tiny Fizzle wasn't going to hurt him, or even slow him down.

But then the Darksider's face paled. Because even though a single tiny Fizzle wouldn't slow him down, a *million* of them was quite another matter.

Billy couldn't help but grin as the entirety of Powers Island seemed to come alive all at once. Literally hundreds of thousands of the Kung Fu Cleaners erupted out of the rock and dirt of the island, coating it like ants on an anthill. Each of them was motionless for a moment. Then Rumpelstiltskin said quietly, "Well, my children, what are you waiting for?" He smiled a tight, thin smile, and for a moment Billy almost thought he could see Terry struggling to appear from within the old man. Then Rumpelstiltskin nodded at his army. "Let's clean up this place," he said.

With that, the tiny Fizzles swarmed over the Darksiders. And suddenly, the battle that had been all but over was in full swing once again. The Kung Fu Cleaners were devastating in their attack, overrunning the Darksiders in a matter of seconds. Nor were they threatened by the zombies, Billy could see: the granite creatures knocked over the zombies as fast as they ran over anything else, the Kung Fu Cleaners apparently impervious to the paralyzing touch of the undead warriors.

The Darksiders immediately found themselves between the Kung Fu Cleaners on one side and the most elite of the Dawnwalkers' remaining fighters on the other, a tight vise that allowed little room for maneuvering or attack. Billy saw the rock giants that the Death's Head Moths had converted to skeletal servants of the Dark swing their huge bone clubs, and a thousand Kung Fu Cleaners were shattered into oblivion, disintegrating into dust under the force of their blows. But for each Fizzle that fell, a hundred more took its place.

The battle was joined again, and as Billy watched, he started believing that maybe—just maybe—they might win after all.

He looked at Rumpelstiltskin. The old man winced in pain each time one of his Fizzles fell, but he was clearly determined to stop the cause of the mess that had been made of the previously beautiful island. Billy remembered that the destruction of a Fizzle caused pain to its master as well, and wondered how long Rumpelstiltskin would be able to withstand the attack. He suspected not long, and worried that if something wasn't done to turn the tide of the battle overwhelmingly in the Dawnwalkers' favor, it might still be lost.

Beside him, he heard a groan, and turned in time to see Tempus fall to the ground. The old man was exhausted, worn out by his years and by the Herculean work he had done with Billy. He was not a Councilor, Billy knew, not one of the great Powers like Mrs. Russet or Fulgora. So his flight with Billy had clearly taken its toll, and weakened him to the point of collapse.

Billy looked back at the battles that raged below. He saw Fulgora, following a horde of Kung Fu Cleaners and followed herself by a trio of her red warriors, all four of the fighters astride their beasts of flame. But then he saw as, one by one, her entourage was picked off. Then Fulgora herself was taken down as a zombie lurched into her steed. The lion Fizzle flamed out of existence under the zombie's deadly touch, and then the dust and movement of the battle obscured Fulgora from Billy's view.

Billy felt a sinking in his stomach. The Kung Fu Cleaners might make all the difference. But the battle was still far from victory. And his friends were suffering.

But what can I do? he thought to himself. But nothing was coming. Again, he felt like a rather poor Messenger, if that was indeed what he was. What use was it to be special in any way, if your specialness couldn't help your friends?

I'm the Messenger, he thought, knowing that he was trying to coax himself into confidence as much as anything else. So what can I do? What can the Messenger do?

Beside him, he heard Rumpelstiltskin gasp with pain. The old man fell to his knees for a moment, and Billy could sense the rock Fizzles stumble when their master did. At the same time, he also saw another group of Dawnwalkers below fall to the ground as they were touched by the zombies.

Then he became aware that Rumpelstiltskin was murmuring; saying something under his breath:

> "Through fires of fate and storms that save
> Through winter's gate and water's grave
> Shall come the One, once lost, now found
> Seen by the Son whose love abounds.
>
> A sword, a spear, and armor strong
> A shield to wear, and dagger long
> To fell the Dark and bring the Light
> To call the spark that ends the night.

*And through it all, one twist of fate:*
*A child whose call will seem too late*
*But though the Dark seems once to win*
*The child will spark the light again."*

It was the Prophecy of the Messenger. It was, if Mrs. Russet was correct, the Prophecy of Billy. Rumpelstiltskin repeated it two more times, and Billy got the sense that the crazy old man was trying to tell him something. Then the frail Brown Power giggled and added,

*"There was once a messenger true*
*Who both came and went through the blue.*
*He used a big blade,*
*And the dead were waylaid,*
*And he felt like he'd soon have to poo."*

Then he looked at Billy and said one more thing: "The Diamond Dais cracked, didn't it. The shard came up, eh?" Once again, Billy almost saw Terry in Rumpelstiltskin's eyes.

And suddenly, Billy knew where he was needed. He didn't know what he had to do there, but he knew where he had to go.

"Rumpelstiltskin," he said, "I need to get into the tower."

The old man smiled, though his smile was weak, and grew weaker as his Fizzles were attacked and destroyed by the thousands. "You know," said the old man quietly, "I think you may be right."

He clicked his fingers, and the granite seat that could travel the earth rose up beneath Billy. Billy sat on it, and in an instant was deep inside the ground. The trip this time was a short one, however, and so within seconds he found himself in the cloistered confines of the Accounting Room.

After the cacophony of battle, the sheer wall of sound that had assailed him through these last hours, the silence of the room was almost deafening. Billy stood from the chair, which sank into the floor at his feet and disappeared, leaving Billy on his own.

The room was empty, save the Counters in their cases.

Billy marched right past them, going to the elevator banks and thumbing the "Up" button. There was an almost immediate "ding," but none of the elevators opened. "Sorry," said the voice of one of them. "You have to get a badge and be Counted and Determined before continuing into the island."

Billy looked at the elevators grimly. "Open," he said quietly.

And one of the elevators opened. Billy stepped in. "How did you do that?" asked the elevator. Then, without waiting for a response, it said, "Doesn't matter. I'm not taking you anywhere. It's the rules."

Billy laughed, and was surprised to hear that the laugh was not the squeaky giggle he tended to make when he was nervous or afraid. It was a deep, confident chuckle. "You *will* take me where I wish," he said. "Take me to the top of the tower. Now," he added.

And with a surprised swish, the doors closed and the elevator began to rise. "How are you doing this? You're breaking the rules of the island," said the elevator, half-heard awe in its voice.

"I am the Messenger of the White King," said Billy simply. "And none shall stop me from delivering my Message." Again, as he had a few times before, he felt like he was being lead, guided by some unseen hand on the road he had to follow, the path that would lead him to his foreordained fate.

The elevator rose silently, and Billy started to feel anxious again. When speaking to the elevator, he had felt almost like he was someone else, someone strong and confident. But now he was feeling like plain Billy again, small and weak.

The doors opened. "Top of the tower," said the elevator in a hushed voice. Then, in a tone that bordered on reverence, it added, "My Lord."

Billy stepped out of the elevator, which as always disappeared behind him, and had a moment to take stock of what was going on around him. It wasn't good.

Darksiders were everywhere, their unconscious forms bearing silent witness that Billy's friends had taken their toll on them. But he knew—as he had known all along—that the fight had never really been in doubt. Not with the forces that had been brought to bear against his friends. He looked around for them, and was almost dismayed to find them, so horrible were their situations.

Ivy was on her knees, screaming and weeping. Billy could hear her saying something about "her friend Sally," and knew she was deep in the Dread, deep in some memory of fear and terror. His heart broke a little to hear it, and broke still more when he realized that Mrs. Black was standing over the Green Power, laughing as she repeatedly threw invisible spells of fear and Death at Ivy, each one bringing a new round of screams.

Billy also saw with horror that Prince—or what was left of him after the Death's Head Moth had had its way—was with Mrs. Black, curled at her feet. Every so often the skeletal snake would whip out and bite Ivy, and Billy could see that where the creature of Death bit her, Ivy's skin grew black and rotted.

Close by them, Cameron Black was standing near Vester. Vester was trying diligently to cast some kind of spell, but it was clear that he had been worn out in the fracas, and all he could manage was a few weak sparks. Cameron laughed cruelly, and threw a spell at Vester. But apparently the fireman had learned a few tricks from Fulgora, for just as Billy had seen her done, Vester conjured up a shield of flame. The shield was smaller than Fulgora's had been, but it was enough to do the trick. Cameron's spell bounced back and hit him in the forehead, dropping him to the ground instantly.

Cameron was back on his feet almost as fast as he had fallen, but he was bleeding from a cut on his face. He snarled, and cast another spell at Vester, and this one got through, knocking the fireman down with a yell. Mrs. Black looked over from her malicious toying with Ivy at that moment, and apparently saw that her boy had been injured, because she screamed, "You will not touch him—or anyone else—again!"

She gestured, and Billy saw a Death's Head Moth—that creature of nightmare and pain, flit over and land on Vester before the fireman could get away. Vester shrieked, the sound high-pitched and surprising coming from the strong young man.

"Not quickly, my pet," said Mrs. Black. "Not quickly, for we wish him to feel it. To feel it coming and feel it being beyond his power to stop."

Sure enough, Billy saw the transformation from living flesh to dead lacework of bone happening slowly this time. The moth had landed on Vester's right arm, and the spell of death moved agonizingly up the fireman's fingers, then to his hand, and then his arm. Billy's friend shouted and writhed with the pain, but there was nothing that could be done to stop the spell.

But worst of all this was what Billy saw next.

Wolfen was standing over Mrs. Russet. Billy almost cried out, because he was so shocked to see his teacher's appearance. She was bruised and disheveled, her clothing in tatters. She raised her crystal scepter, and sharp arrowheads of dark rock hurtled out at Wolfen. But the Dark Master only laughed and batted them away contemptuously. He, too, had a Death's Head Moth nearby him. "What shall it be, Lumilla?" he asked with a nasty chuckle. "Oblivion? Or an eternity as a servant of the Dark?"

Mrs. Russet's only answer was another sweep of her scepter, another swarming storm of arrows. Again, Wolfen laughed. He looked at Eva Black, who now had her hand around Cameron's shoulders, the two of them laughing as well as they watched Vester's arm slowly turn to bone.

"My queen," Wolfen shouted, and Eva turned to regard him with those horrible dark eyes of hers. The scarab broach on her shoulder was moving, Billy could see, its feelers twitching around like it was sampling the death in the air, and loving it.

"Yes?" she said, clearly anxious to get back to her sport with Vester and Ivy.

"Shall we turn her, or destroy her?" asked Wolfen.

Eva opened her mouth to answer, but before she could, Billy found himself stepping forward, and heard himself say, "You shall do neither."

All movement from the three Darksiders stopped. They turned toward Billy.

"Billy, don't," said Mrs. Russet, but Mrs. Black threw a spell at her and the Brown Councilor started gasping, her breath stolen by Eva's spell.

"Well, well, well, if it isn't the irritating and powerless Mr. Jones," said Mrs. Black. She looked at Wolfen, who smiled a predatory smile at her. "I must admit," she said, and the Death's Head Moth that had been crawling on Vester's arm now took off and swooped toward Billy, "it will be a pleasure to hear you scream as I have heard your friends."

"Wait," said Cameron suddenly. "Don't hurt him."

Mrs. Black looked at her son in surprise, and Billy himself felt more than a little shocked. The shock dissipated, however, when Cameron said, "*I* want to hurt him."

Mrs. Black smiled. "My boy," she said proudly, and then looked at Wolfen. "They grow up so fast, don't they?" She nodded at Cameron. "Have fun," she said with an evil wink.

Cameron didn't have to be told twice. He rushed at Billy instantly, hurling spells with deadly rapidity as he ran. Billy ducked and dodged, feeling the spells whip by him with trails of cool fear. One of them glanced off his head, dazing him for a moment, but then he was off and running, zigzagging as he went, trying to avoid Cameron's raging onslaught.

Billy heard Cameron yelling, and looked back to see that the bigger boy was quickly gaining on him. Cameron smiled at him—the smile of victory already achieved—and again threw something at Billy. This time, Billy thought he could see a skull flying toward him, its eye sockets burning with a purple light. The fearful object hit him square in the back, and he could feel the indigo fire that had burned in the skull's eyes spread to his shirt. He cried out in pain, feeling his back blister and his muscles clench in agony, but kept going.

At last, Billy was at the Diamond Dais. He couldn't think what else to do, the pain in his back pushing out most of his thoughts. Cameron was still laughing behind him, the bigger boy clearly sensing Billy's imminent defeat, knowing that the end was near.

Billy clambered up onto the podium, then stood and turned to face Cameron. The bully was only a few feet away now. Wolfen and Mrs. Black were close behind him, walking arm in arm and watching the bully's performance with ghastly glee. Billy glanced over their shoulders. He saw Ivy crying, the Dread sure to permanently take her to oblivion at any moment. He saw Vester, the bones of the Death's Head's spell still creeping up his right arm with the inevitability of Death itself. He saw Mrs. Russet, still unable to breathe, the life slowly ebbing from her as he watched.

Then he looked back at Cameron as the boy leapt lightly up to the Diamond Dais. "Mom?" called the young Black Power.

"Yes, dear?" answered Mrs. Black, her tone of voice light and happy, like they were discussing the best decorations for a birthday cake.

"I'd like to try the Dread," said Cameron.

"Well, do you think you're ready?" asked his mother.

Cameron grinned, and nodded. He smiled at Billy, who backed up until he found his back pressed against the shard at the center of the Diamond Dais. Nowhere else to go.

"Oh," answered Cameron, "I'm ready all right."

"Well, do it right," said Wolfen. "No half-jobs. We want him to suffer, and we want him to die."

"No, not die," said Eva Black. The two Death's Head Moths that still flitted above her and Wolfen started moving towards Billy. "We want him to suffer, and then we want him to become an eternal servant of Death in the midst of it. So that he walks the earth forever, and suffers for eternity."

"You got it, Mom," said Cameron. He frowned in concentration, and held his hands out like he was holding an invisible basketball. Between them there was a spark, and a dark cloud of violet and black appeared, roiling between his fingers. Billy thought he could see writhing bodies in the tiny cloud, souls forever doomed by the imprisoning grip of fear.

Billy had been touched by the Dread before, when Wolfen had cast it upon him. But he hadn't seen this pool of darkness then, and realized that Wolfen had been only playing with him. *This*, on the other hand, was the real thing. This was the thing that had destroyed

Mrs. Russet, that had rendered her into a doomed shell of what she had been.

Cameron smiled again at Billy. The Black Power pushed his hands forward suddenly, and the dark mist he had been holding coalesced and speared forward, shooting toward Billy like a ghostly arrow.

Billy did the only thing he could think to do. And actually, he didn't even really think to do it, he just did it.

He ducked.

Cameron's spell of Dread arced out, and hit directly where Billy had been. But Billy had dropped to the ground, banging his knees on the unforgiving surface of the Diamond Dais, and the spell lanced over him. It hit the shard that speared up through the middle of the podium, and with a deafening concussion, the shard cracked, a piece of it shearing off and then falling to the ground at Billy's feet.

As for the Dread, the instant after the spell hit the diamond shard at Billy's back, he saw the dark projectile bounce back...and hit Cameron squarely in the nose.

For the second time, Billy had to smile as blood starting dripping from the bully's beak. But this time, instead of crying about the fact that he was bleeding, Cameron's eyes widened into terrified circles of fear. "Please, no, don't!" he shouted, his mind already lost in the grip of his terror. "Don't bring the clown to my birthday! I'm scared of clowns! Nooo!" And the boy fell over, writhing and unconscious.

Mrs. Black was clearly stunned. But only for a moment.

"Kill him!" she shrieked. And the Death's Head Moths now flew at Billy, closing the distance between them and him with frightening speed.

Billy knew that, unless he could do something, this was going to be it for him. Avoiding Cameron's blast had been sheer luck. But Mrs. Black and Wolfen...the Black Councilor and the Dark Master would not leave him any room for luck. There would be no bouncing of *their* spells off any crystal shard.

Billy turned, looking for somewhere to run and hide, knowing even as he did so that he hadn't the time to do either. He was doomed, he knew it.

Then he frowned.

Everything around him seemed to slow down, and then disappear. Mrs. Black, Wolfen, the deadly moths, his friends dying in the background. It all faded out, and all he saw was the crystal shard that had cracked the Diamond Dais.

*Through fires of fate and storms that save*
*Through winter's gate and water's grave*
*Shall come the One, once lost, now found*
*Seen by the Son whose love abounds.*

*A sword, a spear, and armor strong*
*A shield to wear, and dagger long*
*To fell the Dark and bring the Light*
*To call the spark that ends the night.*

*And through it all, one twist of fate:*
*A child whose call will seem too late*
*But though the Dark seems once to win*
*The child will spark the light again.*

Billy leaned over and grabbed the shard. The top of it, where it had been broken by Cameron's spell, was rounded and smooth. It fit in his hand perfectly. Billy pulled at the shard, and with a cracking noise that seemed to shake the whole earth, Billy pulled the shard free of the Diamond Dais. He lifted it up, and as he did, the world returned to him.

He suddenly saw the two Death's Head Moths winging towards him, the deadly intent in their minds clear. They swooped down, and without thinking Billy swung the crystal shard in his hands. He moved with an expertise that he could not possibly possess, the swings sharp, quick, and true.

There was a crackle of spent energy, and the two moths fell to the Diamond Dais, each one split neatly in half.

Billy looked at Mrs. Black and Wolfen. They were both staring at him in shock. Then Mrs. Black's face again bunched up into the living embodiment of hate and rage. She raised both fists, and Billy saw that each held the Dread. Wolfen, too, the Dark Master only a second behind her, raised his fists, and two more dark orbs of Dread appeared in his hands.

Billy knew that there was no way he could block all four of the attacks, not if they came at once. And Mrs. Black apparently knew it too, or at least could see it in Billy's eyes, because she laughed. The laugh was tinged with insanity now, and Billy felt almost positive that what had happened to her son had perhaps been the thing that inalterably snapped an already disturbed mind.

"You are mine, Billy Jones," she screamed in triumph, and both she and Wolfen clenched to cast their spells. "Any last words?" she said.

Billy felt a sharp pang of fear, but only for an instant. In the next, the fear dissipated, replaced by that strange sense of being guided. He felt what had been Billy Jones disappear, or at least recede into somewhere deep within him. And what took its place was something different. Something far older, tied to the very Essence of Power.

"My words are these," he said, in a voice no longer entirely his own. And Mrs. Black and Wolfen both paused, as though he had stopped them merely with his words. "The Diamond Dais has cracked, the White King's sword has been found." As he said this, the Diamond Dais began to glow a deep, forest green, the sign of truth being told upon it. At the same time, Billy held forth the shard that he clutched in his hands, and as he did, bits of it fell away, leaving only a diamond blade and hilt—a perfectly crafted sword hewn without hands from a single diamond.

Billy raised the sword in both hands, high above his head, and now the sword began to burn with an inner light, a fire that was not only brighter than the sun, but seemed to pull the sun down from the heavens itself.

"I am the Messenger," said Billy. "And my Message is this: the White King comes. The Dark shall give way to Light, and the worlds shall end at my hands."

And with that, Billy swung the sword downward in a fierce, fiery arc, slamming the blade onto the Diamond Dais.

There was a sound: a pure, bell-tone that was followed immediately by a pulse of energy that had the tip of the sword as its epicenter, and which pulsed outward to flow over Powers Island.

Billy felt the pulse go out, and it was like he was a part of it, as though some portion of him had *become* the energy cast forth by the sword. He could see what it touched, and what happened to those things that it touched.

The ring of energy rode in a white pulse over the top of the tower. It moved slowly at first, then picked up speed. It hit Cameron, then Wolfen and Mrs. Black, knocking the Darksiders to the ground like they were paper dolls in a hurricane. It hit Prince, the snake that had once been Billy's friend and then turned to a servant of the Darksiders, and as it did the snake turned back to fire. It looked around, and Billy could see a subtle smile on the fire serpent's face. It looked at Billy, and flicked its forked tongue, and then disappeared in a pleased puff of smoke, its time as a Fizzle done.

And still onward rolled the power that came from the sword, pulsing forward and touching Vester, Ivy, and Mrs. Russet.

Mrs. Russet gasped, suddenly able to breathe. Ivy stopped crying and fell into a deep sleep, the weeping now replaced by a slumbering smile. And the gray-white bone structure that had slowly been replacing Vester's arm now withered and burned away, leaving only pink flesh behind it.

The ring of energy moved outward, flowing over the river that bisected the top of the tower, touching the dead plants that covered it. And as it did, the river glowed like blown glass, like a flowing diamond of light, and the greenery was restored, the Earthtree claiming the tower once again.

Then the pulse traveled to the edges of the tower and flowed downward, traveling in an electrified ring to the tower's base and then rippling over the island. Everywhere it touched, the fighting Powers were knocked down. It flowed over the zombies, as well, and as soon as it did the undead beings also fell, their skin transforming from the mottled color that had distinguished them and their eyes returning to the normal, closed eyes of the dead who have found peace at last.

It flowed over all, and where it went, everything changed. The Darksiders fled, terrified by the forces that had been brought to bear against them and the sudden dissipation of the most terrible part of their army. The Dawnwalkers brightened with new hope and a rekindling of the happiness and optimism that had been theirs until the recent weeks.

Wherever the sword's power flowed, all were touched, all were changed. And wherever it went, all could hear a voice. The voice of a boy who was not a boy. The voice of youth that was tied into the ages.

"The White King comes," said the Messenger. "And the worlds will end."

# CHAPTER THE THIRTIETH

*In Which Billy sees the End Begin, and knows his Fate…*

Billy blinked and looked around. A circle of faces crowded in on him. His friends. Ivy, Vester, Tempus, Mrs. Russet. Even Fulgora was looking down at him, blood running in rivulets from various cuts all over her, but still looking uncharacteristically concerned.

"What happened?" Billy groaned. His head felt like a gorilla had pulled it off his shoulders and played a rousing game of kickball with it.

"It's over," said Tempus. "It's over, my boy, and we won!"

His friends helped Billy to his feet, and he saw that he had been laying on the Diamond Dais. The sun was up, and birds were singing in the foliage that now cloaked the tower.

Billy almost tripped getting up, though. He looked down and saw the reason why: the White King's sword, the sword that had been prophesied as one of the tools that would end the Dark, was at his side. It rested in a golden scabbard that had somehow appeared and attached itself to a bejeweled belt he now wore, only the diamond hilt of the sword visible above it.

Billy looked around. He could see a still form nearby, a dark lump curled in on itself. "Cameron?" he said.

Vester shook his head. "Cameron and his mother skedaddled," he said. "Along with the rest of the Darksiders—the ones that were still conscious anyway." He nodded at the still form. "That there is Wolfen. And he's dead."

"What?" said Billy, aghast.

Mrs. Russet nodded. "It's true. And it explains a lot."

Billy's head was reeling. "Wolfen is dead?"

Mrs. Russet nodded. "And I think he's *been* dead for a long, long time."

Not just Billy, but everyone now looked at the Brown Councilor in surprise. "Remember how he was able to swear fealty to the

Council, and swear that he had not broken the terms of his exile, all while the Diamond Dais glowed the green of Truth?" she said.

"That's right," said Ivy. "How did he manage to lie like that?"

"I don't think he *was* lying," said Mrs. Russet. When the others looked askance at her, she continued, "We know that the Darksiders have developed new powers. Like that insect—"

"The Death's Head Moth," interjected Billy.

Mrs. Russet frowned, clearly not appreciating interruptions even when she *wasn't* giving a lecture in history class. "Is that what it's called?" she asked. Billy nodded. "Interesting. And do you remember when you first saw it?"

"On Dark Isle, with Mrs. Black," said Billy with a shudder. He would never forget it.

"With Mrs. Black," said Mrs. Russet, nodding as though she had known he would say that. "I think that Eva has reached deeper into the Dark than any Power that has gone before. Even beyond Wolfen, it seems, in her evil quest for power. And she *is* powerful, indeed. She raised an army of zombies, she orchestrated this attack. And I believe that she killed Wolfen as part of it…and then raised him up again."

"But why?" asked Vester. "Why would she do that?"

"Several reasons," answered Mrs. Russet. "First of all, I think that in stealing his life, she stole something of his essence, his power. And Eva would surely want that, even as a much younger girl. She was always a servant of Death and the Dark, and I never believed that she was acting truly when she—like the other Darksiders—swore to keep the Truce after Wolfen's first uprising. But more than that," continued Mrs. Russet in a thoughtful tone, "I think that she always felt betrayed by Wolfen. I think she felt he had abandoned her. And Eva takes those things personally. So I believe she hunted him down, and killed him…and then brought him back as something like a zombie, but more powerful. Smarter, retaining its powers…and totally under her thrall."

Tempus snapped his fingers. "That was why he could tell us he hadn't broken the terms of his exile: he hadn't. And that was why he could swear allegiance to the Council: because if Eva told him to do it, he would have to, and he would have to mean it. But she could then tell him to fight us, and he would flip over in an instant to the other side."

"But if she hated him," said Billy, "why would she bring him back? Why not just use her powers to gather the Darksiders and be in charge on her own?"

"Because everyone knew Wolfen, and believed he had the power to control the Darksiders," said Vester, clearly grasping, as Fulgora would have said, the "tactical implications" of Mrs. Black's plan. "No one would believe Eva Black could do such a thing. No one would follow her, unless it was *through* him."

"Not only that," continued Mrs. Russet, "but I also think Eva always loved Wolfen. And this way, she could have him. Not the thing he had become—not the vanquished Dark Power who had perhaps come to understand the error of his ways—but as she had always envisioned him, and wished him to be. Not weak, but strong. What she saw as his true self."

"Then," Billy said, still looking at Wolfen's still form, "when the White King's sword unleashed its power and destroyed the force keeping the zombies alive...."

Mrs. Russet nodded. "It also released Wolfen." She glanced at the body as well. "May he rest in peace. And may he find mercy in the hereafter."

"So we've won!" shouted Billy.

"Of course we've won!" said Tempus with an impatient snort. "I already said that."

Then, a terrible thought came over Billy. He looked at Tempus. "Tempus, you were knocked out," he said.

Tempus looked at the others uncomfortably. "I wasn't knocked out," he finally said with as much indignation as he could muster. "I was just resting my eyes."

"Whatever. When you woke up, where was Rumpelstiltskin?" asked Billy. He wanted to make sure the old man who had come to the Dawnwalkers' rescue was all right.

The company of friends looked uncomfortable. Mrs. Russet, in particular, looked like she was about to cry.

Billy looked at them. "What?" he asked, a sinking feeling in the pit of his stomach.

Vester pointed, and Billy noticed that one of his arms—the one that had been touched by the Death's Head Moth—hung loose and lifeless. It had been made flesh again, but apparently some things that were damaged could not be completely healed, not even by the sword of the White King.

Billy looked where Vester was pointing, and saw Rumpelstiltskin. The old man was cradled in a giant velvety leaf, propped upward so that his face was to the sky. He was terribly gray and wan.

"How is he?" whispered Billy.

No one spoke for a long time. Finally Fulgora, ever the practical—and tactless—one, simply said, "He's dying."

"What?" Billy hollered. Then without waiting for a reply he scrambled over the side of the Diamond Dais and ran to where the ancient man was laying.

Rumpelstiltskin *was* dying, he could see at a glance. Billy felt tears start to burn behind his eyes as he took in the shriveled form of the man who had done so much to save them all.

"What happened?" asked Billy as his friends slowly approached.

"His Fizzles," said Ivy softly. "Too many of them were destroyed. It took too much out of him."

Billy leaned in to the old man. Rumpelstiltskin squinted, as though blinded by the light, and then smiled. "Well who are you, young man?" he asked.

"Billy. Billy Jones."

The old man smiled. "I knew a Billy Jones once," he said weakly. Then he added, "But you're nothing like him."

Billy smiled and laughed, bittersweet tears running down his nose. He turned to his friends. "Can't something be done?" he asked.

Mrs. Russet shook her head, then moved away, far enough that she was out of earshot.

Billy watched her go. "Shouldn't she be here?" he asked. "Shouldn't she be with him?"

Vester shook his head. "She should, but he doesn't know her. And she can't bear to see him die like that." Without thinking, the fireman reached out his good hand and took Fulgora's. She flinched in surprise, then slowly Billy saw her fingers curl around those of the fireman, the two young Red Powers drawing support from one another in this sad moment.

"How long does he have?" asked Billy.

"Only a few minutes at most," replied Ivy after feeling Rumpelstiltskin's head. "Death is coming to claim him, and the Earthtree sings for his soul."

And with that, Ivy herself began singing, a wordless tune that nonetheless spoke of grief, and loss, and sadness. But it also spoke of hope, and happiness, and life born from the ashes of despair.

Billy felt himself join in the song, unsure of how he knew what the tune should be, but knowing it nonetheless, and singing not just for the passage of Rumpelstiltskin—Terry to his friends—but for all those who had suffered and fought to protect the world of the Powers. It was, Billy realized, the Earthsong, the song of Life. And it was beautiful, because it always went on, throughout eternity.

Then, a noise interrupted him and Ivy. A beating of great wings. A sound of wind and fire. They all looked up, and slowly, gracefully, a form that Billy remembered well dropped from the sky.

Billy's friends all gasped and gaped, and Billy had another one of those "I told you so" moments. This time, however, he actually gave voice to the sentiment.

"See?" he said. "I *told* you that I'd seen a Unicorn."

And so it was. The magnificent flying horse with the horn of gold settled slowly to the earth beside them. It looked at the group, meeting the eyes of each one in turn, then turned to Rumpelstiltskin's still form. The old man was breathing only with difficulty, clearly showing that he was not long for the earth.

Mrs. Russet came running up, concern for her husband etched into her face as the huge animal stepped toward him. "What are you doing?" she cried, anguish in her voice. "What more can be done to him?"

But Billy stopped her, standing in front of her before she could interfere with whatever the Unicorn was doing. "Wait," he said.

The Unicorn nodded at Billy, as though to thank him for his help. Then it leaned toward Rumpelstiltskin, just as the old man breathed one last breath, and then was still.

Mrs. Russet let out a sob of grief, and then that sob turned to a wail of fear as the Unicorn leaned in even closer. Slowly, it dropped its head, until at last the horn touched Rumpelstiltskin's forehead. Then the Unicorn moved, and the horn lightly touched each of the man's closed eyes, then his gray and slack lips.

And as the Unicorn did so, Rumpelstiltskin's skin returned to its former pink color. He gasped and his eyes opened. He looked around at the company, clearly confused.

Then, his gaze fell upon Mrs. Russet. "Lumilla," he said. And with that, Billy saw the steely-eyed teacher disappear, replaced by a woman in love as Mrs. Russet threw herself upon her husband, and kissed him.

The Unicorn pulled away, giving the reunited lovers their space. It looked at Billy, then it looked at Billy's side, where the sword of the White King still hung, and nodded again.

"I know," said Billy quietly in response. "I haven't forgotten what I have to do."

The Unicorn neighed and reared up on its hind legs. And with a great flap of its snow-white wings, it shot into the sky, and was gone.

Billy watched it disappear from view, then turned away from his friends.

"Where are you going?" shouted Vester. Billy ignored him, walking toward the river that ran over the top of the tower. "Hey," said the fireman, "what's going on?"

Still Billy walked. He drew near to the river's edge, and then pulled the sword from its sheath. It gleamed with that inner fire once more, with the enormous power that had called forth victory from the depths of defeat. Billy looked upon it, savoring its beauty, its majesty, then hurled the sword into the river.

"No!" screamed Vester, launching himself toward the river, clearly intending to dive in and get the sword again, bad arm and all.

But before Vester reached the water's edge, a hand shot up out of the river. It plucked the sword out of the air, then both hand and sword slid into the river and were gone in an instant, though Billy thought he could see the flick of a coralline tail as they disappeared.

Vester began wading into the river, but Billy put a hand out. "Don't bother," said Billy. "It's gone. Taken by Blue."

Vester stared at him in horror. "What did you do?" he demanded. "We won the *battle*, not the war. The Darksiders are still out there, and you just threw away our best weapon."

Billy looked at the river, and the coolly flowing waters. He murmured some of the words of the Prophecy:

*"A sword, a spear, and armor strong*
*A shield to wear, and dagger long*
*To fell the Dark and bring the Light*
*To call the spark that ends the night."*

Vester stared at him. "What does *that* mean?" he asked.

Billy smiled. "It means I'm the Messenger, and even though my message has been delivered, I don't think I'm done with this world." He drew himself up to his full height, all five feet nothing of him. "It means there are other weapons," he said. "And I will find them."

# CHAPTER THE THIRTY-FIRST

*In Which Billy must Go Home, and finds that there are still a few Surprises...*

The coming hours and days were filled with reconstruction. The Dawnwalkers had regained control of the island, but much needed to be done. And once again, Billy's friends were at the middle of it.

Fulgora was no longer needed in an immediate battle, but still she secreted herself away with Vester—whom she had appointed as her Knight Marshall—and insisted on planning a defensive strategy for the future. Vester had protested the appointment, pointing out that he was not one of Fulgora's subjects, and besides that, he noted that he only had one working arm so he didn't know what kind of Knight Marshall he could be. Fulgora, typically, had told him to shut up, be quiet, stop making a fool of himself, and get to strategizing with her.

As for Ivy, she went to work with her father—whom they found under a pile of rubble, weak but alive—tending to the wounded and regrowing the island. Soon, the flowers were once again in bloom, and Powers Island teemed with life. There were still evidences of the fighting, but as the Earthtree grew and laced its tendrils and greenery over the whole of the island, even what remained of the destruction was changed, and made beautiful. The island had been destroyed, but out of the destruction had come life, at Ivy's hands.

Tempus was soon at work, too, flying over the island so that he could provide a bird's eye view of the things that needed to be done. He clearly loved the job, laughing and playing as he flitted to and fro, calling down to those hard at work below, always ready with a joke—even though sometimes his jokes were meant to be serious comments, but just came out sounding a little off, or even just downright nonsensical.

Terry was still weak and withered, and Billy knew that he would never again be the strong and tall man that Billy had seen in

Mrs. Russet's memories, but at least he was himself mentally once again, and Billy was glad to see his teacher so happy at the return of her husband, who had been lost but was now found again. The two stayed constantly together, mostly working side by side on the top of the tower, looking at sunrises and sunsets together, and making up for the years they had lost.

But as for Billy himself, he suddenly found himself largely useless. The others tried to include him, he could tell, but there simply wasn't much he could do. Once again, he was a non-Power in a world of Powers, like a blind man in a world of the sighted. But he tried not to let it get him down, mostly spending his time chatting with the elevators—who thankfully no longer referred to him as Boy Number 3583Q—and walking around the island. He walked its mountains and its valleys, forded its streams, climbed its trees, and felt of its power. But still, he was mostly alone, a bit homesick, and largely ignored in the press of work that followed the destruction of what was already being called the Battle for Powers Island.

One night, he was feeling particularly lonely and useless. He sat at the edge of the tower, his legs dangling out over space, looking at the empty scabbard he still had strapped around his waist. A noise alerted him that someone was coming, but he didn't look up. Then a swish of brown robe appeared in his peripheral vision, and with a creaking of old bones Mrs. Russet slowly sat beside him.

They looked over the tops of the clouds for a time, then she finally said, "Are you all right, Billy?"

He nodded, but Mrs. Russet clearly didn't believe him. "What is it?" she asked. "What could possibly be bothering you?"

"I don't know," Billy finally said. "I just feel like I'm not helping anything I guess."

"Not helping!" said Mrs. Russet, incredulous. "Billy, you above all others are responsible for saving this island, for saving the Dawnwalkers and the world of the Powers!"

He looked at her. "Was I? Was I really?" He looked away, then shrugged. "I don't feel like I did much. I don't have any powers, and the only things I really did were when I felt like someone else was guiding me. So it wasn't me that did anything, not really."

Mrs. Russet pursed her lips. "Well, as for you being guided, just because you have a guide doesn't mean courage isn't required. Many a person who has been guided up a mountain has turned back before reaching the summit. And you never turned back, Billy." She thought a moment, and then said, "Besides that, as for your not having powers…I wouldn't be so sure."

Billy felt a thrill of hope. "But, I didn't really pass the Test of Earth, and I haven't done anything other than Glimmer a little that one day at school."

"Oh haven't you?" asked Mrs. Russet, with a glimmer in her eye. "What about the Fizzle?"

"Huh?" asked Billy.

"Vester's Fizzle. Prince," she said.

"What about it?" he asked.

"Don't you remember what you were told about Fizzles? That only a great Power can keep it around outside of that Power's presence."

"So?" asked Billy.

"So," said Mrs. Russet, "as much as I like Vester, and respect him as a smart and good person, he is *not* a great Power. And there's no way that he could have kept Prince alive to protect you the way that Fizzle did."

"Then how did it happen?" asked Billy.

Mrs. Russet smiled. "*You* did it, Billy."

"Me?" said Billy, nearly dumbstruck. "But I didn't mean to."

"No, you didn't," agreed Mrs. Russet. "But I theorize—I *believe*—that you did it nonetheless. Just as I believe that you were the one who turned Fulgora into a dragon each time you were worried she was going to come to harm. You wished her to be saved, and the Elements themselves moved to change her, to save her according to your will."

"But," Billy stammered, struggling with these ideas, "but I didn't want those things to happen. I mean, I wished for *something* to happen, but not those things in particular."

"That may be true," said Mrs. Russet. "But I still think you did those things. You showed control of Red Fire, when you saved Fulgora and when you walked the halls of my Memory to save me from my Dread—something that no one else has ever done before. And when you were in the sea you were able to stay alive and call to Artemaeus to rescue you, with the Power of the Blue. You saw the future when you had a dream while riding with Artemaeus, and saw yourself wielding the sword of the White King, though you didn't know it at the time. That's one of the Powers of the Gray, to see the future. You wielded the White Sword, made of diamond, purest of the treasures of the Brown. And," she continued in what was almost a whisper, "you saved my husband. You called forth the Unicorn, and it brought the Element of Life on its wings."

"What *was* the Unicorn, anyway?" asked Billy.

"I don't know," said Mrs. Russet.

"You don't *know*?" said Billy incredulously.

Mrs. Russet laughed. "Believe it or not, there are a great many things I don't know, Billy Jones," she said. Then she sobered. "The war has just begun. Eva Black was the real power behind this most recent struggle, and she is still at large, and no doubt angrier and more vengeful than ever. The Darksiders have grown more powerful than we had imagined, and Wolfen shows us that we cannot trust anyone to be what they appear. And most important, the weapons of the White King must be found so that the world can be prepared for his return. So though some things have been made clear, there are many mysteries still to solve, many strange things to understand." She leaned in close to Billy, almost conspiratorially. "But I *have* figured out some things," she said.

"Like what?" asked Billy.

"Like who the White King is," she said.

"Well, he's the White King," said Billy, confused.

"Yes, but I think I have discovered his name. And I think you know it, too," said Mrs. Russet.

"I do?" asked Billy. He thought. "No, I don't."

"You mean you haven't figured it out?" she said, and laughed again. "Billy, don't you realize what you did when you drew the White King's sword from the Diamond Dais?" Billy shook his head. The twinkle in Mrs. Russet's eye brightened still further, and she said, "Young man, you pulled the sword from the stone." She waited, then said, "You held Excalibur, the sword of King Arthur, the White King who brought peace to the earth, and who will bring it one day again."

She laughed again at Billy's expression. "But I thought he was a legend," said Billy.

"And so he is," said Mrs. Russet. "But like many legends, this one has its roots in fact." She nodded at the nearby river. "Haven't you wondered why Blue the mermaid wanted the sword so badly?"

"She said it was hers," said Billy.

Mrs. Russet nodded, "And so it was, once, long ago. I believe she was once the original Blue Power, one of the six Councilors who helped Arthur craft this island from raw Element. And it was she who designed the sword, and dipped it in the living waters of the Earthsea, so that it would be ever sharp and true and never broken, just as the seas of the world will never break. Then she cast it into Arthur's hands, and now she holds it in her own, the sword returned to its maker, a woman who had a name long ago, now named Blue the mermaid, but once known as the Lady of Shallot."

Billy reeled, trying to digest all this information. Then he thought of something. "It can't be," he said decisively.

"And why not?" asked Mrs. Russet curiously.

"Because, well...wasn't the sword only supposed to be pulled from the stone by someone who was going to be a king?" asked Billy.

"Interesting, isn't it?" was Mrs. Russet's only reply, and she looked sideways at Billy with an expression he didn't quite understand, but one that made him thoroughly uncomfortable.

"So what do we do now?" asked Billy, changing the subject.

"We look for the White King's weapons. And then we try to find him, and bring him back to us to restore the earth to peace again."

Then Mrs. Russet's expression sobered. "But before that happens, I'm afraid I have some bad news for you."

"What?" asked Billy, a sinking feeling in his stomach.

"When the Darksiders arrived, you remember how Wolfen said they didn't need to come through the Accounting Room anymore?" Billy nodded. "Well, it turns out that's because they somehow managed to destroy—or at least weaken—the spell that separates Powers Island from the rest of the world. So they could just Transport in, rather than having to come through the conduits that were originally required for entrance to the island. And there's been an...unfortunate side effect of that."

"What?" asked Billy.

"Our time has slowed down," replied Mrs. Russet.

It took Billy a few minutes to understand what that meant. "You mean...."

Mrs. Russet nodded. "Yes. Normally the time passed here would be as nothing back home. But with your time on Dark Isle, and the time you've passed here after the broken time spell, I'm afraid several *weeks* have passed back home."

Billy paled. "My parents are going to be worried sick!"

Mrs. Russet nodded. "And that's why it's time to go home."

"But what are we going to do? They're going to want to know where I was! What am I going to say?" He stopped a moment, then added, "And what about Blythe?"

Mrs. Russet's expression darkened a bit. "Blythe is a young girl. Perhaps she was a Darksider because her parents were, and she simply didn't know any better. Perhaps she was a follower and believer, though I didn't see her among the Darksiders whom we found after the battle. Either way, from what you said to me about her, she was someone that was good to you, and whom you cared about."

Billy nodded. "Then," said Mrs. Russet, "let us see what happens, and not borrow trouble. Perhaps you will return to find her still a friend. And perhaps," she added as the twinkle returned to her eye, "perhaps even more."

Billy looked away, embarrassed. To change the subject, he said again, "But what about my parents? And what about school? I missed all that time. How are we going to explain that?"

Mrs. Russet hugged Billy, and then, in defiance of all laws of the universe, his teacher kissed the top of his head. "Oh, Billy, I think we'll find a way to take care of those problems."

"But how?" Billy insisted.

Mrs. Russet laughed long and loud, seeming to find his expression deeply comical, then said, "How will we do it? Why Mr. Jones, hadn't you heard? We can do magiq here."

And Billy jumped. Because he had heard the silent "q."

And he suddenly knew that he would one day do magiq too.

# EPILOGUE

Billy sat and looked at the horror that hunched before him. It was oozy, slimy, something that had once been alive, at least theoretically, but now was only a man-made terror to be visited on those who least deserved it. But no matter how much he hated and feared what was before him, he knew there was only one thing he could do.

He opened his mouth wide, stuck a piece in, and chewed.

"Ugh," he said to himself after swallowing. "I hate Salisbury steak."

He was sitting alone in the hall outside the cafeteria. Actually, not in the hall: he was sitting under a water fountain, hoping that no one would find him here. But someone did.

He watched as a foot in a white sneaker walked into view and stopped in front of his hiding place. The sneaker was connected to an ankle, and the ankle—as Billy knew ankles tended to do—turned into a leg. Billy's gaze followed the leg up. It was a girl's leg, and a nice one at that.

The girl squatted down and smiled at him. "Hi," said Blythe Forrest. She, too, was carrying a lunch tray. She sat down next to him, and looked around. "No admiring fans?" she asked.

Billy shrugged. The "reason" that had been invented for why he had been gone for more than a month had turned him into something of a celebrity. Suddenly all the people who had dismissed, ignored, tormented, or avoided him were now his best friends. He had dreamed about being one of the Popular Kids his whole life. And now that he was one, he could only hope that he wouldn't be one forever.

"Well," said Blythe, "I guess it must be tough, being famous and all." And to Billy's great dismay and horror, she consumed her own oversized helping of Salisbury steak in two gulps that would have been the envy of a three hundred pound lumberjack with a tapeworm.

Billy watched her eat—if you could call inhaling something like a vacuum cleaner "eating"—and a thousand questions ran rampant through his mind. Why was she a Darksider? Was she, as Mrs. Russet had said, one who truly believed in their cause, or just someone who happened to have been born into that group and never really realized what it was? Had she seen him on Dark Isle, as he had seen her, or perhaps later when he and his friends spoke to Blue on the cliff of Dark Isle? Had she fought in the Battle for Powers Island? If so, had she seen him as he bombed Darksiders with Tempus?

Did she know he was the Messenger, and that he had found the White King's sword and defeated the Darksiders, at least for now?

Was she a spy?

That last thought sent a shiver through his spine. What if she *was* a spy? Sent by the Darksiders to gain his confidence, and then destroy him?

"You okay?" she said. Billy nodded. She laid a hand on his arm, and he felt a thrill run through him, though whether happiness or terror was its origin he could not say.

"I never told you this, but right before you disappeared, I got knocked out or fainted or something. Remember?" Billy nodded. With his understanding that Blythe was a Darksider, he knew as well that she had to understand what had happened when the zombie had touched her. But here she was, feigning utter ignorance, and her motives still completely unclear to Billy. But he forced himself not to think about that as she continued, "Well, ever since then, I dunno...." She finished her Salisbury steak and went to work on the potato side course. "I've felt...." She stopped a moment, clearly trying to think of what to say. Then, finally, she simply said, "I've felt like we were friends, Billy Jones. And that's made me happy."

Billy didn't know what to say. Who *was* Blythe Forrest, really?

Then again, thought Billy, who am I? Who is anyone?

We are as we do, came the answer in his mind. And it again felt like it was someone else, someone wiser and smarter and stronger than he was, leading him to something beyond himself.

Blythe had rescued him from Cameron Black.

She had been kind to him.

She had treated him as a friend.

"You gonna eat that?" she suddenly asked, pointing at Billy's almost untouched meal.

Slowly, uncertainly, Billy shook his head.

Blythe reached over with her plastic fork and speared a huge bite of potatoes. She chewed it, and smiled at Billy.

And Billy smiled back.

# ABOUT THE AUTHOR

**MICHAELBRENT COLLINGS** is a lawyer, screenwriter, black-belt martial artist, father, husband, and has a killer backhand on the badminton court. He has written several other books, has published dozens of articles on several continents, and is currently writing a number of television shows and movies.

He resides in Los Angeles, California, with his wife, two kids, and several imaginary friends, all of whom are too cool to invite Michaelbrent to their parties.

Made in the USA
Lexington, KY
23 November 2014